"Get in"—he gestured don't leave until morning. Tr

Charlotte tugged at Alex .... climbed into the unknown car. Slippery stalks of crackling grass poked at her trembling fingertips as she groped about in the darkness. She willed herself through and turned to pull in her son. The two tumbled back into a tousle of hay. Moldy dust puffed in a cloud from the fall to fill her nostrils and tickle her tear ducts. She sneezed. Joe gripped the iron handle of the sliding door and cast a wary eye around the circus grounds behind him.

Martha's warning rang in Charlotte's mind. *You hold onto yourself and hold onto Alex so y'all don't end up like George and Willie.* She wrapped her arms around her son and was startled by a furry rattling at her wrist.

"Mom, it's Printesa!" Alex whispered. He gathered up the purring cat in his arms, and his shoulders dropped slightly, shrugging off some of the tension.

Charlotte and Alex looked down at the little cat and back up at the strongman.

"Don't make noise."

"Thank you—"

But before the words had left her mouth, Joe slammed the screeching sliding door of the railcar shut. Charlotte and Alex were left in complete darkness with echoes of foreboding accented by the throaty whistle of the departing train.

Praise for Sarah Denning

"The rich smells, the growls of beasts, the excitement of exotics, leotarded bodies, and feigned danger beckon when the circus comes to town. Gasps and laughter, thrills and dreams. This story escorts us to a long-past time when the circus was the year's most anticipated event, giving locals an evening of wistful and throat-catching dreams of living a life other than the mundane and droll. Through the eyes of the common folk and the performers, the good and the bad, the innocent and the manipulative, *Circus Train at Sunrise* is a study of people. The wealth of senses versus the dustbowl dryness only serve to suck us deeper. You're warned from the outset that nothing good comes from a circus, and the author draws you in to prove it's true. Nicely done. You can't ask for a better setup for a murder." ~C. Hope Clark, author of award-winning mysteries. www.chopeclark.com

Circus Train at Sunrise

by

Sarah Denning

This is a work of fiction. Names, characters, places, and incidents are either the product of the author's imagination or are used fictitiously, and any resemblance to actual persons living or dead, business establishments, events, or locales, is entirely coincidental.

Circus Train at Sunrise

COPYRIGHT © 2023 by Sarah Denning

All rights reserved. No part of this book may be used or reproduced in any manner whatsoever without written permission of the author or The Wild Rose Press, Inc. except in the case of brief quotations embodied in critical articles or reviews.
Contact Information: info@thewildrosepress.com

Cover Art by *Tina Lynn Stout*

The Wild Rose Press, Inc.
PO Box 708
Adams Basin, NY 14410-0708
Visit us at www.thewildrosepress.com

Publishing History
First Edition, 2024
Trade Paperback ISBN 978-1-5092-5374-6
Digital ISBN 978-1-5092-5375-3

Published in the United States of America

Dedication

To my parents, who always encouraged me to color outside the lines; my sisters, who helped me find my voice again; my sons, who give me strength; and to Jeremiah. My Jay, who helped me create a circus I'd want to run away with.

Friday I tasted life. It was a vast morsel.
A circus passed the house - still I feel the red in my mind though the drums are out.
~Emily Dickinson

Prologue

Fort Worth, Texas
February 1927

The Sterling & Son's dressing tent swarmed with sideshow dancers and showgirls putting the finishing touches on their costumes. Dimly lit and hazy, the air was thick with anticipation for the first show of the season.

Zarina leaned forward through the cloud of cigarette smoke to watch her own reflection as she painted a deep magenta cupid's bow across her lips. She smirked, satisfied with the new shade, and set the lipstick back carefully among the other articles on the dressing table. The thick canvas walls of the tent rattled with a muffled uproar from the center ring yards away, elephants trumpeting as if a part of the jazz band that roared along with the lions.

She stood up, took one last drag, and dropped her cigarette into the sawdust, snuffing it out with the toe of the red-heeled shoe that perfectly matched her red-and-gold-striped leotard. She mingled with the other girls and stepped out of the dressing tent, through the crisp cold night, and into the stifling humidity of the big top behind a row of waiting performers all congregating like moths in the shadows around the flaming light of the center ring.

Amongst the smell of sweat, sawdust, and animals, she caught the familiar whiff of peanuts and buttered popcorn. The unique aroma triggered her adrenaline as she prepared for her performance. Soon, there would be another fragrance wafting through the tent. Sulfur from the fireworks on the human cannon.

She craned her neck to watch the end of the Grand Entry procession and bumped into the woman standing in front of her. The woman whipped around, and Zarina's breath caught in her throat when she realized whom she'd disturbed.

"Birdie, I'm so sorry," she said hastily. "I'm such a klutz."

Birdie simply narrowed her eyes. "Are you wearing my lipstick?" Birdie reached for her face and clutched her chin between sharp fingernails. "You are wearing my lipstick! You better wipe that off your trap before I wipe it off for you—"

"Cannonball, time to get in position," Ian, the crew master, interjected, eyeing the interaction.

She wriggled out of Birdie's grip and followed after the crew master.

"You oughtta know better than to mess with Birdie Bells," he whispered as she stepped into place on the stand by the large wooden spoked wheel of the cannon.

"I just thought it was a pretty color," she said, adjusting her beaded headpiece. Her palms prickled with sweat, and her mouth went dry as the clown cars made a final circuit and zipped out of the ring. She couldn't tell if it was growing anticipation for her own act, which was about to begin, or fear of another confrontation with Birdie after the show.

The lights lowered, drums rolled, and the piano

keys ran a rapid build-up for the human cannonball act. The seasoned performer waved at the crowd as the spotlight swung across a row of elephants to settle on her magenta smile. Past the elephants, the safety net waited her landing after her flight across the ring. Slinking next to the net was the scowling silhouette and flaming red hair of Birdie Bells.

"And now, ladies and gentlemen"—the ringmaster swept his arms toward the cannon—"feast your eyes on the brave, gravity-defying flight of Zarina, the Human Cannonball!"

The band fired up "Entry of the Gladiators" as she hopped into the cannon with an enthusiastic wave. Snare drums rolled, and the fires were lit. A loud bang echoed—the fireworks. Then another, the springboard. She went soaring across the center ring above the tilted chins of the silent spectators. She closed her eyes, breathing in the gasps of the crowd and waiting for the gentle resistance of the woven rope net at the end of her flight.

But she never felt the comforting catch of the net. Under the terrified rapture of the shocked crowd, the net snapped. And so did the neck of Zarina.

Without missing a beat, the crew master called out, "Swing the lights over to the third ring!" The crew did as they were told, and the crowd's attention was directed to an enthusiastic troupe of riderless white Liberty Horses who performed as if nothing had happened.

Someone kneeled down by the limp body and lifted her head in their hands. "Oh my God, she's dead."

The crew master grabbed the nearest body to him by the shirt collar as he waved directions at his crew to fall in and clean the scene. "You, boy! Go get Mr. Sterling!"

The kid wove his way through the crew and ran out of sight toward the boss. One red-headed performer backed slowly away as the crew flooded forward swiftly around her to move the dead performer's body out of view before the next center-ring act.

Back in the dressing room tent, a sideshow dancer listened to the chaos from the neighboring center ring show. She smiled ever so slightly, then slipped a tube of magenta lipstick into her pocket.

Chapter 1

Blowing Through
Ayer, Texas
March 1927

The whistle of the wind rushed through the cracks of the little house to Charlotte's bed, pulling her awake before the hammering bell of her alarm clock. Another Texas dust storm. Coming in gusts or coming in swirls, but always coming with a will of its own and never asking if it was welcome in her home.

Charlotte sat up and let her eyes adjust to the familiar shapes of the still-dark room. The corners of the wooden door materialized, followed by the looming lump of the armoire in the corner. Then the fuzzy curve of the rocking chair on the woven Navajo rug, and the shadowy shape of the man lying next to her, his chest rising and falling in rhythm with the rattling of his snores.

She'd almost forgotten he was home again.

Charlotte went to reach for her husband but changed her mind. Instead, she quietly slipped out of bed, dressed in the dark, and tiptoed into the kitchen. She rested the bedroom door against the frame without allowing it to close lest it wake her sleeping husband with a disturbing click.

Remnants of her dreams still tugged at her mind as

she turned on a low light in the kitchen, struck a match, and lit the gas stove. It had been the one with the horses again. Riding in the rodeo with her father. Someday she'd teach her son Alex to ride like that, but it had been years since she'd been on a horse. Her husband didn't like women to ride, and her place was here. Her home was here.

Charlotte pulled a cast-iron skillet from the drying rack, gathered up the last bits of bacon she'd scraped together, and dropped them into the seasoned center. If she had a good day at the cookhouse, maybe she could pick up a good cut of meat from the store after work. She took the coffee tin from one of the sage-green shelves filled with spices and knickknacks, and a pot for boiling water from beside the line of clean white plates above the farmhouse sink. As she prepared breakfast, she looked around at the kitchen and sighed. The Texas winter wind had blown dirt in through the cracks in the doors again, and it scattered across the wood floor like the cool blue morning light that peeked in through the window.

I'll sweep up again tonight. She set the coffee tin back down next to a bowl of rocks that her son was endlessly collecting and cracked a few eggs in the hot pan.

Pops of sizzling bacon were interrupted by sounds of stirring from the bedroom down the hall. Gravelly snoring was replaced with the groaning of a man getting out of bed when he didn't want to.

Charlotte pulled the pan up from the fire for a moment. A scrape, muffled shuffling, a thud. *What is he doing in there?*

After a few moments, the snoring resumed, and she

set the pan back down, scraping at the eggs as she scrambled them in the same way she'd seen her boss, Saul, do at the cookhouse a hundred times. Sometimes Charlotte felt like a little girl playing house when she made breakfast for her family, and she had to remind herself that she was a grown woman. A wife. A mother.

Charlotte pulled two plates from the rack and arranged the bacon and eggs on each one. Humming a little tune to herself, she set a cup of coffee by her husband's plate at the head of the table and a cup of juice for Alex. She set a bread basket full of yesterday's biscuits on a crocheted doily next to the butter on the oak table and dusted her hands across the apron over her plain wool dress.

Tiptoeing down the hall, Charlotte paused for a moment by her own bedroom door, which was now closed. *It must have been the wind rattling through the house.* She shrugged and went on to her son's room to wake him for breakfast.

After breakfast, Charlotte and Alex trudged against the whirring wind on their daily walk to school and work. Night hadn't yet given way to morning, and the pale moon still dotted the dusty denim sky like a pearl snap button.

Ayer was a small Texas town, hours by train from the nearest city, just a crop of buildings and a few neighborhoods in the middle of miles of flat brown fields. The only variety in the landscape outside of a few splintered wooden fence posts, a handful of wind-worn scarecrows, and the occasional wandering emaciated cow were steady even rows of dirt in the fields with naked stalks where the cotton had been stripped months before and a few lines of feeble trees carefully planted to fight the wind erosion.

Nonetheless, the relentless wind had whipped the dust up into the air, tinting the entire landscape in shades of brown, like murky water in a stream after a dropped stone stirs up the mud.

"Look at those tough little birds. It can't be easy to fly against this wind." Charlotte nibbled on half a biscuit as a scattering of blackbirds cut through the sky across the moon and reorganized themselves into a new formation.

"It isn't easy to walk in it either." Alex shielded his eyes with his hand. "Is it this dusty everywhere, or just in Ayer?"

Charlotte considered the question. "I've only ever been around Texas. It seems like anywhere we went for the rodeo had plenty of dirt, but I do think these dust storms have gotten worse the last few years. People say it's because of the droughts."

"Did you ever wanna go anywhere else?"

"Outside of Ayer?" Charlotte went to take another bite of her biscuit and drew her lips back at the grains of dirt that ground in her teeth. "Goodness, it sure is a dusty day," she muttered, tossing the rest of the biscuit to a stray dog who snatched it up and ran off toward the train tracks.

"I don't know. Beyond Ayer. Beyond Texas. Anywhere that's different."

"Well, I can't say. Your dad's got a good job out at the Stallman ranch, and so we've never talked about going anywhere else. Most people I know in Ayer raise their families in the houses they were raised in, and then they give those homes to their children."

"They never leave? They just die where they were

born?"

Charlotte chuckled. "Yeah, I guess they do."

"I don't want to do that. I won't live my whole life a five-minute walk from a train that could take me anywhere and just stay put while I watch other people have adventures."

"Well, don't forget your mother when you're off seeing the world," she said with a playful nudge.

"How can I? You're coming with me," he responded. "Hey, look at that." Alex pointed down the sidewalk to a group of men putting posters up on the brick wall.

Charlotte directed her attention to the captivating painted scenes revealed beneath the roller when the men stepped aside to work on the next one.

Sterling & Son's Spectacular Circus!
One Day Only!

"The circus," Alex gasped in an awed whisper.

"How wonderful! When is it coming through?" Charlotte asked the man in suspenders and a flat cap.

" 'Bout two months." He tapped at the date on the large poster they'd already plastered and pulled out another large sheet with zebras and purple dancers.

April 14, 1927
Parade at Noon
Shows at 2 & 8

A strong gust pulled two posters out of the other man's arms and sent them cartwheeling down the street.

"Well, shoot." He turned to the man in suspenders, who shrugged, removed his cap, and tucked it into his front pocket.

"I can't wait to tell everyone at school." Alex ran his fingers over pictures of red and yellow railcars, the new images a bright contrast to the chipped dusty bricks beneath them.

The man in suspenders used his roller to flatten down a corner of the paper that had been pried away from the wall by the gust.

"It will create a buzz at the cookhouse, too. Seems like everyone within a hundred miles hopped the train to Ayer when the circus came through last year."

"It was my favorite day. Can we get cotton candy again?" Alex asked eagerly.

"Yes, and funnel cakes—"

"Taffy, balloons, and pink lemonade!"

"Oh, and they'll have your Tesla displays again, I bet."

"And the horse opera for you." Alex quickened his pace. "And the menagerie…"

"Miles of colorful railcars full of exotic animals and mysterious people from faraway places," Charlotte said with a sigh.

By the time the pair arrived at the schoolhouse door, they were almost skipping with excitement.

Charlotte waved goodbye to her son and continued down Main Street, straight into the wind with her hand on her hat and dust dancing across her feet in swirls like ghosts from the fields.

She giggled to herself when she saw Bill from the general store furiously sweeping at the dust on his storefront steps as the wind blew the dirt right back on top of him. He shouted, "Good morning," across the howl of the wind and lost his own hat when he lifted his hand to wave. Looking like a vaudeville clown from one of the circus scenes, Bill quickly dropped his broom to run after his hat, grumbling as he chased it down the street.

When Charlotte arrived at the Winslow Inn and Cookhouse where she worked, she found one of the rolled posters had blown up against the brick wall by the door, along with part of a tumbleweed and layers of dirt. She picked up the large paper scroll, shook the dust off, and tucked it into her coat.

In the cookhouse dining room, a few farmers sat complaining about the dust storm over their breakfast. "The last thing we need is another drought," one said.

"Well, the almanac says this is a rainin' year."

"Lord willing."

"I sure hope you're right," another chimed in. "If the wind keeps carryin' off my topsoil, I don't know what I'm gonna do. I swear every grain of dirt that flies off with the wind is money outta my pocket."

"If only the wind brought something good in with it. All it does is sweep through, bringing tumbleweeds and trash—"

"—and when it sweeps out, it takes the very ground from under my feet."

"Can't plant if there ain't no dirt to put the seeds in."

The farmers all nodded in agreement, humming and grunting and clicking their tongues.

Through the swinging kitchen doors, she found the inn owners, Saul and his wife Martha, sitting together at the butcher-block counter having a cup of coffee.

Saul had effectively been running the cookhouse, Ayer Inn & Cookhouse, as it was back then, since before the war, even though people often assumed it was operating because of the little old white-haired white man who owned several of the city businesses at the time, rather than because of the Black man in the kitchen. It was only after the little old man died and left the business to Saul and Martha that the town realized it was their hard work and good cooking that had drawn traveling ranchers and hungry patrons to the small town for the past ten years. By then, the little cookhouse was already famous for the best grits, biscuits, and gravy in North Texas.

"Good morning, you two." Charlotte greeted them cheerily as she hung up her hat and unbuttoned her coat to hang it on the coat rack by the door. The coat slumped onto the rack and created a new pile of dust on the black and white penny tile. "Goodness, I'll sweep that up."

"Oh, don't you worry, Lottie," Saul said. "That won't be the last bit of dirt that finds its way in here."

"He's right. I done swept up three times already this morning." Martha rubbed at her temples. "You go get you a cup of coffee, hon."

Charlotte quickly swept the dust into a pan with a hand broom and dumped it in the bin. "You've been working too hard. Up early again today?"

"Before the sun as always." Saul patted his wife's hand. "I'm looking to get her a little help with the inn if we can put away enough money to afford it."

"Oh, nonsense, I don't need any help. You two quit your worryin'." She held the warm cup to her forehead and closed her eyes.

Saul and Charlotte exchanged glances.

"You'll never guess what I saw on the way here."

She pulled the rolled-up poster from her coat.

"What's that?" Saul asked.

"The circus is coming to town again!" She handed the poster to Saul and took a waiting cup from beside the tin coffee pot on the stove.

Martha's eyes shot open. "The what?" She set down her coffee cup forcefully, sending a little of the black liquid sloshing over the rim of the cup onto the countertop.

"Oh, glory," Saul murmured, spreading the poster across the counter and looking at Martha out of the side of his eyes.

"The circus!" Charlotte exclaimed. She took her seat beside Martha and hugged the warm cup with both hands.

Martha tutted and wiped the spilled coffee from the counter with a spare rag.

"Here we go," said Saul.

"Ain't nothin' good come from the circus," Martha declared.

Charlotte peered at her curiously over the top of her coffee cup. "I can't imagine anything but good. Everything about the circus is so exciting! Bright and colorful. Why—"

"Don't ask," Saul said.

"She ain't gotta ask. I'm gon' tell her," Martha said. "Haven't you ever heard the story of George and Willie?"

Charlotte shook her head.

"Well, it makes sense you wouldn't have heard it, but every Black family knows the story of George and Willie Muse." Martha looked to her husband for support. "We warned our children again and again.

Didn't we, Saul?"

"Mm-hmm," he responded as he spread out the poster and drank his coffee.

"George and Willie were two little Black boys from Virginia," she continued. "Albino Black boys, which is a thing I've never seen. An' I guess those Ringling Circus boys had never seen it either, because they was rollin' through town and spotted them. Plucked them right from their home and put them in one of their sideshows. Told those poor boys their mother was dead and that their new home was the circus. Meanwhile, their poor mother was sittin' at home sick with worry."

"They just took them?"

"Just up and took 'em," Martha said. "But their mother went lookin' for them. Never stopped. After something like twenty years, she found them. That Ringling Circus had them on display in a sideshow like animals at a zoo. Calling them 'Savages from Afar' and telling everyone they were mute."

"How terrible." Charlotte shivered with horror at the thought of having her own son ripped from her home and thrown into a traveling sideshow act.

"You hold onto yourself and hold onto Alex so y'all don't end up like George and Willie. The circus sweeps through town like this dust storm, stirring up trouble and taking anything that ain't nailed down with it when it goes. Like a tumbleweed in the wind."

Charlotte shuddered, as if shaken by the wind that howled outside the cookhouse walls.

"Look here," Saul said, pointing to the poster. "Human cannonball. They gon' shoot a lady right out of a cannon across the elephants."

She leaned over and looked at the colorful scene, an illustration of a big red cannon with a bright blue star and a woman in red flying through the air over a row of elephants, waving and smiling.

"I wouldn't mind seein' that," Saul said, winking at Charlotte.

Martha tutted again. "Well, you can see it on your own then, Saul Winslow, and good luck! I won't be settin' foot near the whole mess."

"Aw, come on now—"

"No, I mean it. I said it before and I'll say it again." Martha wagged her finger at her husband. "Ain't nothin' good come from the circus."

Chapter 2

Trapeze Bat Extraordinaire

Herman Frances Sterling the Third had everything a man could ever want. He was handsome, well educated, and rich. Frank lived a life of enviable luxury and was often accused of being a profligate. He smoked expensive cigars, drove expensive cars, and slept with beautiful (sometimes expensive) women. Most of all, Frank Sterling stood to inherit an empire—the Sterling & Son's Circus.

This morning, the young bachelor woke slowly as the curtains were drawn, and light rushed through the room in a singular beam, dust dancing in the ray across his bed and tiptoeing to an array of fiery red curls. He slipped his arm out from under the sleeping girl and exchanged a smug smirk with his butler, who handed him a tray with his newspaper, some correspondence, and a tall white ceramic mug full of piping hot black coffee.

"Thank you, Charlie." Frank pulled himself up and took the tray from his man. Even if his apartment wasn't half as nice as his father's swanky estate downtown, he liked the freedom it offered. He could do things his way here without the hovering, suffocating judgment of his father.

"God, how much did I drink last night?" He held

the hot cup to his temples in an attempt to melt away the tension behind his eyes.

"I couldn't say, sir. You spent the first part of the evening at the Jazz Lounge, and the rest..." Charlie shrugged and gestured to the sleeping redhead.

Mention of the Jazz Lounge ushered forward segmented glimpses of the night before. Frank remembered, with a little bit of nausea, roaring trumpets, the clinking glasses of sloshing amber liquid, lace garters, and dice on the table. "Must have been some kind of moonshine. I feel terrible."

"You told me last night that it was excellent moonshine, sir. And something about 'Prohibition be damned, this is Texas! And we'll drink if we want!' "

"That doesn't sound like me," Frank responded, opening up his newspaper. "Did I say anything else?"

"Yes, sir. Now that you mention it, you repeatedly asked me to sing the chorus to 'Blue Yodel,' and you told me to remind you that I deserve a raise," Charlie answered.

"Hmm, that doesn't sound like me either." Frank hummed the tune as he scanned the paper and was both relieved and slightly annoyed to find that he was nowhere in it. He'd been a tad bit less discreet with his exploits than he should have been the last few days, and his new fiancée wouldn't appreciate it. His last one sure hadn't.

But still, *Premier Week for Sterling & Son's Circus!* should be splashed across the front pages of newspapers all over. *New Animals and Attractions! The Biggest Show Yet!* Frank imagined his picture front and center, right under the heading. He'd be standing in front of their newest set of railway cars with his tailcoat and his tallest top hat, thumbs in his suspenders, like his father always did. *I'll talk to Jay at the party on Saturday. He'll get the reporters set straight.*

He could always count on his older cousin Jay to take care of anything he needed. As their logistics manager, it was his job. More than that, Jay had always been the most responsible of the three young men poised to run the circus as Frank's father eyed retirement.

"The driver is here, sir. If you'd like, I can dress you for the meeting at Sterling Mansion."

"Oh damn, that is today, isn't it?" Frank winced at the sting from his headache and the thought of another exhausting conversation planning out the travel season in the dullest part of the day. "That sounds more like a job for Mr. Edwards and the other Sterling. I think we'll sit this one out, Charlie."

His father would be displeased if Frank skipped another meeting, but he'd get over it. Despite an occasional condescending comment or slap on the wrist, he knew his dad would ask him to run the circus when he retired. He was the star and Sonny Sterling's only son, so he needn't trudge out to every dreary business meeting. That sort of thing was more a job for his cousins, Hugh Sterling and Jay Edwards. When Frank was promoted to running the circus, he'd still allow them to run things behind the scenes.

"Very good, sir. Shall I send the car away?"

Frank glanced at the woman next to him and back at Charlie. "No, we'll need it in a few minutes for her. Ring Mr. Sterling's butler. Let him know I won't be attending today's meeting."

Charlie nodded and left the room.

Next to him, the redhead was stirring. She groaned and pulled the covers over her head. "That light's right in my eyes!"

"That's what daytime looks like."

Birdie threw the covers from her head and glared at Frank. "You callin' me a vampire or somethin'?" She bit at him playfully.

"Oh, now that would make a great new act! 'Birdie Bells, Trapeze Bat Extraordinaire! Step right up, folks, but not too close!' I wonder, should we let you continue riding with the girls or move you to the menagerie with the other animals?"

"Aren't you hilarious?" She rolled her eyes. "Besides, you know what I think about that. I shouldn't have to share a car with the girls anymore, not now that I'm a star act. I should have my very own sleeper car to travel in like Lillian Leitzel does for the Ringling Brothers!"

"Ringling Brothers and Barnum & Bailey runs a little bit bigger operation than we do, Birdie. And anyway, you know I can't do that. We've talked about this. Our show's already got a caravan sixty-five railway cars long."

"So what's sixty-six, huh?" she asked, pulling Frank's coffee from his hands and taking a sip. "I've earned it, haven't I? Doesn't my act draw big crowds, Frankie?" She softened. "Imagine how much easier it would be to spend time with your favorite trapeze bat if she had her own sleeper car that you could sneak in and out of whenever you wanted?" She snuggled up to him, kissing his neck and biting at his ear.

The truth was that Frank had already commissioned a new railway car for Birdie. A big spectacular chariot with her name and a painted picture of her likeness flying through the air on trapeze splashed across the side. He'd had it painted along with the new cars for the seals. After all, she was a crowd-pleaser, and he had to compete with those blasted Ringling, Barnum & Bailey blokes. People traveled from towns across counties to get a glimpse of Birdie Bells. But he didn't see a reason to admit any of this to her. Not yet, anyway. Not when there was so much more he could get out of her first.

Charlie reappeared and nodded at Frank, taking his post by the door as he always did on mornings like these.

"Well, you may not have your own railway car, but you can have your very own motorcar for transport home today. Isn't that right, Charlie?" He took up his paper again.

"Yes, sir, the car for Miss Bells is waiting outside."

Birdie glared at Frank and rose from the bed, sheets falling down around her. Charlie blushed and looked away.

"See somethin' you like, Charlie?" She sauntered over to the man and popped open his coat buttons one by one with a single finger "Coffee?" She extended Frank's cup to Charlie's lips, pressing her body against him.

"Will you need anything else, sir?" Charlie asked, hurriedly refastening his buttons.

"Just the car, thank you, Charlie," he said without looking up from his paper. "She'll be down shortly." But Charlie was gone before Frank could finish his sentence.

Birdie giggled and turned back to Frank.

"You're going to give him a heart attack."

"I was just having a little fun." She pushed Frank's paper aside and ran her fingers through his hair. "Anything you wanna see before I go?"

"I think I've seen everything there is to see," he said without looking up from his paper. He still slipped a hand around her hip for one last squeeze before taking back his mug, a little disappointed that there wasn't much coffee left.

Birdie rolled her eyes and turned to examine the room. She marveled at the life Frank lived. Last night they'd stumbled in, knocked over furniture, and thrown clothes everywhere. But today, only a few hours later, the room was clean and tidy like it always was. The chair had been turned upright, and on it were her neatly folded clothes.

Birdie had yet to spend the night in the big Sterling house. Her rendezvous with Frank had always been in his apartment. But she'd been paraded around the mansion once or twice when Mr. Sterling wanted to wow his party guests. It was magnificent. She'd overheard Mr. Sterling telling everyone that all of the rooms were modeled after Bavarian palace bedrooms. Sleeping there in one of those grandiose bedrooms, in one of those oversized beds with the canopy, was one of her personal goals. It would be a little harder to wriggle her way into one of those beds with Frank now that he was engaged to be married again, but Birdie didn't mind a challenge.

She would have her chance that weekend. Mr. Sterling would be throwing another one of his famous soirees, and he had conscripted most of his best circus acts to perform at the party. Birdie tried not to picture the lavish ladies in their elegant evening gowns as she gathered her own tasseled silk number from the chair and began to dress. Thinking of the party gave her the stomach-flipping sensation of reaching for a fly bar in midair that was just an inch too far. Birdie could fly through the air on trapeze without batting an eye. But she hated mingling with rich people at parties who judged her by her birth instead of by what she could do.

She pulled her stockings on seductively at first, but Frank was opening and analyzing his letters, completely uninterested in her movements about the room. She retreated to her own thoughts.

The mansion would be full of innocent-looking marriage-worthy high-society girls clamoring for Frank's attention. Her stomach tightened at the thought of one decorated débutante in particular, Luella Prescott. The society papers called Luella "a model of elegance and sophistication," and her family was rolling in dough. Birdie would have to work a little harder if she wanted to keep Frank's attention with perfect little Miss Prescott on his arm.

"We girls will be having a little get-together on Saturday," she hinted to Frank, hoping she could pull him from the party early, or at least give him something else to think about while he was there.

"You'll have to have a drink for me then," Frank said as he flipped over one note with disinterest and proceeded to open the next one. "Family business."

Birdie considered telling Frank that she'd be there for his "family business" but decided against it. Frank didn't have to know everything. "A woman is entitled to her secrets," her mother had always said. That was about the only useful thing Birdie ever learned from her mother. That and the fact that the only person she could count on was herself. She pushed away the image of her siblings looking up at her, the youngest one shuddering and screaming. The blood on the floor, rolling in a river with the wood grain toward her toes. Then she remembered the last time she'd lost her temper.

Yes, she kept more than a few secrets from Frank. She sighed and gave him one last kiss on the forehead. "Suit yourself."

Birdie let herself out of the bedroom and glided down the stairs to the front door. She caught a glimpse of herself in a gilded hallway mirror and was bitten by the bitter realization that the woman in the frame made a conspicuous contrast to the women she'd be standing next to at the Sterling mansion party. She looked completely out of place even here in this apartment. With her fishnet stockings and silky scarlet dress, she'd look out of place anywhere in the daytime. Although, she had to admit to herself, the dress hugged her curves perfectly and suited her well. And so what if she didn't fit into this stuffy domestic setting; she had no desire to.

Birdie had been feeling dull lately, like a light going out, and her pale skin and the dark circles under her eyes reflected it. She paused for a moment. Was it the persistent snapping that echoed in her memory when she tried to sleep at night or the ghosts from her past that kept her awake? She brushed away the thought. She always felt out of step and out of place in the off-season. Hated going about her life without a crowd to witness her magnificence. Hungered for the power and freedom of flying through the air or contorting her body in a way that no one else on Earth was known to do. Birdie never felt more invigorated than after a show. She licked her finger and rubbed a bit of smeared mascara from under her left eye before slipping on both gloves. She missed the taste of infamy, thirsted for admiration.

"Maybe you are more of a vampire than a woman," she said to the mirror. She needed to get back to work.

Charlie was waiting for her by the back door to discreetly send her on her way in the car, but Birdie didn't feel like slipping out the back today. She opened the front door and pranced down the steps, squinting into the sunlight. *I guess it's close to noon.* The streets were already packed with people going about their business, headed to and from the stockyards. She stopped walking for a moment when the back of her neck prickled, but each time she turned around, no one suspicious seemed to be following her. Maybe she was just feeling the stares of passersby taking in the sight of a burlesque dancer in a flapper dress out in broad daylight.

It wasn't far to the circus grounds. Birdie shook off her suspicions, turned on her heel, and sauntered down the pavement toward home.

Chapter 3

A Long List

"We'll need two hundred pounds of beef for the tigers alone."

Tigers! The customers at Charlotte's table shoveled the last bits of biscuits into their mouths and licked gravy from the corners of their lips. Would feeding hundreds of pounds of beef to hungry tigers be more difficult or dangerous than serving endless plates of breakfast to hungry patrons? All morning the three men had huddled around a sheet of paper discussing prices and schedules, negotiations punctuated by forks clinking against plates and the steady cadence of the early spring's first rain falling outside.

The meeting seemed benevolent enough, except for an underlying tension that vibrated between them, like the flexed but motionless muscles of a predator ready to pounce. All three of the men around the wooden cookhouse table were tigers, running their tongues along their whiskers and surveying which of them was the weakest. She was Mabel Stark, the famous tiger tamer, with a whip, subduing them by refilling their coffee and clearing away their breakfast plates.

Bill from the general supply store sat with his back to the window. She suppressed a smile at the memory of him chasing after his hat in the wind. The other two men were taller and younger with fancy suits, clean-shaven faces, and shiny hair. Definitely from out of town. Charlotte had overheard their names—Jay Edwards and Hugh Sterling. They were with the Sterling & Son's Circus.

"It's a bigger list than last year, Mr. Edwards. Like these fresh herring...Look around you!" Bill indicated the miles of dirt and fields with his hand. "We don't have fish around here, gentlemen. Much less fresh! I'll have to call every supplier in the country...and it's likely to get expensive!" The sheet of paper rattled in Bill's hand as he went on reading the list through the spectacles perched on his bulbous red nose. "One thousand pounds of bread, ninety pounds of butter, three hundred dozen eggs, five barrels of peanuts...peanuts?"

The man Bill was speaking to had tossed his suit jacket on the back of the chair and rolled up his sleeves. He snapped his pocket watch open and closed over his newspaper, the corner of his mouth fighting to suppress a smile as he listened to the red-faced store owner read the list he'd written. "It's essentially the same supply list we discussed in November, Bill. Sure, I've made some adjustments on the consumables because we've acquired some new animals." Jay Edwards lowered his voice and leaned in enthusiastically. "My cousins in India—"

"Regardless of the difficulty, or the expense, the listed items are needed. Can you acquire them, or should we look elsewhere?" The other man, Hugh Sterling, cast a wary glance at Jay and tugged at the bottom of his securely buttoned jacket. His pursed lips settled into an angle of perpetual annoyance. He didn't want to be there. And he certainly didn't seem to want anyone hearing their company secrets.

Jay leaned back slowly as Bill rattled on. Hugh picked up his coffee cup as if to take a sip but scowled at the cup and set it back on the saucer at the table. He flicked a piece of fuzz from his jacket sleeve and returned to his rigid upright posture, crossing his arms and observing the conversation with scornful contempt.

Charlotte tended to customers at other tables, bringing out breakfast plates and glasses of juice for ranchers, farmers, and families. Her regular group of farmers was happy today. They closed their eyes to take in a deep breath every time someone opened the door, savoring the smell of damp earth and the cool moisture of the air.

"Praise God, and keep it coming," one said as she tended to their table.

"The coffee or the rain?" she asked.

"Both!" The men laughed as they held out their cups and thanked her. The farmers' cheerfulness warmed the whole room, a welcome relief from months of drought and fear. In the little farming town, wind brought worry. But rain brought hope.

"A lot of out-of-towners in here today," one of the farmers observed. "Think they washed in with the rain?"

"I couldn't say. It's usually just folks passing through to Fort Worth or Dallas, but it has been busier lately. Poor Martha's about worked herself to death keeping up with all of the guests staying in the inn." She gestured to the rooms above her.

"I'd hate to think of Ayer as a tourist town, but if they bring the rain, then I guess I'll have to change my mind on that." The farmers laughed. "Hey, Miss Charlotte, can you bring us another round of them famous grits 'fore the tourists eat 'em all up?"

At the circus table, Bill was trying to work a deal with the city boys. Jay and Hugh exchanged glances over his head when he leaned over to examine the list again, and Charlotte chuckled quietly. Bill knew exactly where to get all those supplies. He knew it, and they knew it. The tigers had sussed out the clown.

"I know you're still new to this, but we make the same requests in every city and those proprietors always find a way to make it happen," Jay said, "even in California."

Bill scrunched his red nose at the word "California" and readjusted his glasses. "Well, they have the whole ocean to pull fish from in California! We're a little more remote out here."

Jay tried again. "You're right. But they didn't have trouble finding anything on our list in Clovis. There's no ocean by Clovis."

"There's nothing at all in or anywhere near Clovis," Hugh muttered to no one in particular.

Bill's lip twitched and curled a little. "Well…I'm just letting you know it'll be expensive…" He repeated "expensive" as he arranged his napkin and looked up at the city men.

Charlotte chatted with her regular customers as she wiped down the wooden tables. A pair of church widow ladies dressed in purple velvet, Agnes and Agatha, seemed as hungry for gossip as they were for breakfast.

"Tell me, Charlotte. Who are those sharp-looking men at the table with Bill?" Agatha whispered over her cup of tea.

She leaned down by Agatha's good ear. "They're businessmen from the Sterling & Son's Circus."

Agatha leaned back and placed a dainty black-and-white-gloved hand across her chest in surprise. "Bless my soul. Right here in the cookhouse!"

"Did she say the circus?" Agnes asked, quite a bit louder than she needed to, leaning across the table and dropping her napkin.

Agatha nodded knowingly at her friend. "I wonder if one of them is that Frank Sterling I've read about in the papers. I hear he's a cad."

"No, their names are Jay Edwards and Hugh Sterling," Charlotte answered, retrieving Agatha's napkin and replacing it for her. "Could be related though. Maybe."

"Well, I'll be." Agnes adjusted her spectacles and peered over at the table. "Aren't they handsome, too!"

"They're too young for you, Agnes," Agatha quipped as she sipped her tea properly, gazing at the men over her extended pinky finger.

Charlotte cleared away a few more empty breakfast plates from various tables and carried them through saloon-style wooden doors into the kitchen, where she encountered another man who was interested in the conversation at the circus table.

"Who are those dandies over there?" Saul asked, peeking over the still-swinging door at the strangers as he spooned eggs onto a plate for her customers.

"They're with the Sterling & Son's Circus," she said, setting down the armful of dirty dishes and running her hands under the warm water.

"Is that right?" Saul whistled. "Don't tell Martha, on account of how much she hates it, but I don't much mind the circus myself. Last few times I've been, they had some jazz or ragtime groups in the parade or out at the sideshows. Only way to hear a good Black band outside of New York or Chicago."

"Oh, I forgot how much you love jazz." She dried her hands on her apron. "That band last year was really good!"

Saul sang out in deep rich baritone as he added pepper to the gravy, "Pack up all my cares and woe, here I go, singing low. Bye, bye, blackbird..." He placed stacks of hot bacon on waiting plates beside the biscuits. "What are boys from Sterling & Son's doing in town now anyhow? The circus ain't set to come through for a few weeks."

"It looks like they're talking over a list of food and supplies with Bill."

"They're workin' with Bill again?" He turned away from his cooking. "I heard he robbed 'em blind last year. Bought himself a fancy new car after the circus left town from all the money he made."

"I did hear Bill use the word 'expensive' a few times."

Saul drummed his fingers on the countertop for a moment, thinking. "You know, I've got a cousin over in Abilene who gets our supplies to us for half the price Bill can get 'em. I bet I can beat his prices and still make a killin'," he whispered.

Charlotte considered that for a moment. "Do you think we'd make enough to hire some help for Martha?"

He nodded, thinking. "You know what, I bet we sure could."

"But what would she say if she knew you were

working with people from the circus? She hates the—"

"You let me worry about Martha." He winked. "Get me a word with those circus men!"

Charlotte pricked up her ears when she went to drop off breakfast plates at a table near the circus men, but the chatter from other customers and the steady drumming of rain against the windows drowned out their conversation. Charlotte moved a little closer and strained to listen.

"As Mr. Edwards has already stated, we won't agree to tentative prices," Hugh said to Bill.

"Well, these other items..."

"Listen," Jay said, "Hugh and I will be here at the inn until tomorrow morning. Why don't you prepare the costs of these added items for us, and we'll look it over together this afternoon."

"Oh, but of course. I'll just put off everything else I was planning to do today and scour the country for fresh fish and peanuts." Bill rose abruptly with a scrape of his chair against the hardwood floor. "Come see me this afternoon. I want payment up front!" With that, Bill scurried out the door, tipping his hat at a few of the locals on his way out.

"I guess breakfast is on us," Jay said to Hugh.

Hugh flicked at a crumb on the table. "I can't understand why Sonny sends us out to the middle of nowhere to work with the local riffraff. It's such a tremendous waste of our time."

"It's good to build these local connections," Jay said. "Ayer didn't do as well as it could have for us last year, and Mr. Sterling wants us to make sure everything is perfect this time. You know we can't afford to skip a dime even on one show this year or we'll be belly up.

Besides, it's all part of the game. Look at them." The pair looked up from their conversation to see the Ayer residents at other tables staring at them and murmuring in low conversation. Their acknowledgment spooked Agnes and Agatha, who abruptly turned away and started fidgeting with their teacups.

"What exactly am I looking at?"

"The people! Our presence here generates curiosity and excitement," Jay said, smiling at the remaining onlookers. "Isn't that the heartbeat of the circus? Curiosity and excitement?"

Hugh slumped back in his chair and rolled his eyes. "Well, even if that's true, I don't see why I had to come along. It seems more a job for you and Frank, if anyone."

"Frank's never been in for this kind of thing. You know he's more about the show than the numbers."

"Must be nice." Hugh pulled out a cigarette and fiddled with his lighter. "Frank gets to choose where and how he contributes while we toil away like slaves for our master. Must be nice to be the son of the king."

"We've all got a part to play."

"But for how long? When Sonny retires and gives this all to Frank, one of two things is going to happen. Either Frank will get rid of the likes of us in favor of…more attractive assistants…or he'll bumble it all up and we'll both be out on the pavement."

"Frank will be just as successful as Sonny and we'll support him," Jay said. "Starting with the supplies for Ayer."

"Speak for yourself. I've got better things to do than answer the summons of that too-big-for-his-britches hillbilly. Besides, didn't you hear he expects payment up front? How do you expect to manage that?"

"We will both go," Jay said firmly. "I'll handle it."

Hugh sat back up and looked at Jay defiantly.

"Don't worry. It won't take long." Jay opened up his newspaper and started scanning it. "Then you can sneak off and do whatever it is you always do when we're sent out in place of the advance men."

"I'll have you know that I—"

"Excuse me," Charlotte said as she refilled the men's coffee cups, "I couldn't help but overhear you were looking to purchase some supplies for your circus and, I thought…I th-thought that—"

"Did anyone ask what you thought?" Hugh snapped. "Can't you see that I was speaking?"

"Calm down, Hugh." Jay closed his newspaper. "Don't mind him, ma'am."

Charlotte hesitated. "I-I didn't mean to intrude…I just saw your list and thought you might want to talk it over with the proprietor of the inn. That is, my boss, Mr. Winslow."

Hugh huffed and pulled the list from sight. "This has nothing to do with you or Mr. Winslow. This list is Sterling & Son's business!"

"I didn't mean to offend you, sir." Charlotte sensed the watchful eyes of all the customers in the cookhouse as she continued. "I just…well, I love the circus. I can't bear to watch Bill charge you an arm and a leg when I know that Mr. Winslow is much more pleasant to talk to than Bill. He's fair and reliable—and I do believe he could get you all the items on that list."

"Even the fish, you think?" Jay began writing something down in the black book in front of him, crossing out numbers and writing new ones.

She brightened. "Yes sir, he has a cousin—"

"You can't be considering this! Mr. Winslow is a colored man." Hugh cast a ferocious glance up at his waitress, and Charlotte remembered that Mabel Stark didn't always leave the tiger cage unscathed. Maybe it was time to turn tail and run for the kitchen, but the sight of Saul nodding enthusiastically behind the doors and giving her two thumbs-up sent a new wave of determination through her. *I can't let him down.* Rooted to the spot, she stood a little taller, facing the men. *Saul and Martha deserve this.*

"Your sense of propriety seems to be second to your stomach, Hugh. I saw you gobble up those grits and gravy." Jay finished what he was writing and closed his book.

Hugh crossed his arms and looked out the window.

"As for me, I've never cared for those distinctions or understood why they're used to keep a man from going about his business." Jay turned to Charlotte. "You believe Mr. Winslow can provide us with everything you've heard us discussing?"

Charlotte nodded.

"It can't hurt to talk to him. If he can get us everything we need at a better price than Bill..." Jay snapped his pocket watch closed and popped it back open. "Might save you that trip to the general store this afternoon."

Hugh grimaced in disgust and took a long drag from his cigarette. "Have it your way, Jay."

Jay smiled at Charlotte and gave her the nod she'd been waiting for.

Charlotte quickly took Bill's empty coffee cup and Hugh's full one and ran back to the kitchen triumphantly. "They wanna talk to you, Saul!"

"Atta girl, Lottie!" Saul said as he untied his apron and threw it on the counter. He clapped her back on his way out and lumbered through the swinging doors with confidence and purpose.

Heart pounding, she finished up the breakfast Saul had left at the grill, fighting the urge to let everything burn and rush back to the circus table. She dished out a new set of breakfast plates, took a deep breath, and headed back out to tend her tables. She circulated the room in measured steps, topping off cups of coffee at other tables. Saul was seated at the table across from Jay, who nodded intently and seemed interested in what he had to say. *Stop staring, Charlotte*. She wiped at a clean table nearby and waved off one of the farmers who tried to get her attention.

"And these last few items, well, I can get these for you very near cost at that. I've got a cousin who's a fisherman. Water's down around here, of course, but the rain is promising! We'll get you those herring. Don't you worry!" Saul clasped his hands together with excitement.

"But can you get it here on time on such short notice?" Jay asked. "It's crucial."

"Without a doubt. I'll get to work on this, and you can count on us having it ready at the train tracks by the Friday after next, no problem!"

"Let's get this in writing and move forward," Jay said, extending his hand to Saul. "We'll pay you on the day. Half on delivery, half at the end of the night."

"Thank you, sir!" Saul shook his hand enthusiastically. "You won't regret it, sir!"

"We'll see about that," Hugh said, snuffing out his

cigarette. "Settle up with our waitress, will you, Jay? I've got a few things to see to."

Charlotte briefly made eye contact with Hugh as he rose to leave and cringed at his indignant and superior expression. If she never saw Hugh Sterling again, it would be too soon.

Jay looked after Hugh with concern as he pulled his pocketbook from the jacket on his chair and flipped through the cash inside. "Thank you," he said, handing the money to Charlotte. "Please keep the change." His eyes were stormy gray, like the spring clouds that promise rain to wash away the dust and revive suffering crops.

"Thank—" Her voice caught in her throat when his fingers brushed against hers. Speechless, flushed, and flustered, she tucked the money into her apron, turned away quickly, and ran to the kitchen.

"Did you hear that, Lottie?" Saul exclaimed as he burst through the kitchen doors and shook her by the shoulder. "I'm selling them everything! My God, that list was as long as my arm." Saul guffawed with laughter and excitement. "Martha's going to find out she's wrong. We're fixin' to get a whole lot of good from the circus!"

The mention of Martha's warning sent a chill down her spine.

"You take home an extra basket of bread and meat tonight for your family, Lottie," Saul said. "You take that and some cinnamon rolls, buttermilk, whatever you want. You've earned it. The whole lot! I can't believe it!"

Chapter 4

Simmering

Charlotte lit the fire at the stove, browning butter in her cast-iron skillet as she unwrapped the raw roast from the brown paper. Aromatic spices from years of home-cooked meals rose up from the well-worn pan. Saul had taught her how to cook a good pot roast years ago, and he'd given her a good-looking cut of meat to take home after their success with the circus men. Small, but plenty for her little family. Much better than the potato skin pie she'd been planning to pass off as their meal that night. The roast would take a few hours to cook in the oven after she'd seared it, so they'd be eating later than usual, but it would be worth it. Her husband loved a hearty meal. She tapped her tired toes on the wood floor as she peeled the carrots and potatoes, humming a tune to herself and listening to Alex chat about his day.

Since she'd gotten home, the two of them had tidied up, started a fire, swept the persistent dust from the floor, and now Alex was sitting at the kitchen table with his books and papers.

"This new book is so interesting. Look at this part about atmospheric electricity." He picked up the book to show her a page full of smudged pencil notes. Charlotte ordered books for her son every few weeks from Bill at the general store. They just about ate up her small salary from the cookhouse, but she didn't mind.

She wiped her hands on her apron and sat across the table from her son. "You're right, that is interesting," she said, flipping to the title page of the book. *Electricity, the Science of the Nineteenth Century, a Sketch for General Readers* by Emma Marie Caillard. Charlotte smiled. Never having finished school herself, she felt a sense of pride and awe to hold a book about science and electricity that had been written by a woman. "Fascinating!" she said, handing the book back to Alex, who immediately turned it back to the pages on lightning.

"And look here, where they describe the Leyden jar," he continued.

"Oh, I remember the Leyden jars." She chuckled. Alex had built about four different kinds of models using leftover milk bottles or any other glass jar or bottle he could obtain. "You had me worried you were going to burn the house down!"

"I would never." He laughed as he added a bit more to his sketch. "On purpose…"

"If we had to lose a house on our way to you achieving your dream of being a famous scientist, I guess that would be all right," Charlotte said. "I've heard living in a box isn't as bad as they say…"

Alex rolled his eyes.

"Perhaps you could engineer a very nice box for us," she went on.

"I'm not going to burn the house down, Mom. But I do want to give the Leyden jars another go. They have new schematics on them here, and I'll need to make some adjustments. I just need a few supplies."

"A few supplies?"

"I've made a list," he said through the pencil in his teeth as he examined the book. He ripped out a sheet from his sketchbook and handed it to her. "Do you think you could get these things for me?"

Charlotte took the list and laughed as she read over it, imagining she felt about the same way Bill or Saul did when they saw the circus list earlier that day. "I'll see what I can do," she said.

"See what you can do about what?"

Charlotte jumped at the sound of her husband's voice. *Is it six already?* She stood up quickly. "I'm sorry, Pete! I didn't hear you come in. How was your day, dear?"

"Fine…it was fine." Pete's lanky frame stood stooped and shadowed in the open door in a swirl of dry dust despite the rain falling steadily behind him. In his silhouette, Charlotte could make out his spurs and the pistols he carried on either hip.

"How about this rain?" Charlotte went to greet her husband with a kiss.

Pete grunted as he looked back over his shoulder at the rain before closing the door behind him. He stepped into the light of the kitchen and took off his cowboy hat to reveal sun-bronzed cheeks covered in dirt and stubble and obstinate blond curls wet with sweat that pushed up against the crown of his head where the rest of his hair was flattened from a long day under his cowboy hat. His eyes were dusty brown flecked with gold, piercing, though they were less lively than they'd been when she met him. Hardened from long days squinting against the sun. There had been a dozen years, a few new towns, and a World War since their whirlwind romance, but Charlotte still saw the handsome young buck she'd fallen in love with when she looked at Pete. She still felt like she was lucky to be his wife, just as she had felt lucky to be his girl all those years ago. Out of all the women who'd fawned over him, he had chosen Charlotte.

Pete leaned over to set his hat upside down on the chair by the door slowly, taking in the room before speaking again. "What's all this?" he asked, waving a calloused hand over the books and papers strewn about the table. Charlotte could tell by his posture, the furrowed lines between his eyebrows, and the change in the air since he'd stormed in; Pete was in one of his moods.

"We were just cleaning up," she said, hastily tucking away Alex's list into her apron and sorting the books and papers into a pile. She always felt like a tightrope walker in the Texas wind when Pete came home angry. One wrong step could send her plummeting.

Pete threw his cowhide coat over the chair where his hat lay and eyed Alex suspiciously with that piercing gaze of his as the boy hastily gathered his things from the table into a stack in his arms. "Set those books by my chair, Alex. I wanna look through 'em."

Alex nodded silently and set his books by the round wooden foot of Pete's dusty threadbare armchair in front of the fire. A pang of helpless guilt tugged at Charlotte. Her son was tiptoeing the tightrope too.

"We've got pot roast for dinner! Won't that be nice? I'm just about to put the meat in the oven."

"Why've you been sittin' around when dinner ain't even in the oven?"

"I'm sorry, I—"

He leaned on the doorpost and let out an exasperated sigh. "How long is it gonna take?"

"Just an hour or so. I'll hurry." She turned back to the stove to tend to the roast, rotating it to the last uncooked side with a pop and sizzle of the melted butter in the skillet.

"An hour! You know I've been working out in this soppin' mess all day. I'm chilled to the bone and starvin'!" Her husband stomped off into the back rooms leaving a trail of muddy bootprints.

Alex joined Charlotte, looking up at her with big silent eyes and offering help. He had his father's hair, the same thin frame, but she saw herself reflected in his eyes. She ruffled his dusty blond hair and asked him to set the table as she opened the oven and placed the simmering pot of meat and vegetables in to cook.

Pete reappeared and took his seat by the fire, collecting his pipe and assembling tobacco into it from a tin he'd pulled out of his pocket. The familiar woodsy smell of the pipe wafted through the room and mingled in with the savory smell of the simmering meat.

"That's the kind you like, isn't it? Did Bill start carryin' it again?" Charlotte gestured to the pipe as she brought a glass of water to her husband.

"Nah, this is from Fort Worth." Pete leaned up to tuck the tin away into his back pocket.

"I'm glad you could find it! I'd recognize that smell anywhere, like sarsaparilla. I used to get excited and nervous when I was that seventeen-year-old girl out at the ranch if I smelled the smoke from that pipe. It meant Pete, the handsome new bull rider, was somewhere nearby."

Pete laughed. "The handsome new bull rider that your father told you to stay away from."

"I was in love; he knew that. No one could have stopped me." She managed a weak smile to hide the rising lump in her throat. Charlotte still couldn't talk about her father without evoking echoes of the gasping desperation of his last rasping breaths. The daring rodeo star confined to his deathbed by something as common as the Spanish flu. Her palms became clammy at the memory of his once-strong hand resting inertly in hers, heavy with the weight of all the things they never got to say to each other because she got swept up with Pete and waited too long to visit home.

"He sure tried though, didn't he." Pete took the glass in hand, relaxed his shoulders, and sank back into his chair. "I thought he was gonna have me horsewhipped when I told him we were movin' on."

"Well, you took away his best trick rider." Charlotte rested against the arm of Pete's chair.

"And you took away his best bull rider." Pete placed a hand on her leg.

"Your father was great, Alex. You should've seen him."

Alex looked at the two of them together and smiled, his posture relaxing.

"Still am! I just don't get to ride bulls much these days. Rex has me doin' all the mundane stuff out at the ranch. Mendin' fences, breakin' wild horses. It ain't the good ol' days no more, Charlotte. Least Rex'll have me going back out to Fort Worth again soon."

"Again?" Charlotte leaned back in surprise.

"Next week."

"Next week? But you just got home!"

Pete grunted and took another puff from his pipe, clearly done with that discussion. "Where did you get meat for a pot roast from anyway?"

"It's the most amazing thing," she said, sitting across the fire from her husband. "There were some city men from the circus at the cookhouse today, and they were talking about buying some supplies…" Charlotte hesitated, as Pete picked up a book from the top of the pile and looked it over, absently puffing at his pipe. *One foot carefully in front of the other*. She continued, "I-I was able to help Saul get some business with the circus men and he gave us all of this food because—"

"Ain't that meat done cooking yet?"

She sighed. "I'll check."

Alex arranged plates and silverware on the table. For the benefit of her husband, Charlotte peeked under the lid of the dutch oven pot where the meat simmered on a bed of bright orange carrots, chunks of onion, and starchy red potatoes. She knew it would be an hour yet at least before the colors deepened and became soft under the prodding of her fork, but Pete was likely to boil over before the vegetables.

"Get outta the kitchen, Alex. Come over here and tell me about this book you're reading." Pete squinted at the book and flipped through the pages.

"Yes, sir." Alex looked tentatively at his mother before leaving the kitchen to take his seat by the fire across from his father.

"What's all this?"

"That is a new book about electrical science. It explains the different ways electricity can be harnessed and used. For example—"

"Electrical science?" Pete said. "How come you

never bring home books on horses or cattle or anything useful?"

"I'm just not interested in—"

"Here, read me this first page here." He handed the book to Alex.

"Well, Dad, this is the preface. I could read you the part about—"

"I know what a preface is. I said read it!"

"Okay." Alex began timidly to read. "The aim which the writer has proposed to herself in the present little work, is to give such an outline of modern electrical science—"

Pete snatched the book from Alex. "Herself? Is this book written by a woman?"

"Yes!" Charlotte chimed in. "Isn't that wonderful?"

"No, Charlotte! It ain't wonderful." Pete turned back to Alex, waving the book dangerously near the fire. "This is the sort of nonsense that'll get your ass kicked, Alexander. When you start workin' out at the ranch in a few months, you'll need to know about horses. Cattle. Agriculture. Not some made-up 'electrical science' crap written by a woman. You'll get laughed off the ranch with this bullshit."

"But, Dad, it isn't made up, it's—"

"No, you can't waste time on this. We've gotta get you learning about something useful. I want you to do well out there, son. Hold your own." Pete squinted at the book again and hit it against the arm of his chair, sending up a tiny cloud of dust. "I'm gonna talk to that Miss what's-her-name about this. Giving Alex this crap. Charlotte, I want you to tell her this is unacceptable."

"Yes, dear, I'll talk to his teacher." Charlotte bit her lip as she cranked up the heat in the oven, hoping to hurry dinner along.

"This is exactly why I've been sayin' that schoolin' is a waste of time. I don't see the point in goin' if you ain't even learning nothin' you can use in life out at the ranch—"

"Did you hear that the circus is coming to town?" Alex changed the subject.

Pete set the book back on the pile and took a measured puff of his pipe.

Alex continued excitedly, "Last year, Mom and I went out there as soon as the railcars arrived. Watching them set up was almost as fun as seeing the show. Can we go, Dad?"

"The circus." Pete stared into the fire as he continued puffing at his pipe. "Seems like a waste of money to me."

"I bet you'd love it if you give it a try. They've got horses and cows and—"

"I see horses and cows every day, son."

"I've got a little extra money set aside, Pete," Charlotte said proudly, walking around the dinner table with its waiting plates to join the boys by the fire. "We could all go."

"Yes, let's all go!" Alex cheered.

"I didn't say we don't have money. I said it was a waste of money." Pete's scowl deepened. "And what do you mean you have money 'set aside'? You hiding money from me again?"

She took a wobbling step back. "No. No, I just—I just set aside a little extra when I have good days at the cookhouse...so y'all can have bacon with breakfast or-

or days like this, so we—"

"Good days at the cookhouse." Pete snorted. "What, like today? When you come home with kitchen scraps instead of money?"

"Kitchen scraps? That's not—"

"That Saul don't treat you right out there. I don't like how you work yourself to death in that kitchen, servin' food to all those strangers, and then that bastard don't even pay you right for it."

"Language, Pete," Charlotte chided meekly, trying to tiptoe the tight line of the wire without getting blown over. "You know I enjoy working in the cookhouse."

"No, you don't! Of course you don't." Pete stood up from his chair and took her by the shoulders, speaking more gently. "Let me take care of you, Charlotte."

"You do take care of me, Pete." She searched for the flecks of gold in his eyes through the blur of tears forming in her own.

"I make plenty of money, honey. And I work my ass off for it. What's the point if you don't let me take care of our family? You could stay home as the other wives do." His thumbs dug into her collarbone, and his fingers pressed deeper into the softness of her arms.

"I know you work hard, Pete. I'm grateful. I-I…I just don't want to sit around and wait for you to bring money home. I want to be useful."

"You are useful, honey. You can be real pretty when you want to be. You could do your hair up more, get a little better about havin' dinner ready on time. You got real good at the cross-stitchin' for a bit. You could do that again."

"I like working at the cookhouse with Saul and

Martha. It isn't enough to—"

Pete dropped his hands from Charlotte's shoulders and staggered back. "Isn't enough? Do you know how many women would kill for a man like me? A husband who provides for them. Especially after the war!"

"Of course, I do. I just—"

"You make me look like a bad husband for allowing you to work in that dump, Charlotte. Let me do the work so you can rest. You just look so tired all the time."

"No one thinks you're a bad husband. I just haven't had time to freshen up yet, I'm fine." Charlotte did her best to smooth her hair as she swallowed the swelling lump in her throat. "I've been trying to tell you, I actually—I had a great day, a wonderful day at the cookhouse! I—"

"This is exactly what I've been sayin' for months now. We have gotta get Alex out there at the ranch with me! Once he starts doing his share and makin' us real money, then you can stay home like a proper wife and have dinner ready for me on time when I get home."

Alex shrank back, eyeing his books nervously. "Dad, I don't want to—"

Charlotte stepped between her husband and her son.

"My work at the cookhouse," she said, her trembling voice growing louder, "is the only reason we have this dinner tonight! There's no money at the ranch! You haven't brought home anything in weeks!" Charlotte swallowed hard as her husband's red skin cracked into white lines at the edges of his narrowing eyes, the left one flickering beneath a pulsing vein in his forehead.

"What did you say to me?" Pete swelled up to his full height, left arm pulled back as if ready to draw on his pistol.

"I'm sorry, I—I'm just trying to say that…that my job at the cookhouse—my job at the cookhouse is good for all of us"—Charlotte's words trembled with her voice—"and dinner tonight, well, dinner tonight—"

"Dinner tonight?" Pete roared. "What dinner?" He gestured to the empty table. "I don't see no dinner, do you?" He upended the armchair, knocking over the pile of books, which slid inches from the flames. A cloud of dust settled slowly around him as he continued his tirade silhouetted against the orange glow of the blazing furnace. "Your job is supposed to be here! At home. Bein' a good wife and mother. Not off at the damned cookhouse around all those men! Not letting our son read all this nonsense because you're too busy playin' waitress to pay attention. I don't trust that Saul as far as I can throw him. And you're like a sad stray dog, grateful to that negro for tossing you his leftovers." He strode over to the door and put his cowboy hat back on his head. "It's probably old rotten meat anyway."

Alex scampered over to the pile of books, pulling them away from the fire and gathering them up in his arms.

"Pete," she begged, "please."

"I ain't eating that charity food."

"It isn't charity food. I've been trying to tell you I—"

"I'm going out for a real dinner, and when I get back, we'll finish our discussion. I'm done with your back talk and all your questions, woman! You're gonna learn how a wife's supposed to be, and you're quitting that damn job!"

Charlotte froze in fear, barely breathing as she watched her husband stomp across the room toward their son.

"And you—" Pete pointed at Alex. "You're done with these stupid, good-for-nothing books!" Pete snatched Alex's book from the top of the pile in his arms. "You're done learning from women. It's time you learned to be a man!" Pete looked at the book with disgust. He threw it into the fire.

"No!" Alex's eyes filled with tears as he helplessly watched the book warp and burn in the flames. He dropped everything he was holding and seized the drinking glass from beside the chair. He tossed the water from the glass onto the book, but the flames only swallowed the splash with a sizzle of steam. Charlotte filled a bucket of water and raced to the fire.

Steamy smoke billowed out from the drowning fire and mingled with the smell of dust and pipe tobacco to overpower the clear richness of the marinating meat in a musty gray haze. The glow of the flames reflected in Pete's burning eyes through the smoke. He started to speak but closed his mouth resolutely and disappeared into the back rooms. Distant shuffling and slamming shook the walls as Alex cried into his hands. Gently, she took the wet and charred pile of paper from him and placed it back in the fireplace. There was no saving the book.

Charlotte sank to the floor and wrapped her arms around Alex, shielding him from the angry glare of her husband as he stomped past them through the kitchen.

"This is your fault," he said, pointing at her as she hugged her son. And with a slam of the door, Pete was gone.

Chapter 5

The Sterling Mansion

Guests had been arriving at the Sterling mansion for almost an hour, trickling up a series of marble stairs and through pillared arches to the grand main entrance. The fashionable Fort Worth elite mingled in the mansion's main room, which through gigantic glass doors overlooked the veranda and a square of crisp green grass, carefully manicured and dotted with statues and fountains.

Inside, the ceilings of the center room were unfathomably high, and a pair of bright green birds soared back and forth across the balconies, resting from time to time on one of the many iron branches extending from the railings that had been designed for them, or in one of their ornate cages about the grand hall.

"Oh, look! The Moores," Jay's wife exclaimed. "I can't believe they'd show their face in public after that fraud scandal with the oil and the post office. From prison right into this fancy ballroom. Jay, what are those pillars made of? Is that marble?"

His wife continued making observations about the room and the people in it as she sipped on a tall glass of champagne and adjusted the beads on the sheer glittering overlay of her new dress. Vanessa looked as if she could have been made out of marble as well. She was tall and classically pretty, with pale porcelain skin and dark curled hair that had been carefully coiffed into a large and fashionable arrangement at the back of her head accented by draping beads and feathers. Her face had the lines and structure reminiscent of Roman times, and Jay often thought her profile looked like the countenance of Pompeia or Agrippina from the back of an ancient coin, which was fitting because she was and had always been very occupied with money.

"I wanna meet Frank's fiancée. Did you know they say her family made their money pushing moonshine out in some one-horse town before one of her uncles was shot dead at his kitchen table?" Vanessa had taken a recent interest in society news and in accompanying Jay to anything where she might mingle with the people she'd seen in the newspapers. "Half the family moved up here to the city to get away from the scandal! But I heard everyone in the family carries a gun, even Luella! On her thigh like a gangster moll—"

"Surely that's malicious gossip." Edna Sterling approached the couple. A scalding flush rose up Jay's neck and burned his cheeks under the formidable deep-set eyes of his aunt.

"Hello, Jay." Edna kissed him on the cheek affectionately. "Vanessa, so good to see you again, dear."

"Hello, Aunt Edna," Jay said. "Please allow me to apologize. Vanessa and I didn't intend—"

"Well, surely you'd wanna know if you're letting a bunch of moonshiners and murderers into your house, Edna!" Vanessa insisted.

Mrs. Sterling, as cool and composed as ever,

simply raised an eyebrow and looked past the pair. "Well, speaking of outlaws, I do believe I see my long-lost son headed this way to grace us with his presence."

Frank strode over to the trio to greet his mother, and she smiled warmly as he kissed her on the cheek and received one from her in return.

"Now, why am I an outlaw?" he asked his mother, taking a glass of champagne from a nearby waiter and raising it with a smile at guests passing by.

Edna wiped two or three shades of lipstick from her son's cheek as she spoke. "Because it's criminal how long it's been since you visited your loving mother. Now, I had lunch last week with the ladies from my quilting club, and they were asking about you…"

As Mrs. Sterling chatted merrily with her son, her husband reveled in the flattering laughter of a small gathering of guests near the fireplace. Herman Frances Sterling the Second, or "Sonny" as he was affectionately called by everyone who knew him, had a big round belly, a big round head, and a big round laugh. His leathery skin crinkled by the eyes, and his mouth often rose into the lopsided charismatic smile of a man who was handsome in the prime of his youth.

"Oh, do you like that painting?" he asked without waiting for a response. "I had it redone from the one at the Louvre—that's in Paris, you know. It's three feet bigger, of course. Have you seen the statue in the library?" The gaggle of guests shuffled after Sonny on their customary mansion tour.

"Oh, dear. I'd better save your father from himself. So lovely to see you, Jay," Edna said, pausing stiffly before going on. "Good of you to bring your wife."

His jaw tensed.

"Well." Frank sighed and he clapped Jay on the shoulder. "Ready for a few hours of smiling and small talk?"

Jay smiled politely at his wife while she carried on with someone next to her about the quality of the champagne and leaned in closer to Frank. "Actually, you just saved me. You know I've got your back, and I love your family, but I was ready to leave this party about half a minute after we arrived. This is more your scene than mine."

"No, I'm with you." Frank sighed. "I've been spinning my wheels here in Fort Worth. I'm ready to get this show on the road."

"I don't care if this is your scene or not, Jay. You better slap a smile on and show me a good time. And keep that pocket watch outta sight. I'm here to have fun." Vanessa spoke to Jay without looking at him, surveying the room instead.

"Well, good! Someone oughta get this guy to loosen up a little." Frank adjusted his tone and turned to Jay. "Actually, I'd like to discuss something important with you. Who do you know in newspapers?"

"Speaking of the papers, I want to meet this famous new fiancée of yours, Frank! I've read all about her in the *Fort Worth Press*! She was right under that story about the missing Indian heiress, Maude Mudd. Of course, Luella's a different kind of heiress, isn't she!"

Frank shifted awkwardly to his back foot. "I'm not sure she's here yet, Vanessa."

"If I were her, I wouldn't let you out of my sight!"

"Well, don't mention that to her if you don't

mind." Frank managed an awkward laugh.

"Actually, I did see Luella Prescott, if you're looking for her," a stranger piped in. "She arrived a few minutes ago, looking fabulous. They're all on the veranda."

"In this cold weather? We can't have that! Let's go invite them all in, shall we?" Vanessa said, taking ownership of the home and the stranger. They looped arms and proceeded toward the giant steam-glazed glass doors.

"Oh. No. Maybe we should—" Frank reached out as if to pull them back.

"I know. I'm sorry," Jay apologized. "She insisted on coming tonight."

"Well, she's your wife, Jay. Of course, she's welcome," Frank said as the two men made their way to the veranda. "I just don't want any of her comments to cause a stir. Luella gets upset so easily, you see."

Frank's quick strides toward his fiancée halted as he was distracted momentarily by a voluptuous brunette, but Jay politely ushered him through another group of guests clustered around Sonny as he showcased the architecture on the veranda.

"Well, all the stone for those columns had to be brought in from Italy. That's the only place in the world you can get that color!"

The guests sipped their champagne and nodded along in admiration.

Frank and Jay filtered through the crowd to the women to find that introductions had already been made. Vanessa was trading her empty champagne glass for a new one as Luella gracefully turned to greet them.

Shoulders back and chin high, Luella had the

confident look of a woman who knew that every eye was on her and liked it that way. Her sparkling blue eyes seemed to speak to everyone individually as she looked at them, even when she herself wasn't saying a word. They were the kind of eyes that could make a person feel like they were in on a secret.

"Well, look at that," Frank said. "The most beautiful woman in the world has made her way to the Sterling house."

Vanessa's eyes darted from Luella to Frank, and back to Luella again.

Luella rewarded Frank with a warm smile and playfully kissed him, leaving a bright red, perfectly formed print on his cheek where the other prints had been wiped away by his mother. "Hello again, Jay! I've just met your lovely wife," she sang, extending her gloved hand.

Jay searched for a hint of irony in the statement as he took her hand to kiss it.

"Oh no, you're the lovely one," Vanessa said. "And so fashionable. Your short haircut!"

"Oh, you're too kind," Luella said, waving at guests behind Vanessa.

Vanessa patted at her own locks and went on. "Personally, I'd never be able to part with mine. Everyone loves my hair long, you know. They're always telling me how pretty it is. And anyway, I know it's very in vogue now, Clara Bow and all that, but the magazines say it won't last. I don't want to be stuck with short hair when it goes out of fashion!" Vanessa took a cigarette from the woman next to her and mimicked the movements of the other women in the circle in holding it out above a tilted hip. Jay patted at his pockets for a lighter, but she fluttered her eyelashes at some man who appeared from nowhere to light it and disappeared just as quickly to another pair of waiting red lips.

Luella edged backward politely. "Your hair is lovely, and it was nice to meet you. But I must—"

"Your frock is so stylish too! I saw one like that in Harolds when I was buying mine, but I chose this one." Vanessa smoothed her hand over the fabric of her new dress.

"Your dress is very pretty." Luella exchanged glances with Frank.

"Thank you, it is my color, isn't it."

Jay jumped in. "You look very nice, Vaness–"

"But your dress—it's so short and form-fitting. How do you hide your gun under there?" Vanessa said, reaching toward Luella's thigh to lift the hem of her dress.

Luella jumped back from Vanessa's hand and stared blankly at her for a brief moment before turning back to Frank. "Darling, where can a girl get a drink around here?"

Frank took the hint and extended an elbow. Luella grasped onto his arm as if it were a life preserver in choppy waters.

"Catch up with you later, Jay." He winked. "Enjoy the party, Vanessa!"

Vanessa smiled obliviously and waved at the couple as they disappeared into the crowd.

"Vanessa, I—" Jay had to end the embarrassment before it began.

"Everyone says she's so pretty, but I don't see it," Vanessa hissed. "That boy haircut isn't doing her any favors! And she's so classless! First thing she wants is a drink!" Vanessa took a sip of her champagne. "I guess when you come from a family of moonshiners!"

"We don't want to offend anyone, dear."

Vanessa rolled her eyes and turned back to her new friends. Jay turned over his watch inside his pocket. He looked up at the parrots circling overhead and back at his wife as she tilted her chin back in chirpy insincere laughter at one of the circle's comments. Vanessa was just as ridiculous as one of the feathered fliers and somehow even more out of place at this party.

It's going to be a long night, Jay thought, waving off a waiter who was carrying a new tray of drinks toward them and smiling politely at Sonny and Edna, who looked on with remonstrance from across the veranda.

Chapter 6

Dinner in the Dark

Guests wandered into the dining room at the gong, shuffling around the mile-long banquet table as they searched for their names among the place cards.

Sonny gracefully led his wife Edna on his arm to the head of the table, followed by the exotic birds who flew in behind them, and with his other hand, hooked his thumb in his suspenders. He had the content and satisfied look of a self-made man, the kind of man people seemed to root for. In a world where so many people despised the wealthy, people of all classes willingly gave Sonny Sterling their money and seemed happy for him to have it. And thank goodness they did. Jay had learned in recent meetings that the Sterling bank balance, despite all appearances, was bordering on zero. Everyone surrounding Sonny Sterling stood with their hands out, waiting either to be paid or for a ticket to the show.

"Good evening, ladies and gentlemen!" he boomed. "Welcome to our humble home."

The guests' laughter echoed off the marble tiles, tickling the crystal chandeliers.

"Edna and I are honored for all of you to join us tonight as we kick off the season with our opening week here in Fort Worth! Please, help yourselves to as much food and drink as you wish! After all, it's the last party we will have here for a while. At the end of this week, Sterling & Son's will be taking our little show on the road!"

Laughter again. Sterling & Son's traveling circus was as little as Sonny's home was humble. Even if keeping the luxurious lights on was getting more and more expensive, harder and harder to maintain, he showed no sign of slowing. Sonny was more insistent than ever on every show raking in the cash to appease investors and bill collectors.

"I know I'll see all of you at the show here in town this week, and that you'll all bring all your friends and family. But for now, it's time to eat! Please have a seat. And enjoy the show!" He paused and smiled again. "Oops! Old habits. Enjoy your dinner!"

The guests laughed and began taking their seats. Ever the appropriate hostess, Edna had carefully arranged the name cards, and Jay was pleased to see that Vanessa was seated between Hugh and himself. He wouldn't have to make apologies for either one of them tonight if they could occupy one another in conversation.

Though monitoring Hugh on the road often proved tiresome, Jay really felt sorry for him. As a child, Hugh's mother had run off to California with some gold miner, and little Hugh was the one to find that his father had put a bullet in his brain soon after. He and his younger sisters had been effectively adopted by Sonny and Edna shortly after that, but Hugh was already damaged. He always seemed to simultaneously avoid violence and cause it by stirring up mischief, something that hadn't faded with age. His taste for trouble usually meant an ear that was ready for gossip, and it was an ear that Vanessa found before they'd rested in the chairs pulled back for them. "Did you hear about the secret marriage of the Indian heiress?"

Jay leaned over and placed a gentle hand on his wife's shoulder. "Look at the oysters. I made sure they'd have your favorite foods tonight. Deviled eggs, potatoes—"

Vanessa batted him away and returned to her gossip with Hugh. Jay pulled his hand down awkwardly and rested it in locked fingers on his napkin. Down the table across what seemed like miles of hors d'oeuvres and garnishes, Frank was basking in the glow of Luella's loving gaze as he told some joke. Edna wiped away tears of laughter and rested her hand on Sonny's arm as he related a wild story to a group of captivated diners. Even one of Sonny's parrots was enraptured by him, sitting on his shoulder with a cocked head as if it were listening to the story too.

Jay racked his brain for a story to tell that might make Vanessa look at him the way Luella looked at Frank. Or elicit the warm touch of her hand on his arm. He'd even settle for the way that parrot looked at Sonny. Jay opened his mouth to speak, but he couldn't think of a joke that was funny enough. The steady swell of gossip and laughter rang in his ears until he was unable to pull forward any sort of quip that might enchant his wife. He shut out the conversations at the table, picked up his fork, and resigned himself to running numbers in his head one more time for the initial departure.

"Do you have children?" the familiar man next to Jay asked between bites.

Jay paused with his own fork halfway to his mouth. How long had the man been trying to talk to him while he was absorbed in logistics? Sonny invited potential investors to his parties from time to time. Was this one of them?

"I do. A daughter named Sadie."

"Daughters are wonderful, aren't they!" the man said, dusting crumbs off his fine jacket. "Mine are all grown of course. Where is little Sadie tonight?"

"She is with a friend of mine and their family this evening," Jay said, dabbing at his mouth with his napkin. "She's not quite old enough for dinner parties."

"Isn't she the lucky one," the man said with a wink. "How old is she?"

"Seven!" Vanessa cut in.

"Our daughter is six, dear," Jay said, annoyed that she'd infiltrated a new conversation. Were she and Hugh bored of their gossip already?

"Hello, I'm Vanessa Edwards," she said, ignoring Jay and extending her hand across him.

The man took her hand and kissed it a few inches from Jay's face. "Nice to meet you, Vanessa. Butch McNeil."

"Of the McNeil ranch? Where all those celebrities visit?"

Butch chuckled as he smoothed his silver hair. "Guilty." He had a charming sparkle in his eye.

This is just the kind of thing she would know, Jay thought, *the name and reputation of a local oil tycoon, but not the age of our only daughter.*

"Hugh, this is Butch McNeil." Vanessa leaned back so Hugh could wave down the table, increasing Jay's discomfort.

Jay looked up at the decorated ceiling above them, observing illustrated scenes of fairy tale romances, each scene featuring the painted faces of a young Sonny and Edna in place of the characters.

"Oh, I know Hugh," Butch said. "I hear you're the man we have to thank for all this free booze tonight!"

Jay retreated into his own thoughts as Butch, Vanessa, and Hugh continued their conversation. Though he disagreed with everything the oil tycoon was saying, he noticed Butch was enjoyably charismatic and obviously rich. He could understand why Sonny had chosen to invite him.

"It's a brilliant loophole, the way religious men are able to get their hands on alcohol without having to abide by the damned Prohibition police. And I tell you, if you're going to be religious, I prefer a Catholic religious family to a Protestant one! You know at the Rockefeller parties, there's not a drop of booze or a hint of dancing. What's all that money for anyway?" Butch took a long drink from his wineglass.

"Well, if you need to come to confession, you know where to find me. And it's quality wine I've supplied you with tonight. You're almost never likely to be struck blind or fall over dead when you drink it—unlike that awful moonshine poison." Hugh slid a sly smile at Vanessa.

It didn't surprise Jay that they'd already found a way to gossip about Luella's alleged family associations. Jay did wonder where Hugh had obtained the alcohol they were drinking, but that always seemed to be a secret only Hugh and Sonny shared. Jay wished Sonny would let him in on it so he could ensure they weren't getting themselves into the kind of trouble they couldn't get out of, but Sonny always dismissed Jay's concerns when it came to circumventing Prohibition.

"Well, I'm glad about that. I wouldn't be caught dead drinking that hooch." Vanessa's tone carried a level of snobbery that was new to Jay. Or was it jealousy? "But Hugh, I don't understand. Since when are you a religious man? I thought you were just a traveling salesman like Jay."

"Darling, I'm no traveling salesman. Nor is Jay. But yes, I attended seminary school in 1918."

"Did you really?" Vanessa asked, taking some potatoes from the serving tray held beside her.

"I had a sudden calling," Hugh said, dismissing the passing tray with his nose up.

"A sudden calling that started when the draft notices started going out and ended just as suddenly when the war was over," Jay said.

Hugh shrugged.

"What does being a preacher have to do with the war?" Vanessa hesitated with her fork in the air above her potatoes when she noticed Hugh let the tray pass by. She set her fork down without taking a bite.

"Jay's just pointing out that they couldn't draft me when I was in seminary school, darling." Hugh smiled, raising his glass. "The gift that keeps on giving!"

"Oh! Hugh, you clever fox!" Vanessa's enthusiasm disappeared as she turned to her husband. "Well, why didn't you think of that? You could have skipped the whole thing too?"

Jay felt his face grow hot. He welcomed the tray and shoveled two servings onto his plate as he spoke. "I was drafted. I did my part. And Hugh isn't a preacher, Vanessa. He got—" Jay stopped himself. "He decided to rejoin the family business before he finished because seminary school wasn't for him."

"Thank you," he said to the waiter who moved along to Butch.

"Jay is the only noble one among us, I'm afraid," Hugh said, eying Jay with a mixed expression.

"Noble or stupid," Vanessa said, looking at Butch. "I don't see how it's our problem, what happens over there. Men killing each other over nothing and leaving us women at home with all of the work, responsibilities, and worry. It isn't right."

"Perhaps if you could point out 'over there' on a map, darling," Jay muttered under his breath. He could feel Vanessa's glare burning into him as he continued digging into his meal with fervor.

"Well, good for you, Jay. The right thing to do," Butch said. "I was too old for them to bother with, of course, but my oldest daughter was a nurse. Saw some terrible things. I pray to God there's never another war. Where did you serve, Jay?"

"A nurse! How good of her, serving her country," Vanessa cut in. "Tell me about the Rockefellers! What is their house like?"

As the chatter went on across him, Jay was finally able to eat his food and run numbers in peace.

He had just taken a bite of the roast duck when the lights shut off without warning. Gasps and confused mumbling reverberated off the marble walls. As his eyes adjusted to the complete darkness, a bright light flashed with a bang at the end of the long table, where Mr. Sterling was sitting. The spark took speed and traveled, fizzing and spitting, down the length of the table.

Jay leaned forward, searching through the darkness, worried for Sonny's safety. He reached beside him to make sure his wife was all right and felt her leg jerk away from his hand. Behind him, horse hooves tapped in sharp unison and the same staccato clicking echoed across the other long side of the table too, amongst the whispers, excited gasps, and the scuffing of chairs.

The light returned, blinding the confused guests. Above him, bodies tumbled from the ceiling enveloped in long ribbons of purple cloth. Jay exhaled with relief as he realized what was going on. He looked past the dazed and blinking dinner guests across from him to see that they were not horses he'd heard enter the room but zebras. Zebras adorned in complete circus dress, with gold sequined saddles, jeweled reins, and violet feather plume headdresses. Above them, the glittering aerial acrobats soared, jumped, and twisted in the cloth. Spinning in unison to the floor, the acrobats held their silky purple cloth in one hand and extended the other in a graceful, dramatic curtsy.

"The Sahara Sisters!" guests exclaimed as the room erupted in applause.

The now grounded women, all adorned in identical glittering jeweled corsets and tiaras with sheer amethyst veils gracefully falling from their hips and shoulders, waved at the dinner guests. The six sisters stood sumptuously in their high heels next to the exotic zebras, who lifted their front hooves in unison. The dinner guests clapped and cheered.

"Well! That Sonny sure does know how to surprise a fella, doesn't he?" Butch exclaimed, drawing in a whistle as he ran his eyes over the sisters.

Jay chuckled to himself. Why shouldn't Sonny's dinner party be as spectacular as a center ring show? He was sure to hook a few investors tonight.

"Ladies and gentlemen, may I present the Sterling & Son Circus's Sisters of the Sahara," Sonny boomed, extending an arm across the row of ladies who were now sitting sidesaddle on their zebras. "Please follow these lovely ladies to the garden where we will resume our party with drinks, dessert, and dancing!"

"Did you know about that, Jay?" Vanessa hissed as she clapped.

"No," he said. "Not the details anyway. I just knew Sonny had something in store for us."

"I thought you said Mr. Sterling involved you in everything," she muttered with disapproval, taking one last bite of her dinner and fussing with her dress again.

"Sonny always has a surprise or two up his sleeve," Jay responded.

"Well, you could have told me. Horses and half-dressed women in the dining room while we're eating; it's disgusting. Honestly, it's a wonder one of those birds didn't leave droppings on our entrees."

"It might end up in the papers," Jay said hopefully. But his wife simply rolled her eyes, unimpressed, and patted at her lips with the cloth napkin.

As the guests rose to follow the parade of purple plumes, Jay fell in line behind Butch McNeil, who suavely offered Vanessa his arm and led her to the veranda.

Chapter 7

Party on the Veranda

"That's go time, people," the crew master announced at the first sign of purple feathers. The jazz band put out their cigarettes and took up the horns. Tigers paced in their cages in the center of the lawn. Past the manicured square, the lights of the Ferris wheel flickered on and the large metal structure shuddered and began to turn. A series of showgirls and waitresses in glittering uniforms were dispatched across the veranda, greeting guests with trays of drinks and delicacies.

Hazel drank in the scene around her with wide eyes. A poor girl from a small dusty Texas town, she'd never been anywhere like the Sterling mansion.

"We're moving up in the world, ain't we," Hazel said to the performer next to her.

The girl laughed and slipped on her cigar box. "I've worked worse places. At least you get to keep all your clothes on out here."

"Not if I play my cards right." Hazel pulled the red ruffles of her costume down in the front, pushing her breasts up at either side to make sure her cleavage was center stage.

"Just stick to your job, and don't mingle too much with the dandies. The boss don't like it much when we get outta place." The girl slapped on her showtime smile and greeted guests as they poured onto the lawn.

Hazel pursed her lips and patted at her hair as she tried to distinguish the men in suits.

"Get to your mark, cannon girl!" the crew master shouted.

Hazel batted him off as he prodded her forward and headed to the corner where the cannon was waiting for her, scanning the crowd as she strolled proudly through it.

Finally, her sights landed on the man she was looking for. Frank Sterling. She let out a disappointed sigh when she saw the girl standing next to him. Beautiful. Rich. Classy. The other girls were always talking about the perfect and pretty little Miss Luella Prescott. It would be hard to break him free of a doll like that.

From her point of view, though, Frank didn't seem the least bit interested in the dainty little princess beside him who wore his ring on her finger. His focus was elsewhere. Hazel followed Frank's gaze upward to see that it was fixed on their circus star, Birdie Bells, perched at the edge of the roof, dressed in a glittering two-piece leotard that revealed her impossibly slim, milky-white torso, ribs protruding. Birdie was smiling at the spectators below her with a superior air, one hand holding a trapeze bar and the other proudly extended to its full length among the bright speckled stars of the night sky as if to suggest she'd invited them to participate in her act as long as they didn't outshine her. Her delicate foot was draped daringly in pointed toe out into the open air above the square like a skeletal marionette.

"A fiancée *and* Birdie Bells?" Hazel clicked her

tongue, providing commentary to the charged air around her. "For some men, I guess even two-timin' just ain't enough."

The drums rolled as Birdie leaped from the rooftop, flying through the air on trapeze across the square. Gasps of astonishment rippled through the guests as a combination of fear and wonder overtook the crowd. "What happens if she falls?" someone whispered as Hazel weaved through the crowd unnoticed toward her cannon.

Tonight, as with every time she performed, there was no net between Birdie's weightless escapades and the full gravity of the dense ground beneath her. Nothing to catch the performer should she slip or stumble. Nothing to protect the captivated crowd from her falling body should she miss the trapeze bar, even by a hair's width.

"If she falls, she dies," another answered.

The upward gazes of the crowd had reduced the throng of people to a lawn of statues with a singular purpose. The guests watched the alluring star twist and fly through the air above them with bated breath. Every performance by a star like Birdie could be the last performance. Birdie knew it. Each person watching knew it. They didn't want to miss a thing.

Hazel rolled her eyes and looked back to Frank and his fiancée, noticing Luella's flushed cheeks and tight-lipped expression. Her innocent little face wasn't pointed upward. It was turned directly toward Frank, making her and Hazel the only two out of a hundred people at the party who weren't looking at Birdie. *She knows. A woman always knows when there's someone else*, Hazel thought as she approached her cannon. She returned to a familiar memory then. She thought of the way she'd sat alone on that wooden porch last year, waiting for her cowboy to come home with one hand on her belly and the other on her pistol. Time hadn't dulled the searing pain in her chest. She decided that a woman didn't always know when her man was a liar.

Hazel recognized the fire that raged in Luella's eyes as she left Frank's side and disappeared into the crowd. She'd felt it herself before too.

"There you are! Did you get lost? Hurry up!" The crew ushered Hazel toward the cannon stand.

As she slid down into the body of the cannon to wait for her cue, she thought about that look in Luella's eyes and she couldn't help but wonder if dallying with Frank might be more dangerous than flying through the air without a net.

Without warning, an alarming jolt released the springboard, sending Hazel hurtling through the air right into the middle of Birdie's act.

Her body spun out of control. In an instant, Birdie's flaming red hair materialized as Hazel flew toward her, the twilight sky around them a blur of cascading lights. She squeezed her eyes tightly closed, expecting the inevitable collision. Seconds stretched into an eternity. The sound of her own heartbeat was deafening, but somewhere beyond the rhythmic thumping, rang the muted cadence of the big brass band, a cheering crowd, and the screeching screams of Birdie Bells.

When the swirling subsided, Hazel forced her eyes open one at a time. She peeked past her red-tipped toes tangled in the white knotted ropes and found a pair of wide-eyed men and a cluster of champagne-clutching partygoers looking up at her. Beneath her body, her fingers grasped the smooth sturdy strands of the net. She'd landed safely, just as she'd done in practice shows a dozen times, in the net across the square. Above her, Birdie was swinging on trapeze through the night sky. Unharmed and unfazed, she confidently and competently completed her act as if Hazel hadn't just blasted right through the center of it.

A handsome man who looked similar to Frank but for his clean-shaven face and smooth gray eyes reached out a hand to Hazel. "Are you all right?"

Hazel felt a flutter as she took his hand and untangled herself from the net to step down onto firm manicured grass. As he released her hand and looked over to Frank, she adjusted her costume again to make sure her best features were well represented. The man was tall, like Frank. Hazel liked tall men.

"Who set this up, Jay?" Frank asked the man. "Why would they send the cannon girl plummeting right through the middle of the trapeze act?"

Annoying that Frank called her "the cannon girl" as if he didn't know her.

"I was just about to ask you the same thing!" Jay said. "Birdie could have been scared off her mark! Both girls could have been done for!"

Frank threw his hands up. "Don't look at me. I had no idea about any of this!"

A deep booming voice joined the conversation. "Well, you would, if you ever attended a family meeting, Frank."

Hazel recognized the man as Sonny Sterling and stood up a little straighter.

"This was all discussed this morning."

Frank shot a confused, betrayed look at Jay, whose expression denied understanding.

"Were these surprise acts intended as some sort of punishment to me, Father?" Frank fumed furiously.

"A punishment? How could you be so dimwitted, Frank? It's advertising! A chance to wow our guests! You'd know about this if you had half a head for business."

Frank swelled up as if preparing to respond, and she wanted to reach out and comfort him, but Jay interceded. "Sonny, I get trying out the new cannon girl, but why'd they shoot that cannon off right in the middle of Birdie's act?"

"Well, that was not part of the plan." Sonny turned to Hazel. "What happened, girl?"

Hazel looked up at the men from under her lashes, assuming the posture of a damsel in distress. "I don't know, sir. I slid into that cannon, and it shot off without warning."

"Is that right?" Jay asked her.

"It is, sir," she said, looking into his eyes a long while before turning to Frank. "But lucky I was already in, right, Frankie? I think it went good, don't you? The audience seemed to like it…"

"This isn't an audience though, is it," Frank said scornfully, ignoring Hazel and speaking to his father. "It's just a bunch of people trying to socialize and eat their dessert."

"It's always an audience, son." Sonny rubbed at his temples. "Don't you get it? It's always a show. You think this is a dinner party? You show up and drink the booze and flirt the night away. You spend money you don't have on things or people who'll never give it back…"

Hazel looked back and forth between the men. She'd never seen a similarity before between the handsome ringmaster and his bald, round, aging father, but when both brows were furrowed, she could see the resemblance clearly. She tried to hide a smirk as she looked on, watching the two prepare to do battle.

"These aren't party guests. They're our meal ticket. I'm trying to reach into those deep pockets so we can get the show on the road and start making money again. As it stands, I can't even pay for the food tonight, much less your little girlfriend or your last bill at the Jazz Lounge. We're—"

Sonny stopped speaking abruptly, looking at Hazel and then over to Jay.

"Let's get you something to drink," Jay said, extending his arm to her.

Hazel's disappointment at missing the argument was quickly forgotten when she felt Jay's bicep straining against the sleeve of his jacket beneath her fingers. "Oh, you've got some nice arms under there, don't you?" she asked in her most sultry voice. "I bet you could sweep a girl right off her feet."

Jay didn't answer. Instead, he led her to the center of the square where bartenders in clean black tuxedos were stacking crystal glasses into precarious pyramids and arranging trays of drinks and desserts to be carried throughout the veranda by maids from the house and Sterling & Son's employees. Hazel reveled under the jealous stares of her fellow performers. She pulled her shoulders back and fluttered her eyelashes at a few onlooking Sahara Sisters as she clutched Jay's arm a little tighter.

"Well, here you are," he said, gesturing to the bartender to pour Hazel a drink and releasing his arm from her grip. "Enjoy the party."

"But wait…" Hazel licked her red lips to make sure they were glistening. "Aren't you going to show me around a little bit?"

"No. I'm afraid I'm needed elsewhere," Jay answered politely.

I sure would like to shake the manners offa him. I bet he's real fun when he ain't so proper.

"I don't see no lady with you." She lowered her voice to a sultry hum and stepped in closer to Jay. "Nobody needs you more than me." She wrapped her fingers around the back of his neck and pulled him in for a kiss, but he stepped backward with surprising quickness. Hazel pushed out her bottom lip into a pout, but his expression told her the conversation was over. Jay turned around and stepped resolutely through the partygoers away from her.

Hazel took the drink offered her by the bartender and grimaced at the unwelcome wave of nostalgia as the familiar taste hit her lips. It was better than the fake stuff she'd pushed in the city but reminiscent all the same of a time she'd rather forget. Each bubble rising from the bottom carried memories of the most joyful and most painful year of her life. Evaporating just as quickly and gone like so many promises.

"You won't get anywhere with that one, honey." Hazel turned to see Mei-Ling, one of the girls from the Sahara Sisters act, sipping a glass of champagne. "Why don't you try some lower-hanging fruit."

"Oh, please, if Birdie can snag Frank, surely I can catch that one."

"You're no Birdie, toots. Besides, plenty of girls prettier and sharper than you have made a run at Mr. Edwards. He doesn't mess around with us. He's married."

"I like the married ones. You can have a little fun without giving nothin' up." Hazel tried to look for Jay through the crowd.

"You mean, you don't have to feel like you're not pretty enough if a married guy doesn't go for you."

Hazel snapped her attention back to Mei. "Don't you have some cigars to peddle or something?"

"Don't you have some men to give a nickel dance to? We all know where you came from. Birdie told us she pulled you off the cooch tent. Though none of us can understand why."

Hazel glared at Mei. "Maybe you didn't notice, but I'm a headliner act now."

Mei flipped her long black ponytail over her shoulder. "You know the last cannon girl died, right? Just missed the net. Splat. You think Birdie put you there 'cause you're special or did she put you there because she hopes you'll hit a wall too?"

Hazel's mouth went bone dry. Before she could reply, Hugh Sterling and a tall, slender woman with long hair, a large nose, and a black beaded dress came careening toward the table for another drink. Hazel locked eyes with Hugh for a moment before turning to take a new glass of champagne from the top of the delicate structure next to her.

"You two know each other?" Mei asked, looking at Hazel and Hugh.

"Don't be ridiculous," Hugh scoffed. "I don't associate with hoochie-coochie girls. I'm not Frank."

Her insides burned at that comment. *These boys act like they don't know you when they're at fancy parties.* The stories she could tell.

"I was just tellin' Miss Hoity-Toity to stay away from those Sterling boys," Mei said, still observing Hugh with skepticism.

"Why should I stay away from Frankie when he's the one helpin' me? He says if I keep practicin', I can catch a trapeze in midair when they shoot me out of the cannon. He says I'm gonna be a star—"

"Oh, that's a genius plan!" Hugh laughed mirthlessly. "Go after Birdie's act!" Mei joined him in laughing, along with the woman in the beaded dress.

At the same moment, Hazel spotted Birdie beelining toward her through the crowd in a fury, the party guests parting like the Red Sea around her.

"What the hell were you thinking, Hazel?" she shouted. "Blasting yourself through my act like that! You think you can take the spotlight from me?"

"No, no, no, I—"

"What were you saying, Hugh? These girls wanna take my place?"

Hugh opened his mouth to speak but let out a hiccup instead.

"What, you two think you can be up on trapeze now?" Birdie glared at Mei and Hazel.

"Never!" Mei uttered immediately.

"Because I can have both of you out on your asses—"

"She was tryin' to cozy up to Jay Edwards!" Mei blurted, pointing at Hazel. "That's what we were talking about."

Why'd she go sayin' a stupid thing like that? Hazel

wanted to shove Mei right into the tower of glasses behind her.

Hugh cocked his head to the side as he looked back at Hazel, his face a muddled mixture of surprise and annoyance, like he thought he was the only man who deserved her attention or her time.

"Jay Edwards, huh." Birdie turned to the tall woman in the beaded dress. "That's your husband, right?"

Hazel's eyes grew wide as they landed on the woman who swayed before her with flared nostrils and narrowed eyes. *I'm prettier than she is*, Hazel thought, allowing her wide eyes to settle back to their narrow glare and straightening her back to thrust her chest out. *Her body looks like a sack of elbows. She ain't got nothin' for a man to play with.*

"Watch out," Birdie continued. "If this coochie-dancing carnie thinks she can go from dancin' for dimes to talent acts like trapeze, she sure will try to transform her low-class self into the wife of a Sterling. What, you wanna take her husband so you can saunter around at these parties like you belong here?"

Hazel gripped the glass in her hand harder and tried not to notice the ripples across the surface of the liquid as her body began to tremble in anger and fear. "I ain't trying to take your husband, miss," she said through gritted teeth. "It was a misunderstanding—"

"You can have him." The woman's pinched face flushed, and she sneered at Hazel in disgust. Party guests had paused their conversations to look on at the scene in interest, and Hazel burned beneath their judgmental stares. Jay's wife lifted her chin. "But I doubt anyone would take you seriously enough to marry you anyway. You're more the 'secret drunken mistake' type of girl, aren't you? You don't belong here. You'll never belong here. Except perhaps as one of Sonny's spectacles and displays."

The woman looked to Hugh, who confirmed her statement with a nod and then let out a cackling laugh that filled Hazel's eardrums like the screams she'd heard from Birdie moments before. "We should put her in a cage with the tigers!" Jay's wife leaned on Hugh, who laughed along with her, joined by all of the party guests nearby.

"She got that right, don't she, Hazel," Birdie said mockingly. "You could never be a real wife."

A flicker played at the corner of Hazel's lip as she thought about that man who'd stood across from her in the little church, saying "Till death do us part" with a straight face, then left her facing the slammer alone—or worse, in the kind of crowd they'd been running with. She'd told Birdie about her stupid mistake in confidence, and now the whole world was witness to her disgrace. "Oh, is that what you are, Birdie?" Hazel spat through gritted teeth, " 'Cause I don't see no ring on that finger. You ain't no better than me or none of the girls, and your stupid little act is only fun to watch because everyone hopes you'll miss your mark and fall." She steadied her shaking hand to take a long drink of the champagne from her glass.

"You think that net will always catch you? Girls like you get broken all the time. You're a dime a dozen. You could never be me. You could never do what I do."

The time to back down had long passed. Hazel stepped in closer to Birdie. "I don't know, babe. I'm a pretty fast learner. I can twirl around and do the splits quick as any gal. Just ask Frankie." She pushed the corners of her red lips upward into a wide, confident smile. "Your man and your act—they're both up for grabs."

Birdie stumbled backward, stupefied. She wasn't accustomed to being challenged.

"She might be safer in the tiger cage!" Hugh snorted with laughter and tried to push Mei into the mix, but she resisted and continued edging slowly backward.

Hugh and Jay's wife continued laughing, drawing in the people around them to join in mocking the girls. Hugh handed drinks to all of the party guests nearby.

Birdie looked wildly at the growing crowd, enraged by the laughter. "No one else can do what I do! No one!"

Hazel rolled her eyes, laughing with the crowd, pretending she wasn't terrified.

Birdie grabbed Hazel's wrist and pulled her within an inch of her face, growling at her with all the malice of a predatory wolf. "Listen here, you little slut. If you ever try to wreck my act again, I'll kill you." With that, Birdie turned and stormed off through the crowd.

"My, my." Hugh giggled as the partygoers dispersed. "If that isn't the pot calling the kettle black."

"What do you mean?" Jay's wife asked, sipping a fresh glass of champagne.

"Oh, Vanessa, don't you know?" Hugh's eyebrows rose and fell as his face spread into a satisfied grin. "Birdie is notorious for her less-than-professional relationship with Frank." Hugh extended his free arm out to point in Birdie's direction but caught the tray of a passing Sahara Sister instead. Panicking, the girl tried to catch the tray as the glasses tipped, but the entire collection of glassware toppled toward Hugh, showering him in champagne, flutes shattering at his feet. The remaining guests around them, who'd all but lost interest in the interaction when Birdie left, began to laugh and whisper, covering their mouths to hide their laughter as they turned away from the scene.

"You *stupid clumsy cow!*" Hugh shouted, staring down at his suit as the sticky champagne ran down his jacket front.

"I'm so sorry, I—" The girl bent to clean up the glass, and Mei knelt to help her.

"Don't worry, Sasha," Mei said, glaring up at Hugh. "It wasn't your fault."

"Sasha." Hugh narrowed his eyes at the girl as he removed his jacket. "I'll remember that. Take this to the servant hall and get it cleaned."

"Yes, sir," Sasha uttered through her tears. She turned to Jay's wife. "Miss, are you—"

Vanessa brushed her off and turned back to Hugh. "You mean, Birdie Bells is"—she lowered her voice to a whisper—"sleeping with Frank Sterling on the sly? I can't believe it! It's too awful!" Pure delight washed over Vanessa's face as Hugh confirmed her question with a smug nod.

"Why do you think Birdie gets paid more than all of the other performers?" Hugh continued. "She has a personal dressing wagon. And *now* she's got herself her very own freshly painted railcar." Hugh rolled his eyes and let out an exasperated sigh. "Honestly, it's ludicrous the special treatment she gets." Hazel had to agree; she'd given special attention to all the right people and didn't have anything to show for it.

"That's not fair, Mr. Sterling," Mei said, addressing Hugh. "Birdie is the best performer I've ever seen. She'd get special treatment in any circus. Sex can't get you everywhere."

"Oh, honey," he said in a mocking tone, glaring at Hazel meaningfully before turning back to Mei. "It can if you're doing it right. Just ask Birdie Bells."

Chapter 8

Dancing and Dessert

When Jay found Frank and Sonny again, the rich oil tycoon had joined them, and they were back to smiling and schmoozing.

"I've got no one to give my ranch to when I die," Butch said. "My daughters married worthless city boys, and my wife died years ago. I'd kill for some fresh young blood around the place, but they've all said the family business is too much for them. Oh, they like the money. Just don't want the work. You're lucky your son has taken up the family business, Sonny. Of course, maybe if they just had a little circus to manage, my kids would have been up to the task."

"A little circus?" Frank and Sonny questioned in unison, matched in their defensiveness.

"Well, don't get me wrong. You're to be commended on your bright and shiny dancing girls and your little petting zoo." Butch chuckled. "But it's hardly the same as managing an empire like McNeil Oil."

Sonny and Frank were again unified with expressions of suppressed resentment.

Jay piped in, "I've heard your ranch is impressive, Butch. About how much land do you own out there?"

Butch swirled the brandy in his snifter. "I've got

almost a million acres, fifty miles long and twenty-five miles wide!"

"A lot of rigs?" Jay asked.

"Oh, too many to count, son." Butch winked at Sonny. "And of course I've got the refineries."

"That's a lot to manage. You make it look easy!" Jay said.

Butch grinned. "It's a well-oiled machine, if you'll pardon the pun."

"I can appreciate that," Jay said. "The same might be said for us. Next week, Frank here, along with Sonny, will take the little family business on the road. They'll load up their two hundred workhorses and two hundred show animals and no less than eight hundred employees into a caravan of sixty-six railcars. We'll leave at dusk and arrive in Ayer before sunrise where we will unpack the entire show—which is larger than the town where we are performing—run a parade and two full three-ring performances, only to break down the entire show again that night and load up the whole production. We'll get a few hours of sleep on the train, arrive at the next city before dawn, and do the whole thing all over again."

"Well, that is—" Butch attempted to contribute to the conversation, but Jay didn't allow him to finish his thought.

"During performances, our setup will occupy fifteen acres and see more than seven thousand spectators filter through. People will rail in, come by motor car, or even horse and buggy to watch the show. We'll do that almost every day for the next six months. We don't simply occupy a space, we create it. Every day. And we take it down and roll out of town with unmatched efficiency. Sterling & Son's Circus isn't a little show. It's an extravagant corporate conglomerate specializing in the spectacular. Our circus will drag people out of the menial and catapult them into a world of mesmerizing magnificence. And do you know who will be out in the center ring, every night, announcing the spectacle to the thousands of viewers from the edge of their seats to the edge of the town?"

"Why, I—"

"Frank Sterling," Jay said with finality. "You want to invest in young blood? Here it is. Frank isn't set to inherit the Sterling & Son's Circus, Butch. He is the circus. As long as you have him, you'll have a good show."

"Damn right," Sonny said, patting Frank on the back.

"Well, that sounds like something I can put my money on," Butch said with an exaggerated sip of his brandy. "I never pass up a chance at young blood."

Hugh and Vanessa stumbled over to the group, panting to catch their breath as the orchestra was finishing their last number before a break. Jay extended his arm to invite his wife to the conversation, but she brushed past him. Jay caught a glance between Hugh and Butch but was unsure how to interpret the significance.

"Hello there, Butch," Vanessa said, giggling. "Hugh's tired of dancing. Care to show me around the floor?"

"I'm not much of a dancer." Butch feigned modesty. "But they say old dogs can learn new tricks. Jay, you wouldn't mind, would you?" Butch handed his drink to Jay without waiting for an answer so he could take the hand of his wife.

"Better watch out before Mr. Oil Money dances off with your wife." Hugh winked at Vanessa.

"Well, I—" Jay frowned.

"Jay doesn't dance," Vanessa said dismissively with a hiccup that shook her body. "Or if he does, maybe he can dance with the circus girl."

"The circus girl? What are you talking about?" Jay asked.

"Oh, you know, Birdie, or Hazel, or Floozy whoever," she said with a wave of her hand.

"Birdie or Hazel? Jay, what's she talking about?" Frank asked.

"I honestly have no idea," Jay said as the music stopped. "Vanessa, maybe it's time for us to turn in." He took her arm gently.

"Don't touch me!" she snapped, pulling her arm away and spilling her champagne all over herself. "My dress!" She shoved Jay backward with her champagne-free hand and stared down at herself in dismay.

Jay threw his hands up and exchanged glances with Frank. He was trying to be patient, but this was getting ridiculous.

"Vanessa, let's get you inside, honey—" Frank took her arm gently.

"You can't tell me what to do, Frank!" she said, whirling around to face him. "I'm not one of your circus girls."

"That's enough, Vanessa," Jay said firmly. "I'm sorry, she's had too much to drink. We're going."

"Good idea," Frank said, his face red from either anger, embarrassment, or both.

"I'm not going with you," she spat at Jay, looping

her arm firmly in Butch's. "You don't deserve me."

"Vanessa—"

"Darlin', maybe you oughta listen to your husband," Butch said, patting her arm.

"No! I'm going to be like Birdie Bells. She gets whatever she wants. Just look what she gets out of Frank! Just for sex? Well, I'm much more beautiful than Birdie. And classier. I haven't been getting enough—"

"So it's true."

Jay's heart dropped when he turned to see Luella. Her piercing blue eyes were set on Frank, a single tear streaming down her cheek. How could Frank do this to her?

"Luella, Mrs. Edwards here is a little bit walloped. Let's not listen to anything she says, hon." Sonny took Luella's arm. "Let's get you inside."

Luella stood stoically for a moment, her mouth set in a quivering line as she made eye contact with everyone in the circle one by one. She looked like a wrongly accused prisoner of war bravely facing the firing squad, and Vanessa had unleashed the first shot.

"Luella." Frank stepped forward, reaching out for his fiancée.

Vanessa burst into drunken laughter. "Come on, sweetie. Don't say you didn't know!"

Hugh pulled his lips between his teeth in an attempt to be serious, but his laugh escaped in a snort. The rest of the group stood speechless and mortified, the silence amplifying Vanessa's heartless laughter.

"Vanessa, please," Jay hissed under his breath. But his plea was trampled under the rising cadence of the gossiping crowd and the drunken laughter of his wife.

Luella pulled her hands to her face in despair. She turned and ran past the caged tigers into the house. The music had started to play again now, a happy, upbeat tune.

"God dammit, Jay, get a hold of your wife!" Frank yelled over the music. "Luella!" He ran through the crowd after her.

Sonny leveled a knowing look on Jay as if to say "take care of it" before melting into the crowd.

But Jay didn't have a chance to do anything. When he turned to look for Vanessa, she was already back on the dance floor, smiling and laughing with Butch.

That evening, when Jay had his hand on the door of his guest room in the mansion, he prepared again for what he would say to his wife. He'd spent the better part of the last two hours cleaning up her mess with Frank and Luella, along with apologizing to Sonny before receiving a long list of things he would need to do before the circus officially began travel season the next week. They'd picked up a few new investors, and Jay now had the green light for several necessary purchases that had been put on hold.

With all there was to do, Jay didn't have much time to set things right. But at some point in the evening, he had developed an idea. *I'll ask Vanessa to come with me. Her and Sadie. I'll remind her that I love her. Ask her what she wants and how I can make her happy. We've got to fix our marriage. Our family.*

But he never had a chance to say those things. When he opened the door to his room, he found his wife frantically packing her suitcase.

"What are you doing?" he asked as he looked around at the complete disarray of the room, his hand still on the doorknob.

She hastily gathered her jewelry from the table and tossed it clumsily on top of her undergarments, focusing on one of the gaudy baubles before leveling a stony, defiant gaze on Jay. "Isn't it obvious? I'm leaving you." The bitterness in her voice sent a shiver down his spine.

He shut the door gently, feeling the weight of it rest in the frame as the metal mechanism clicked into place. He took a deep breath. "What are you talking about?"

"I've finally found someone who will appreciate me."

He hadn't expected that. "Found someone? A man, you mean? Why—"

Vanessa's smirk slowly spread across her face. She cocked a hip and folded her arms.

How could there be someone else? Who? Then he recognized the importance of the word finally. He collected himself.

"I see. So that's why you've been asking to come to all the parties," he said. "You didn't have some renewed interest in spending time with me. You've been using me to take you out so you could go hunting for a new husband."

Vanessa swayed a little where she stood. Her dress was already ruined. Stained down the front, probably champagne. The sheer black overlay had a rip where she had stepped on it, probably while dancing with—

"Don't tell me it's that old dinosaur from dinner."

"His name is Butch McNeil, and he's no dinosaur. He's a millionaire. He looks at me like I'm the most beautiful woman he's ever seen, and he said any man who could call me his would be the luckiest man in the world."

Her words cut like a dagger.

"Is that what this is about? The way I look at you? You don't feel like I appreciate you enough—"

"Enough?" Vanessa's shrill laugh rattled Jay's clenched teeth. "You don't appreciate me at all! And you haven't looked at me in years."

"That's not true—"

"But Butch does. He looks at me. And he thinks I'm gorgeous and fabulous, and he wants some young blood in his mansion. He says he'll marry me if you give me a divorce. He called you a cocky little prick." That laughter again.

"Vanessa, you can't be serious. We're married. You have a daughter. This is all so sudden. We need to talk through this logically."

"It isn't sudden for me. I've been done with you for months. Years even. You are such a dull, unexciting, uninteresting—"

"Okay, you've made your point—"

"You aren't fit to lick my shoes," Vanessa spat as she clutched a wad of silk from the wardrobe and threw it into her suitcase.

Jay rolled his eyes. "I've got to say, your timing is impeccable. You're aware that I'm about to be on the road for months."

She ignored him, pushing the clothing aside to jam in a pair of shoes. She pulled the top of the suitcase down and pushed on it with her full weight to force it together.

"I can fix this. Let's sleep on it and talk about it when you've sobered up."

"I'm gonna sleep on it. But I'm gonna sleep on it

next to Butch." She slammed the case closed and popped in the snaps.

"You can't—"

Vanessa picked up her bulging suitcase with some effort and made her way to the door, glaring at Jay with startling sobriety. "I'm going to walk out of here and into Butch McNeil's room. And I'm going to let him do whatever he wants to me tonight."

She might as well have sucker punched him. Anxious mortification seeped through his body from its center point in his sternum.

Vanessa took a step closer to Jay's face to twist the dagger. "I can't wait to watch the look on his face when he takes off all my clothes. I bet he'll look at me like I'm the most delicious thing he's ever seen."

His mouth was too dry to speak. Vision blurred from the blood pulsing in his eyes. As his hand squeezed the cast-iron doorknob, he had to make a conscious effort not to snap it off the door. He imagined throwing it against the vanity mirror. Something about the way the glass would shatter and fall on the table felt satisfying.

"Don't beg me to stay," Vanessa said, taking a step back. "I've made up my mind."

Jay took a deep breath. He felt his strength returning as he regained control of his emotions. He relaxed his grip on the doorknob, turning it gently. Jay opened the door for his wife.

"I wasn't going to beg," he said coldly. "I was going to say that Grandpa Butch's guest room is that way." He pointed down the hall. "And I'll get the paperwork drawn up as soon as possible so you two can live happily ever after."

She rolled her eyes and crossed through the door frame.

"And what's the plan for your daughter, Vanessa?" Jay asked as she passed him. "Are you going to drag her into this filthy affair too, or is it your plan to send her off to some boarding school?"

Vanessa paused for a moment, running her tongue over her front teeth as she considered his question.

Something in her coldness stirred up confusion and disgust in Jay. As he looked at her face, he recognized her Roman features in a new light. The other side of the coin was heartless. Less the lady from a mosaic and more the semi-barbaric empress, fueled by ruthless ambition.

"She's your daughter too," she said, avoiding eye contact with Jay. "You figure it out." Vanessa hesitated for a moment, then stood up straight and tossed her hair over her shoulder.

And with that, Jay's wife marched down the Sterling mansion hall to another man's room.

Chapter 9

Rat in the Kitchen

Charlotte shuffled briskly to work, tugging her scarf around her. The Texas wind was back, this time bringing sand that stung with bitter cold. Every grain of dirt flew at her face like a tiny piercing bullet. She could understand how great statues and monuments crumbled, not in one great storm but eroding over time from every relentless wave of damaging wind. Every stinging grain of sand.

"Good morning, Charlotte," Agnes and Agatha said in unison as they approached her on the sidewalk. The purple pair stopped right in front of a Sahara Sisters circus poster, and Charlotte couldn't help but notice that the feathers in their hats resembled the plumes atop the pictured zebras.

"You on your way to work, dear?" Agatha asked.

"Actually, I'm just on my way to Bill's to pick up a few supplies and books for my son," Charlotte replied.

"Bullets for your gun? I guess Bill does sell everything," Agnes mused.

"Books for her son, you old ninny," Agatha shouted.

"Oh, sweet boy, how is he?" Agnes asked.

"He's great." Charlotte forced a smile, straining the cheek muscles she hadn't been using since her husband's latest outburst. Was her son okay? Lately Alex hid from Pete or tiptoed softly around him. How much longer could she protect her son from her husband's temper? Like a plate-spinning circus performer, she'd been dancing and dodging to keep her balance. Reaching far. Muscles cramping from unnatural distortion, lungs burning from holding her breath. Anything to keep the plates spinning. But lately, it felt like she was losing control.

"Charlotte, are you well? You look like you haven't slept in days," Agnes shouted.

"Oh, I…" Charlotte touched at her face instinctively. Agnes was right, of course. The image of Alex's face when his father threw his book in the fire and stormed out, a combination of panic, anger, and helpless fear, had been playing on Charlotte's mind throughout the waking and sleeping hours. What would happen to Alex if the plates dropped?

"Don't be rude, Agnes. You look lovely, dear, but maybe get yourself something too." Agatha opened her purse and pulled out a few coins to press into Charlotte's hands. "Too often we mothers spend so much time caring for our children that we forget to take care of ourselves."

"Oh, thank you, but I can't take that." Charlotte returned the money. "You're too kind."

"I insist," Agatha said, unwavering. "You're always so lovely to us on our brunches. What with our own children moved on—"

"She's right. You do need money for your lunches." Agnes nodded confidently.

"Oh heavens." Agatha sighed.

"But I—"

"Just take it. We're both nearly dead, you know. You can't spend it when you're dead," Agnes shouted.

"Well, she's not right about much, but she's right about that." Agatha closed Charlotte's fingers in around the coins.

"Thank you," Charlotte said, fighting the urge to cry from the unexpected kindness. "Thank you very much."

"You watch out for that Bill," Agnes shouted again as they sallied down the sidewalk. "He's on a tear today!"

Charlotte pulled open the door of the general store and stepped in beneath a frayed rope that pulled at the iron bell. The howl of the wind outside was replaced with the hum of low conversation and the sound of shoppers' shuffling feet. A pair of women stood in the back corner of the store examining delicate glass jars with gloved hands near a shelf that held rows of gleaming bottles. Powders, perfumes, flowery soaps, and beauty ointments. It was a section of the store with frivolities she usually ignored.

Charlotte turned over the new coins in her pocket. She had enough to order Alex a new copy of his book and still get a little something for herself.

Behind the counter, Bill perched precariously upon a wobbly ladder. His head, bald on the top with tufts of white hair fluffing out unpredictably around the sides, bobbed as he lined up an armful of canned goods on a tall shelf.

"Good morning, Bill!" Charlotte said pleasantly as she pulled the list Alex had written for her from her basket.

Bill turned to see his new customer, and focusing

his beady eyes on her through his spectacles, he immediately scrunched his round red face into an angry snarl. "Don't 'good morning' me, Charlotte Baxter!"

She took a step backward. "I'm sorry, Bill, I—"

"Do you know how much money you cost me? Stealing business away from me for that Saul Winslow at the cookhouse?" Bill waved his short arm in the air unsteadily, tottering a little before shoving the last can on a shelf haphazardly and marching down from the ladder toward her. "That was underhanded and sly, Charlotte Baxter, and don't you deny it!" No longer a few steps above the ground, Bill was shorter than everyone else in the room, but his volume always exceeded his stature.

"Oh." Of course, Bill was unhappy about losing the Sterling & Son's Circus order. She hadn't thought about that. "I'm so sorry, Bill. I didn't—"

"You didn't what? You didn't think I'd find out it was you who told the city boys I was charging too much?" He perched his hand on his hip. The store was stiflingly silent and suddenly impossibly hot. Other shoppers peered at the conversation curiously from behind dusty wooden shelves of beef jerky and a rainbow of swirled candy sticks. *Alex loves those.* She fiddled with the coins in her pocket.

"That wasn't it at all, Bill. I'm so sorry. I just—"

"You just nothing! I'm not sure what you think you need in here"—Bill pulled the list from her hands and tore it in two—"but maybe *Saul Winslow* can get it for you! Because I won't!" Bill tossed the torn paper into the air and turned on his heel, marching to the back of the store in a huff.

Her shoulders slouched under the weight of the

judging eyes of the general store customers. She swallowed hard and knelt to collect her torn list from the floor.

Alex wouldn't be getting those supplies today after all. Or a new copy of his book. And he definitely wouldn't be getting any of those candy sticks. Charlotte left the store feeling hopeless and defeated.

When Charlotte arrived at the cookhouse, Martha was hard at work, wiping down a table by the door. "I think it's going to be another busy day. The inn is all booked up, again. I probably could have rented out the closets if I wanted to!"

Charlotte nodded, mechanically taking the cloth and bucket from Martha. "A busy day, good."

"Are you all right, hon?" Martha asked, pausing to look at her with concern.

"Yes, of course," she said, shaking off her thoughts. "Let me take over with these tables. I'm not worried about it being busy; I love busy. You work too hard, Martha."

"God bless you, Lottie," Martha said, putting a hand to her cheek. "Okay then, I'll go up and get the rooms sorted. Make sure you get some breakfast for yourself when you get a chance."

Charlotte thanked her and finished up the tables. She traded her cloth and bucket for a coffee pitcher when a few customers came in from the porch. They were men she knew vaguely, who worked out at the ranch with her husband.

"Coffee?" Charlotte asked.

"Yes, ma'am." The first one took a cup from the table and held it out. "How are you this morning, Miss Charlotte?"

"Good, thank you," she answered. "Gettin' ready for the big day tomorrow."

"Big day?"

"Well, the circus, of course," Charlotte said. "The whole big train caravan is rolling in tomorrow. Haven't you seen the posters?"

"The circus! Fancy that, Jim."

"I ain't going. Them carnies make me nervous." Jim shuddered. "It ain't Christian."

"Who cares about that; I'll make some money in those gamblin' tents. And then I'll spend it all on them hoochie-coochie showgirls." The man whistled and then blushed. "Sorry, Charlotte."

Charlotte smiled and filled the other coffee cup. "You're not alone, Daryl. I wouldn't miss seeing the circus for the world. We need a little fun around here. I bet the whole town will be buzzing tomorrow. You know, Saul's providing those circus people with all the food. For the people and all those animals."

"Boy, I bet that's a lotta biscuits," Daryl said.

Charlotte brought milk and juice out for a family with two young children, and she smiled, watching them play. "I miss that age," she said to the mother, gesturing to the toddler playing with a model train at the table.

"You have kids?" the mother asked.

"A son. He's ten now," Charlotte said, stabbed by a pang of guilt as she remembered her own son's tear-filled eyes watching his book burn. "My son likes trains, too." Charlotte knelt down and rolled the toy train back and forth to the little boy as the family ordered a round of pancakes.

The routine of work seemed to melt away the early

morning's disappointment. Maybe Charlotte had wobbled for a moment, but she had been able to go on with the show. Keeping the plates spinning was something she'd become very good at. By the time she went to the kitchen to gather the next round of breakfast plates, everything was right side up again.

"Martha told me I'd better remind you to eat some breakfast yourself, Lottie, before it gets too busy out there," Saul said, pouring pancake batter onto the sizzling surface of the griddle. "Why don't you get yourself a cup of coffee."

"That's advice I don't mind taking." Charlotte poured herself a cup of coffee, mixing in a little milk and taking a welcome sip. She leaned against the counter to catch her breath for a moment and gazed thoughtfully at the batter as it bubbled.

"Hot coffee and flapjacks always remind me of my childhood," she said. "I used to get up before sunrise every day with my father to share a cup of coffee and some pancakes. They weren't as good as yours, of course, but the ranch cook did his best."

Saul chuckled.

"I'd spend the whole day on horseback, either taking care of things around the ranch or out at the rodeo. My dad made sure I could hold my own with those cowboys. Other girls my age were learning to sew and read. I was out building fences and tying hogs, or flying around on a stallion for rodeo fans."

"How old were you?"

"About Alex's age, I guess." She swallowed the lump in her throat.

"I worked alongside my daddy about that age too. They were long days. Hard work." Saul paused for a long while. Charlotte imagined he was reliving his childhood too, though she couldn't tell whether it was a happy one or not. " 'Course, when Martha and I had children of our own, we said we wouldn't make 'em work. We wanted them to have schoolin' and opportunities."

"They're both happy and successful now," Charlotte said. "You must have done something right."

Saul laughed again. "I'm not sure I can take much credit. You know, they always did end up helpin' us out around here, even though that wasn't what Martha and I intended for them. When they come home, those are their favorite stories. They love to talk about good ol' times at the cookhouse."

Charlotte sipped her coffee.

Saul flipped a row of flapjacks to show perfect golden undersides. The buzz of customer conversations floated in from the dining room.

"Pete wants Alex to come out and work with him on the ranch."

"Does he?"

"The thing is, I loved being out with my father. I don't want to rob Alex of that. I don't want to rob Pete of that, but— "

"I think work is good for kids, helps build a good work ethic. But I don't know if it would be the same for Alex out there working with Pete as it was for you with your father, or for me with mine. As for me, I'da done anything to get to go to school."

"I always felt I fell a little short since I didn't finish either. Alex has already learned so many things that I never did." Charlotte downed her coffee and placed the empty ceramic cup in the sink.

"You trust your instincts, Charlotte. You know what's best for your son." Saul piled fresh pancakes on a stack of plates.

Charlotte ushered breakfast plates through the swinging doors to the precious little family. The mother lovingly cut the pancakes in little bites while her children hung on her arms, asking excited questions about clowns and cotton candy. The woman's husband gazed affectionately at his wife and children. It was a perfect, beautiful little family.

Charlotte rounded the tables, topping off waters and coffees before heading back into the kitchen to find that the biscuits were done for Jim and Daryl. She whistled a little tune while she plucked biscuits from the hot metal tray and bounced them between her hands. She tore each one in half, letting the steam escape from the middle, and arranged them golden side down on the plates, then ladled piping-hot peppery gravy over the fluffy white mountains of bread. She picked up the plates with a smile and headed out happily to bring the hot plates to her hungry customers.

Before Charlotte made it to the table, the bell above the door chimed as another customer entered the cookhouse. A cowboy with a pistol on each hip and a cluster of flowers in his right hand. His spurs jangled with each scraping step across the floor.

Charlotte froze in place.

"Well, they'll just let anybody in here!" the man shouted as he reached the table with Jim and Daryl.

The ranch hands stood up awkwardly, extending a hand to Pete.

"Mind if I join y'all?" he asked.

"No, er, by all means." Daryl pulled out a chair for

Pete while avoiding a questioning gaze from Jim.

"Pete," Charlotte said, approaching him. "Hi! I wasn't expecting you!"

She set the plates down in front of Jim and Daryl.

"Thank you, Miss Charlotte," Daryl said, digging in.

"Well, I thought I'd surprise you!" Pete smiled broadly and proudly handed his wife a cluster of petunias.

Charlotte took the flowers and hugged her husband. "That is a nice surprise—"

"It ain't easy findin' flowers in this cold weather, but I like to take care of my girl, don't I."

"They're beautiful, thank you. I'll go put these in water and get you some coffee."

"And some eggs!" Pete smacked his belly with one hand after the other as he looked around the room. "And bacon, and—what are you boys having? Is that biscuits and gravy?" He gestured to the plates in front of Jim and Daryl as he sat down. "Some of those too."

Charlotte noticed the mom from the little family she'd been taking care of smile at her as she carried the flowers to the kitchen. She took a deep breath as she passed through the doors, found an empty cup for the flowers, and filled it with water.

"Saul," she said over her shoulder, making an effort to sound carefree, "Pete's here!"

Saul turned around from the grill slowly and looked at her with concern.

"He surprised me." She shrugged her shoulders quickly, turning off the faucet and setting the flowers on the counter. "Isn't that sweet?"

Saul glanced at the flowers, then held Charlotte's

gaze for a moment and turned back to the griddle. "Well, yes," he said. "That's real nice."

"Yes," she said. "So nice. Well, he sure is hungry!" Charlotte went to pick up a biscuit from the hot tray and burned the side of her hand. With a sharp intake of breath, she threw the biscuit onto the plate and brought the burned skin quickly to her lips. After a moment, she pulled her hand away from her mouth and shook it in the air, clenching her jaw angrily as she clumsily poured gravy over the biscuit with her other hand.

"Saul, can I have some eggs and, um, some sausage on this plate, please."

Saul turned back toward Charlotte, prepared the plate, and handed it back to her deliberately. "You let me know if you need anything else, okay, Charlotte?"

"Yes. Of course. Don't be silly," Charlotte said, taking the plate quickly.

Why didn't he call me Lottie? she thought as she went back out through the swinging doors into the dining area.

"Well, I told Rex, ain't no need to call a vet for that! I shot ol' Goldstar between the eyes from twenty paces." Pete held up his Colt .45 and aimed it at the imaginary horse. As he cocked the hammer, the decorative cylinder rotated revealing the intricate design etched into the side. Pete bellowed out a "bang" and a hearty round of laughter before lowering the hammer back down and holstering the gun.

"Here you are, hon." Charlotte set the plate in front of her husband.

"What's this?" Pete said, looking at his plate scornfully. "Where's my bacon?"

"Oh, I'm sorry, you did say bacon, didn't you."

She rubbed her hurt hand.

"I guess this'll be fine," he relented dejectedly, picking up his fork to take a bite. Pete looked over at Jim's and Daryl's plates for a long moment before reluctantly cutting into his own biscuit.

"It's been a busy day," Charlotte said as she poured Pete a fresh cup of coffee and topped off the cups in front of Jim and Daryl. "You know, with the circus comin' tomorrow, Martha said—"

"You know, boys, my wife always works so hard."

"You're right," Daryl said. "She does. Charlotte's a good woman."

Pete narrowed his eyes at Daryl for a moment before turning to Jim. "Your wife work, Jim?"

"No," Jim said slowly, "she doesn't. Although she lets me know all the time that wrangling the kids is tougher than wranglin' cattle."

The men laughed. Charlotte backed away from the conversation to check on her other tables.

"Charlotte," Pete said, throwing his fork down. "There's not enough gravy on this."

"Oh, I'm sorry. Let me go get some more for you," she said, reaching for the dish.

Pete grabbed her wrist as she picked up the plate, and she winced, dropping it with a clatter and splattering gravy out onto the table.

Jim and Daryl sat forward alertly in their chairs, Daryl dabbing at his mouth slowly with his napkin.

"What's this?" Pete said, pointing to the mark on her hand.

"Oh, it's…well, I burned myself getting the biscuits—"

"Burned yourself." Pete raised his voice. "You're

injured?"

"Well, yes, I mean…well, I wouldn't say injured. It hurts a little, but—"

"That's it!" He pounded the table with his fist, threw his chair back, and marched toward the kitchen.

Charlotte ran after him fearfully.

"Saul Winslow!" he yelled, plowing his way through the doors into the kitchen.

Saul turned around with measured composure. "Good to see you, Pete. What can I do for you?"

"You can take better care of my wife, that's what! You know she's injured?"

Saul looked at Charlotte with concern and confusion.

"Show him your hand," Pete barked.

"It's fine really," Charlotte said, reluctantly holding up her hand. "I just burned it—slightly—on the biscuit pan earlier. I—"

"It's not fine at all!" he bellowed. "My wife comes in here day after day, working these ridiculous hours in this run-down shed!" Pete gestured to the kitchen in dismay and grabbed his wife's arm to wave it at Saul. "No wonder she's injured! And what are you going to do about it? Nothing! Send your slave right back out to work I guess, huh!"

"Now hang on a minute," Saul said, setting down his spatula gently and wiping his hands on his apron slowly. "Lottie knows we care about her, and I'd never have her workin' when she doesn't want to."

"Are you saying she'd rather be here than home?" Pete was in a full-out yell now.

"Not at all, Pete. Why don't you sit down and have some breakfast, and we can talk calmly when things slow down."

"Oh, I had your breakfast," Pete roared. "And it's tasteless pig slop and no wonder why!"

"Hey, now." Saul was fighting hard against raising his own voice.

"You can find someone else to be your slave," Pete yelled, adding a hateful word that turned Saul to stone against it.

Charlotte closed her eyes in shame and embarrassment. She took measured breaths and imagined herself in the center ring again, balancing the tall poles with plates spinning faster than she could control.

"Pete, please," she whispered, tugging at his shoulder.

"No—" Pete brushed her off and continued laying into Saul. "My wife is done working here! You hear me? Let's go, Charlotte!" He attempted to pull her through the double doors, but she slipped out of his grasp.

"Go home, Pete." She took a step backward toward Saul. "I can't leave work right now. We're slammed. They need me."

Pete clenched his fist and stepped toward Charlotte.

Jim appeared from the other side of the doors and placed a calm hand on Pete's raised shoulder. "Hey now, there's no need for all this. Why don't you ride on out back to the ranch with us? We're headed back that way, aren't we, Daryl."

"I've got a few more things to do in town," Daryl said, pushing past both men to stand between Charlotte and her hovering husband. "Pete, you take my horse."

Peter Baxter looked like a wild bull in the ring as he glared one by one at the men in the kitchen who'd slowly inched themselves closer to him. His nostrils flared and jaw clenched, he looked ready to charge. But he backed down.

"I don't need your horse. I've got my car," he said, glaring at Daryl. "And anyway, I'm not going back out to the ranch. Rex is sending me to Fort Worth on important business."

Jim and Daryl exchanged glances, and Daryl shrugged.

"All right then," said Jim calmly. "All right. Let's all pay up and go our separate ways."

"Hell naw, I'm not payin' for nothin'." His cold eyes burned when he laughed. "In fact, I need a little cash to go buy myself a real breakfast 'fore I hit the road." He glowered at Charlotte, doubling down when she hesitated. She slowly reached into her pocket and gave him the money she'd intended to use to buy Alex's supplies.

"Oh, come on, darlin', a little more than that. Your husband's got a long trip ahead of him."

Charlotte bit her lip, fighting back tears. She reached slowly into her pocket and took out the coins that sweet old Agatha had given her that morning.

Pete snatched the coins and shoved them into his own pocket. "Thanks, hon." His tone darkened as he leaned in. "I'll deal with you when I get back from Fort Worth."

Charlotte swallowed hard and managed a frail nod. The plate-spinning act had finally spun out of control, and she was standing in a pile of broken shards. The men in the kitchen stood frozen as they watched Pete glare at his wife before backing through the doors out of the kitchen and turning to the guests in the cookhouse dining room.

"Y'all look real close at your food before you eat it," he hollered belligerently as he made his way to the door. "There's a rat in the kitchen!"

Chapter 10

Circus Train at Sunrise

The sun doesn't rise without announcement in the early days of spring on the flat Texas plains. First, the beginnings of light pervade the air, not in color or in warmth, but just in the way the darkness isn't welcome anymore. As the night packs up to leave, some of the bolder bugs and animals come out, rustling, or chirping, or buzzing, or warbling. They gently usher in the cold yellow light of morning with the crack of the sun across the plains. The roosters rustle on their perches and crow at the dawn.

But on this Ayer morning, when the sky was still navy blue, the whistle of the circus train announced the day, scattering lizards and bugs off the railroad tracks before the sun could peek across the horizon to nudge them or the roosters could open their eyes.

This was the day the circus came to town. It would begin not with the sunrise but with the arrival of the circus train caravan and the rising of the Sterling & Son's big top.

In his railcar, Jay sat at his desk with his schedule book, pocket watch, and a copy of the *Ayer Gazette* for the last three days, preparing for the day ahead. He spun his round gold wedding ring on the table and watched it slow its rotations before eventually settling on the wooden surface. He held it up in the air to examine it rather than put it back on his finger.

I'm going to let him do whatever he wants to me.

Jay looked at the ring with disgust, ran it over with his thumb one more time, and threw it in the wastebasket. Something about the echo of the metal clink as it hit the bottom made the ring seem heavier than it was, like he'd just dropped something that weighed a thousand pounds. Jay took out his schedule book and tried to go over his plan for the day ahead. The words in the book floated past him.

She's your daughter too. You figure it out.

He'd made the call to a highly recommended boarding school and spoken to a nun who somehow spread fear and formality even through the telephone.

"All our young ladies are required to wear uniforms and attend Mass. Miss Edwards will adhere to a daily schedule of mathematics, manners, grammar…"

It took everything in him not to hang up the phone as he imagined boxing his playful little girl into a black and white uniform and drilling grammar into her until she became a "well-mannered young woman with all of the requirements for a good and godly marriage."

"Godly marriage? My daughter is ten. This has been a mistake," Jay said. "Please remove us from your list."

After some protesting from the nun, Jay decided to tell her, just for fun, that Sadie would instead be traveling across the country with him.

"A girl traveling with her father for business will never make for a polite young lady ready for a respectable marriage. Girls need structure. Feminine guidance," the nun replied.

"Well, her mother's run off, but there are plenty of women in the circus," he quipped.

"The circus? You can't be serious, Mr. Edwards. The circus is a godless, dangerous place. It isn't suitable for an adult, much less a child."

"Thank you, but we have plenty of children in the circus, so Sadie will be just fine. We put them in the cage next to the cigar-smoking monkeys."

He hadn't had to hang up. The nun had done it for him.

Jay glanced over at the bunk where his daughter Sadie lay sleeping, and joy and warmth overcame his bitterness. Maybe this whole experience would prove a new kind of adventure for both of them.

He flipped open his pocket watch and checked the time. Four twenty-six a.m. They should be arriving any minute. Jay tucked his schedule book in his lapel pocket and stood at the ready by his door. When the train slowed, letting out a sigh of steam as it shuddered to a halt, he flung open the door of his train car and took a deep breath in.

Time to get to work.

Surveying the expanse of bare land before him, Jay was pleased to see that the advance men had properly laid out the flares to direct the supply wagons where to go. They would set up not far from the tracks. Close enough for a quick load-in and load-out but far enough toward town to draw attention and leave some space clear for passengers coming in and out by rail. A few hours from now, this blank canvas of grass and dirt would be a bustling hub of activity larger and livelier than the whole of Ayer itself.

The caravan was broken into four sections, all

carefully choreographed by Jay. He looked down the stretch of rail and back at his pocket watch. He expected the second section to arrive in twenty-nine minutes.

Behind him, the door on the other side of his split car opened, and his best friend and right-hand man, Benny, came tumbling out. Benny was still buttoning his charcoal-gray vest, followed by his wife, Pearl, who placed a coordinating fedora on his head and straightened his tie before handing him a palm-sized parcel wrapped in a white hankie. Pearl would be taking care of Sadie today, along with their two children and all of the circus kids who went to school. She adjusted her sleep bonnet, waved at Jay, and kissed her husband on the cheek, returning inside their train car for a little more sleep. Benny trotted down the ladder and came to stand beside Jay. The two looked out at the sprawling landscape in front of them in silence.

"Ayer doesn't look much different than the hills of France when it's dark, but for the flares," Benny said as he unwrapped the handkerchief, broke off a piece of the breakfast bread inside, and handed it to Jay.

The two had met in the trenches of France as members of the American Expeditionary Forces in 1918. Benny was a part of the African-American National Guard soldiers of New York's 15th Infantry Regiment who unloaded at the docks, and Jay was managing logistics with the 36th Infantry Division. Regardless of their intended roles, Benny and Jay developed knowledge of trench warfare from their French allies, as well as the kind of close friendship that only comes from traumatic shared experiences. After the war, Benny and his family joined Jay with Sterling

& Son's.

"A little less scary, don't you think?" Jay mused.

"Fewer French people."

Jay chuckled and took out his pocket watch to check the time.

"Why do you still use that thing when the rest of us wear wristwatches?" Benny joked, pointing at his own watch.

"This keeps better time than any clock or wristwatch," Jay said, snapping it closed and tapping the case. "Besides, you know it was a gift from my mother." Jay tucked his watch into his jacket pocket.

"I can't believe you convinced Sonny to start with Ayer again after it was such a dud last year," Benny said. "You think all the work you put in will turn it around?"

"You're right. Sonny hates Ayer. He thinks it's a dusty little speck on the way to nowheresville. But logistically, it just makes sense to stop here. It's the halfway point between the Winter Quarters in Fort Worth and our next stop in Abilene, which was over our standard limit of two hundred miles a night. We were just wasting money and fuel by passing it by."

"Every mile's a dollar." Benny smirked.

"Between me and you, if we don't rake in the cash on this first show, we won't have enough money to pay for the second one. Sonny made it clear that this better be a spectacular success, or the losses will come out of my hide."

Jay took out his book and read off his checklist. "I've been communicating directly with the rail master to coordinate the train schedule. I offered excursion tickets that included entry to the big top and a flyer with a description of the most exciting sideshows. I monitored the advance men's advertising placement personally both in Ayer and in the surrounding towns..."

"Are there surrounding towns?" Benny joked.

"I talked to a rancher named Rex Stallman, the biggest employer in town, to make sure that he paid all of his employees earlier this week so everybody's got money in their pockets. If all goes according to plan, I'm predicting we pull in an extra five thousand dollars in Ayer."

"That'll pay for the next show and then some."

"I sure hope so. All I have left to do is check on the advance men and meet up with our supplier."

"Is that the new guy you told me about?"

Jay nodded. "Saul Winslow. That was a bit of a risk, but it's where a good chunk of our profit is coming from, so pray to God he comes through."

"Well, let's get to it," Benny said, dusting the crumbs off of his hands and tucking his hankie into his waist pocket. "You want the Rolls or a Tin Lizzie?"

But before he could answer, a large white delivery truck approached them and came to a stop only feet from the pair. The driver's side door opened, and a massive man stepped out. It was Saul Winslow. "Thought I'd save you the trip."

Jay and Benny exchanged approving glances.

"The cold stuff is in here." Saul gestured to the truck behind him. "Everything else is down at the tracks."

"It isn't often I meet someone who anticipates my needs, Mr. Winslow," said Jay as he shook hands with Saul and introduced Benny. He made a note in his book. "I'll stop back by the cookhouse and settle up with you after our second show."

Saul nodded and put his hands in his pockets. "My wife thinks I'm crazy, trustin' a circus man to pay me before he hops on his train and rolls out of town."

"No need to worry there, Mr. Winslow. Sterling & Son's don't go about stiffin' vendors. Not with Jay in charge anyway," Benny said. "Come on, I'll bum a ride with you to the cookhouse tent and help you unload."

Jay took out his pocket watch and looked behind him. *Right on time*, he thought as the crew unloaded the flat cars. They'd set up the run ramp, a sturdy set of wood and iron planks that created an efficient path from the end of the flat car to the ground. The horse teams were already pulling the first wagon down the run. Simultaneously, another crew was staking off the locations for the various tents and marking off the area for the big top.

Jay was pleased. Everything was going according to plan so far, already better than last year. Maybe everything today would go off without a hitch. He headed back to the tracks to greet Sonny, who was just stepping out of his private railcar.

"Looks like the boys are ahead of schedule, Jay!" Sonny said, hooking his thumb in his suspenders as he watched the workers at the cookhouse fire up the grills and connect the industrial-size refrigerators to the generators. A second crew had erected the dining tent beside the temporary kitchen and were now setting up tables beneath it with the unified rhythm of a chorus line.

"We found a better supplier this year," Jay mused, still watching the workers intently.

"Makes a difference," Sonny said.

"Sure does."

The two men continued discussing plans for the day, completing their conversation without making eye contact, all the while watching the workers.

"All four sections should be here by six thirty a.m., and the Farmer's Almanac says the sun will rise at six forty-six this morning," Jay stated.

"Well, if the sun doesn't show up on time, dock his pay." Sonny winked. "I guess I oughtta go wake up ol' Frank and Hugh. Frank's got an idea for the Grand Entry he's been itchin' to tell me about!"

Sonny headed toward the private train cars, the first section of the train. For decades, Sonny traveled with the circus in its entirety every year and had a full luxury train car to himself, but for the past few years he had been entrusting more of the circus travel duties to Frank, Jay, and Hugh, ducking out of a few of the performances to enjoy time at home as he prepared for retirement. They still retained his car, and to Jay's dismay, due to the lack of efficiency, his luxury home away from home traveled with the circus caravan whether Sonny occupied it or not.

Behind his car were the split cars for family and management. These cars were similar in style and function to Sonny's but were split down the middle so that each train car contained two private units. The first of these was occupied by Frank, and its door was currently under the banging fist of Mr. Sonny Sterling.

Frank slipped out, still in his pajamas and robe, and the two hashed it out for a bit on the steps before Frank hurried back into his car and Sonny moved on to Hugh's railcar a few sleeper cars down.

Past the feuding father and son, the second section pulled in, steam billowing past the blushing horizon into the lightening sky. On cue, half of the crew lined up at the arriving train and began immediately to construct the run ramp when it stopped. This train would contain the poles and equipment for the big top, and it would take at least a dozen workers, half a dozen horses, and a handful of elephants to construct it.

The honk of a Model T behind him disrupted Jay's thoughts. He turned to see Benny grinning at him.

"Ready to check the big top location before they start the setup?"

Jay nodded and hopped into the passenger seat. He glanced back at Sonny, who was red in the face, still pounding on Hugh's door.

They drove past the cookhouse and dining area, where a young boy in overalls and a cap was running a flag reading *hotel* up the pole, to show workers breakfast was ready to be served. Jay scoped out the blacksmith tent, horse and baggage tents, and the barber's tent on the way, and Jay was pleased at the progress for each of those too. Scoping out the area for the big top and menagerie with Benny and the advance men for Ayer, Jay was happy to see that everything was well laid out. He gave them the go-ahead to raise the poles.

Upon arriving back by the train cars, a collection of observers clustered to watch the circus set up. This didn't bother Jay. In his opinion, the setup of the circus was much harder to coordinate than the show itself.

The door to Hugh's compartment was flung open, and workers rushed about it while Sonny yelled at them. Frank was descending the stairs from his railcar, and Jay went to meet him.

"What's going on?"

"Well, uh, I don't know for sure, but I imagine my dad just figured out that Hugh's not where he's supposed to be…"

Jay looked at him quizzically.

"We might have partied a little too hard last night," Frank said, rubbing his head. "Hugh met up with some group of guys, and uh, I don't know if he made it onto the right car."

Jay groaned. "I thought he learned his lesson after getting kicked out of seminary school."

"Well, this is the circus, Jay. It ain't seminary school."

They both turned to watch Sonny yelling at an errand boy.

"Well, at least you made it onto the right car. Glad I didn't have to pull you out of Birdie's or somethin'."

Frank nodded slowly.

"Good God, Frank," Jay said in shock, "You're worse than Hugh! After everything with Luella the other night?"

"Well…" Frank glanced back at his car. "Luella's not here, is she—"

"Is Birdie in your car right now?" Jay cut in.

"Come on, you know how it is with these women," Frank said, adjusting his tie. "You gotta stay ahead of them before they get the best of you."

Jay ran his thumb over his naked ring finger involuntarily.

"Oh hell—" Frank put his hand on Jay's shoulder. "I'm sorry, I didn't mean your wife."

Jay looked at the car and back at Frank. Past Frank,

the third section was coming in. It would still be another thirty minutes before the last section arrived carrying the performers, supposedly Hugh with them, and the full sleeper car they'd commissioned for Birdie.

"I don't care about my wi—my *ex*-wife. All these people sleeping where they shouldn't be is messing up the schedule."

"Aw, come on, Jay. It can't make that big a difference—"

Jay checked the time. Six a.m. He fought off the mental image of Vanessa sauntering into the bedroom of that old oil tycoon and snapped his pocket watch closed.

"I don't have time for this."

Chapter 11

Arrival

"All right, folks," Saul said, with a clap of his hands as he strode through the cookhouse dining room, "it's almost eleven o'clock! Let's all head on out and watch that street parade!"

Customers dabbed at their mouths and checked their watches, excitedly gathering their things and leaving money on the table for their food. They chatted cheerfully amongst themselves about where on Main Street would be the best spot to see the spectacle.

"Y'all enjoy the parade. We'll be open after for lunch!" Saul stood at the door, thanking customers and shaking hands as they left the cookhouse. "And make sure you go see that circus today—they've got a show at two and another one at eight!"

Looking out the window as she gathered up a few plates, Charlotte could see all of the businesses on Main Street were doing the same thing, ushering customers out onto the street so that they could lock up and head out with the crowd to see the much-anticipated Sterling & Son's Circus Parade.

Martha went over to the window to join Charlotte in watching Ayer's sleepy street populate with eager spectators. "This circus has shut down the whole town," she observed.

"Did they shut us down, or wake us up?" Charlotte asked.

"Leave those tables, ladies!" Saul said. "We can clean them up when we get back! We don't want to miss it, come on!"

"That man has lost his mind," Martha said to Charlotte. "You go get us a good spot, honey," she said to Saul. "We'll hurry out, I promise."

"Okay, okay," Saul said, "you gon' lock up then?"

Martha nodded. "Well, he must be excited to see that parade if he's rushing off and leaving money out in plain sight like that!" She gathered up people's tickets and the money they'd left and tucked it into her apron.

Charlotte laughed and continued gathering dishes. The two women carried their plates to the kitchen.

"I know I've had my fair share to say about the circus," Martha said, hanging up her apron, "but I want to thank you for helping Saul get that deal selling them their food and supplies. I've never seen him walkin' so tall."

"Oh, that's kind of you," Charlotte said smiling, "but I hardly did anything."

"Yes, you did! Saul's talking about hiring an extra maid now. Someone to help me with the inn. You've been a great help to us, hon. You always have." Martha set her plates down in the sink and rinsed her hands. Her smile faded as she dried her hands on her apron. "Listen…I wanna talk to you about yesterday. About your husband…"

Charlotte's whole body tensed at the mention of her husband, shame and embarrassment washing over her again. She'd apologized for Pete and his behavior, his language, so many times, but it never seemed to make things better. "I am so sorry—"

"No, no, it isn't that. I want to tell you that…" Martha paused thoughtfully. "You know, I had a sister who was married to a man like Pete. We didn't know him, but he seemed like a nice man, and she thought he hung the moon, but…well, turns out he wasn't as nice as she thought. She was always apologizin' for him. Stood by him, for a long time…" Martha's eyes began to water.

"What happened?" Charlotte asked.

"He started hitting her," Martha said, dabbing at her eyes, "and still, she stayed. Had children, too, precious little things."

Charlotte untied her apron as she listened, focusing on the familiar roughness of the fabric strings. The thready bumps of the stitches.

"He beat her half to death one night," Martha said, looking at Charlotte. "She ended up in the hospital before we knew what was happening. Broken ribs. Eye swoll shut."

Charlotte held her apron tightly.

"Well, once we found out—the family you know—we come out there and we scared him off. My momma and daddy, they took her and the children in, and they've been helping her get through it. But he broke her. She's never been the same."

"I'm sorry for your sister," Charlotte said, taking Martha's hand, "and for you. That must have been hard."

"It was." Martha nodded, dabbing at her eyes with the back of her sleeve.

"But that isn't me. Pete's not like that," Charlotte lied. "He's a good man. Better than I deserve. I don't know why he has these outbursts like yesterday. And I'm so sorry that he said those things and made a scene—"

Martha squeezed Charlotte's hand. "I don't want you to be sorry. I—"

"—but he really is a good man, and I love him. He's not perfect, but he's my husband."

Martha took Charlotte's apron from her hands and hung it up beside hers. "I know I don't know what things are like in your marriage or how Pete is at home," Martha said, "and you gotta do what you feel is best for you and for your family. For that little boy of yours."

Charlotte's jaw clenched, and she let go of Martha's hand so that her fingers wouldn't do the same.

"I just want you to know that you always have a place here at the inn if you need it," Martha said, gently taking her hand again. "That's what I want to say. That if you ever need a place to go, you and Alex, y'all come here. We love you, Saul and I, and we wanna do anything we can to help. If you need it. If you want it."

"Thank you." Charlotte forced a smile and stood upright. "Well, we don't want to miss the parade! Saul will be wondering where we are!"

Martha smiled and patted her hand. "You're right. I'll go lock up."

By the time Charlotte and Martha joined Saul, Main Street was so crowded they could hardly turn their heads without bumping into someone. The anticipation in the crowd was palpable. Music and the clopping of horse hooves floated over the brick streets toward the waiting crowd.

Saul put his arm around Martha and smiled at

Charlotte. "Let's see where all that money comes from, huh?"

At the far end of the street, rows of black horses pulled a larger-than-life wagon topped with a dozen uniformed musicians, glistening circular horns, and shining pipes.

"Martha, it's the jazz band!" Saul said. "I feel as giddy as a child!"

Charlotte laughed as she tried to imagine Saul as a small giddy little boy. Surely it was impossible that her goliath friend had ever been anything but large, serious, and strong. She leaned over to Martha. "I guess the circus brings out the child in everyone."

Gasps of awe and wonder waved through the crowd as the wagon rolled by carrying the roaring jazz band. It was as wide as three horses and twice as tall as any car Charlotte had ever seen. As it passed, time seemed to stop. She caught a glimpse of her own mesmerized face in the mirrors that decorated the sides between exotic illustrations and floral embellishments. Something about seeing her face on the wagon gave her a fleeting moment of childish joy too.

The bandwagon passed, revealing across the square the little family that she'd served pancakes to the day before. The little girl pointed in wonder at the elephants as they stomped by, raising their trunks to let out the loud trumpeting call that signified the arrival of the circus to everyone in Ayer. Each elephant was decorated with a glittering performer atop its head, some standing, some sitting, all waving and smiling.

The mother laughed and the father put his arm around her, kissing her on the cheek. The two smiled at each other as the children hugged them, bouncing with energized amazement at each new section of the circus parade. *We could be like them*, she thought, *if only we tried a little harder*. Large clowns in tiny cars were zipping through the street in figure eights. In the middle of the zippy zoomers, a pair of tall stilt walkers in endlessly long striped pants stalked whimsically down the street, waving at the children so far below them.

When Pete gets home from Fort Worth, I'll talk to him, she thought. *If he wants me to quit my job, I'll quit. I'll be a housewife, and we'll be happy.*

Charlotte drew in a sharp breath as a regal procession of horses distracted her from her thoughts. The well-trained riderless horses trotted in a uniform line that would make military generals raise an impressed eyebrow, lifting their hooves and pausing to extend their bodies in a deep bow every few feet. In front of Charlotte, they stopped and rose up on their two back legs, tapping at the air in unison.

"Oh, Martha, look!" she said, covering her mouth with her hand. "How beautiful!"

Martha smiled and patted Charlotte's back comfortingly. A pang of guilt stabbed at her. How could she leave the employment of these kind people who had been so good to her? She'd left her father for Pete, and didn't she regret it?

As she marveled at the animals performing in front of her, Charlotte remembered her father and the first time he'd introduced her to his horse, Whiskey. She had looked up at him in wonder as he stood by the powerful glistening chestnut stallion. As tall as her father was, he still looked small in comparison.

"The great thing about horses, Lottie," her father said, "is there's no pretending with them. They see right through you to your soul, and they expect you to look past them into theirs. And if your soul is true, they'll love you forever. You'll have a friend for life better than any person you ever met."

Charlotte reached up to pet the beautiful animal and pulled back for a moment as Whiskey's broad neck twitched involuntarily beneath her hand. Her father smiled and put his hand over hers to run it smoothly and confidently over the horse's shiny coat. Charlotte was breathless when her father picked her up and put her on the horse for the first time.

She closed her eyes, remembering the warmth of hugging Whiskey's huge neck, feeling his mane on her cheek. The still and steady look in his eye when she'd run her fingers between his ears. Charlotte had a sudden longing to break through the crowd and touch one of the magnificent animals in front of her.

"To ride a horse again," she found herself saying out loud.

The horses pranced on.

The next dozen horses were also riderless but had strapped to them a long red velvet rope that attached to a rolling wagon. On top of the wagon was a set of bars decorated by flying gymnasts who spun around and around one bar before flipping onto the next one, a woman with bright red hair and three identical tanned men in identical striped leotards. The crowd gasped and cheered as the woman leaped straight up into the air from the highest bar, twisting and spinning above the moving wagon only to drop perfectly into the waiting hands of a striped muscle man standing at the edge of the wagon below her. She stood on top of his hands as he raised her high enough for every onlooker on Main

Street to see.

Charlotte joined the crowd in an eruption of applause.

"What in the world!" Martha said. "Have you ever seen anything like that?"

"Never!" Charlotte said, pausing her clapping to wipe a tear from her eye.

The rest of the parade continued on—tumbling acrobats, a preview of the menagerie in gilded cages pulled by workhorses and led by zebras. Charlotte watched them in a daze. When it was over and the crowd was slowly dispersing to collect their things or find some lunch, Charlotte found herself drifting back to the cookhouse almost in a trance. A silent spectator to the parade of thoughts marching through her mind.

She almost ran right into two men walking toward her.

"Oh, I'm sorry!" she said, jolted from her daze by the near miss. "Daryl. Jim. Hi!"

"Mornin', miss." Jim tipped his hat. "Did you enjoy the parade?"

"Yes! Wasn't it wonderful! Are you boys stopping by the cookhouse for lunch?"

"Well—" Daryl started.

"Oh no," Jim cut in. "We've gotta head back out to the ranch. Lots to do."

"I bet so! Y'all are probably shorthanded with my husband out in Fort Worth."

"Fort Worth?" Daryl said. "Pete's—"

"That's right, we've got more work than we know what to do with." Jim laughed awkwardly.

"Lots of work," Daryl echoed. Neither of the men would make eye contact with her.

"Well, I'll see y'all soon then." Their shifting glances and the insincerity of the conversation unsettled her.

"Yes, ma'am, you take care," Daryl said, tipping his hat.

Jim yammered at Daryl as they walked away. "You want him to shoot you like he shot that horse?"

Charlotte brushed off the awkward conversation and made her way to the cookhouse, energized by the buzz of excitement from the crowd she was wading through. Her palms tingled from enthusiastic clapping, and her heart felt full of hope and joy. She couldn't wait to take Alex to the eight o'clock show, and she couldn't wait to make things better with Pete when he got home. She kept imagining the way he would hug her and kiss her when she'd tell him she would quit her job, the way the man on the street had hugged and kissed his wife.

The afternoon at the cookhouse was somehow even busier than the morning. Charlotte didn't catch a breath until almost four. She finished cleaning the last of the tables, thinking about Alex, Pete, the circus that night, her father, and the horses from the parade.

She became so lost in her thoughts that she almost didn't notice the bell clanging above the door when a new customer came in or the dull clicking of heels on the wood floor as they walked over to her table. But she couldn't ignore the sudden chill that gripped her spine when the customer stood in front of her, hand on the opposite chair, and declared, "So you're Charlotte Baxter, then."

The hand dragged the chair back, and the customer sat at the table across from her.

"I've been looking for you."

Chapter 12

Cards with Clowns

"I couldn't have asked for a better matinee, Jay," Sonny boomed. The midday count was coming in high. Ticket sales were better than expected.

"The work Frank put in with the performances in Fort Worth was a huge part of that success, sir," Jay said, acknowledging a grateful smile from his cousin.

"I guess you aren't good for nothing after all, are you, Sterling Jr.?" Sonny smacked Frank on the back with a force that caused him to lurch forward and spill a little whiskey on his sleeve.

"You just make sure load-out tonight is a well-oiled machine," Sonny said to Jay, "and maybe I'll let you call the shots more often."

"Are you kidding, Dad? There's nobody in the business who can manage a schedule better than Jay. Load-out will be flawless."

After the eight p.m. show started in the big top, the real show would begin for Jay. Everything would be packed up and ready to go in particular and well-timed order before the show was over except for the big top and the performers' dressing trailers, which would go last after the performers left the tent and finished changing out of their costumes.

"I'll be honest. I was a little concerned that the

things going on with…your personal life…would cause a distraction for you. That thing that happened with Vanessa—"

"Quite the contrary," Jay cut in. "In fact, it might be the first time in years that I'm able to focus. My wife—my ex-wife—caused more harm than good, I'm afraid to say." Jay made a mental note to get the paperwork drawn up.

Sonny shifted uncomfortably in his chair. "Have a drink with us. You've earned it."

"Thank you, but you two enjoy that whiskey without me," Jay refused politely. "I think I'll go check on Sadie in the school tent."

The fresh spring sunshine felt welcome on Jay's smiling face as he stepped out of Sonny's luxury train car, closed the door, and donned his hat. Sonny and Frank continued congratulating each other through the walls behind him as he descended the steps.

Jay took out his watch: five p.m. He'd been awake for thirteen hours, and the day was only two-thirds of the way through. He dipped into his own private railcar to enjoy the gentle dimness, calm quiet, and personal space for a moment. He couldn't help casting a longing glance at his cleanly made bed with its cool soft pillow but resolutely turned away. He rifled through the items on his table and picked up a new pen, the employee ledger, a tape measure, and the schedule for his midday rounds. He tucked the pen into his lapel pocket and dropped the tape measure in next to his pocket watch. Leaving the comfort of his dusky quiet train car behind him, he stepped back out into the vivid afternoon and squinted into the sunlight.

Benny had left a few cars near the tracks. He'd be

driving Sonny and Frank out to the big top in the Rolls Royce after dinner. Jay chose the hunter-green Model T and made a mental list of all the people he needed to check in with as he sat in the driver's seat and closed the door.

"Hey, hang on!" Frank shouted, coming out of his father's luxury train car. "Can I bum a ride over?"

Jay nodded and gestured to the open seat for Frank to join him. Frank removed his hat with a flip of his wrist and hopped in next to Jay.

"I wanna check on a few things before we get the show rollin' tonight," Frank said, running his fingers over the brim of the hat. "Dad's in a great mood. I finally got him to agree…"

Jay's thoughts turned again to his daughter. He found that he had spent much of the day replaying the admonishments from the boarding school nun and worrying if a life on the road with the circus was the best thing for a six-year-old girl. Would she be happy? Would she resent him? Would she miss her mother?

"…I mean, I know it's the equestrian director's job, but he's so out of touch. If we wanna keep drawin' crowds, we've got to keep it fresh!" Frank prattled on.

"I agree," Jay said, hoping Frank wouldn't notice his thoughts had been elsewhere. It was okay to miss little changes to the details of the show itself. His main concern was load-out.

"But the order of the acts is still the same?" Jay confirmed.

"Oh yeah, yeah," Frank said.

"Where is all this enthusiasm coming from?" Jay teased. Frank was so lethargic in the winter season that apathy seemed to be his reigning characteristic, but of course Frank always thrived on the road. "I wish you could transfer some of that gumption to Hugh…"

"I haven't seen Hugh all day now you mention it. He didn't seem real pleased at hearing my dad brag about how impressed he was with your ingenuity setting up this stop in Ayer."

"That makes sense. He wasn't particularly eager to complete any of the tasks I gave him."

"Don't worry about Hugh. He's always sour when he ain't the one getting praise. He's been like that since he was a child. Always clamoring for Dad's attention. Hey, by the way, I'm sorry for my dad bringing up things with…your ex-wife. We all just hate what she did to you."

"It's all right," Jay said. "I'm angry, I can't deny that. But I wasn't lying when I said things are easier with her gone. We were miserable for years."

"I'll be honest, I never liked her very much."

"Learn from my mistakes, Frank. It's better to be alone than with the wrong woman. Luella seems like a real nice girl."

"I don't know. She might be a nutcase just like the rest of them."

Jay raised an eyebrow and peered sideways at his cousin.

"Dad said she's coming out to the show tonight. She told him she'll be coming to every single show. Did you know that?"

"I didn't, but that's nice that she wants to come support you."

"Support me?" Frank said cynically. "You mean check on me."

"Can you blame her?" Jay laughed. "Remind me.

Who was that in your trailer this morning again?"

Frank shrugged his shoulders. "Not who you think."

Jay considered asking Frank what he meant but decided against it. "Well, either way, it isn't too crazy for her to be a little worried, is it?"

"It's more than that. You know she hired a gumshoe to follow Birdie around?"

Jay shot a questioning look at Frank.

"Yeah. Birdie told me about it last night. Says a guy has been following her for a few weeks now. She caught him off guard and says he wouldn't say what he was or who hired him. She says she gave him a piece of her mind and gave him some names for people he ought to follow instead of her for a real scoop. Of course, she didn't share those names with me."

"Well, Birdie's a little dramatic."

"I know. She's crazy too. All these women are looney. But if Luella shows up tonight, I'm gonna confront her about it. That's just too much. Besides, life on the road is life on the road. If she doesn't get that, she's not for me."

Jay parked the car at the edge of camp. Part of him wanted to shake his cousin by the shoulders and tell him to quit juggling circus girls. But Jay thought of the time. He had too many things to get to, and he needed to go find Sadie.

"See you tonight," he said, grabbing his book and stepping out of the car. "You can find Benny later if you need a ride back to the tracks."

"Thanks, pal," Frank said, donning his hat and grinning with that circus-fueled enthusiasm. "See you tonight!"

Jay checked off his list, working his way through the sideshows toward the school tent, observing that everything was in order. He checked in with a few of his point people to ensure that they'd load the sideshow tent poles to the rear as soon as the grand parade was complete. He confirmed the order with them and let them know to begin packing up at eight fifteen when everyone was settled in the big top. Jay consulted his list. He still needed to check in with the cookhouse and menagerie, who also needed to pack up and load-out before the show was over, but it occurred to him that Sadie might enjoy seeing the animals and they could sit down together for an early dinner. He could meet with the superintendent of menagerie when he and Sadie went to look at the animals together and talk to the steward at dinner. He capped his pen and tucked it back in his pocket. That would work perfectly with his schedule.

Jay was grinning, pleased with his plan, when he was distracted by a group of cackling clowns sitting at a makeshift table behind the hot dog stand. Still in their makeup, but wigless and shoeless, with partially unbuttoned shirts and unfastened suspenders, the clowns made a disorderly display that displeased Jay. He didn't mind them having some downtime, but they'd all been instructed to do that in their train cars or dressing rooms away from the watchful eyes of the circus patrons. He was just about to tell them so, when he saw past the tallest clown to a little card player in an oversized floppy patchwork hat at the far end of the table.

"Sadie!"

The clowns turned around, startled. At the sight of

Jay, they quickly started pulling their wigs onto their heads and adjusting their suspenders.

"Hi, Dad!" Sadie said cheerfully, waving with one hand and protecting a fan of cards in the other as a dirty-faced little boy next to her leaned over to sneak a peek at her hand.

"What's going on here?" Jay asked angrily.

The clowns mumbled various responses in unison. Jay recognized one of the older clowns, Maurice, who'd been with the circus even longer than Jay.

He should know better than this! Jay thought as he shot Maurice a look that said the same.

"It's called poker!" Sadie said.

"Poker! You're teaching my daughter poker?"

"Your daughter?" Maurice asked, rising up from the embarrassment of Jay's harsh gaze. "Well, that makes sense then, don't it? She and my grandson here, they've been running this table! Smart little thing hustled Jimbo outta ten cents already and bluffed her way through that hand too. She sure did."

The dirty-faced little boy nodded and gave the grinning Sadie a thumbs-up.

"I let her win," Jimbo muttered, snatching his hat from Sadie's head playfully.

Jay was speechless, unable to identify what he was feeling.

"Uh, I think we oughtta, uh…" The clowns started to gather their things.

"Wait!" Sadie said, sitting up proudly and spreading her cards out on the table. "I have all these aces."

The clowns groaned collectively, tossing their cards on the table in frustration. The older clown laughed. "See that, boss! Little card shark you got there! Reminds me of a young Mr. Edwards, she does!" Maurice ruffled Sadie's hair as he chuckled. For some reason, something about the affectionate interaction tugged at Jay.

Sadie beamed up at her father. "I won, Dad!"

"That's…" Jay surveyed the scene in front of him, still processing the situation. *The circus is a godless, dangerous place to be*, the nun had said.

"That's wonderful, Sadie…" Jay turned to the clowns. "Gentlemen, find someplace to be."

The disheveled performers gathered the rest of their things quickly and scattered. Jay opened his mouth to speak but was interrupted when one ran back to scoop up the rest of the cards. Jay glared at the clumsy clown as he tipped his hat and tiptoed away, clutching a cluster of cards to his chest.

"Aren't you supposed to be at the school tent?" Jay asked Sadie.

"Oh no, we finished our lessons early," she said.

"Early? But the schedule—"

"Miss Pearl says we don't have to go by the schedule all the time," Sadie declared matter-of-factly.

"Everyone goes by the schedule," Jay said, pulling out his pocket watch, "all the time."

"Miss Pearl said you'd say that," Sadie said, smiling up at her father. She reached up and took his hand.

His shoulders relaxed, and a smile warmed his face. *Load-out will be fine*, he thought. *Everyone knows what they're supposed to do and I can send Benny or Hugh to confirm if I need to.* Jay slipped his watch back into his pocket without opening it.

"Well," he said, kneeling down. "Why don't you tell me what you'd like to do then?"

Sadie was thoughtful for a moment. "Can we get cotton candy together, Dad?" she asked, eyes shining brightly. "I've always wanted to try some! And maybe a balloon?"

Sadie's excitement seemed to transfer to Jay. Warming, he forgot his own exhaustion as he felt the charge of the renewed energy he'd witnessed in Frank. "You got it," Jay said to his daughter, tucking his book away and forgetting about the time.

Chapter 13

The Cat and the Crystal Ball

Charlotte stared at the waxy red lip print by the foreign signature of the letter clutched between her trembling fingers. Cheap perfume drifted up from the shaking paper and stung her eyes and nostrils.

My Cowboy,

While you're out with those boys getting them horses, I'll be here at home by my little self and thinking about how I'm gonna tear your clothes off and cover your body in kisses as soon as you step back through that door. Don't be out too long, sugar. You've got a woman who loves you waiting back home.

Xoxo

Your wife!

Charlotte let the letter fall from her hands to the floor by her knees and sorted through the other strange documents in the box with disoriented fingers. She couldn't even understand what she was looking at. More letters. And then the cash. A big old handful of cash.

She picked up a photograph and dropped it just as quickly, rubbing her hands on the wool of her dress as if to rid them of the residue.

You know I ain't lyin'. The voice from the cookhouse replayed in her mind. *You're the one who's lyin'. Lyin' to yourself.*

Her stomach was turning, eyes burning, head spinning. Her face felt sore from her mouth turning down. *I'm going to be sick*, she thought. She put the lid back on the box with her shaking hands and ran to the bathroom to vomit. She collapsed beside the toilet and held her head in her hands.

So, it was true.

If she was honest with herself, Charlotte had known that opening the box would change things. She had known about its existence for some time now, even though Pete took special care to retrieve it only when he thought Charlotte wasn't looking. Every time she heard the muffled thumps from the back room, she wondered what he kept there, in the back of her mind. But she always respected his privacy too much to look. Or maybe she was afraid he would come home to find her digging through his secret things and unable to explain herself. How angry he would be. But that didn't matter now. Ten years. All this time…the thought made her stomach retch again.

Charlotte pulled herself up to the sink and washed her mouth out. The water swirled down into the drain, and she wished she could follow it. She lifted her heavy head and looked up at her face in the mirror, running a finger along the dark crescents under her tired eyes. Charlotte scowled at her own reflection, dead and pale with colorless lips and lifeless eyes.

I was never good enough, she thought, splashing some water on her face and looking into her own puffy eyes again. *What if I just wandered out into the fields?* She could collapse into the crop stalks and let the dust fill her lungs, fading away into the land with the next dust storm. She could throw herself onto the train tracks. In front of the circus train as it sped out of town. It would be dark. It would be quick. Would her husband be relieved?

Her eyes welled up with a new wave of tears.

"Mom!" Alex's bright voice rang out from the living room. "If we want to make it through the menagerie before the show at eight, we should leave soon."

Charlotte drew in a sharp breath and turned away from the grave reflection. She dried her face with a towel and straightened her posture, turning her thoughts to her son. "Coming," she shouted, opening the door. Charlotte paused for a second. The box.

"Just a minute." She ran back to the bedroom and opened the box again, staring in shock once more at the contents inside. Shaking herself out of her trance, she grabbed the photograph, the papers, and all of the money and shoved everything into her purse. On a whim, she pulled off her wedding ring and set the tarnished band gently in the middle of the empty box, letting her eyes rest on the lonely circle for a moment and blinking away tears. Dead or alive, here or gone, Charlotte knew in that moment that she could never be Pete's wife again. She placed the lid back on the box carefully like a casket and returned it almost ceremoniously to the hole in the ground. She replaced the floorboard above the box, pulled the Navajo rug back over it, and scooted the chair back on top of the floorboard. Pete wouldn't be home for a few days, but it would still be better if his hiding place looked as if it hadn't been disturbed.

"Okay," she said, stepping out into the living room

where Alex was waiting, "Let's go get some cotton candy!"

****

"It looks even better than last year. We're going to have so much fun," Alex said as they approached the circus grounds, his wide eyes taking in the extraordinary display before him.

Charlotte smiled and pulled Alex close to her, squeezing his shoulder. "We certainly are."

The circus grounds swarmed with happy families and excited children carrying cotton candy and balloons. Larger-than-life posters for every kind of attraction and game plastered every available surface, all surrounded by electric light bulbs and flashing lights. The cacophony of animal noises and excited conversations acted as a backdrop to the shouting pitchmen. Even the wind took a break for the day, as if it too stood still in awe of the spectacular pageantry of it all. Charlotte's senses were overwhelmed with the smell of popcorn and sugared nuts and funnel cakes. It was almost enough to make her forget the desperate despair that was gnawing at her stomach. All the unanswered questions.

"Balloons!" Alex pointed to a nearby cart. Digging through the crumple of papers in her purse to reach the coins at the bottom, Charlotte purchased a red balloon for her son. As she tied the ribbon around his wrist, he said, "Don't you want one too, Mom?"

"Oh no, that's all right," she said.

"One for my mom too, please," Alex said, proudly handing his money to the man.

"And one for you, my lady." The man smiled, bowing ceremoniously and handing a balloon to

Charlotte too.

"Well, thank you both," she said, smiling.

Alex and Charlotte meandered through the menagerie, balloons bobbing, and marveled at all of the different animals, everything from lizards to llamas. Alex leaned through the gilded bars to touch a giant hippo and swore he'd never be the same. They ate pink cotton candy on white paper cones and browsed sideshows. They giggled at the World's Smallest Circus, mice in tiny clown costumes, and gasped at Serpentina the Snake Charmer with her perilous pythons. They tossed balls into numbered holes for points, tested their strength at the hammer and scale, and threw rings onto bottles.

Charlotte and Alex had almost made their way to the biggest tent, following the signs that read *Big Show This Way*, when Alex spotted another tent. "Ooh, Mom, what's that?" he said, pointing off the main path. "Can we go in there?"

"I think we have time," Charlotte said, glancing again at the crowds making their way toward the show. "If we hurry."

The tent looked like all the others on the outside, red and white canvas formed in a striped pyramid and pegged to the ground with fraying yellow rope. But when they stepped inside, Charlotte and Alex were transported to an ethereal atmosphere, unlike anything they'd ever seen.

The inside of the tent was smoky and hazy, dimly lit with a few hanging lanterns of various heights and sizes with intricate black metal designs on the outside and low flames within. Gauzy fabric in jewel colors draped from the center top of the tent to the floor, some pinned around the outside halfway down and some falling freely. The periphery of the tent was decorated with large illustrated books on pedestals, statues, and interesting paintings. Somehow all of the sounds and smells from outside the tent were gone as if refusing to pass an unseen barrier out of respect. Charlotte couldn't identify the aroma in the tent, some sweet spice that made her think of the fireplace at Christmastime or of lying in the flowers to gaze at clouds in the long afternoons of summer. A few other circusgoers were milling around the tent too, murmuring in confusion and wonder, pointing at eclectic artifacts.

"Whoa!" Alex said, spotting something in the center of the tent. Charlotte pushed past a beaded berry-colored curtain to see that there was a small round table in the center of the tent with a deck of cards, some low-burning candles, and a large glowing glass ball, which Alex was now holding.

"Alex!" Charlotte hissed, rushing to the table to take the ball from him. "Don't touch things in here."

"But how does it glow?" He continued examining the glowing orb in her hands, trying to turn it over to look at the bottom.

"I think we should get out of here," she whispered, placing the glass ball gingerly into a circular wooden frame on the table.

But before she could turn to leave, a hand placed itself on top of hers. The body that belonged to it was enveloped in shadow.

"Welcome to the Temple of Knowledge." A deep and raspy woman's voice floated through the darkness. Charlotte couldn't place the accent. She jumped and pulled her hand away, reaching about to pull her son closer.

"I am Madame Rusalka," the voice continued as a body floated forward from obscurity to join it, "fortune teller and medium to the spirits and ancient arts." As she spoke, she wove a graceful arm through the smoke, and a limber little monkey jumped down from within the fabric jungle and ran up to sit on her shoulder, playing with the beaded scarf Madame Rusalka was wearing on her head.

Charlotte had never heard of anything like that before, but circus sideshows were famous for exaggerating the truth a little to make a few dimes.

"So you tell the future?" Alex asked, mirroring Charlotte's skepticism.

"Sometimes, *băiatul meu*," Rusalka replied stepping into the light cast by the glowing crystal.

"Will you tell me what makes that glass light up? Is it an electric charge or…"

"Perhaps." Madame Rusalka pulled out a chair for Charlotte and gestured for her to sit.

"Oh, no…we should go. But thank you," Charlotte stammered. "We-we want a good seat for the show, so—"

"If you allow me to read your palm, I will tell your future, and I will tell your little boy there how the crystal ball it glows."

"Please, Mom!"

Charlotte sat down reluctantly and extended her palm.

"What is your name?" Madame Rusalka asked.

"Charlotte."

"Charrolatah," she repeated. The way Rusalka rolled her *R*s and accentuated the "t" made Charlotte's name sound like four syllables instead of two. Rusalka leaned forward, and Charlotte peered through the smoke at the figure in front of her to see a beautiful confident face under long dark waves of hair. Rusalka had large gold hoops in her ears and gold and silver bangles on both of her wrists. Her large eyes were a translucent amber lined in dark kohl with thick lashes and shimmery green shadow on her eyelids, which drooped slightly as she stared intently at Charlotte.

"I see that you had happy childhood." Madame Rusalka ran her finger along the lines in Charlotte's palm. An involuntary chill shuddered up her arm.

"Hmm. That's odd, I see a…" She stopped at the end of a line where it split to go another direction. Madame Rusalka looked up meaningfully at Charlotte and then at Alex.

"Hmm," she repeated.

"What?" Charlotte asked, peering at her own palm as if to glean an answer. Alex leaned over to look too, and shrugged.

"You miss something about your childhood, don't you, Charlotte. Regret maybe. What is it?"

She blinked, feeling lightheaded in the smoke. "Well…I guess everyone misses something about their childhood, don't they?" She glanced around the tent. Where had all of the other people gone?

Madame Rusalka held Charlotte's gaze patiently and turned her chin down and to the right slightly, studying her silently. The room itself seemed full of slow and gentle movement vibrating in the growing effervescence of the glass on the table, and Charlotte found herself swaying in the chair like the sheer fabric or wisps of smoke in the breeze.

"I suppose..." Charlotte thought for a moment. "I mean, I imagine I miss my father."

"A kind man. Strong and patient."

Charlotte nodded.

"You never knew mother?"

Charlotte shook her head, dropping her gaze to her dusty boots.

"Childbirth take her?"

Charlotte nodded without looking up. She glanced at Alex. She never talked about her mother even though he had asked her about it many times. After all, she'd taken the life of the woman who gave birth to her. Taken her from her father and then left him alone to die...

"Something else, then. Something that used to be passion for you. Before you forgot how to be free."

"Forgot how to be free?" She glared at the infuriating woman. Her eyes darted to the exit, but a persistent image overtook her vision. The dreams she had at night. Of the way she felt when she was the most free.

"Ah! It's there." Madame Rusalka pointed at Charlotte enthusiastically, her bangles jangling. "What is it, Charlotte?"

"The horses." The admission escaped involuntarily. It was less a response and more like a sound her breath made when she exhaled. Hardly audible.

Madame Rusalka sat back in her chair with a satisfied smile. "The horses," she said, twisting at one of her loose curls. "You used to be like a wild stall-i-on too, didn't you, Charrolatah? Before you were domesticated." Madame Rusalka said the word "domesticated" with staccato.

"Domesticated?" Charlotte repeated with growing irritation, her voice shedding the stammer. "I don't wish I was a child. I don't wish I was an untame horse. I am very happy being 'domesticated,' and I love being a mother." She smiled at Alex.

"And a wife?" Rusalka asked, casually petting the paw of her monkey.

Blood left her face as she stared into the unwavering amber eyes. "And a wife. Of course." Charlotte jumped a little as she felt something warm and furry rub against her leg. She looked down to see an inky-gray cat by her ankle. Charlotte pulled her leg away, but the cat jumped onto her lap, paced a circle around her legs, and settled in comfortably, the silky body vibrating in a contented purr.

"That is Printesa," Rusalka said. "She was somebody's house cat in Arizona, but when circus came to town, she found me and jumped onto my train car and now she lives with us."

"You stole someone's cat?" Alex asked incredulously.

"I didn't steal her, *băiat*. She is a free spirit, like me." Rusalka turned to look at Charlotte. "She chose her own path."

"So the cat ran away," Alex said flatly.

"Maybe she wasn't running away from something," Rusalka said, still looking at Charlotte. "Maybe…she was running to something."

Goose bumps rose in waves across Charlotte's wrists. She pulled down at the sleeves of her coat and shifted uncomfortably in the chair. Charlotte and Rusalka stared across the table at one another for a moment before distant music began, shaking them from their trance.

A muffled voice floated through the tent. "Come one! Come all! The show is about to begin!"

"Oh, Alex! We've got to go find our seats or we'll miss the show!"

"You don't want to miss the horses."

"Yes." Charlotte laughed uncomfortably as she gently nudged Printesa from her lap. "Well, you're right. I-I do love to watch the horses." She was ready to shake off this haze and hurry out of the confusing tent.

"But, Mom! She said she'd tell me how the ball glows!"

"Don't worry, *băiat*," Rusalka said. "I'll see you again very soon."

"We should go," Charlotte said, lifting her purse to the table. She became flustered as she encountered the papers and cash she'd haphazardly stuffed in her purse at the house, reminding her again of that awful feeling. But she pushed past them to find a few coins resting at the bottom.

"Ah, there they are," she said, looking up from her bag with money in her hand.

But Rusalka was gone. The monkey hopped across the table and snatched the coins from Charlotte's fingers, then disappeared through the smoke.

"Let's get out of here, Alex," Charlotte whispered, snapping her purse closed.

As they stepped out of the smoke into the clear air, they could see a steady stream of laughing families and couples pouring into the big top. Charlotte thought about the horse show and felt as giddy as a child as she took her son's hand, almost skipping to the upbeat music as they made their way toward the main tent at the center of the circus yard for the show.

Chapter 14

The Human Cannonball

Jay stood with Sonny, Hugh, and Benny at the outer ring in the shadows, watching guests take their seats. Jay swelled with pride, thinking about the times they'd had to dress the house, arranging spectators so that it appeared fuller than it was. There was no need for that today. They even had people sitting in the cattle guards in rows below the stadium seats.

"Packed house," Sonny said to the group. "Even better than this afternoon! I swear, I'da never thought I'd see that in this little town, but you pulled it off, Jay!"

"Thank you, Sonny."

Benny jabbed Jay with his elbow and mouthed *wow* with an excited nod. Jay responded with raised eyebrows and chuckled silently. But over Benny's shoulder, Hugh was scowling.

Jay pulled out his pocket watch and waited for the second hand to make one last trip around the watch face before the night's show began. "Three, two, one." Jay gestured to the light operators to begin the show. Lights out. Music began. Four cylinder spotlights did circle eights around the ring before landing on Frank, who stood proudly in the center bedecked in red and gold, full tails, beams gleaming off rows of shining buttons.

The drumroll punctuated the excitement with rapidly building pit-a-pats.

"Ladies and gentlemen," he announced, top hat in hand, "boys and girls! Welcome to the Sterling & Son's Spectacular Circus!"

"Okay, Hugh," Jay whispered, eyes locked on the center ring as the pageant of animals and performers began to parade in for the Grand Entry spectacle. "Tell the crew to start packing up the cookhouse and give the menagerie the go-ahead too."

"Excuse me?" Hugh challenged. "I'm not doing that."

Jay turned slowly to look at Hugh and took a measured breath. "We've gotta get load-out started now if we want to stay on schedule." Jay caught a nostril-burning whiff of Hugh's breath and paused at the sight of his droopy glazed eyes and the droplets of sweat forming on his forehead. "Hugh, have you been drinking?"

"Listen, 'boss,' you don't get to tell me what to do or ask me where I've been. Get one of your lackeys to run your errands."

"Hugh, do what he asks," Sonny ordered.

Hugh froze in fury but couldn't refuse Sonny Sterling.

"Yes, sir," he said through gritted teeth, and after glaring at Jay, he turned and stomped off out of the big top, kicking at a pile of hay on his way out.

Jay watched him for a moment, frustrated and confused.

"Benny, could you—"

"Done."

Benny headed out of the tent after Hugh to make

sure he delivered the message.

"Well, son, I'm headed to the other side," Sonny said, clapping Jay on the back as he left. "I'd call our first stop a success. Great job."

Jay snapped his pocket watch closed and kept his focus on the center ring. The Grand Entry was over, and the crowd was laughing at the clowns. Up at the top of the scaffolding towers, Birdie was getting ready for her act. It was always hard to see up in the rafters because of the way the lights swung around. They could blind you sometimes. But Jay knew the circus schedule beat by beat and knew when and where to check to make sure everything was running smoothly, although he remembered Frank had told him there would be some changes. He squinted at the other four posts to make sure the other aerialists were in position. Hard to see for sure, but he thought he counted the right number of bodies.

Back in the center ring, the horses and their riders had begun their dressage to a mildly impressed audience.

Benny reappeared beside Jay. "Hugh told me he didn't need a shadow and to run on back to my master," Benny reported, "but far as I could tell he was on his way to start load-out for the cookhouse."

Jay nodded. "Thanks, Benny." And then, "I'm sorry about him. It shouldn't be a problem. They know what to do. I'll double-check that everything is on track after Birdie starts her act."

"And now, ladies and gentlemen." Frank flourished his arm as he pointed to the corner of the ring, the light and captivated eyes of the audience following his gesture. "The Human Cannonball!"

The light landed on the piano player as he excitedly hammered on the keys. The band joined in to play "Entry of the Gladiators."

"Popcorn! Popcorn!" a pitchman hollered, exchanging red-and-white paper bags for change as other viewers peered around the purchasers to see what would happen next.

Misty smoke rose from the ground, and every light lowered but the ones that settled on Hazel and the cannon. Hazel extended a proud graceful arm to the crowd, waving to the captive audience. Her smile was too big for her painted face, but it wasn't the fake showgirl's grin that she'd put on like a piece of costume jewelry night after night in the sideshow tents.

Hazel wasn't standing in a line of nameless girls. She wasn't pretending to be something she wasn't. She was exactly where she'd always wanted to be. The center of the ring, music playing for her. All eyes on her. Her own eyes glistened, and a pair of proud, joyful tears played at the corners through thick fluttering eyelashes.

Hazel climbed into the cannon carefully, giving a final wave before sliding in completely. The drums rolled deafeningly, and the fires were lit. A loud bang echoed, and then another, and a third. Hazel's body went hurtling out of the cannon. Spinning and flying through the air across the ring as the audience roared and cheered.

But at the end of its trajectory, Hazel's body flung full force against the rubber mat and flopped lifelessly to the ground below. There was no attempt to rise. No movement at all. Her body lay still, headpiece broken and carelessly askew above the golden hair that was slowly reddening with the steady billowing of blood. Hazel's mouth gaped open, no longer smiling. Her eyes stared into the empty space in front of her vacantly, a single tear rolling down her cheek. And the arm that had been extended in a wave only moments ago now lay lifelessly beside her.

The crowd was silent.

Murmurs and confusion slowly filled the ring in place of the happy music as the musicians ceased their playing and stood up to get a better look.

"What's happened? Did they send her off too early again?" someone asked.

"Direct the lights to the zebras," Sonny barked. "Now!"

On cue, three of the lightmen swung the cylinders around to focus on the zebras. The Sisters of the Sahara, who stood resting, recognized immediately what they were meant to do. They glanced at each other and quickly mounted the zebras, moving through their act mechanically in an attempt to distract the crowd.

But Frank stood frozen in the last spotlight, staring at Hazel's body. The crowd followed his gaze, as they always did, to make out what lay in the darkness. Jay waved his arm, caught Frank's eye, and gestured toward the girls and zebras.

"L-L-Ladies and gentlemen! The…Sisters of the Sahara!" Frank took a deep breath and continued in a more confident tone, raising his extended palm out toward the lighted zebras. "Five princesses riding zebras from their palace in the faraway desert. Here, tonight, for your entertainment!"

But it was too late. A loud scream of terror escaped from a seat near Hazel's body and another as the crowd recognized what had just happened. Hazel, the human cannonball, was dead.

The crew stumbled through the dark to reach the body. Jay was already there.

"Hazel! Get up!" someone shouted, shaking her lifeless body by the shoulders.

"She's not moving!"

"Listen to me. We've got to get her out of here," Jay said. "You two, put the body in the palanquin and carry it to the medical tent."

With a nod, the two strongmen retrieved the palanquin that had carried the ballet girls and brought it to where the body lay, gently picking up the body and placing it inside. Silently, they lifted the palanquin atop their shoulders and carefully carried it out of the center ring, through the red and white tent flaps into the night. Jay paused for a moment, watching their solemnly moving silhouettes against the moonlight before turning around to the crew who was gathered around him, wide eyes looking toward him, waiting for instruction.

"You"—Jay pointed at three prop boys—"move the net forward to cover where the body fell. Throw straw over the blood. Someone get to Frank and tell him to skip the next act and move viewers to the third ring."

Two boys moved toward the net, and one took off in a sprint through the dark toward Frank.

"Benny," he said, "find Pearl and the kids. Get them back to the train cars, please. Ask her to keep Sadie there."

"Got it, hoss," he said, nodding confidently.

"Jimbo," Jay said, picking a clown out from the crew. "Get Sonny over here, now."

Jimbo nodded and hustled to the other side of the ring, his oversized shoes stomping through the sawdust. Jay turned back to the crew.

"Birdie was supposed to be the next act, but we've gotta skip it. Maurice, send someone up the scaffolding and tell her."

"Yes, sir." Maurice turned to the remaining crew, who looked around nervously. No one wanted to deliver that news to Birdie.

"That'll be you, Kip," Maurice said.

The boy shook his head and took a step back. Another of the clowns elbowed the little pitch boy and gestured toward the trapeze act. He scowled and reluctantly took a few steps away from the group before putting his cap on and running over to the scaffolding to begin the climb.

With this disaster managed for the moment, Jay's thoughts returned to load-out. He looked all around him and threw up his hands in frustration.

"Where's Hugh?"

Chapter 15

This Stays Between Us

Jay squeezed through the crowd toward the medic's tent to check on the body. The circus grounds were swarming with a swirling blur of stampeding spectators and circus personnel. Just steps in front of Jay, half-dressed clowns bumped into a cluster of crying families in their church clothes as an elephant meandered between them led by a bewildered menagerie staff member.

"Watch where you're going. You can't run over paying circus patrons," Jay shouted at Jimbo, pulling him back by the collar. "Grab some guys and help the menagerie staff."

"Yes, sir, sorry, sir. I just—" Jimbo gawked at the scene unfolding before him. "I ain't never seen—"

"It's a sad fact, but accidents happen in the circus all the time, Jimbo. We've got to keep our heads about us and get back on track."

Jimbo nodded and ran toward the animals, dragging a few more clowns along with him.

With load-out tumbling around him like a pile of cards, Jay found it hard to prioritize a body that was only getting colder, but no less dead. Jay took out his black book and stood in the middle of the chaos unfolding around him. He crossed off the load-out timeline and sketched in a new timeline. With some quick figures and readjustments of the railcar lineup, he made a plan to get everything back in order.

But he'd have to do it alone. Benny had the most important job, ensuring the safety of Sadie and the children. It was clear that Hugh wasn't willing to help, nor could he be found. Frank couldn't help. He was occupied in the center ring, trying to continue the performance as the show limped on.

Frank had completely dropped the ball. Much of the mess before Jay was due to Frank's inability to manage the accident. He'd gone completely off-script and been unable to redirect most viewers' attention to the rest of the show. He'd also completely skipped several of the acts. None of the performers knew when they should go on or when the show would be over and half of them had just wandered out into the circus grounds. Why had Frank been so shaken? It wasn't his first time to switch up a show on the fly.

With a sigh, Jay marched past the medical tent. The body would have to wait. If load-out was going to get back on schedule, he'd have to manage it personally. His first stop was the cookhouse tent, which to his absolute frustration, had not even started packing up. He felt his anger rise with every step he took toward the tent.

"What are we doing here?" Jay shouted to the steward. "You should be packed up and rolling up the ramp right now!" He gestured angrily toward the train tracks.

The steward jumped up from the table and dusted off his apron.

"Mr. Edwards, we—we was waiting for your say-so like we was told, an' I didn't wanna get out of order—"

"Waiting? My say-so came with Mr. Sterling," Jay said.

"Mr. Sterling? I haven't…I didn't…"

"Mr. Hugh Sterling came here half an hour ago and instructed you to begin packing up."

"Oh, Hugh Sterling. Yes, boss. He came here for a nip, but he didn't have no instructions or nothin'. 'Cept that he said you'd be over when it was time and that you didn't want us doin' nothin' without your personal say-so or we'd get outta order. Lemme get the bread boy, boss. He'll tell you so too, sir. He was there." The steward looked around in a panic for someone to help him.

Jay was fuming. Not only had Hugh neglected to do as he was asked, but he'd sabotaged load-out purposely. Ruining the schedule. Compromising everyone's safety. Jay looked out of the cookhouse tent at the scattered crew tripping over each other.

"I could kill him," Jay murmured under his breath. Realizing that the steward looked terrified, Jay collected himself.

"Well, I'm saying so now, Mr. Brown. Load out."

"Yes, sir, right away, sir." The steward turned to his crew. "Boys! Load out! On the double!"

Jay knew his next stop needed to be the menagerie, but it was clear across the grounds. He could make a quick stop at the medical tent first and then head to the animal trailers, with the hope that they were doing what they were trained to do, but the suspicion that they too probably had new orders from Hugh. *Why would he do this?*

"Boss! Boss!" Maurice approached Jay at a trot, panting.

"What is it?" He cast a glance at Maurice and paced on. "Walk with me."

"We need you back in the big top, we—" The old clown paused to catch his breath before running to catch up to the fast-walking Jay. "We need you to look at somethin', boss."

"I'll get there when I can. It'll have to wait."

"But, boss—"

Jay stopped in front of the medical tent and looked at Maurice. "It will have to wait," he said firmly as he lifted the flap of the tent. The old clown nodded and reluctantly turned to jog back to the big top.

"Edwards!" the medic said, running up to Jay. "Glad you're here. I didn't know what to do."

"What do you mean you didn't know what to do?" Jay asked in exasperation. The medic was an old army friend and usually so competent and efficient.

"See for yourself." The medic dropped his cigarette in the dirt and snuffed it out with his boot. They both headed for the table where the body lay under a white sheet. On his way to the table, Jay was pleased to see everything else in the tent was properly packed up and ready to go. He pulled out his pocket watch. Nine thirty p.m. "Good God, the cookhouse, sideshows, and menagerie should all be loaded up by now."

The medic pulled back the sheet to reveal Hazel's face, which had been cleaned of all the blood and makeup. Jay understood instantly why the medic was confused. He staggered back, fighting off wartime flashbacks. Jay and the medic stood together in silence for a moment. The medic lit another cigarette and offered one to Jay, who shook his head, refusing.

"Did you find the—"

"No. That'll take some time. Wanted to talk to you before I got started."

Jay nodded and stared at the body for a moment while the medic puffed on his cigarette. "Cover it back up," he said. "I'll figure something out."

"But—"

"Listen. Tell no one what you saw. For now. This stays between us."

The medic nodded and placed the sheet back over Hazel's head.

"Just stay here. Wrap up the body, and wait for me. I'll be back soon with a plan."

The medic nodded, taking a long drag of the cigarette.

Jay snapped his pocket watch open and closed for a few moments while surveying the tent, shaking off the sensation that the second hand was ticking along faster than usual.

"Good job packing up. I'll send some guys over to help get you loaded after we figure this thing out." Jay pushed through the fabric opening and marched toward the menagerie. The tent behind him hovered in the darkness above all the crates, boxes, and equipment that still needed to be loaded like the cloth draped over the corpse. *This can all go in behind the cookhouse. It won't throw off setup too much tomorrow morning.*

"Jay!"

Sonny, red in the face and surrounded by nervous errand boys, charged toward him. Casually following a few steps behind him, hands in his pockets and a smirk on his face, strode Hugh.

"What the hell is going on out here!" Sonny bellowed. "We've got to get out of town!"

"You're right, sir, I—"

"I told you this town's bad luck! You get these bastards packed up now! I don't care how you do it, but *get us back on schedule!*"

"Yes, sir."

"Get me out of here! Where's Benny? I need someone to take me back to my train car. I want the Rolls."

"I'll take you, sir," Hugh volunteered, emerging from the shadows.

"Fine. Let's go." The entourage followed Mr. Sterling as he spun around and stomped off toward the cars.

"And Jay—" Sonny turned around abruptly, his crew bumping into each other as they stopped to turn too. "I'm not giving one red cent to *anybody* who says they want their money back. *No refunds!*"

"Yes, sir."

Sonny and the rest of the crew turned to march toward the cars, but Hugh stood smugly planted in the middle of them as they surged past, grinning at Jay. The two locked eyes for a tense moment before Hugh turned and walked away.

Who knows what kind of chaos is waiting for me at the menagerie. Jay took a deep breath and once more checked his pocket watch. "How am I going to salvage this?"

A tug at his sleeve distracted Jay. He pulled his elbow away, but the tugging persisted.

"Boss...Boss—"

"*What?*" Jay shouted, turning around. He looked

down to see the terrified face of a kid with streaks of sweat down his dirt-covered face, pulling at his sleeve. He recognized him as the kid who'd played cards with Sadie and the clowns earlier that day.

"I'm sorry, kid," Jay said, lowering his voice. "What do you need?"

The kid hesitated, looked around him, and gestured for him to come closer.

Annoyed, Jay leaned in. *I don't have time for this.*

"My Grandpa Maurice, he told me to just come give this to you, boss," the kid said, reaching in his shirt. "Said just to give it to you and tell you where I found it and ain't nothin' else I need to do."

He handed Jay a bundle of old burlap cloth.

Jay knew what it was by the weight of it before he unwrapped the cloth.

"Where did you find this?" he asked calmly.

"Well, boss, when I went up there…climbed up them towers to find Miss Birdie Bells like you done asked me to…well, she wasn't up there. But when I climbed back down, I saw this just layin' there by the ladder."

"What do you mean, she wasn't up there?"

"Miss Birdie, sir, she wasn't up there up them towers. Nobody was up there. Nothin' down the rails neither 'cept this." The boy gestured to the item in Jay's hands. "I didn't know what to do, so I called my grandpa over and he wrapped it up. He was gonna have you come see it, but then he said you was too busy so I oughtta just bring it to you."

"Who else knows?"

"Nobody 'cept me and my grandpa, and whoever else left it there, I guess." The boy shrugged.

Jay thought of Hazel's head under the sheet in the medic's tent and covered the item back up in much the same way with the burlap. "Thank you. You did the right thing. Go on back and finish packing up."

"Yes, sir." The boy nodded and turned to head back to the big top.

"Hey, kid," Jay called out. The boy turned around.

"You and M—Grandpa Maurice...keep it under your hats, okay? This stays between us."

Benny walked past the boy as he shook his head and ran back to the big top. "What's all that about?" he asked.

"Benny." Jay tucked away the burlap parcel. "Thank God. How are the kids?"

"They're all right," Benny said, eyeing Jay's jacket curiously. "Pearl's got 'em."

He sighed with relief. "Was Sadie scared?"

"She'll be all right."

Jay nodded.

"I've got a lot to catch you up on," he said, retrieving the black schedule book from his pocket.

"Seems like it," Benny said, looking around. "Where's Hugh?"

"That's part of it." Jay rolled his eyes.

Benny clicked his tongue. "Makes sense. I've got the Tin Lizzie over there. Big top?"

Jay nodded. "We've got to stop at the menagerie first."

"Menagerie?" Benny paused, noticing the faraway look on Jay's face. "Well, that's no problem. It's on the way."

Benny cranked up the car as Jay popped the trunk open, placing a few things—including the burlap package—inside. Benny opened his mouth to speak before closing it again as they sat together in the car.

"It's a gun," Jay said, looking straight ahead as he spoke. "That kid just brought me a gun." Jay met Benny's confused stare. "I think someone used it to murder Hazel the cannon girl."

Chapter 16

The Escape

Charlotte took Alex by the hand, and they made their way through the bottle-necked crowd out of the big top. She felt disoriented and confused as they stepped out into what had previously been an area full of tents and fun attractions but was now a scattered mass of skeletal structures, closed carts, half-erected tents, and flickering lights.

"Mom, what's going on?" He asked again, "Did that woman die?"

Charlotte couldn't look at her son. She knew he would have more questions when he saw the concern on her face, and she didn't have answers. People were frantic.

"Let's just get safely home, Alex. We can—" Charlotte stopped dead in her tracks among the fleeing spectators, unable to speak as her eyes widened at the sight before her.

"Mom?" Alex tugged at her hand.

At first, Charlotte was unsure, but then he made eye contact with her. Fierce and piercing. Fear flickered throughout her body and rose up to meet the unspoken words caught in her throat in a silent scream.

It was Pete. Shoving aside anyone in his path, he made his way upstream through the surging crowd toward Charlotte and Alex.

Isn't he supposed to be in Fort Worth?

Charlotte tried to reconcile the man in front of her with the man she knew as her husband, but she had never seen that wild look in Pete's eyes before. It was insatiable and unrestrained fury. Charlotte remembered the implied threat he had leveled on her at the cookhouse when she'd disobeyed him. What would he do when he got home to find his secret box empty except for the lonely wedding band?

A more terrifying thought occurred to Charlotte. What if he already had?

He'll kill me.

As Pete pushed through the crowd, Charlotte noticed his intense focus wasn't fixed on her. It was on her son.

Looking down at Alex, Charlotte had no choice. She turned and knelt down eye to eye with her son. "Alex, I need you to trust me," she yelled above the noise of the crowd. "Can you do that?"

Alex opened his mouth as if to ask a question, but upon seeing her face, he closed it and nodded solemnly. Charlotte let go of her own balloon and untied the string from Alex's wrist.

"No—" he protested.

"I'm sorry," she said, letting go. She released her grip on the string.

Alex's lip trembled. A tear escaped and rolled down his cheek as he watched the cheerful red souvenirs from their perfect day together slip away into the darkness of the night sky above them. Charlotte squeezed his hand as she looked around frantically. Above her son's head and behind him, a maze of tents and carts were packing up. Feeling her instincts take over, she knew that would be the best place to hide from Pete.

"Stay with me, no matter where we go. No matter who you see."

Alex nodded, wiped his cheek on his shoulder, and tightened his grip on Charlotte's hand. Without another word, they began to run. First, a hard right through a small break in the crowd, and then directly forward into the chaos of the circus packing up. The fortune teller's tent was still up. A perfect place to hide. She lifted up the side flap and ushered Alex in. She followed and pulled him down close to the ground, the reassuring weight of the closed thick canvas tent panel resting on her shoulder. Her chest was heaving, heart beating fast. She pulled her son to her in a comforting, if not too tight, hug. She ran her unsteady hand over his head, trembling fingers through his hair, trying as hard as she could to cut through the darkness with her eyes.

A match lit.

In the small light provided by the flame, dark eyelashes slowly rose and fell. Bright emerald eyeshadow shimmered behind the languid lashes, and under them the amber iris glowed. The flame was lowered to the end of the cigarette, briefly showing bright red lips that said, "I told you I would see you again, Charrolatah."

"Please," Charlotte whispered. "Don't give us away, we're—"

"I know. Wait here." The woman left the tent, leaving a trail of scented smoke behind her.

"Mom, I'm scared."

Charlotte rubbed her son's back and used every

effort to steady her voice as she spoke. "Tonight might be a little scary, Alex, and a little confusing...but everything is going to be okay. Do you trust me?"

The weight of the silence seemed to pull down the smoke as Charlotte waited for her son to answer.

"Okay."

She gave her son's hand a reassuring squeeze and turned her attention to the activity outside the tent.

Madame Rusalka was talking to someone just feet away. The words were indistinct, but Charlotte strained to hear them as she pressed her ear against the fabric of the tent.

A sliver of navy light appeared as two figures entered.

"Joe will take you where you need to go," Madame Rusalka said with certainty. "He knows why you run. He will help you."

Charlotte's body gave an involuntary jump as a large hand appeared within inches of her chin.

"Come with me," a deep voice rumbled.

Recalling the fury and purpose in Pete's searching eyes, Charlotte slowly trusted the strange hand in front of her with her own, hesitating for a moment before resting her hand gracefully in his palm. The calloused fingers encircled her delicate wrist in a tight grip. She brushed away the thought that he could snap her arm with the flick of his own wrist if he wanted to.

"Let's go," she said to Joe, or to Alex, or maybe to herself. As they rose to follow, she turned to say thank you to Madame Rusalka, but she was nowhere to be seen. All that remained in the tent was the orange glow of a smoking cigarette.

Joe moved fast, and Charlotte had to alternate

between a jog and a fast walk to keep up. She wanted to ask where they were going, but there was no point. What was the difference, as long as it was away from Pete?

"Get down," Joe said, shoving them behind a pile of metal poles. Charlotte and Alex crouched low.

"We've still got the scaffolding to pack up, Joe!" someone called out. "Load-out's all outta whack, and Mr. Edwards is bout to strangle all of us if we don't get a move on!"

"I'll be there soon, taking care of something important for the boss," he shouted back.

"All right, all right," the voice said. "Hey, sir, you can't be back here! Circus crew only in the backyard."

Charlotte peered through the poles to see who the man was talking to and prayed it wasn't Pete. Squinting through the darkness, she couldn't see.

The man continued to argue with someone, and Joe knelt down beside the poles. "Do you see train car back there painted with tigers picture?" Joe asked, his accent reminiscent of Rusalka's.

Charlotte followed his gaze to a long line of train cars surrounded by busy workers with swinging lanterns and flashlights, pointing and gesturing as they loaded up in chaos. Some of the train cars were illuminated from the inside, and Charlotte felt drawn to them. The same way she'd felt drawn to the main tent only hours ago, though it felt like another lifetime now. Even in that strange moment, she had the understanding that she'd never skip into a circus tent again floating with naiveté.

She spotted a car with large painted illustrations of roaring tigers. "I see them."

"Meet me there." Joe turned and headed toward the voices.

Charlotte peeked out around the poles. She couldn't see very far. Surely no one would be able to see her and Alex if they stayed out of the light. Still, though, Pete would be looking for two figures about their size moving together.

"Alex," she said. "Do you see the car with the tigers on it?"

Alex nodded.

"I want you to run to it, find a shadow, and stand still. I'll follow you after ten seconds. But, Alex—"

"I know, Mother. Stay off the tracks." Alex smiled.

Charlotte put her hand to his cheek. "Okay, go!"

Alex did as he was told, and Charlotte watched after him with her heart in her chest. Her own shallow breaths roared in her ears over the racket of rattling wood, the clinks of pegs being pulled from the ground and tossed in buckets, and the tumbling rustling of heavy canvas tents cascading to the ground. If Pete recognized Alex, she knew he would grab him and carry him away from her forever. She tore her gaze from his running silhouette and looked back to where the men had been before, and all around her. She saw no one.

Charlotte fled toward the train car. Through a stampede of animals groaning against their handlers. Toward the swinging lanterns. Toward her son. When she was almost there, a man grabbed her arm with a strong grip. It was impossible to see who it was through the darkness. Gasping for breath, she stumbled and attempted to pull away, but the man was too strong. The ear-splitting roar of a lion behind her shook her spine.

Charlotte felt like prey, growing frantic under the fingers pressing into her flesh.

"Where is boy?"

Charlotte's body relaxed as she recognized Joe's voice, but the surge of fear left her heart pumping rapidly and her hands shaking.

"He's at the train car...the train...the car with the tigers." Her voice was trembling.

"Good," he said, relaxing his grip.

Charlotte searched through the darkness for Alex as Joe led her toward the car. The intermittent illumination from the lanterns revealed glimpses of brightly painted railcars. Bars on the windows. Curves of large letters. Flashes of claws and teeth.

"Mom!" Alex shouted, running to hug her. Charlotte embraced her son and looked up at Joe. The behemoth strongman hovering over them could have been made of stone. He was enormous and densely stoic, made even more extraordinary by the shadows that danced across his gigantic tattooed body. In the erratic winking light, Charlotte couldn't tell design from shadow.

Joe studied the cars and stopped at one just two cars past the tiger car. He grabbed a rusty iron handle and inched the screeching door open a few feet. This one wasn't warm and inviting like the other cars. Just cold blackness. She shuddered, unable to see or imagine what awaited her inside.

"Get in"—he gestured to the dark abyss—"and don't leave until morning. Train rolls out soon."

Charlotte tugged at Alex, and they climbed into the unknown car. Slippery stalks of crackling grass poked at her trembling fingertips as she groped about in the darkness. She willed herself through and turned to pull in her son. The two tumbled back into a tousle of hay. Moldy dust puffed in a cloud from the fall to fill her nostrils and tickle her tear ducts. She sneezed. Joe gripped the iron handle of the sliding door and cast a wary eye around the circus grounds behind him.

Martha's warning rang in Charlotte's mind. *You hold onto yourself and hold onto Alex so y'all don't end up like George and Willie.* She wrapped her arms around her son and was startled by a furry rattling at her wrist.

"Mom, it's Printesa!" Alex whispered. He gathered up the purring cat in his arms and his shoulders dropped slightly, shrugging off some of the tension.

Charlotte and Alex looked down at the little cat and back up at the strongman.

"Don't make noise."

"Thank you—"

But before the words had left her mouth, Joe slammed the screeching sliding door of the railcar shut. Charlotte and Alex were left in complete darkness with echoes of foreboding accented by the throaty whistle of the departing train.

Chapter 17

The Delivery Truck

"I knew I was an idiot for trusting those hustlers in suits to pay me what they owe me." Saul clenched his fist as he looked out at the scrambled chaos that was the circus packing up.

"You know what I think," Martha said, crossing her arms.

"I know, I know," Saul muttered through clenched teeth. "And looks like you were right." He pounded his fist against the steering wheel. "I'm a damn fool."

"You're not a fool." Martha laid a hand on his arm, taking a moment before she spoke again. "I imagine that girl dying like that threw folks into a panic. Just be patient."

That girl dying. Saul couldn't shake the thought that he'd seen her at the cookhouse. *It's so hard to tell with those kinda girls. They all look the same. Red lips and legs and cleavage.* He and Martha had sat so far away from the center ring, up at the top, that he hadn't gotten a good look at the cannon girl.

I dragged Martha into this mess, took her to the circus, and she sees a girl die. Talked her into lettin' me work with these guys, and they leave us high and dry payin' for more food in a day than we use in a year.

"I'm not going to be patient," Saul said, opening

the driver's side door of their delivery truck. "I'm going to find Mr. Edwards before they leave and tell him to pay me what they owe me."

"But—"

"Get in, Martha," he said, peering toward the big top. "They're still packing up. If they're going to stiff me, they're going to have to say so to my face. I'm not going to sit here like a hobo with my hand out waiting for money while the train rolls past."

Reluctantly, she climbed into the passenger seat next to Saul and nodded her head in agreement.

They drove the truck toward the big top lights faster than she liked, weaving through stacks of broken-down sideshow tents and horse-drawn trailers in the darkness. She gripped her husband's arm in fear as they jolted to a halt outside the half-assembled tent beside a hunter-green Model T.

Both of them looked out the front windshield wide-eyed and silent as a pair of elephants pulled the tent down alongside a bustling crew and a handful of workhorses. No longer wearing embellished costumes or parading around the center ring, the elephants looked more like the tired workers who labored along beside them than the elegant animals that had entertained them just a few hours ago.

"Wait here," Saul said, hopping out of the van and slamming the door. Martha nodded and looked back up at the elephants in awe.

Saul was right. He found Jay right in the middle of the tear-down. His jacket was off, shirt untucked, sleeves rolled up, and he was carrying a stack of some wood and metal assortment toward a rolling cart. He looked deep in thought, ragged, and frustrated.

Definitely not approachable. But as a Black man who owned a business in a small Texas town, Saul had learned a long time ago that he had to ask for what he deserved or he'd never get it. He wasn't going to turn back now.

He doubled down and marched toward Jay, who wiped his forehead with the back of his sleeve, pulled out his watch, and snapped it shut angrily.

"Mr. Edwards," Saul said, startling Jay. "I'm here about—"

"Mr. Winslow!" Jay answered with a weary smile. "You're just the man I want to see."

"I am?"

"Yes, I owe you some money. Come with me."

Saul nodded and followed him out of the light toward the cars.

"Hey, Benny," Jay shouted to the man Saul had met earlier, who was directing a group of workers. Benny headed over to join them, pulling out a ring of keys from his pocket.

"Thanks," Jay said and unlocked the trunk of a Model T parked next to Saul's truck. He rolled quickly through the combination on a briefcase, popping it open to reveal a stack of cash and papers.

"I'm sorry I didn't come find you sooner. We're behind schedule, I hate to say, and I'm down a few gents…" Counting out a few bills quickly, Jay extended the cash toward Saul and then paused, looking behind him at the van. "You brought your delivery truck."

"Well, uh…yes…" Saul was unsure how to interpret the statement.

Jay went to close the briefcase and then stood in front of it silently for a moment, both hands on the top corners, keeping it open. His fingers drummed the lid as he contemplated something. The air between them was clammy, and the clatter of the workers behind them was disorienting.

Saul edged backward. Martha was right. This was a mistake.

Jay looked over at Benny, who nodded in silent agreement.

"Saul," Jay said after what seemed like forever, "I've enjoyed doing business with you. You're efficient, resourceful…trustworthy. I wonder if I could trust you with another bit of business." He looked over at his friend as he spoke.

"What's the law like here in Ayer, Saul?" Benny jumped in.

"The law? Well, I guess it depends what it is…and who you know…" Saul looked back over at Martha. "I should go."

"Wait…" Jay pulled out a few more bills and then shut the briefcase. He spun the combination dial and slid it back inside the trunk.

Saul paused, looking from Jay to Benny for an answer to what was going on.

"Were you at the eight p.m. show tonight?" Jay asked.

"I was…we were." Saul gestured to his wife, who observed them guardedly from the passenger seat.

"We had a mishap with a performer—"

"We saw that."

"The thing is…" Jay looked behind him to make sure they were alone. "I'm not sure it was an accident. But I need some time to investigate."

"What does that have to do with me?"

Jay handed Saul the money.

Saul flipped through the bills. It was almost twice the profit he'd made on the sale. He shoved the money in his pocket. "What do you need?"

****

Saul, Jay, Benny, and the medic rolled the cart toward the back of the truck and opened the doors.

"I'm gonna have a hell of a time explainin' this to Martha," Saul murmured as the four of them carefully placed the tightly wrapped white package inside. "She always says nothin' good comes from the circus."

"You'll need this," Benny said as he handed Saul a bundle wrapped in burlap.

Saul nodded and placed it in a crate in the truck.

"You'll let me know what you find out," Jay said, dusting off his hands and gesturing to the medic to roll the cart to the load-out area.

"Yes, sir. See you in a few weeks." Saul nodded, shutting the van's back door. He watched Jay walk away for a moment before ambling around to the driver's side door and reluctantly opening it. He sat silently and slowly in the seat and started up the vehicle before turning to meet the wide questioning eyes of his wife.

"Is that—?"

"Yes…it's…"

"A body? A dead body! Oh, uh-uh. Hell. No."

Martha opened the passenger side door to leave.

Saul reached across her and closed it.

"Saul Winslow, what in the world?"

"I can explain," he said as he leaned back over and put the van into drive.

"Oh, you can explain that, huh?" She looked back

at the white sheet-wrapped body lying in the back of their truck between empty crates and bottles. "Well, let's hear it then!"

Saul took a deep breath.

They backed up from the big top, turned toward the tracks, and headed through the darkness toward home.

Chapter 18

Hiding in the Hay

Charlotte was jolted awake by the steely screech of the railcar door and a fresh wave of sunlight.

"Where are we?" Alex asked, sitting up and rubbing his eyes.

"Abilene," a gruff voice answered from behind the door. Charlotte blinked as her eyes adjusted to the light and the enormous silhouette of Joe materialized.

Charlotte wasn't sure at what point in the worry-filled night she'd finally fallen asleep, but it felt like it had only been moments ago. All night, her thoughts had pounced and clawed at her with the same unpredictable ferocity of Printesa the nocturnal huntress, digging through hay and scratching claws against rusty metal at a spine-tingling pitch.

The photograph. The strange notes. That letter. Charlotte wished she could feed the contents of her purse to the cat like one of those troublesome indefensible rats. But it was too late for that. Instead, the items from the box scattered across the forefront of her consciousness and formed themselves into a question, like pieces to a puzzle that wouldn't fit no matter which way she turned them. A puzzle she had to solve in the dark.

"Best to act like you belong. Run off into town or

find some work to do," Joe said.

Charlotte nodded, dusting hay from Alex's shoulder. "Thank you."

Joe nodded solemnly and moved down the line to the next car.

Printesa seemed to know it was time to get to work too. The energetic little gray cat stretched and jumped lithely from her lap to the ground as if she hadn't spent all night hunting mice. Her white-tipped tail flickered nimbly behind Joe's ankles as he continued down the railcar line.

Charlotte plucked a few cat hairs from her skirt and stood up, her back stiff from a restless night of rattling along the Texas plains in the makeshift bed of hay on a metal floor. Holding out her hand, she pulled Alex to his feet, and the two climbed down out of the train car into the cool morning.

"There's nothing like a Texas sunrise," she said to Alex, staring out at the tangerine horizon blushing pink against the pale blue sky. There was something comforting about the sun rising in the same familiar way even though they were in a new place. A reminder that the sun, like the trains on their tracks, had a bigger purpose than simply passing through Ayer.

Across the street, a pair of men raised a red and yellow banner that said *hotel* up a pole next to a large tent with tables and a kitchen setup. "Let's go see if we can find something to do at the hotel over there. I bet we can get you something to eat, and we'll make ourselves useful…" *Until I figure out what to do…*

"Okay." Alex hung back near the train car.

"And then we can see the animals and the circus all over again tonight."

"Oh…" He took a small step forward. "Well, that does sound fun."

"Of course, it will be fun. How many people get to see the circus two days in a row? And haven't you always said you'd like to ride the train and have your own adventure?"

"Yeah, I guess we are on our own adventure, aren't we?" He squatted down to look at the mechanics under the car. "This is a different train than the one I usually see at the tracks in Ayer, and I've never been this close to one before. I wonder how it works…"

"There'll be time for that later," she said, holding her hand up against the glowing sky.

Alex bounced up. "Can I touch a hippo again?"

"Absolutely."

They left the train behind them in pursuit of the hotel, passing a man-made lake that reflected the pink hues of the promising skyline along the way. She stopped to take her son's hand eagerly as they prepared to cross the street and gripped her purse tightly with the other. "But first, let's get some food."

As they neared the tent, the clinking of plates and scraping of spatulas on a metal griddle acted as a symphony to articulate her regret for leaving Saul and Martha without a word. She made a mental note to write them a letter soon so they wouldn't worry.

Charlotte looked around for the most important person in the kitchen area. She spotted an intimidating man at the grill, who was keeping an eye on some eggs while also waving the large rectangular spatula at others in the tent as he shouted at them to perform various tasks.

"Excuse me." She approached him sheepishly.

"If you's wantin' to watch the setup, miss, you'll hafta go over there behind those lines," the man said, gesturing to a growing collection of spectators with his spatula.

"Oh no. I-I mean, thank you, but—" Charlotte stepped back to allow a stream of waiters in white shirts and aprons to rush past her.

"I need a job," she finally conceded.

The man stopped what he was doing to survey Charlotte and her son, pulling a ratty red bandana out of his shirt pocket to wipe his sweaty forehead. "A job?"

"Yes, I'm a waitress. Or I've been a waitress anyway, and my son is very helpful. Can you give us something to do here in the hotel?"

The man let out a laugh that rose up from his big round belly and filled the tent like the smell of eggs and bacon. "This ain't a hotel, miss. This here's the cookhouse! You seen that flag, I guess? That just tells the staff and performers that the food's hot!" He tucked his bandana back into his pocket while still looking over the pair.

"Oh…" Charlotte was embarrassed. "Well, that's even better because I worked in the cookhouse back in Ayer."

Alex elbowed his mother and pointed to a group of performers just sitting at the tables to eat their breakfast inside canvas-separated areas. It seemed like there was a hierarchy in who sat where. People they'd seen in the center ring the night before sat clustered together in one section, while men in overalls or work shirts with flat caps sat huddled together in another.

"That's Serpentina, Mom," Alex whispered, too quiet for the man to hear. "And look at that lady's neck!"

A woman with a tall stack of rings on her longer-than-usual neck was nodding and sipping her juice as Serpentina spoke animatedly about something, weaving her arms through the air like one of her snakes as she spoke.

Charlotte nodded at her son and looked back to the cook. Her stomach let out an audible growl.

"Stowaways, huh?" The man studied Charlotte for a moment, noticing their fascination with the performers. "Down on your luck?"

"Something like that." Charlotte squeezed her son's hand a little tighter as she looked up at the man hopefully. He scratched at his ear as he looked from Charlotte to her son. The kindness in his eyes reminded Charlotte of Saul, and she blinked away tears.

The large gruff cook gave her a gentle nod of understanding.

"Well, I could always use more help in the kitchen, that's for sure," he boomed affably. "Try it out today, and we'll see how it goes."

"Thank you!"

"Don't thank me yet. *Hey, Kip*," the man yelled.

"Yes, sir." A young man about Alex's age appeared with an armful of wooden boxes containing butter.

Charlotte remembered the long list of consumable needs that the circus men had presented to Saul and how she'd gaped at line items like the ninety pounds of butter on that list. Standing in the middle of the endless tents rising and people bustling all around the circus grounds lent some sense to the seemingly absurd requests though. There was no doubt that all of those supplies would be used today.

"Set that there." The steward nodded to a stack of crates as he flipped the eggs. "Kip, I want ya to take this kid—what's your name, kid?"

"Alex."

"Hi there, Alex. I'm Chuck Brown. I'm in charge around here, all right? They call me the steward here at the cookhouse."

Alex nodded as Mr. Brown put a large greasy hand on his shoulder.

"Kip, take Alex with you today. He can help you carryin' stuff and all a' that. You listen to Kip, got it, Alex?"

"Yes, sir," Alex said, looking at Mr. Brown, who gave him a friendly wink.

"He'll be a good'n. I can tell." The steward patted Alex's shoulder and went back to working at the grill.

"Do you think," Charlotte asked as politely as she could, "that he might have some breakfast first? Before he starts at work? I can pay—"

"Well, of course he can! You're one of us now, ain't ya!" The steward picked up two filled plates and shoved them toward the boys. "You boys eat up while you give him the ol' rundown, Kip. Then y'all go on an' get to work."

"Yes, sir!" Kip said, taking the plate. "Come on, kid."

Charlotte gave his hand a squeeze and let go.

Alex took the plate tentatively and looked back at his mother.

"We'll meet up in a bit to go see the animals," she whispered.

Alex nodded and followed after Kip, carrying his

breakfast plate, turning to look at her one more time before the two slipped through the canvas into the dining area.

Though she smiled confidently and waved assuredly, every bone in her body ached with guilt, weariness, and uncertainty.

This isn't permanent. I'll figure things out for us. We'll find a new home, and I'll get him back in school as soon as I can.

"Here's an apron. Oughtta be clean," the steward said, grabbing a wadded clump of white fabric from a pile in a nearby crate and shoving it toward her. "You can eat too, on your break."

Another gnawing growl from her stomach told Charlotte that her break couldn't come soon enough.

Though she found herself longing for the comforting regularity of Saul and Martha's cookhouse, Charlotte found it easy to fall into step with the other waiters.

"You just carry out a plate with eggs, bacon, and biscuits to everybody who sits down. Performers and crew all get the same thing," a kind woman who looked to be about her own age advised her. "Let the busboys pick up the dirty plates. They'll bring them over to the wash station behind the cookhouse tent."

Charlotte nodded, piling three plates across her arm. "When do we get paid?"

"End of the day most days. Every now and then they skip a day if we don't have a good turnout." The woman picked up her own collection of plates and ran them out to waiting diners.

Charlotte followed and deposited steaming plates in front of jovial circus performers and crew. Though she wore exhaustion like a heavy coat about her shoulders, the diners in the tent bubbled with a bright excitement that distracted her from her weariness.

"They got them a nice little shoppin' street down where the parade's at," an overall-clad crew member mumbled to another through a mouthful of eggs. "I'ma spend last night's money on somethin' for my girl."

"You talkin' bout Jeannie-Lou? She ain't yer girl, Herschel. She's everybody's girl."

The table laughed as Herschel jabbed at the man next to him. The men weren't so different from Charlotte's regular farmers in Ayer, with their easygoing smiles and casual banter. Their energy and hopefulness slowly warmed her enough to shed the exhaustion in favor of making her own plans.

Two or three days of this will put a little money in my pocket and get me far enough from Ayer so that Pete can't find me. Then we can start over. I could use my maiden name and find a job…figure out a place to live…

A sweeping quiet overtook the tent and shook Charlotte from her thoughts. A row of men in crisp black suits had entered the tent, cutting through the cookhouse dining space like a hot knife through butter as they marched through, silence and shifting in seats melting out around them. The crews finished their plates quickly and stood up to leave if they could, or adjusted their uniforms and sat up a little straighter if they still had food to eat. Even the loud and colorful performers stopped midstory and took on a pale rigid posture, eating their breakfasts with measured bites.

Her breath caught in her throat at the first figure in the intimidating line. *Jay*. He was easy to remember, tall and handsome, with a military stride, strong, confident posture, and a clever face. He'd been at the cookhouse in Ayer the day Saul got the big order for the circus. *He's the one who coordinates all of this.* Her fingers fluttered beside her at the memory of his hand brushing hers. She adjusted the tray she was carrying to both hands. Behind Jay was a man who was similar in appearance but with bright hungry eyes, a full beard, and a carefree sort of walk. He had been in the center ring the night before. She shuddered, remembering the awful accident. Then Hugh, the other man who'd been with Jay at the cookhouse, sauntered in behind them. He was unmistakable too.

She didn't recognize the last man. He was older and portly, with one thumb hooked in his suspenders. He was the most intimidating of all, and he didn't seem happy. Charlotte could understand why the mood in the tent had changed. She made her way back to the kitchen and tried to look busy.

"Nice try, new girl," one of the waiters said. "You go take care of the bosses."

Charlotte opened her mouth to protest, but as she looked around at the other waiters, she felt it would be pointless. "Oh, all right," she huffed.

The waiters laughed. "Good luck," one whispered.

Charlotte gave him a half smile and made her way to the bosses' table, smoothing her hair as well as she could along the way with her free hand. She found a straw of hay in the nest of hair at the back of her neck and tossed it on the ground.

"I don't give a damn what it was, Frank." The older man pounded his red fist on the table as he spoke to the younger bearded one. "We've got to get it back on track. We cannot afford another disaster like last night. We're going back to the old lineup."

"But, Dad—" Frank stopped when the man held up his hand.

"End of discussion." He held out his coffee cup for Charlotte to fill it and turned to Hugh. "Find me a new cannon girl. We've got to get her trained during the parade so she can be ready to go by the two o'clock."

"Can I choose anyone?" Hugh asked.

"Absolutely not—" Frank sat forward in his chair.

"Just have her ready by the two o'clock," the man demanded.

Charlotte poured Hugh's coffee next and watched hesitantly as he took a sip before moving on to fill the other two cups.

"Thank you," Jay said, looking at Charlotte briefly as she filled his coffee cup and then looking back up at her again as a flash of recognition crossed his face.

"What are we doing to fix the load-out crisis?"

Jay returned his attention to the table. "I'm on top of it, Sonny," he said. "I've identified the source of last night's fiasco—beyond the obvious—and it won't happen again." Jay glared at Hugh as he responded to Sonny.

Hugh's eyes sparkled as he downed his coffee and held out his cup for more. "We've got to cut Jay some slack. He was probably distracted, what with everything that's going on in his personal life."

Jay's face flushed, and Charlotte felt angry for him without knowing why. It crossed her mind to spill some of the hot coffee in Hugh's lap "accidentally." *What's wrong with me?* Charlotte filled the cup and quickly escaped to the kitchen to get their breakfast.

"Survived so far, huh!" Chuck said as he wiped the corner of a plate. "No, don't take those, take these. Hey, you. Help her carry these out."

Charlotte and the other waiter approached the table carefully and sat the plates down, leaving just as quickly.

"I'll go get them some more coffee," Charlotte said.

"The old one will want tabasco too. For his eggs," the other waiter whispered hastily before disappearing into the kitchen.

Charlotte heated up the tin coffee pitcher on the griddle again and returned to the table. She refilled the cups and set the hot sauce in front of Sonny.

"Thank you," said Jay, eying Charlotte again.

"I get that it'll be easy to train someone for the cannon, but who's going to want to after what happened last night?" Frank asked the group.

"Who cares who wants to. They'll do as I say! I'm going to move Sasha from the Sahara act. She'll be perfect."

"No, you can't do that! If you take Sasha for the cannon, you'll have to have someone else in the Sisters of the Sahara act, and that's a lot harder to do," Frank contended. "I think you need to find—"

"Frank, it's Hugh's call," Sonny said, shaking hot sauce all over his eggs violently. "I don't care which girl we stick in there. We've gotta pack those seats. Just take care of it."

Hugh smiled and nodded, taking a bite of his breakfast and chewing slowly.

"Now!"

Hugh looked startled and offended. He dropped his

fork, gathered his jacket, and left the tent wiping crumbs from his face. Charlotte stifled a giggle as she picked up the plate and cup to take it to the dishwasher but ran almost face-first into a boy Alex's age who looked at the dishes in her hands with confusion.

"I'm not used to having help with dirty plates," she apologized. "Thank you."

The boy took the plates and shuffled out of the tent. Charlotte found her way back to the kitchen, where Alex was collecting bread in a crate from a worker.

"How is everything going so far, hon?" she asked him.

"It's all right," Alex said, adjusting the heavy crate. "How much longer are we doing this? I want to see the animals with you, Mom. Maybe we can get a new balloon?"

"I'd love that," Charlotte said. "Can you hang in there a little longer?" She ruffled his hair.

Alex nodded. "And then we'll go home? I left all my books and…"

Charlotte's voice caught in her throat. What could she say to him?

"All right," Kip said as he picked up a crate of his own. "Enough chatting. Let's go, Alex."

"Coming, coming." Alex winked at his mother and followed the older boy carrying his crate.

What am I doing? Charlotte wondered as her son shuffled off toward the sideshow tents.

Chapter 19

Thirteen Hundred Suspects

Jay stared at the load-out page from the night before in his black book with mixed emotions. Every line and splash of ink represented a botched plan and minutes wasted in confusion. As he turned the page to the orderly load-in schedule, a series of clean lines and check marks gave him a sense of satisfaction. The morning setup in Abilene had gone perfectly despite the chaos of the night before.

Nice try, Hugh. He jotted down that night's load-out schedule, hopeful that it would resemble the clean coordinated list on the mirroring page. But as he sat alone at the wooden cookhouse table, pen poised atop his impending agenda, he couldn't decide which worry to focus on first. He set the pen on the blank page and rubbed his temples with his fingers. The tense morning meeting made it difficult to concentrate. He'd felt blindsided by Sonny for doubting him, betrayed by Hugh for sabotaging him, confused by Frank for how he'd fallen apart, frustrated with his crew for letting panic overtake them after the accident—

The murder, Jay corrected himself, taking up his pen again. He tried to shake off the image of the dead circus girl on the medic's stainless steel rolling cart, the corner of the white sheet pulled away from her pale face, the black and purple circle at the crown of her…

It was no accident. Someone had murdered Hazel. The bullet hole he'd seen in the top of her head couldn't be explained in any other way. *But who would want to kill her, and how could they pull that off right under my nose?* Trusting Saul with the body and the gun had bought him some time, but not much time.

In place of his to-do list, Jay wrote the word "Suspects" at the top of the page. Crew members and performers bustled around at their tasks, preparing for the parade. Jay had thirteen hundred names he could list. Who could he trust? He thought through everyone he knew. Outside of Benny—

"You're all alone."

Jay looked up. It was the waitress who'd been taking care of them that morning.

"What?" He closed his book abruptly.

"Your buddies left you." She smiled as she gestured to the empty seats.

"Oh." He laughed. "Yeah…"

"It doesn't look like you miss them. Coffee?"

Jay nodded and held out his cup. "It's a little easier to think when they're gone," he admitted. "Thank you."

"I can imagine," she said, picking up their plates.

"I know you, don't I? You were our waitress in Ayer, the one that introduced us to Saul Winslow."

The waitress blushed and nodded.

"Well, I should thank you. That turned out to be a fantastic arrangement." Jay sipped his coffee. "I think I heard Mr. Winslow call you Lottie, is that right?"

"Yes, it's Lottie…Cameron. It's Lottie Cameron. And your name is Jay?"

"You have a good memory," he said, setting his

cup down. "So, Lottie, what are you doing here? Why aren't you back in Ayer?"

The waitress shifted from one foot to the other. "I...I guess I decided it was time to run away with the circus." She smiled. "My son and I...it seemed exciting...so we hopped on the train."

Jay nodded, certain that wasn't the whole story. *Why do I care?*

"I'm not in trouble, am I?" Lottie said. "I know technically we're stowaways, but—"

"Oh no, it happens all the time," he said with an unconcerned wave of his hand. "We take on help in every city we tour through and often take on extra passengers, but...you don't seem like the typical runaway circus girl, if you don't mind my saying so." Jay forgot himself and looked into the waitress's eyes a moment too long. She broke his gaze and looked down at the table. "So you said your son is here too? What is he doing?"

She raised her chin and beamed at the mention of her son. "He's found some work as a bread boy. They're very nice in the kitchen. They've offered to train him."

"Glad to hear it," Jay said. "Mr. Brown runs a tight ship over there, does a great job. You know, I've brought my daughter too. This is her first time traveling with me."

Lottie set the plates back down and looked at Jay with interest. "Is she enjoying it?"

"I think she is. She seems to have taken to playing poker of all things."

Lottie chuckled. "A good skill."

"With clowns," he added.

Lottie's laugh reminded him of the way Frank and Luella had laughed together at the party. How he had wondered what that felt like.

"And how about you?" she asked.

"What?"

"How are you doing?"

"How am I doing?" he repeated, confused.

"Yes, you." Lottie laughed again. "It seems like you manage a lot." She gestured to the whole of the circus grounds. "At least, I know you order all of these supplies and seem to run the show with your handy black book and pocket watch there. And you've got a little poker player along for the ride with you. How are you doing?"

Jay looked down at the book under his drumming fingers and back up at her. He couldn't remember the last time someone asked him how he was doing. "Well," he said, "to be honest…I'm a little tired."

She nodded sympathetically and added a little more coffee to his cup.

"It might take more than that." Jay chuckled. He drew in a long breath as he fumbled with his pocket watch. "I love my daughter," he said, taking on a more serious tone. "And I'm really glad I'm not missing out on all of the…you know, the day-to-day things."

"Like when they lose a tooth, or their favorite breakfast food?"

"Or her favorite animal in the menagerie—"

"And just watching them learn things about the world that you forgot you ever knew?"

"Just like that," he said, leaning forward. "You know, there was this great moment yesterday, when she took my hand and told me it was the best day she'd ever had."

Lottie listened intently and leaned forward too, tucking a stray strand of hair behind her ear. Her hair was pinned up behind her head.

He wondered how long it was. If he took out the pins, would it tumble halfway down her back? What would it feel like in his fingers? "But then of course—" Jay sat back. "Did you see the show last night?"

"I did." A shadow passed over her face.

"I wonder if this is a suitable place for Sadie. I worry about her witnessing things like that…" *Why am I telling her all of this?* "I apologize. I've filled this conversation with an unnecessary amount of personal speculation. I don't usually—"

"Well, I don't know what is right or wrong for your daughter, but it sounds to me like you're doing a wonderful job as a father. I mean, for her to tell you it was the best day she ever had—that's something!"

Jay was speechless for a moment.

"I went to work with my father when I was about Sadie's age, maybe a little older. I didn't realize it at the time because he made it seem like our life was a great adventure, but he didn't have a choice either. My mom had died, and it was just the two of us. But to me, my father and those cowboys…that was my family."

"An adventure…" He gazed into her eyes again. "I do sincerely hope Sadie feels the same."

"I imagine my father asked himself a lot of the questions you are asking, but I remember my time with him fondly. I wouldn't change it for the world." She reached across the table to pat his hand. "I'd be willing to bet your daughter feels the same."

A wave of relief washed over him. "Thank you,"

he said, fighting the catch in his throat.

"You know, it's funny," she went on, taking back her hand. "I'm telling you that it's good to have your daughter on the job with you, but I've fought so hard to keep my own son from being out at the ranch with his father."

Jay reached awkwardly for his coffee, nearly knocking it over. "Oh…his father…wants him working, huh?" He couldn't keep himself from glancing at her ring finger as he recovered the handle and brought the cup to his lips.

"Well, he…he did, but I wanted my son to stay in school. That was always a fight. It was different though. He wasn't always a nice man. He wouldn't have been…I…" She bit her bottom lip. "Well, it doesn't matter now because he's dead."

"Oh, I'm sorry!" Jay said, almost convincing himself that he meant it. He set his cup back down, unsure whether he'd had a sip of what it held. He rested his hand on his black book and absently flipped at the pages with his thumb.

"And here we are…" She sighed. "And my son is working as a bread boy instead of learning in school." Her eyes were downcast. "Despite all that fighting to keep him in school, here's the spot I've put him in. I didn't even pack any of his books."

Lottie ran an anxious thumbnail along a scratch in the wooden table. He wanted to reach out and take her hand.

"Hang on a minute." Jay slammed the table and snapped his fingers, startling her. "He doesn't have to work. We have a school."

Lottie looked up at him hopefully. "A school?

Here?"

"Yes, it travels with the circus. My mother had insisted on it—it's a long story. Sadie is there now." He tossed his watch in the air, caught it, and slipped it smoothly into his pocket. "Let's go get your son. I'll take you both." Gathering his book and paper, Jay stood up swiftly and marched toward the kitchen.

But Lottie didn't follow. Jay looked over his shoulder, confused to find her still seated, wiping at her eyes.

"You're crying," he observed, sitting on the bench beside her, wondering if he'd miscalculated. Made some mistake. "I'm sorry. Did I—"

"That's wonderful," she said, flinging her arms around him. His pulse quickened under the warmth of her cheek on his neck. "Thank you. Thank you so much."

Jay sat up stiffly under the hug, not sure what to do with his hands.

"I'm sorry," she said, pulling back, "I—"

"We'd best make haste in finding your son," Jay said, retrieving his pocket watch. "We don't have much time before I need to get things rolling for the parade."

"Yes," Lottie said, composing herself. "Yes, let's go now." She gathered the dirty plates back up and then sat them back down again, restacking them in a perfect pile before wiping her hands on her apron. She shrugged her shoulders quickly and followed Jay to the kitchen with a new bounce in her step.

"You was gone forever, girlie! We was placin' bets on if'n you got your head bit off!" the stout steward said with a hearty chuckle when he spotted Lottie. Upon seeing Jay step through behind her, his belly stopped bouncing, and his face went white. "Mr. Edwards, uh, is everything all right, sir?"

Lottie's eyes danced from the steward and back to him.

"Mr. Brown, everything tasted great, thank you."

"Thank you, sir! And don't worry, sir, I've already talked to the crew, and we'll be packed up and rollin' out at eight fifteen, no ifs, ands, or buts, sir." As he spoke, the steward was standing at attention, his shoulders pulled back and belly protruding.

Lottie silently observed the interaction with a twinkle in her eye.

"I wonder if you could help us locate—" Jay looked at Lottie, realizing he hadn't asked the name of her son.

"Alex," she said, drying off her hands on her apron.

"Oh, yes, sir, excuse me, sir." The steward took a step back from Jay and looked around uncomfortably before resorting to a shout. "Kiiiiip!"

Jay winced at the steward's volume.

"Somebody find me the bread boy!" Mr. Brown shouted. "Sorry, sir, they, well, they run all over, ya see. I think they oughtta be 'bout roundin' the horse tent, that is the horse-opera performers' area, sir." The steward was wringing his hands as he spoke, sweat trickling down the side of his blotchy face.

"Chuck," Lottie said gently as she set her hand on his forearm, easing his tension almost instantly. "Do you think you could point me in the direction of the horse-opera performers' arena? I'm sure I could go find him if you don't mind my stepping out for a bit."

"Not a bit, Lottie. You go on and do what you need

to." Mr. Brown smiled at her gratefully as he mopped sweat from his forehead with his hat. "That is, if it's all right with you, Mr. Edwards, sir."

"Of course. I'll escort her. Thank you, Mr. Brown."

As they left the tent, Mr. Brown relinquished a grateful lopsided grin at Lottie and placed his sweaty hat back on his head. Jay was perplexed. He had never seen a softer side to the cast-iron cook in all the years he had known him, but somehow Lottie had brought it out of him after just one day in the kitchen. And didn't he find himself confessing feelings he'd never expressed after just one conversation with her too? Jay looked at Lottie with a new kind of interest, but he wasn't sure what to say. He took his pocket watch out and checked the time. The steward's mention of load-out reminded Jay of Hugh's frustrating misdirections the night before.

"It would be good to head toward the horse tent to see how the performers are coming along. It's really more Frank—young Mr. Sterling's area. But I've got a few things to check in on. He's supposed to be finding a replacement for one of our acts."

"An act in the horse opera?" Lottie's eyes grew wide.

Jay confirmed her question with a nod and surveyed the circus grounds as they walked, making sure that everything was on track and looking for Hugh. He took a moment to consider the idea he'd been pushing aside since the night before. Hugh had been so unpredictable and irritable lately, and he wasn't where he was supposed to be during the show. Could he have been hiding in the shadows with a gun somewhere, waiting to shoot Hazel?

"I think you scared poor Chuck half to death," Lottie said.

"Huh?" How long had Lottie been talking?

"I said I think you scared poor Chuck—Mr. Brown—half to death," she said, looking up at him. "He seemed like a whole different person when you went back there. You command a lot of respect around here, don't you?" She reached down to pet a gray cat that was trotting along beside him.

Jay shrugged. "He's just respectful of the chain of command."

"Yes, but it's more than that. Look at everybody." She gestured to the crew and performers as they walked by. "Don't you see how people stand up a little taller and work a little harder when they see you?"

Jay looked around. He hadn't thought about it in a while, but he did notice people acted differently around him.

"They don't necessarily do that around everyone who wears a suit here," she said. Something about the way she said it made Jay want to stand a little taller around her too.

"Hi, Joe." Lottie waved at a passing strongman carrying a stack of trunks.

Joe's hard face broke into a gentle smile. "Finding your way, Lottie?"

"I am! Thank you!"

Have I ever seen that guy smile? Jay remembered how the man had solemnly carried out a dead body from the center ring just the night before.

"You know, my cousin accused you of being too observant, miss," Jay teased. "Maybe he was right."

"I'm sorry. Sometimes I speak out of turn."

"No, no," Jay said. "I like it. It's refreshing. Any other observations?"

Lottie paused, looking up at him skeptically. "Hugh—he's your cousin?"

Jay nodded.

"Your cousin's a jerk."

Jay laughed. "I can't disagree with you. Although I should tell you not to talk about the bosses that way if you're going to stick around here."

"Sorry," Lottie said, looking back down at the ground with an adorable scrunch of her nose.

"Are you?"

"Am I what?"

"Going to be sticking around?" Jay stopped walking for a moment, anxious for her response.

"I don't know," she said, stopping too. "I haven't…my plans are a little…"

What was she thinking as she stared at the ground, playing at the dirt with her boot? The cat rubbed against her leg for a moment before she picked it up.

"Well, I think…" Jay took a step closer, a surge of excitement rushing through him. Her hug a few moments ago was so warm. He desperately wanted to reach out and touch her again, but something stopped him. Excitement turned to panic under the full force of her eyes looking up at him, waiting to hear what he'd say.

"I think…" Jay broke off and took a step back. "Did you bring your cat with you?"

"What?" Lottie looked down. "Oh no, this is your cat. Well, a circus cat, so…This is Madame Rusalka's cat, Printesa."

"Madame Rusalka?"

She set the cat down, and it strode off toward one of the performers' tents just as Frank came storming out.

"I'm gonna kill Hugh!" Frank fumed. "He's pulled Sasha, and there's nobody here that can ride. The equestrian director won't spare anybody. I think he keeps forgettin' that I'm his damn boss. But I guess Dad talked to him and told him not to make any changes to the original show, so now the old stick-in-the-mud is squarely rooted—who's that?"

Jay glanced at Lottie standing awkwardly behind him.

"Oh, uh, this is—"

"Lottie Cameron," she said, stepping forward and reaching out to shake Frank's hand.

"Hi there," Frank said, giving Jay a sideways glance.

"I'm sorry. I know I'm out of place," she said, gesturing to her waiter's apron. "I'm just looking for my son, Alex. He's one of the bread boys?"

"We're gonna take him over to the school tent," Jay said.

"And she needs you to help her with that, huh?" Frank said with a sly smile.

"So what's your problem," Jay said, changing the subject. "You need someone to ride the—"

"I can ride."

Both men turned to see Lottie standing confidently with both hands on her hips.

"I'm sorry, what?" Frank asked.

"I heard you saying you need somebody who can saddle up." Lottie shrugged. "My dad was in rodeos for years. It's been a while, but—"

"Wait! Cameron, as in the famous trick rider Clive Cameron?" Frank blurted.

The waitress nodded.

"Now I see why you brought her over here! Why didn't ya say so? God, I remember watching him as a kid. He could jump from horse to horse like it was nothin'. Talk about sold-out shows..." Frank turned back to Lottie. "And you can ride like your old man?"

Lottie shrugged. "I'm not a rodeo star, but I can ride—"

"Well, goddammit girl, get in here!" Frank took her by the hand and pulled her toward the tent.

"Oh! I-I—"

"Thanks, Jay!" he shouted. "Clive Cameron's daughter right here in our circus, I'll be damned!"

"But wait," Lottie said, looking back helplessly. "My son—"

"I'll take care of it," Jay offered before he knew what he was saying.

Lottie looked at him with fear in her eyes as Frank tugged her inside the tent. The overwhelming need to comfort her drew him a few steps forward. "You can trust me. I'll get Alex to the school tent."

She mouthed *thank you* as she disappeared into the tent with Frank. Jay stood rooted to the spot for a moment breathing in the air she'd just occupied, fighting the urge to follow her.

Chapter 20

Three Bangs

As performers bustled preparing for the parade, Jay stood as singular and stoic as the persistent thought of Lottie, cemented in the center of his mind amidst schedules and planning and the swirling questions of the murdered cannon girl.

"There you are!" Benny came jogging toward him. "I've been looking all over for you. I've got the updated numbers for the supplies and the..." Benny looked curiously at the tent in front of them and then back at Jay.

"Sorry, I got sidetracked." Jay broke his dazed fixation and turned to his friend. "I've got to find a bread boy and take him to the school tent."

Benny opened his mouth to speak and then closed it.

Jay lowered his voice. "And I'd like to take a look at that cannon."

"You think someone tampered with it? It was the net last time, wasn't it?"

"Yes, but this is different from last time. The net and cannon both seemed fine." Jay replayed the scene in his mind, picturing Hazel's broad ignorant smile as she climbed into the cannon. "All I know is the girl flew across a center ring full of witnesses and somehow ended up with a bullet in her brain by the time we got to her. I've got to figure out if someone shot her when she was loaded in the cannon, flying through the air, or when she'd already hit the ground."

"How'd somebody shoot her without anybody seeing it?"

"That's the million-dollar question, isn't it."

"First Zarina, now Hazel. That cannon's bad luck. I hope Sonny puts it up for good."

"Oh, he isn't. We had a meeting this morning, and he's allowed Hugh to choose a replacement—"

"Hugh?"

"Indeed. And he's chosen Sasha. She'll perform as early as this afternoon."

"On the fly like that with no rehearsal? Who'll they get to replace her in the Sahara Sisters act?"

Jay couldn't decide how to explain Lottie, but an involuntary smile crossed his face as the image of her laughing across the breakfast table snuck in. "We have a lot to catch up on."

Ahead of them, Jay spotted two boys carrying empty crates. One, he recognized as the little poker player, Maurice's grandson, who'd handed him a gun the night before. Next to him, a boy about the same age with light hair and Lottie's eyes was struggling to keep up.

"Good morning, boys." Jay approached the pair.

"Mornin', sir," Kip said, standing up straight and batting at the boy next to him to do the same.

Jay smiled. "Are you Alex?"

The boy nodded.

"Alex here, he's a good fella, sir. Please don't can 'im," Kip said. "I'm sorry we took so long at breakfast, sir. It's just that he's trainin' and everything. Gotta tell him how it all goes and all."

Alex looked at Kip with wide eyes and back at Jay.

"Thank you," Jay said to the boy, "I'd heard that you were kind in the kitchen, and that you'd taken on the job of training Alex. It looks like you've been performing your task well."

"Thank you, Mr. Edwards, sir!" The boy's face lit up.

"But I'm afraid I need to steal your protégé so he can pursue his education."

The first boy stared blankly at Jay.

"He's taking Alex to the school tent," Benny clarified.

"Oh, I see. Well, that's all right, ain't it," the boy said, taking Alex's empty crate with his own. "He's a good kid, but by golly, he talks a lot. Asks a lot of questions."

Jay looked at Alex, who hadn't yet spoken a word, and smiled. "Thank you, Kip."

"Good luck, Alex!" the boy said as he turned toward the cookhouse.

"Sorry, sir," Alex said, "but where did you say we are going? I kinda feel like I should ask my mom…"

"I'm sorry," Jay said, placing the knee of his clean black suit on the ground to be eye to eye with Alex. "I should have introduced myself. I'm Jay Edwards, the managing director of Sterling & Son's Circus, and this is my friend, Mr. Brooks. Your mom asked me to find you and bring you to the school tent."

"Hiya, Alex." Benny shook the boy's hand. "You're a brave man. You know who's the teacher in that school tent?"

Alex shook his head.

"A mean, feisty woman—my wife!" Benny shuddered and winked.

Alex giggled, and Jay heard traces of Lottie's laugh. Benny got along easily with Alex, and Jay admired him for it. He could have a genuinely pleasant conversation with anyone. Jay always learned a little bit about people from watching Benny.

Alex turned back to Jay. "What does a managing director do?"

"Good question," he said, thinking for a moment. "I manage the other directors, the supplies, schedules, finances, equipment, and all the day-to-day problems that arise. I keep the train moving."

"The train!" Enthusiasm illuminated the boy's face. "I'm so interested in the train! Is it really powered by steam? How does it work? I saw it has two leading wheels, eight smaller ones—"

"That's right. We call those driving wheels."

"Eight driving wheels," Alex repeated. "And two trailing wheels. Is that a 2-8-2?"

"It is. This train is a 2-8-2 Mikado, made in Chicago."

"Wow. So it runs on steam, right? How do you get the water?"

"Did you see the lake where we stopped the train? It's a man-made lake just for trains like ours. Our engineers will refill the train while we set up and run shows today."

"What if you run out?"

Jay laughed. "Kip was right. You do ask a lot of questions."

"I like figuring out how things work." The boy

shrugged.

"So do I," Jay said, encountering a thought. "Hey, Alex, how do you feel about making a quick stop by the center ring on our way to the school tent?"

Jay could taste the tension in the big top almost immediately. Benny's smirk told Jay that he could sense it too.

"Morning, everyone," Jay said, approaching the cannon crew. "How's it going?"

The crew looked around at each other, drawing nonverbal straws for who would speak first.

"Good morning, boss," one finally said. "We're all right, just trying to get the new girl trained on the cannon and, uh—"

An angry head popped out of the barrel of the cannon.

"I am not a new girl! I've been a trouper with Sterling & Son's longer than you, Ian!" Sasha retreated back into the cannon and continued shouting, "I don't wanna be here any more than you want me here!"

"That's how it's going, boss." Ian, the lead crew member, put his hands in his pockets and dropped his shoulders.

Jay nodded. He approached the cannon and placed his hand on the barrel. "Sasha, why don't you come on out for a minute."

Scrambling and muttering from inside the cannon preceded two arms that thrust themselves out of the opening, followed by Sasha, who pulled herself out. "Mr. Edwards," she said as she struggled to swing her legs out of the device and onto the ground. "Mr. Edwards, no disrespect, but I really do not want to be the new human cannonball girl."

"I can under—"

"Was I doing bad in the Sahara act? No one ever said nothin' to me about it if I was!"

"I don't make those decisions. You'd need to talk to Frank and Hugh about that."

"Hugh!" She huffed. "That son of a bitch. He just stuck me here out of spite, all because I spilled champagne on him at that party. I bet he hopes I'm the third dead cannon girl—that's why I'm here."

"Uh, Miss Sasha." Benny made a sideward glance at Alex. "Take it easy."

"Sorry, kid," she said, dusting off her arms. "Mr. Edwards, can I please go find Frank or Hugh and talk to them about this? I'd really rather stay with the Sahara act. It ain't easy workin' with them zebras, you know! Y'all could put another sideshow girl in this cannon!"

Jay thought of Lottie's face as she was dragged into the zebra tent. If Sasha went back to the Sahara act, they might pull Lottie for the cannon.

"I'm sorry, Sasha," he said, "but Hugh's decision is final." Jay ignored Benny's raised eyebrows.

"I'm actually here to check on the cannon mechanism and ensure your safety. Why don't you take a break while I work with the crew to make sure everything will be in tip-top shape for you this afternoon."

Sasha didn't look happy. She gave a firm nod and beelined out of the tent.

"So Ian…" Jay turned back to the crew. "Give me a rundown of how the cannon works."

"Well, sir…" Ian knelt down and removed an outside panel. "It's a basic springboard mechanism. We get it cranked back so it's holding the tension here, and then on the signal, we release it and let 'er fly."

"So it isn't really a cannon?" Alex asked. He looked around at the surprised adults. "Sorry."

"No, that's all right, kid. You're right, it isn't really a cannon. It's kind of a giant slingshot."

"Wow," Alex said.

"How do you determine the trajectory?" Jay asked.

The crew looked at Jay quizzically.

"He means how high and far she flies, Alex," Benny announced.

"I know," said Alex, looking up at Benny, who winked.

"Right, well, we angled it the same as we had done for Hazel"—Ian pointed to the wheel—"and we have it fixed here where that mark is so it don't move on us. But the thing is we haven't been able to test it with Sasha yet because she ain't keen to give it a go. We did test it on Herschel, though"—Ian gestured to a gangly, grease-covered crew member with bulging eyes and big red ears in half-buttoned overalls standing over by the net—"and he did have the, uh, trajectory we was hopin' he would. Mostly."

"I did land in the net, boss," Herschel shouted from the other side of the ring where he and another crew member were securing the net. He drew back and spat in the dirt inches from the shoe of the other crew member who glared at him.

"Barely," the crew member said as he shoved Herschel over a few feet and got back to work.

"But don't try to put me in one of them girly costumes, boss," Herschel shouted at Jay as he regained his balance, stuck his thumbs in his trousers, and gave a comical curtsy. "I ain't got the figure for it."

Alex and Benny chuckled as Ian rolled his eyes. "Can we send him off with the clowns, sir?"

"Let me look at the springboard again," Jay persisted. "Can you set it off for me, without anything or anyone on it?"

"Sure thing, boss." Ian pulled the release, and the board flew up. Ian looked at Jay and cranked it back.

"It seems safe to me," Jay said. "I'd like to go check out the net, and I'll have Frank come look over everything too.

"Yes, sir," Ian said, closing up the panel. "I still don't know what went wrong with Hazel, Mr. Edwards. We all feel awful bad about it. But we did everything just as we've always done, and I looked real close at the cannon this morning on load-in. Nothing was off about it."

Jay nodded. He stepped up to peer inside the cannon. His first thought was to look for blood or a bullet, but of course, the medic had told him there was no exit wound. Looking at the rim of the cannon, however, he could see a small splatter across the red paint that could have been blood. Jay looked at the angle of the cannon and studied the scaffolding and surrounding seats, imagining where someone would have to be standing if they were to take the shot at the cannon girl. If they shot her while she was in the air, he thought, looking at the seats, they could have been anywhere within this range. But how did they know they wouldn't hit anyone else?

"Sounds like someone jumping off a diving board, doesn't it," Benny said to Alex as he mimicked the springboard sound. Alex giggled.

"Well, that's why we light off them two

fireworks," Ian said, turning to Benny and Alex, "to give the illusion that we've lit off the cannon and cover up the sound that gives away the trick."

"Three," Alex said.

"What?"

"There were three fireworks."

"No kid, just two." Ian gestured to the crew to unload the next set of props for inspection.

"What did you say, Alex?" Jay was jolted from his thoughts.

"I just…" Alex hesitated. "Well, I heard three fireworks last night when they did this. Bang, bang, bang. I remember because I was trying to figure out how it works."

Ian shrugged at Jay. "We good here, boss?"

"Yes," Jay said, looking back at the seats and the scaffolding. "Yes, Ian. Thank you."

Three bangs. Alex was right. Jay remembered it too. One of those was the gunshot. Someone shot the cannon girl while she was still in there, and they must have known the fireworks would disguise the sound.

Jay followed the line of sight from the cannon up into the scaffolding. *That narrows it down a little bit.*

He took out his book and made a note and then put his hand on Alex's shoulder. "You're a smart kid, Alex. I can see why your mother wants you to keep learning."

Benny raised an eyebrow, and Jay knew he'd ask him who Alex and his mom were as soon as he got the chance.

"Let's get you to the school tent."

Chapter 21

A Horse With Stripes

"Where are the horses?" Charlotte asked, looking around at the performers and animals. Workers were diligently assembling rows of stadium seats, a steady rhythm of chants and hammering. A pair with a clipboard and a tape measure were methodically testing the security of pegs and poles, tugging at ropes and poking at knots. Two identical girls with long black ponytails, angular eyes, and bold red lips were draped casually against a railing, smoking cigarettes and whispering, like cats flicking their tails as they surveyed a mouse. The intensity of their gaze on her every move made it hard to imagine they weren't whispering about her.

"Horses?" Frank removed his jacket and adjusted the cuffs of his shirt sleeves. "Well, they're right there. Why don't you hop on and show us what you can do." Frank tossed his jacket over the railing and gestured at one of the women to join them.

Charlotte's boots seemed heavy on her feet, sinking into the sawdust. There had been a misunderstanding here. "Sir," she said, cocking her head and looking at Frank, "aren't those—?"

"Zebras." One of the women led the largest in a lineup of zebras over to the pair. She assumed a mocking voice. "Regal zebras from a faraway palace in the Sahara."

The other women snickered.

"I can't ride a zebra," Charlotte protested, looking back at Frank. "I can ride horses, but—"

"Eh, it's just a horse with stripes." He waved away her comment as if it were smoke in the air.

"But I'm not a Sahara Sister, I'm not..."

"You think these girls are really from the Sahara?" Frank laughed and was joined in his laughter by the women against the rail.

"You see Mei-Ling over there?" He gestured to the delicate woman with porcelain skin and long black hair who was holding the reins of the zebra. "I picked up her and her two sisters when we were in San Francisco."

"Doesn't he just love bragging about that," Mei said, petting the nose of a zebra beside her.

"What can I say?" Frank placed a hand on Charlotte's shoulder. "I have an eye for beautiful women."

His squeezing fingers sent a wave of uneasiness through her, and she fought against the urge to wiggle out from under his hand.

"And the other two girls—well, they're just talented gymnasts and easy on the eyes. So we outfit all you ladies in purple sequins, showing off all the right features..." He looked Charlotte up and down and winked at her. "And we call 'em sisters. It's the circus, baby. No one cares if you're really sisters. No one cares if you're really from the Sahara. Ada over there is from New Mexico."

"I'm from Texas, asshole," a girl shouted from the railing as she puffed on her cigarette.

"Whatever." Frank shrugged.

"But that doesn't change the fact that I've never ridden a zebra," Charlotte protested.

"Looks like today's the day." A charismatic smile spread beneath his well-oiled beard. "Hand her the reins, Mei!"

Mei approached Charlotte gracefully and confidently, holding the reins just out of Charlotte's reach. "All right, greenie, let's see what you can do."

A cluster of girls had formed around the two whispering observers to form a small unwelcome crowd. The women watched with casual semi-interest as they puffed on their cigarettes.

She turned back slowly to the zebra. How different could it be? "Thank you." Tentatively, Charlotte took the reins from the woman and examined the saddle. It was unlike anything she had ever seen. There were glittering jewels and a confusing assortment of ribbons and velvety fabric. *Underneath all that, it's just a saddle.* Charlotte hiked her skirt up, put one foot in the stirrup, and swung her leg over. Her boots adjusted to the stirrups like an old memory.

"Feels like a horse, sort of," she admitted as she adjusted herself on the zebra's back. It was flatter and broader than what she was used to.

"See, look at that," Frank said, clapping his hands together. "Take the ol' boy around the ring, huh?"

"Okay." Charlotte fidgeted in her seat a little before taking a deep breath. She signaled that it was time to go with a gentle kick to the ribs. The zebra stood obstinately, as if it hadn't noticed the command. She clicked her tongue and kicked again, a little harder this time.

He snorted and tossed his head back, braying. She tightened her grip for what came next. The zebra whipped his head to and fro wildly before taking off in a manic jolting sprint. A chill of panic seized her as she held onto the striped neck for dear life. The animal bucked wildly as it raced around the ring before running into the side of a wall panel, crushing Charlotte's leg against the wobbly wall and sending her toppling over the edge into the sawdust.

The now-calm zebra proudly cantered over to the line of others and stomped its hoof in the dirt. The girls laughed hysterically, pointing at Charlotte and leaning on each other for support as they mocked her fall. She rubbed at her aching leg and reached up to pull hay and shreds of wood shavings from her hair.

"I thought you said you could ride?" Frank said, jogging over to help her up.

"I can ride," Charlotte said, spitting sawdust out of her mouth, "a horse."

Frank laughed. "Well, it's just a—"

"I know, I know." She grasped his hand to stand up. "A horse with stripes."

Frank smiled, flashing a wide row of glistening white teeth. "That's right. Got another try in ya, Miss Cameron?"

She nodded reluctantly and dusted off her apron.

"So to get him movin'," one of the girls said, "we just give 'im a little love pat on the shoulder. Try that." The girls along the railing tried and failed to suppress their laughter.

"Okay." Charlotte stepped tentatively back over to the feisty animal and hopped on, wincing. The fall had been a hard one, and she could already feel tenderness in her tailbone where she'd landed, beyond the pain in her leg. She adjusted herself on the zebra's back and took a deep breath as she reached her hand forward to the zebra's shoulder. "All righty, here's your love pat. Let's go."

The zebra whipped its head back and bit her hand, sending up dust as it stomped its front hooves in place furiously.

"Ouch!" She clutched her throbbing fingers to her chest as the girls doubled over with laughter. Her chest burned as she looked at each laughing Sahara Sister, reminded of the girl who'd sat across from her at the Winslows' cookhouse. "Look at you and look at me." Tears stung at her eyes. *Who am I kidding, trying to pretend I'm one of these girls?*

Charlotte jumped off the zebra and headed for the exit of the tent, when through the blur of her tears, she spotted Madame Rusalka, the Romani woman, sitting in the shadows petting Printesa calmly. Rusalka stared into Charlotte's eyes with a mesmerizing intensity that froze her in the moment and made her forget her intention. Charlotte looked down at her aching fingers and her dirty apron. She heard the mystic woman's words echo in her mind. *You used to be like a wild stall-i-on too, didn't you, Charlotte?*

"Well, that's too bad," Frank said resignedly. "We'll short the act tonight, girls—"

Rusalka lifted her chin, and Charlotte stood up a little taller as if she were a marionette on a string. She held her own head higher and pulled her shoulders back to match the fortune teller's proud posture. Charlotte broke Rusalka's gaze and turned to march past Frank and back toward the zebra, untying her apron as she walked. As she approached the animal, she balled up her apron and shoved it into the hands of the nearest laughing Sahara girl. She placed one hand on either side of the zebra's nose and looked it dead in the eye. Lottie remembered her father's words. *There's no pretending with them. They see right through you to your soul, and they expect you to look past them into theirs...*

"You're not a horse with stripes," she said to the animal, staring deep into the dead center of the glassy black eye. "You're a wild animal." She held firm until she felt the restlessness beneath her fingers melt away. Then she hiked up her dress and swung up onto the zebra's back, gripping the barrel of his body with her thighs.

"Well, so am I," she said as she whipped the reins and clicked her tongue. "Go!"

The zebra resisted and stood still, but this time she could feel something coursing through the muscles beneath her. A flex in the shoulders like it was ready to perform instead of fight. She repeated her command with more confidence.

This time, the animal moved one flexed leg forward in a step that became a walk and eased into a canter. Charlotte praised the zebra, kicking at its ribs to go faster. The pair raced around the ring. Like a speeding steam engine along a well-traveled track, zebra and Charlotte rode their course. It was faster than she expected, but the wind rushing in her ears thrilled her. The galloping body beneath her was synchronized with her goal but still not under her control. Fear and uncertainty gave way to excitement and courage. As they made a second lap, flickers of familiar comfort and confidence began to return to her from some distant place. She pulled the reins up and to the right as she slowed the zebra to a trot for a third lap. The animal resisted for an instant but relinquished more quickly this time and slowed to a stop in front of Frank, who was clapping ecstatically.

"Well, there we go! Looks like we have ourselves a sixth Sahara Sister!"

Charlotte was excited by the pace of her own breath. She smiled and looked up at the seats. But Madame Rusalka was gone.

"You know, Lottie," Frank said, encircling her waist with his hands to help her hop down, "you'll just sit on the zebra's back and look pretty while it trots along in a line behind the other zebras. We don't expect you to race around or do tricks or dressage or anything."

"But I thought—"

"No, no. We just need a warm body to fill in for the act. We save the trick riding for the horse opera. Great job, though!" Still holding her hand, he turned to the girls who had ceased their cackling. "Mei, will you get Lottie here to meet up with Birdie so she can get her an outfit?"

"An outfit?" She hadn't thought about what she would have to wear. The idea of putting one of those tiny purple outfits on her body was horrifying.

"I'll admit"—he leaned in, staring at her chest as if he could see straight through her clothes—"I'm looking forward to seeing you in it."

Charlotte stepped back and swallowed hard.

Frank chuckled and took up his jacket from the railing.

"Y'all get everything sorted out, and we'll line up

for the parade at ten thirty," Frank said as he walked out of the tent whistling a tune.

"Do I really have to wear an outfit?" Lottie whispered to Mei.

"Yes, of course you do." Mei laughed. "Who would pay money to see you do anything dressed in that?"

Charlotte rubbed her neck and looked down at her scuffed leather boots before following Mei out of the tent. She ran her hands over the seams of her dusty woven wool skirt as they walked and imagined the constricting glittery ensembles she'd seen on the dancers and performers the night before. She hadn't given a second thought to what the fabric was made of when she watched the show, but now she wondered how it would feel cutting into her skin in place of her comfortable and well-worn day dress. *I've mastered a zebra. Surely I can master sequins and fancy tights.*

"Who's Birdie?" she asked.

"Who's Birdie?" Mei stopped abruptly and shot Charlotte a reproachful look. "Don't let her hear you say that."

The two trekked past the performer's tents to the dressing area. Charlotte found herself looking around, hoping to catch a glimpse of Jay. Would he be impressed with her if she told him she could ride zebras? That might not be such an impressive thing here, where everyone was attractive and their talents always on display. Thank goodness she hadn't seen Jay and embarrassed herself by bragging about something so unimportant and trivial. Still, it would be nice to know that Alex was settled.

"Where's the school tent?" Charlotte asked.

"Why would I care about that?" Mei said, rolling her eyes.

"It's just that Jay—Mr. Edwards—took my son there this morning, and I—well, I hope he's doing okay." She bit her lip, thinking of the way Alex had looked at her when he asked if they could go home. "It's our first day here, and I just hope that he—"

Mei stopped in front of a long yellow trailer and looked at Charlotte with narrow eyes. "You don't want much, do you?" she snapped as she reached up and knocked on the door of the trailer.

"My advice," Mei said, lowering her voice to something just above a whisper, "stay away from all the Sterlings, 'Jay—Mr. Edwards' included. Messing with them is nothing but trouble for girls like us. Trust me. The last girl that tried to kiss Mr. Edwards is dead."

Charlotte's chest alternately stung with jealousy and burned with anger at the mention of the dead girl. Of course, she'd had something to do with Jay too.

The trailer door opened, and Charlotte took in a sharp breath when a woman stepped into the open space. She had pale, freckled skin and flaming red hair, which fell in wild curls around her pointed chin. She was the girl who had spun gravity-defying somersaults off the gilded wagon in the parade the day before.

So that's Birdie.

"What do you want? I'm getting ready." Birdie was dressed in what Charlotte could only imagine was underwear, silky cream-colored panties and a brassiere, with an open flowy robe of the same color tossed casually on her sharp shoulders. Charlotte blushed and looked away. She had never seen another woman's navel before.

"Birdie, this is Lottie Cameron. She's taking Sasha's place in the Sahara Sisters act, and Frank asked me to bring her to you for a costume and…" Mei eyed Charlotte skeptically. "Well, I guess to make her look presentable and all that."

"Did he now?" Birdie said, stepping down and brushing sawdust from Charlotte's shoulders.

Charlotte stood still and tried to project an image of confidence, though her heart was pounding in her ears.

"Let's go, tomato. We'll see what we can shine up." Birdie disappeared into the trailer.

Charlotte looked back at Mei.

Mei snorted.

"Don't let her eat you alive. See you at ten thirty, Lottie Cameron." She laughed and walked back the way they'd come, leaving Charlotte standing alone at the doorstep of the mysterious yellow trailer.

Chapter 22

Looks Aren't Worth the Trouble

Nothing good can come from going in there. Charlotte stared at the larger-than-life painted image of Birdie soaring across the length of the bright yellow dressing trailer before returning her focus to the dark space beyond the open door. Her mind was involuntarily invaded by that crude woman with laughing eyes, sitting across from her and casually shattering her reality. The cackling sisters in the zebra tent. She considered turning away. Going back to the cookhouse. Or better yet, finding a way home.

But the memory of Pete pushing his way toward her with the intent of taking her son reminded Charlotte that there was no home to go back to. Glancing back over her shoulder at what lay behind her, Charlotte realized the only direction she could go now was up.

She swallowed hard and gripped the railing, tediously aware of the weight of her boots as she stepped laboriously up the steps into Birdie's dressing trailer.

I'll step in as me, and I'll step out as me, no matter what I look like.

"I've got Sahara Sister costumes in here somewhere," Birdie shouted from somewhere in the space. "Who knows what sizes or if they're current, but maybe you won't look too out of place."

Charlotte felt like she had stepped inside a genie bottle from *The Arabian Nights*. Plush fabrics and cushions decorated the space, and silk garments and feathered accessories were flung randomly about the room beside neckties and beveled glasses of various sizes and colors. Directly before her was a sitting area with a counter covered in every kind of makeup a girl could apply, and in the corner of the room was an ebony-paneled screen decorated with images of ivory-faced women dancing around a palace surrounded by knotted winding trees. Posters of Birdie were plastered to every available surface. Everything had the nose-tingling intoxication of flowery perfume.

"Don't touch anything!" Birdie poked her head out from behind the panel and glared before disappearing again.

"Okay," Charlotte responded meekly, still in awe of the space around her. She'd never felt more out of place in her whole life.

Her thoughts were cut short as she caught sight of the dingy reflection in the lighted mirror of the dressing table before her. Charlotte bit her lip, understanding now why the Sahara Sisters had seemed to find the idea of her as one of them so hysterical. These girls were jewel-toned, glittering, sensual, and bright. Charlotte smoothed her shapeless dress, sending up little clouds of fiber and dust. The woman in the mirror was frumpy and colorless. Unremarkable and dull. Still covered in layers of grimy shades of brown from the Ayer dust storms.

She took a step backward. She could still go back to the cookhouse. After all, Chuck would be wondering where she'd run off to. And she was hungry. But something in Charlotte knew her days waiting tables were behind her.

What if Rusalka was right that I'm not just running from Pete. Maybe I'm running toward something. She thought about the way her soul quivered a little when she looked into the eyes of the zebra and felt it relax beneath her fingers. The same way she felt when the man at breakfast had looked into her eyes a little too long.

Charlotte studied her reflection in Birdie's mirror and tried to peer through the dingy layers of dust and domestication to see what might lie beneath. Next to the mirror was the poster of Birdie, the bright-haired beauty soaring through the blue sky uninhibited.

What would it feel like to be remarkable?

As if in answer to her question, Birdie stepped out from behind the dressing panel with an armful of purple glittering garments.

"All right, toots, one of these oughtta fit the bill."

"Those look smaller than my underwear." Charlotte gestured to the cluster of fabric on Birdie's arm, discouraged by how little of it there was as she tried to imagine how it would look on her body.

Birdie frowned. "Ya know, this is the part where you squeal with glee and thank me for being so gracious," she quipped.

"I-I—Of course, I…thank you." Charlotte shuffled her feet as she attempted to melt into the walls.

Birdie eyed her suspiciously. "What brings you to my door, Lottie?"

"I, uh—well, they, the sisters and, um, Frank, they said I needed to…" Charlotte pinched at her dress and shrugged.

"No, I know that," Birdie said dismissively. "But what brings you *here*?" She lifted her free hand purposefully, sweeping the space around her.

"Oh. I..." Charlotte's heart pounded. How could she admit out loud that she'd imagined—even for a moment—that she could be anything other than what she'd already become. "This was a mistake. I don't—"

"Don't get your panties in a twist," Birdie said, moving between Charlotte and the door. "I don't really care who you are or where you came from as long as you stay out of my way."

Charlotte nodded, taking a step backward.

"What do you think of Frank?" Birdie circled Charlotte, sizing her up.

"Frank?" Charlotte asked, confused.

"Yeah, Frank sent you over with Mei, right? He must have noticed you have some talent or some potential. You're clearly not from another circus, so where did you come from?"

"I don't know if he noticed anything like that. They just needed another rider for a zebra and—"

"But he chose you."

"Well, I think it was because my father was—"

"What do you think about him?"

"W-w-what? What do I—"

"Frank. What do you think about Frank?"

"I-I'm not sure I think anything about him...He seems...nice, I guess."

"And handsome," Birdie cut in.

"I guess so," Charlotte admitted, remembering Mei's warning, "but he seems like one of those men whose looks aren't worth the trouble."

The silence was painful.

"Ha!" Birdie laughed out loud finally. "You know what? I couldn't have said it better myself! Looks aren't worth the trouble…"

Charlotte exhaled, feeling she'd passed some sort of test. "Frank is yours. I mean…mean that…y-you two are…"

"Yeah. He's mine, but I'm not his. But ya know what? I wish I'd been as perceptive as you. I'm not sure any man is worth the trouble."

"It's a lesson I've learned the hard way," Charlotte said. It was the most honest thing she'd said all day.

"Well, Lottie," Birdie said as she sat down on a velvet sofa, "I'm not sure where you came from or who you are, but we've got to turn you into a Sahara Sister before the eleven o'clock parade. Sterling & Son's counts on me to make sure all the girls look glamorous, no matter what they give me to work with…"

Charlotte took a deep breath.

"Come on, off with all that." Birdie brushed her hand toward Charlotte's garments. "Let's try some of these on."

"I…right here?" Her cheeks flushed.

"Go behind the screen if you want." Birdie waved her hand casually as she took a glass from a nearby table, sniffed it, and took a sip.

Charlotte nodded and made her way timidly toward the screen, stepping behind it to see an array of clothing from corsets and feathered headpieces to a man's white shirt with Birdie's lipstick on the collar.

"You know," Birdie said from the other side of the panel, "stumbling into the Sahara act is a pretty big deal. I know girls who'd do anything to get a gig like that. They fight and claw for years. Some of 'em die tryin'."

"Did you have to?" Charlotte asked as she slipped slowly out of her dress. "To fight hard to get to where you are?" She peeked between the panels.

Birdie tipped up her head and downed the liquid in her glass. Her legs were crossed and her toe pointed circles in the air, but her eyes looked tired and her face seemed steeped in a sullen sadness.

"Of course I did. Anybody who's anybody has. Done things we never dreamed we'd do to get to where we are. I could tell you stories you wouldn't believe…"

Charlotte stepped out of her boots, folded her dress neatly, and placed it on top of them. Next to them, crumpled on the floor, she saw clothing she recognized and recoiled instinctively. "Did you know the girl who…who…" She didn't have the courage to finish her sentence.

"The girl who died last night?"

"Yes."

Birdie stood up and poured another drink with her back to Charlotte. "I did," she said. "Obviously. We all did."

"What was she like?" Charlotte found herself asking, unable to stifle her curiosity.

"Honest to God truth?" Birdie came around the panel and stood before her. "She was a man-stealing, lights-hungry, empty-headed whore." Birdie handed a glass to Charlotte. "She tried to steal the spotlight, tried to steal Frank, tried to have it all. And it killed her."

Charlotte took the glass and stared into it, unfamiliar with the liquid inside. It looked like water, but the smell of it burned at her nostrils. She looked back up at Birdie, who clinked the glass and smirked at her.

"It's not gonna hurt ya," she said. "Might loosen you up a bit though. You seem like a real prude. And I can't handle all that stuttering."

Charlotte took a drink from the glass and coughed. "Why are my eyes burning?" she said over a tingling tongue.

"Well, that's vodka, baby! Smaller sips maybe, or pinch your nose if ya have to."

Birdie laughed, but somehow Charlotte wasn't self-conscious or hurt the way she had when the Sahara Sisters had laughed at her in the ring. Instead, she found herself laughing too. She took another sip.

"What was her name?"

"Huh?" Birdie asked as she took a gulp from her own glass. "Oh, the dead girl. Her name was Hazel."

"Hazel." The name burned in Charlotte's mouth like the cheap vodka from the glass.

"Why are you so interested in the dead girl? It ain't like she's the first nitwit to die in a show."

"I'm just curious about her," Charlotte said, taking another sip. "What do you mean it killed her? Trying to have everything."

"I mean that every girl oughtta know that you can't have it all. Look at me. D'you think I could do what I do and have the family life? No. I gave that up a long time ago." Birdie took a swig from her glass. "A long time ago."

"But Hazel didn't? Give it up?"

"She gave up nothin', and she gave up everything. She was stupid. All over the place. Got herself a good gig here, then ran off one summer and married some rancher who left her. Rex something. Then her dumb ass came right on back here, and she tried to take over the spotlight after no practice, no work. Then she starts sleepin' with Frank because that's easier than working for a spot in the center ring."

"Frank got her the job on the cannon?" Charlotte asked.

"Frank didn't get her shit. I put her on the cannon. And she was ungrateful." Birdie pointed a finger an inch from Charlotte's nose. "I hope you don't think Frank can get you anywhere. You see how it turned out for Hazel."

"Yes," Charlotte said, taking another sip of the burning liquid, "I don't want to be anything like Hazel."

"You've been hiding something," Birdie said.

She was caught off guard, "I...I..." she sputtered.

"You've got a figure!" Birdie exclaimed as she pulled the waist of Charlotte's undergarment tight around her stomach with one hand. Birdie sat her glass down and cupped Charlotte's breasts with both hands, pushing them upward and examining her thoughtfully. She tensed and fought the urge to flinch.

"Some girls have all the luck," Birdie said, letting go and traipsing back over to her sofa to sort through the costumes. "Here, I think this one will suit you best now that I see what we're working with."

Charlotte took the garment gingerly.

Birdie pulled at the pant leg of Charlotte's undergarment with disgust. "Oh, sister," she said, dropping the pant leg. "We've got a few things to take care of first." She disappeared to the other side of the screen. Charlotte stood waiting awkwardly, alternating her focus from the dainty purple fabric in one hand to the glass of vodka in the other while Birdie rifled through a drawer.

Birdie returned with a bar of soap and a metal razor. "Do you know what this is?" she asked.

"Of course I do," Charlotte said, "My husband—that is, my late husband—um, used to use one to shave—"

"Well, you can understand why I thought you'd never seen one," Birdie said, gesturing to Charlotte's legs. "We already have a bearded woman, a bear, and a gorilla, so you're going to need to get rid of all that before you put on your Sahara Sisters costume."

Charlotte and Birdie stared at each other for a moment.

"You want me to…"

"Everything below the neck, babe," Birdie said, taking the costume back and handing the soap and razor to her.

Charlotte gaped at the razor and back at Birdie, who had her hand on her hip.

"You don't have a lot of time. Shower tent is just across the yard by the cookhouse where they wash the dishes," Birdie said, turning to her dressing table. "They'll give you two buckets of water. You're gonna have to find it on your own. I've gotta get ready too."

"The shower tent…I'm going to have to walk around outside in my underwear with all this?" Charlotte looked at the razor in her hand, scrunched up her nose, closed her eyes, and gulped down the rest of the vodka. She set the glass down carefully next to a cluster of other empty or almost empty glasses. "Can I borrow something to cover myself with?"

Birdie let out an exasperated sigh. "See what I mean? Such a prude." She pulled a floral lavender robe from the arm of a nearby chair and handed it to her. Charlotte had never worn anything so luxurious. She ran her fingers slowly over the slippery silk, feeling the effects of the vodka set in.

"Then I'm gonna find you some undergarments from this century and…well, I'll get rid of all these other…clothes. Somehow they even make the floor look uglier. God, did you wear that on purpose?"

Too dazed to protest, she nodded and turned toward the trailer door, pulled the borrowed garment over her underwear, and stepped out in public. She wasn't even slightly aware of what a shower tent would look like, but surely she could find help from someone along the way.

Looking down at the soap and razor in her hand, panic fluttered with the idea that she really would be putting on some costume and riding a zebra in front of a bunch of strangers. Charlotte felt the earth beneath her bare feet and squeezed a few blades of grass between her toes as she looked around the circus yard at the blur of the performers preparing for the parade. Somehow, she was melting into the blur while still completely separate from it.

No turning back now. She tugged at the edge of the robe and set off for the shower tent.

Chapter 23

No More Bread

Charlotte was keenly attuned to her borrowed silk robe slipping across her now-hairless legs as she made her way across the circus grounds back to Birdie's trailer. At the shower tent, Charlotte had decided to throw away her long underwear rather than put them back on. She felt a fleeting chance at friendship with Birdie, and she was eager to impress her, or at least to save herself from enduring any more insults about her frumpy old underwear. But now, she wondered if she shouldn't have kept them for the journey back as the robe rippled across her body, threatening to expose the smooth skin beneath it.

The cookhouse tent loomed before her, though it wasn't on her way. Charlotte winced with guilt as she thought about how she'd abandoned Chuck for the Sahara Sisters act without a word. Surely a quick detour wouldn't put her too far behind. She pulled at the belt of her robe to secure it more tightly and moved her bare feet quickly through the dirt and grass toward the cookhouse tent.

As she shuffled toward the kitchen, a boy headed the same way carrying crates of bread.

"Kip, isn't it?"

"Yes, miss." The boy stopped and looked at her

quizzically.

"It's Lottie, Alex's mom. You helped my son this morning. Did he make it to the school tent okay?"

"Oh! Yes, ma'am, that's right. Sorry, you look different. I didn't see whether he made it out to the school tent, but he did get picked up by Mr. Edwards and Mr. Brooks."

She blushed at the mention of Mr. Edwards and adjusted her robe again.

"He's in with them, then he's okay, miss. They'll get him where he's supposed to be. Don't you worry."

"Thank you, Kip."

"I never did go in the school tent. My Grandpa Maurice said I didn't have to if I didn't wanna. And I sure didn't. Alex though, he'll like school right enough, bein' that he—"

"Yes, he asks a lot of questions." She smiled. "Are you bringing those to Chuck?" She gestured toward the crates, and the boy nodded.

"I'll come with you. I'm headed that way too," Charlotte said. "So how long have you been with Sterling & Son's?"

Kip scrunched up his forehead and readjusted the crates. "I don't know. Maybe forever. Can't say I remember what it's like to do anything else, miss. My mother sent me with Grandpa years ago, and I've been out here earnin' my keep ever since."

"Oh, I see."

"I make real money, you know. I can buy all the candy and baseball cards I ever want. Grandpa says most kids can't do that."

"So you like it then?"

"Like it?" Kip looked up at Charlotte like he didn't

understand her question. "Are you nuts? I love it! You know I been to six of these United States and about a hundred towns? Plus that, Grandpa's pals with the menagerie man, and I know the names of all them animals. Even the elephants let me feed 'em peanuts if I want to."

"That is good to hear. I hope Alex will enjoy circus life as much as you do." The idea warmed her. She didn't plan to be on the road with the circus forever, but Kip's enthusiasm was reassuring.

"He will, miss. You tell him to come with me next time after the show. I'll teach him how to hold the peanuts so the elephants don't slurp his hand up with their nose."

"That's kind of you, Kip." Charlotte suppressed a giggle. "I wonder if I could ask one more favor of you? I have a letter that I'd like to send to some friends back home."

Kip shrugged. "Seems easy enough. I drop off mail for folks sometimes, although you can leave it with the post car."

"This letter is important to me. Could you see that it gets where it needs to go?"

"I can."

"I thought you could. I'll get it for you when we find Chuck."

As she drifted into the comforting smell of biscuits and sugared ham, Charlotte briefly considered throwing an apron over her silly robe and joining the waiters again. It would be so much easier to serve a table than ride a zebra dressed as a showgirl. But somehow, that morning already seemed to be far behind her. She'd left easy in the dust when she had chosen to take Alex and run.

"*Kip! Where's that bread—*" Chuck roared from the kitchen. "Oh, there you are. Set it here—Lottie? That ain't no waiter's uniform, girl."

"Hi, Chuck," she said sheepishly, tugging at the collar of her robe. "I just stopped by because, I wanted to tell you…" She stumbled over her words awkwardly as the waiters who'd become her friends that morning paused in their bustling to take in the sight of her. "I guess they want me over in the Sahara Sisters act now and—"

"Sahara Sisters?" Chuck whistled. "Well, look at you, Miss Lottie, movin' up in the world after 'bout half a day."

The whispers of the waitstaff fell against her like new rain. She rubbed her newly smooth legs together and looked down at her toes as blood rose to her cheeks. "Oh, I don't know about that—"

"Well, I do! That's a good act, Miss Lottie. More money too. So I guess you won't be servin' lunch or breakfast around here no more then, will ya?"

"That's why I stopped by. I didn't want to—" When Charlotte looked up, she found clusters of warm smiling faces nodding at her. What was the look on their faces? Was it admiration? Maybe she shouldn't have taken their whispering for judgement.

"Well, go on, you center-ring star. Don't you forget your friends in the kitchen now!"

Chuck's smile was the biggest. *If I don't win over the Sahara Sisters or the zebras, at least I've got friends in the kitchen.* She smiled. "How could I? Can I leave my things with you?" She gestured to the apron area, tensing at the sight of her purse as she remembered everything that was in it.

"Sure, sure. I'll keep 'em safe."

Charlotte went to her purse to retrieve the letter for Kip and handed him a coin with it too. "For your trouble." She winked.

"Thanks, miss!"

Chuck observed the interaction shrewdly without comment.

"Half a day ain't a record for me by no means, but I never scared off a mother and her son in the same mornin' before," he said finally.

"If you scared me, would I be back here to apologize?"

Chuck smiled sheepishly. "All right, go on then. Oh! Take you a couple slices a' bread there. You'll wanna get a bite in before you go prancing around the city." Chuck grabbed a handful of bread from the crate nearby. Charlotte's mouth watered as she reached for the bread. She hadn't had anything in her belly since their escape the night before except coffee and—what was it, vodka? Gin?

As Charlotte took the bread, her robe slipped a little off her shoulder, and she scrambled to catch it with the bread and the soap and the razor in her hands.

Chuck pulled her robe back up for her and gave her shoulder a friendly pat.

"Go on, Lottie! You're gonna be late, and I hear Miss Birdie's a force to be reckoned with if you don't look right for the show."

She nodded and took a welcome bite of the warm bread as she scurried off toward Birdie's trailer. When she approached the trailer, Charlotte knocked but didn't hear a reply. Worried about the time, she opened the door and went inside. She set down the razor and soap carefully beside Birdie's things and considered the costume lying on the velvet couch that Birdie had told her she was meant to wear. Beside it were tights and skimpy undergarments like the ones she'd seen Birdie wearing. Charlotte took another bite and chewed slowly as she eyed the ensemble.

Now or never.

Setting the other half of her bread down beside Birdie's makeup and dusting the crumbs off her hands, Charlotte gathered up the apparel and went behind Birdie's dressing screen. Even alone in the trailer and behind a screen, she was embarrassed to stand without the protection of her borrowed robe. She peeled it off slowly and hung it carefully on the corner of the screen before quickly slipping into the undergarments Birdie had set out for her. Charlotte tugged at the edges of the foreign fabric on her body. There didn't seem to be enough of it. She wasn't sure exactly where everything was supposed to sit, and she realized it had been a long time since shc'd looked at her own body.

My figure doesn't quite look like Birdie's. She studied herself in the mirror.

Next, she pulled on the tights, stumbling and losing her balance a little as she lifted one leg and then the other, groaning in pain as she extended her hurt leg. In the mirror, a big bruise was forming on the side of her thigh. But as she pulled the thin fabric past her belly button and ran her hands along her hips, the tights made her legs look surprisingly long and smooth.

A little more optimistic, she picked up the sparkling purple costume she'd been obsessing over for her entire trek to the shower tent and back. What would it look like? How would it fit?

She turned the tiny purple dress over in her hands both in awe of and terrified by the lightness of the fabric. Where to start? She found a row of cloth buttons on the side and undid them one by one. Eager to wear anything other than just the tights and tiny undergarments, she unbuttoned the costume quickly and clumsily. As she worked to pull the thick string loop from the top button, her finger slipped and the fabric flurried to the floor. Charlotte cursed herself for her clumsiness and knelt to pick up the garment.

She stopped when something on the floor caught her eye.

Under Charlotte's boots, which were set nicely beside the folded brown wool clothes that Birdie had threatened to throw away, was a note. Charlotte hesitated for a moment, hand halfway to the note.

She pulled her hand back and picked up her costume instead. She finished undoing the buttons with shaky fingers but continued to eye the slip of paper, and the other pile of clothing that hovered just outside of recognition in her recent memory.

She stepped into what she assumed were holes for her legs and worked her body through the unbuttoned bodice. Charlotte pulled the costume up to her shoulders and slipped her arms in one side and then the other, having to take her arm out once and try again when she pushed her fingers through a jumbled mess of sheer purple fabric. Taking a deep breath, she decided it was time to quit imagining the worst and confront the reality of the image in the mirror. Charlotte turned to look at herself. She inspected her reflection from her toes, slowly up her body to her bottom lip, which sat tucked between her teeth under the scrunched nose above them.

She turned to the side and twisted her body to hook the slick round cords around the fabric buttons. The inside of the bodice had fabric bands that tightened uncomfortably around her midsection, but the outside was thick and smooth, covered in sequins and jewels.

With each newly fastened button, a little bit of breath left her body. She tried to focus on her fingers as she fumbled with the fasteners, but that slip of paper beneath her boots was always in the corner of her eye.

She ran her hands along the bodice of her costume and looked in the mirror, trying to reconcile the reflection with how she imagined herself to look. The costume was tight. Uncomfortable. She spilled out of the top a little bit. But it did fit. Charlotte decided she was content with how she looked. After all, Birdie had said she had a figure. It must be true.

I could use some encouraging compliments from Birdie right now. She pulled at the top of the bodice to even out her cleavage and fluffed at the feathers on her hips. Charlotte looked at the mirror. Was this the kind of woman who could join the circus and ride a zebra? Her eyes fluttered back down to the note.

She thought of Pete's secret box again. The notes. The photograph. *Didn't I say to myself that I should have looked in Pete's secret box years ago? What does it hurt to read it and put it back?*

Charlotte took a deep breath and reached for the note. Quickly realizing that she had less mobility in the new costume, she sucked her stomach in, bent straight over, and picked up the slip of paper. As she unfolded it slowly, a scent slipped out like a haunted memory. She pulled her nose into the fold and caught a whiff of harsh perfume.

That isn't Birdie's. She tried to align the smell with the unpleasant sensation that tugged at her memory. Pulling it back down, she saw there wasn't much to it.

I know who you really are.
I know what you did.
Back off.

The bottom of the note was sealed with a reddish-purple kiss. It was an unusual lipstick color that Charlotte hadn't seen before, but the lip print looked familiar. She was filled with questions as she looked at the paper in her hands. She was jolted back to reality when the door flung open with a bang, rattling the trailer. Her tightly constricted chest flushed with adrenaline.

"Go to hell, Frank!" Birdie shouted as she stepped into the trailer and slammed the door behind her.

Charlotte didn't have time to fold and return the note. She patted at the hips of her costume to find a pocket she could slip it into, but of course this ridiculous costume didn't have pockets.

"You're dead, Sasha," Birdie muttered through gritted teeth. "Dead."

Charlotte looked down at her chest and determined that there was only one place to put the note. Rolling her eyes, she quickly folded the paper and shoved it between her breasts. Looking around her, she stepped back into her boots and kicked at the clothes around them.

"Who's in here?" Birdie snapped.

"Hi, uh, sorry, I—" Charlotte crept out sheepishly from behind the panel.

"Oh, it's you," Birdie said.

"I...p-put on the costume you set out for me."

"God, stop it with your stuttering!" Birdie ran her thumb upward along her cheekbone and flicked away an unwelcome tear. "It fits?"

Charlotte clunked out into the middle of the trailer and held her arms out awkwardly. "It's a little tight."

Birdie studied her for a moment with a clenched jaw. Air escaped her pointed nose in measured breaths.

"Are you all right?" Charlotte asked gently.

Birdie glared at her before looking away toward the dressing table. "Is that yours?" she asked, pointing to the bread.

"Yes...do you want some?"

"Do I look like I eat bread?" She laughed. "I haven't had a bite of anything like that in ten years, toots—and neither should you if you want to keep squeezing into that costume."

Blood rushed to her cheeks. "You're right. I look ridiculous. I'll change back—"

"Why are you wearing those boots? You don't really think you can wear those with a sequin leotard?"

"Well, I—"

"What's that? Are you wearing your knickers under your tights?" She flicked at the fabric and feathers on Charlotte's hips.

"Yes, I...Am I not supposed to?" Charlotte tugged at the fabric, smoothing the tiny skirt back down.

Birdie rolled her eyes and flew over to the dressing table where she used the end of a makeup brush to knock the bread off the counter into a wastebasket is if it could infect her with calories by contact. "Get back over to Mei. Tell her to find you some heels, and for

God's sake, put some makeup on. You'll need your hair done up too. I don't have time to fix this mess. She'll know."

Charlotte stared at Birdie blankly.

"Dust out, dummy!" Birdie turned her back to Charlotte and chose a glass from the counter and poured gin into it with a shaky hand.

"B-Birdie, I—"

"Are you d-d-deaf? Get your pudgy stuttering ass out of my trailer!" Birdie spun around and hurled the beveled glass at Charlotte.

The glass flew inches from her face and shattered against the colorful poster behind her. She barely shielded herself from the splinters of glass and droplets of gin that splattered everywhere. The poster wasn't so lucky. Broken glass dragged a long scratch through Birdie's perfect picture, and ink bled blurred lines into the letters *Watch Birdie Fly!* Birdie turned back toward the table and fumbled around for another glass to fill without apology or explanation.

Charlotte bit her lip and shuffled back to the dressing panel. It wasn't her first time on the wrong end of a bad fit, but she thought she'd left that behind her in Ayer. She gathered her clothes, stepped over the shards of broken glass, past the illustration muddied and dripping with gin, and scurried out of the trailer.

Fighting back tears, Charlotte looked around the circus grounds and tried to remember where she'd come from with Mei before. She knew they were nearby, but where? Surely they'd be somewhere close to the main tent. She stomped awkwardly in her boots across the grounds toward the big top, fighting the urge to pull out the scrap of paper scratching at her soft skin.

Was someone trying to threaten Birdie? Or had Birdie threatened someone else?

Charlotte was deep in thought, contemplating the meaning of the strange note when she mindlessly stumbled right into a man in a suit.

"I'm so sorry!" Charlotte exclaimed.

"Try walking with your eyes open. It works wonders for me," the man said, clearly perturbed.

Charlotte's eyes traveled up to the man's face slowly, and she quickly looked away upon recognizing him.

"Can I help you?" Hugh said.

"I—no." *He doesn't recognize me.* "Well, actually—sir, I…well, I…"

Hugh looked past Charlotte, clearly annoyed he was being held up.

Birdie's criticism *Quit that stuttering!* rang in her ears. She took a deep breath.

"I'm looking for the Sahara Sisters," Charlotte said with feigned confidence. "I need to meet up with them for the parade."

Hugh snapped his attention back to Charlotte. "The Sahara Sisters? They found someone?" He seemed disappointed.

"That's right," Charlotte said, standing up taller. "I'm a Sahara Sister now."

"You?"

"I…yes."

Hugh narrowed his gaze. "You look like you just crawled out of a pigpen. Has Birdie seen you?"

"Of course she has. I've been practicing, that's all. Can you show me where I should go to finish my makeup?"

"It's that way." Hugh tossed his forefinger over his shoulder to suggest vaguely an area behind him while still skeptically scanning Charlotte. "But I doubt there's enough makeup in that tent to make you look like you belong in the center ring." He turned his attention to his hands, examining them and flicking off a bit of dirt from under his fingernail. He seemed to be waiting for her to leave, as if he didn't want her to know which direction he'd be going.

"Okay, well…thank you." Charlotte edged away and continued in the direction she'd been going before she ran into him. She glanced over her shoulder and saw him slip briskly between the train cars and out of sight. She'd better keep her eyes open for answers to her questions and anything else that could get in her way.

Chapter 24

Accidents Happen

Jay strode slowly through the circus grounds with his brow furrowed and his hands in his pockets. He'd just gone over expectations for the day with Sonny and received clear instructions to call and report the previous night's accident to the authorities in Ayer when he went into town.

Jay played the events from the night before over and over again in his mind, searching for any detail he might have missed. *And now, ladies and gentlemen— Frank extending his arm toward Hazel as the light followed—the human cannonball!*

The piano player. The band. Music mingled with questions swirling in his mind. That night he'd looked out at the crowd, counting spectators, but now in his mind he turned his attention to the other side of the crowds. Up in the rafters.

Wispy gray smoke rising, lights lowered. He followed the line of sight from Hazel climbing into the cannon back up to the top of the scaffolding. Nothing. A blinding spotlight obscured the figures behind it into blackness.

Bang. The first firework. Sparks flared in his mind, and the crowd waited anxiously behind them.

Bang. The shot. Up at the top of the scaffolding,

the barrel of a gun extended into the light. He followed the arm up to the face. The face...

Bang. Hazel's lifeless body flung morbidly across the forefront of Jay's mind as he fought against his fading memory and strained to see the face of the stranger in the scaffolding. Hadn't there been four men instead of three?

But instead, he pictured Hazel lying lifelessly in the sawdust, his daughter clapping wildly behind the cannon, completely unaware of what happened.

Whoever the murderer is, they could have missed. They could have shot my daughter.

Jay knew what Sonny wanted, what he would want even if he knew the truth. His main concern would be to save face for Sterling & Son's. They couldn't have a scandal now, not when finances were so shaky. But Jay couldn't let someone get away with murder in the center ring of the Sterling & Son's show. *Not while I'm running things.* Jay clenched his fist.

And he couldn't brush it off as an accident, whatever he'd been told to do. Whoever shot Hazel might kill again. Performers, crew, and even spectators expected Jay to keep them safe. He couldn't justify allowing a murderer to walk free if they were spending all day with Sterling & Son's Circus and traveling with them at night.

He fought to see the face in the shadow, the face behind the gun. But it was a black void. He would have to keep investigating. For now, all he knew was that the person who shot her was either very reckless, or very cocky. Maybe both.

As his cousin approached, Jay couldn't think of anyone who fit that description better.

"So did you see Frank's new Sahara Sister?" Hugh mused.

Jay raised an eyebrow.

"Oh, he didn't tell you? Frank pulled some girl up out of nowhere to fill Sasha's spot. Probably one of the floozies he rotates in when he's bored with Birdie."

"Lottie's not a floozie," Jay snapped, quicker than he meant to.

"Lottie, huh?" Hugh raised an eyebrow. "Well, don't get too attached. If she isn't in Frank's roster yet, she will be. They always are."

"Where are you off to?" Jay changed the subject.

"Me? Why, I'm going into town for the parade." Hugh scowled at the question. "Don't go looking for me. I'll be back by the first show."

"I'm headed that way too, actually," Jay said. "Let's ride together."

"Oh no, I—"

"I insist," Jay said firmly. "Benny!"

"Yeah, boss." Benny hustled over to the pair.

"You got time to drive us out to Main Street? We're gonna scope out the parade route."

"I can drive myself." Hugh's words floated between the three, seeming to land on no one in particular.

"Sure thing, sir. The Model T is by the tracks."

"Great, let's all go now, then." Jay and Benny looked expectantly at Hugh.

"Model T?" Hugh scoffed. "Take the Rolls."

The ride to Main Street wasn't far. The circus grounds were setting up only a few blocks away from the parade route, but with the throng of people already gathering along the street's edge, the drive a few blocks down would move slowly, just long enough for Jay to get some questions in.

"So have you seen Sasha try out the cannon yet?" Jay asked Hugh pleasantly.

Hugh turned his whole body to look back at Jay before slowly readjusting himself to face forward again.

"No, why would I?"

"No? You seemed so set on choosing her for the cannon, I assumed you'd want to make sure she was a good fit."

"Oh, Jay, you're so tedious. I'm not concerned with how well a human body flies out of a cannon. Surely the crew can manage that."

"Even after the accident last night?"

Hugh ignored the question. "If she doesn't work out, we can just throw another one in there." He shrugged. "Or maybe one of the monkeys."

"Fair enough," Jay said, trying another approach. "But for what it's worth, I think Sasha was a good choice. She's skilled and smart. Smarter than Hazel anyway."

Jay watched Hugh carefully for a flicker of any emotion he could try to read.

"We wouldn't want another *accident* like last night's, of course." Jay emphasized the word accident again.

"Of course not," Hugh said, sitting a little taller, "which is why I chose someone from a skilled act, naturally."

"Right," Jay said. "So smart."

Hugh couldn't hide the self-satisfied smile that emerged from the compliment.

"I might head out to the range for some shooting

today if either of you gents wanna join me." Benny looked into the rearview mirror at Jay as he spoke.

"The range? Do you shoot for fun now?" Hugh looked over his shoulder at Jay, regarding him with a raised eyebrow.

"From time to time." It was a lie. Jay hadn't held a gun since he left France.

"Really? I had no idea. Personally, I abhor guns," Hugh remarked before turning back around. "But you should know that."

Jay hearkened back to the dark days after Hugh's father had shot himself, decades ago. No church funeral, no priest. Just wide-eyed children beside a gaping hole in the ground with no mother to comfort them even if they had been crying.

Jay broke the uncomfortable silence. "What are you up to downtown? Gonna grab a bite for lunch or anything?"

Hugh shifted in his seat. "Uh no, I—Yes…Sonny wants me to make sure the parade is…"

"What does Sonny need you to do?"

Hugh set his jaw and looked out the side of the car. "How's Vanessa?"

Benny coughed, apologized, and kept driving.

"Vanessa?" Jay asked.

"Your wife."

"Not my wife," Jay said definitively. "Some guy named Butch's wife, maybe. She signed the papers about as quick as I could send them."

"Butch? You can't mean Butch McNeil, the rich oil tycoon from Sonny's party? Our new biggest investor?"

Hugh knew exactly who it was. Jay was fairly certain he had helped to orchestrate the whole debacle.

Don't let his snarky comments rattle you.

"That's the one." He responded without emotion.

Hugh snorted and slumped back down in his seat. Jay allowed himself to enjoy the small victory.

"Well, good luck, Butch," Benny hailed, matching Jay's smile as he looked at him in the rearview mirror.

"Good luck, Butch! He did me a favor." It felt nice to laugh about it. Usually, on a day like this, he'd be headed into town to call his wife and check in on her and Sadie during the parade, maybe listen patiently to some gossip or endure some sort of lecture about money or how often he was gone. But today, he would be calling a man from a cookhouse to ask about a dead body. He chuckled, realizing the second conversation was ever the more preferable.

"Well, I'm glad you're taking it so well," Hugh responded stiffly.

Benny parked the car, and the three gathered their things.

Jay tried again. "So what is Sonny's task for you regarding—"

But he didn't get an answer. Hugh had scurried off into the crowd before he could finish the question. Jay peered over at Benny, who stood beside him with his hands in his pockets, also watching Hugh.

"I gotta be honest," Benny said. "I can't see it. You think he could fire a gun in the middle of a crowd and time it perfectly?"

"Hugh's always full of surprises. And he's seen the show just about as many times as anybody, so he'd know where Hazel would be and the best place to hide. Although I never thought he was paying much attention."

"But what reason could he have for killing some dime dancer turned cannon girl?"

"I don't know," Jay admitted, "but he's definitely up to something."

"Want me to follow him?"

Jay nodded.

"See you in an hour," Benny said as he melted into the crowd after Hugh.

Turning toward the street, Jay took out his pocket watch and made a mental note of the time. Ten fifty-two. They'd start to head this way from the tracks soon. Jay adjusted his hat and smoothed the lapel of his jacket coat as he ran a mental count of the growing parade spectators. Abilene was always a good turnout for them, and if the gathering crowd here at the parade was any indicator, it was going to be another great year.

His thoughts were interrupted by the music of the bandwagon. The parade had begun. He migrated toward the front of the street crowd. Normally annoyed to be surrounded by strangers, Jay wasn't bothered by them today. Their enthusiasm to watch the procession matched his own. He looked back at his pocket watch and imagined the parade lineup in his head, predicting the time that each act would make its way in front of him.

Usually, Jay didn't stay to watch the parade. He would dip into a shop somewhere for a moment of peace and a telephone to use. But today it would be more than a lineup of music, clowns, and animals that he'd seen a thousand times. It would be another opportunity to see *her*. Jay opened his pocket watch. Eight more minutes.

For the first time in a long time, Jay experienced

the anticipation of the parade as the crowd might. Maurice stuffed into a tiny car among the clowns brought a smile to his face. He chuckled with the crowd when the stilt walkers wobbled as if he didn't know the wobbles were planned and practiced. Jay glanced at his pocket watch again, watching the second hand tick its way to the twelve in what seemed like slow motion. Five minutes. He would see her again in five minutes.

He took in a sharp breath when Birdie went soaring through the air above her rolling trailer just as everyone in the crowd around him did. *I'll have to bring Sadie out with me next time.* Jay made a mental countdown of the last thirty seconds.

Finally, the act came through that Jay had been waiting for. The Sahara Sisters. Glancing at his pocket watch, Jay smiled. Right on time.

He was thankful for his height as he scanned the act for their newest member over the tops of the bobbing heads in front of him. A surge of excitement rushed through him as he recognized a glittering purple figure at the back, waving and smiling atop a zebra. Though she looked drastically different from the woman he'd laughed with that morning, Jay knew her instantly. It was Lottie.

He lifted his chin and rocked up onto the balls of his feet to see her better, even though he was several inches taller than the bobbing heads around him. What a corker! This morning, the mysterious waitress from Ayer had reappeared at the circus cookhouse like she belonged there. By midmorning, she'd made friends with half of the circus staff, and now here she was showcased riding through town on a zebra in the Sterling & Son's Main Street Parade.

He watched her as long as he could, even wading through the crowd to follow the zebras. The smile she wore for the crowd looked different from the one he had seen at breakfast but no less dazzling. Though she was dressed exactly like the other girls, doing the same things they did, she seemed to stand out from the ensemble. Jay had seen hundreds of pretty performers on display for Sterling & Son's over the years, but he couldn't take his eyes off Lottie.

To his surprise, Lottie turned toward him. She rested her chin on her shoulder and locked eyes with him. The buzz of conversation from the spectators around him faded into a ringing in his ears. He brushed away someone tugging at his jacket. The crowd pushed around him, and he allowed himself to dissolve back into them, letting distance and the people separate their gaze.

"Jay," someone said as if from a distance.

His heart pounded, punctuating the sound of the crowd around him as it rushed back in to fill his ears. How would he explain to Lottie why he'd been staring at her? Had she smiled at him?

"Jay Edwards!"

Startled, Jay turned to see Luella Prescott.

"I'm so sorry, Luella," he said, removing his hat.

"Goodness, Frank was right. You do take your work seriously!"

Jay turned back to see Lottie, but her back was to him now, and she was waving at spectators down the street. "Yes," he said, turning back to Luella, "I have been accused of that before. What are you doing in Abilene?"

"Well, I come to every city, silly," she said. "Every

city, every show."

She looped her arm in his, and they migrated with the crowd down Abilene's sidewalks, embedded with mica that sparkled like diamonds in the noonday sun. "Take me to lunch?" She fluttered her eyelashes at him.

"I'll have to decline. Unfortunately, I have some things to attend to. Surely you're here to see Frank. I can—"

"Oh, Jay," she said, waving a hand before her, "I'm here to see you! You're a free man now. Take me to lunch."

Jay stopped and looked at her for a moment. "What's this really about?"

She rolled her eyes. "Oh fine," she said. "I wanna talk to you about that Birdie Bells."

"I'm not responsible for—"

"I've found something out about her, and I want to talk to Frank about it. I think you should fire her."

"She's our star attraction, Luella. They aren't going to let her go no matter how much you may dislike her."

"Oh, this is more than simple dislike. She's a murderess."

Jay pressed his lips into a thin line and cocked his head.

"I know you think I'm being dramatic, but it's true. I hired a private detective to confirm she'd been spending time with Frank—even before the party—and he dug up quite a bit more than even I expected."

"Don't you think that's a bit excessive?" Jay asked.

"Certainly not!" she exclaimed. "And anyway, it might interest you to know two things. First, my detective saw more than one of those little circus girls traipsing in and out of Frank's downtown den.

Including that dead girl. We'll be getting rid of that apartment. Second, Birdie Bells is really Beulah something-or-other, and she's wanted in some county somewhere for killing a man."

"Luella, that's quite an accusation." Jay stopped in front of the store in Abilene where he always used the phone.

"See for yourself." Luella took a card out of her purse and handed it to Jay between two gloved fingers.

He examined the card and took his black book from his pocket. "The Pinkerton Agency? You picked some heavy hitters." He tucked the card into his book. "I'll look into it."

"See that you do." With that, Luella turned on her heel and marched down the glittering black sidewalk toward the circus grounds. Her commanding strut and the reflection of the winking specks of sunlight on her proper day dress almost made her look like a circus girl too.

He stood at the door for a moment, contemplating what Luella had told him before ducking into the sandwich shop to make his phone call.

As the operator patched him through, Jay went over what he would say to Saul. Part of him still contended that reporting the death as an accident would be the quickest ticket to wrapping up this mess. But as he opened his mouth to speak, he knew that kind of lie could never leave his lips.

"Mr. Edwards, hello, sir," Saul answered formally. He covered the phone and mumbled to someone. "All right," he said, lowering his voice to something just above a whisper, "so I, uh, I talked to the sheriff like you asked…"

"Yes?"

"Well, Mr. Edwards, the thing is, the sheriff says he recognized her…the, uh, the dead girl."

"What do you mean he recognized her?"

"Well, he says he got called out to the Stallman ranch a few weeks ago about a fuss with her. She was throwin' a fit and attacking Mr. Stallman's wife or something like that, so they brought her in. But when Mr. Stallman came up to the station, apparently he wasn't who she thought he was. Said she kept yellin' at him that he wasn't Rex Stallman, and she wanted to see the real Rex Stallman."

"Does he think that has to do with her murder?"

"Well, nah, Sheriff says they smoothed everything out, and Rex didn't press charges. She apologized and left scot-free. But the sheriff thinks that probably ain't her right name," Saul said. "You have another name for her besides Hazel Stallman?"

Jay took out his book and flipped through to his notes on Hazel.

"Well, that was her married name, although I'm not sure I've ever known her to have a husband. We did have another name for her in our pay ledger, Hazel Beauford. I can try to find some more information about her and the husband," Jay said, "and I'm doing a little digging on my end as well for suspects."

"That's what I told him. An' he agrees we should keep it on the hush until we know more. Stallman is a big deal around here; the sheriff doesn't wanna upset him. I'll tell him about the name."

Jay paused as a waiter led a smartly dressed little old man to the restroom. The man hobbled by at a snail's pace, stopping to tip his hat to Jay as he passed.

When the hallway was clear again, he tucked in closer to the phone and spoke with a low voice into the mouthpiece.

"What about the gun?"

"The sheriff took the gun back with him, and he said he'd bring someone back in a day or two for an autopsy. They'll wanna find the bullet and see if it'll match."

"Thank you, Saul. I know this is a considerable amount of work, and I want to assure you you'll be adequately compensated."

"Oh, that's all right, I'm not—my wife hasn't been real happy about it, but I explained to her how you're tryin' to do right."

Jay smiled, remembering the woman's expression as they loaded the body in the delivery truck. "I can imagine," he said. "Where are you keeping the body now?"

The line was silent for a moment. "Well, uh, sheriff and I moved her into the ice house, bein' that he wants to keep it quiet for now…but if Martha finds out I'm keepin' a dead circus girl next to the groceries, there'll be two bodies instead of one out there—oh shoot, gotta go, Mr. Edwards!"

The line went dead.

Jay laughed as they ended the conversation. He'd been right. That was much more enjoyable than a rant from his now ex-wife.

Chapter 25

The School Tent

Charlotte hopped off the zebra and handed the reins to a man from the menagerie who led the animals to be fed and brushed before the matinée at two. She tugged at the ends of the new ponytail resting on her shoulder and took in a deep breath as she looked at the Sahara Sisters walking arm in arm together in front of her.

"Not bad, new girl," one of the Sisters said with a wink as she passed Charlotte to catch up with the others.

Charlotte blushed and smiled. *Am I one of them, now?* Riding through the parade, Charlotte had been filled with a sense of worth and freedom that she hadn't felt since she was a child. Only days ago, she'd felt important just to be able to share news of the circus and the parade, and now she'd just spent the last half hour smiling and waving as part of the grand spectacle.

At first, she'd thought it was risky. Being so visible. What if her husband followed them? What if he saw her? But when she searched the crowd for the vengeful glare of her husband, she'd seen instead another set of eyes. And just like that, the knowledge of his presence had become the most important thing in the world. Out of everything there was to see, Jay had been looking at her.

A woman dressed in a gold sequined costume joined the women and looped arms with Mei. Another Sahara Sister placed her arm on the woman's shoulder and handed her a handkerchief for her red eyes and wet cheeks.

Mei looked over her shoulder. "You've got an hour, Lottie," she said. "Get somethin' to eat. Then you need to meet us back in the dressing tent to go over what you'll do in the show today one more time."

Charlotte nodded, pressing her hands against the constricting bodice of her costume.

"Is that her?" the woman in gold whispered, glaring at Charlotte. One of the Sisters nodded.

"Don't be sore at her, Sasha. She ain't got nothin' to do with Hugh. She wasn't even here when he moved you."

"Seems fishy that she showed up out of the blue, though, don't it?" The woman shot one last disdainful glance backward at Charlotte before turning back and walking with the Sahara Sisters toward the dressing tent.

Just past the women, Charlotte caught a glimpse of a beaded scarf headed in the other direction.

Madame Rusalka.

She followed the scarf as it disappeared into the crowd of performers and workers, listening for the jingling of Rusalka's bracelet bangles. Where was Printesa? The edge of the scarf disappeared behind a red and white striped tent.

Charlotte ducked inside, noticing the scent of woodsy spice that was quickly replaced by a leathery smell that reminded her of her father. She was standing in front of a row of majestic white horses, each being brushed and saddled for the show. She approached the first horse and ran her hand along his sleek nose.

"That's Pegasus." A scrawny man with dark skin and tufts of scraggly white hair handed a wooden brush to Charlotte.

"Hello, Pegasus," she said, running the brush down the horse's neck and over his shoulders, which shuddered under the bristles. Pegasus lifted his front hoof and tapped at the dirt before him.

"You been around horses, ain't you," the man asked her with a lift of one of his bushy white eyebrows.

"All my life," she answered. "This one seems special." Pegasus lowered his head and bumped Charlotte with his nose.

"I'd agree with that," the man said. "Pegasus done come from a ranch that was 'bout ready ta shoot 'im on account-a he ain't submitted to 'em. Here, though, Pegasus is the star o' the show."

"Shoot him? That's criminal! Thank goodness he got away from those awful people and made it here to the circus where we care for him properly. He doesn't look like trouble to me."

"He ain't no trouble with me 'cause I knows one thang about horses; you can't try to own 'em. Can't never really own nor break a stallion. It's a contract, see. He's here 'cause he wants to be here. I respect him and he respects me. Soon as that respect ain't there, yous gonna have problems. That's why some of those men just shoot 'em; they ain't got the patience or the know-how and they sure ain't got respect."

"My father always said that a horse is a good judge

of character," Charlotte said, still looking into the eyes of the horse. "You must have good character for such a beautiful horse to trust you."

"Why, thank you, miss." The man studied her feathers and sequins for a moment. "You in an act?"

"Yes," she said. "The Sahara Sisters."

The man drew in a whistle. "You in da wrong tent, miss!"

"You're right." Charlotte chuckled. "These horses don't have stripes."

His fluffy eyebrows bunched together, and he scratched his head under his hat.

"I like them better that way," Charlotte whispered to the horse. "Horses without stripes are the best kind of horses."

The man shrugged and readjusted his hat before moving on to secure the saddle of the next horse. Charlotte handed him the brush and gave Pegasus one last scratch behind the ear. But as she went to leave, hushed voices outside the tent caught her attention.

Frank stood with his back to Charlotte, deep in conversation with someone in starched jeans and a cowboy hat. The man was small and tan, wiry looking with stark black hair poking out from under his cowboy hat and tired brown eyes. He pulled a box of sugar cubes for the horses from his starched shirt pocket.

Well, that's a good idea. I should try giving those to the zebras.

"*Es no bueno*, Frankie. I can't change the show with you again. Señor Sterling told me he wanted us to go back to how we did things before the girl died." The man crossed himself and shook his head solemnly. "I don't want no more death on my hands."

"I am Señor Sterling too, and you'll need to listen to me just as much as to my father." The intensity in his tone was matched by his posture.

"Well, with respect, not yet." The little man stood staunchly in the shadow of Frank's hovering frame.

Charlotte couldn't see Frank's face, but she imagined it was growing red when the hands on his hips balled up into a fist. She tiptoed around the side of the tent and hurried out of the shadow it cast toward the middle of the circus grounds.

She had hoped she'd be able to tell where the school tent was without asking, but standing in the swirl of preparation, everything around her looked equally unrecognizable. She stopped a young man from among the meandering crew and asked for directions, trying to hide her amusement at the formal way he spoke to her when he took off his newsboy cap and swept it through the air to the west, indicating a series of tents past the cookhouse.

The smiles and nods of approval from strangers who crossed her path on the way, along with the heavy shadow that accompanied every blink of her newly painted lashes, served as a reminder of her new appearance. Charlotte found herself gliding more gracefully toward the school tent despite the stiffness in her legs from the ride. A new sense of freedom fueled her, and she tipped her chin up and took longer strides in an effort to be the kind of woman who could embody the beauty of the jeweled bodice and soft sheer fabric that danced alongside her when she walked.

The school tent looked like a circus act from the outside, but the inside of the tent felt just like the schoolroom that Alex had been learning in before. Not the makeshift version that Charlotte had imagined at all. Another unexpected sight met her eyes, and the glance was enough to make her heart leap. Jay was in the tent, speaking with a woman by a large chalkboard on wheels. She tore her eyes from the sight of him, reminding herself that she was there to find her son. In the front of the class, she found him. Alex was alternately engaged in conversation with the children around him and eagerly drawing in his sketchbook. He looked just as happy as she'd hoped he would be. Charlotte let out a sigh of relief.

The woman speaking to Jay called out to her, "You must be Alex's mom!"

Charlotte smiled as Jay and Alex both turned around at the same time. Jay's eyes widened and his jaw dropped, though whether he felt it was a good surprise, she couldn't tell. She managed a shy wave and was rewarded with a reassuring smile.

Alex jumped up and ran over to her. "Mom! What's...? Is this your new waitress uniform?"

Charlotte laughed and hugged her son. "You'll never believe it! I'm not working at the cookhouse anymore. They've asked me to be in an act! I ride a zebra!"

Alex's excitement was matched by his surprise.

Charlotte laughed. "I've been dying to hear about how you're doing! Are you enjoying school?"

As Alex told her about his new classmates, and how much the teacher loved science, she stopped her gaze wandering to the figures behind him. She told Alex all about the zebras and the parade and felt a sense of pride to see that her son seemed excited about their new adventure.

"Alex, it may be a few days, maybe a few weeks, that we travel with the circus. Now that I'm...is that okay? Will you be okay?"

Alex took her hand and smiled. "I'm having fun, Mom!"

Relief and joy surged through Charlotte. She wiped at a runaway tear, hoping it didn't ruin the makeup Mei had so carefully applied. Jay was watching the two of them, and she felt embarrassed that he'd seen her cry for the second time in one day when, before this, she couldn't remember the last time she'd allowed herself to cry.

"But you won't have anything to do with the cannon, will you?" Alex asked.

"No, no," she said, "I'll follow the Sahara Sisters on a zebra and keep the animals under control while they perform stunts in the center ring, since I'm unable to do any of those kinds of things—"

"Good," Alex said, leaning in. "Because I don't want you to have anything to do with the cannon."

"The cannon? Why?"

"I think something is going on," Alex whispered.

"What do you mean?"

"Kip, that boy I was working with for a little bit...he told me he found a gun last night. A pistol. He gave it to Jay—that man over there."

Charlotte quickly glanced at Jay and returned her attention to her son.

"Jay told him not to tell anybody about it. And he was asking Kip a lot of questions about where exactly he found it when we went to the big tent."

"When you went to the big tent?"

"Alex, is this your mother?" A little girl with

blonde pigtails in a gingham dress skipped over to Alex and Charlotte.

Alex rolled his eyes. "Mom, this is Sadie."

"Sadie." Charlotte smiled, seeing something of Jay's gray eyes in the little girl as she shook her outstretched hand. "So nice to meet you. I am Alex's mother, but you can call me Lottie." Charlotte went to kneel to speak to her eye to eye, but her stiff thighs were a throbbing reminder that she'd better stay upright if she didn't want to fall over.

"Alex doesn't know how to play poker," the little girl said matter-of-factly.

Alex crossed his arms and looked away.

"Well, it's our first day with the circus, and there's been no one brave enough to teach him." Charlotte lowered her voice. "I heard you're very good at poker."

"I am." Sadie lifted her chin proudly. "I can teach him, if you'd like."

"There are a lot more important things to learn about than how to play cards with old clowns," Alex grumbled.

"All Alex seems to care about is science," Sadie said, still speaking to Charlotte. "I suppose he's not introduced you to our teacher yet. Would you like to meet Mrs. Brooks?"

Charlotte suppressed a giggle. "That would be delightful, Sadie."

"Very well, follow me." Sadie confidently led Charlotte and Alex to the front of the classroom where Jay was speaking with the teacher.

"Daddy, Mrs. Brooks, this is—"

"Lottie Cameron." The woman stepped forward to shake Charlotte's hand. "Yes, I've heard a lot about you."

"Oh, I…"

"I told her how we build Leyden jars at home," Alex said, "and she says we have all the supplies here that we need to make more! She said Mr. Edwards is going to help us. To get the supplies."

"That's kind of him." Charlotte looked up at Jay from under her heavy lashes when she spoke.

"Not at all," Jay said, his eyes sparkling.

Mrs. Brooks seemed entertained. "You've met Mr. Edwards, I presume."

"I have." Charlotte smiled. "He was so kind to help Alex and make sure he found his way here."

Charlotte placed her hand on her stomach as she looked up at Jay, finding it difficult to catch her breath under the constricting corset. As he stared into her eyes again, this time she was bold enough to hold his gaze instead of looking away.

"I'm so glad he did!" Mrs. Brooks said, breaking the silence. "Your son is such a smart boy, and a quick study! I'm so pleased he'll be learning with us."

"Thank you, Mrs. Brooks."

"Call me Pearl."

Charlotte tore her gaze away from Jay and looked at Pearl for the first time. The woman's smooth voice and gentle manner reminded her of Martha, and for a moment, she missed home. "Pearl," Charlotte said, "you can't know how much it means to me that you're teaching my son. I'm so grateful."

Pearl smiled. "It's a pleasure to have him. My children are here too." She waved at a pair of smiling children. "But you two better hurry on out of here! Y'all need to get ready for the matinée!"

Jay jumped and reached for his pocket watch.

"Don't worry about Sadie and Alex. They're doing great. We've already eaten lunch, and we'll all be at the show in a little while. You can come check in with me after."

"Okay." Charlotte hesitated. "Alex, I'll see you—"

But Alex gave her a quick hug and returned to the table with his new friends.

"Did we just get kicked out of school?" Charlotte asked Jay as they left the school tent.

"You know what, I think we did." The sparkle hadn't left his eye.

"Thank you for taking care of my son," she said. "He looks so happy. I...thank you."

"He's a smart boy. I can see why it's so important to you that he keeps learning."

Charlotte smiled, grateful to be understood.

"And anyway, I think it's good for Sadie to spend time with a kid who likes learning. Her mother always told me she hated school. None of the schools or tutors were ever good enough...but Vanessa, my ex-wife, she always had an angle. She was never telling the whole truth..." Jay looked back at the school tent. "If you don't have the truth, you don't have anything, you know?"

Charlotte bit her lip.

"Well, thank goodness Sadie's mother is out of the picture now. I'm just happy to see that she's able to settle in with Pearl."

I should tell him the truth about Pete. "Your daughter is adorable," she said instead, "and she seems very adaptable."

"Thank you." A charming crinkle formed at the

corners of his eyes when he smiled. "It sounds like she's going to make sure that Alex has a well-rounded education."

When their shared laughter subsided, the silence was not an absence of speech but instead charged with more conversation than could take place in a few paces.

Jay finally settled on a statement. "So it looks like you made the act."

Charlotte blushed. "Oh, yes. Well, they didn't have many other options, I think. But I…"

Jay stopped walking to focus on listening to her. One pair of eyes made her more nervous than a whole city crowded along the sidewalks. His attention obliterated her train of thought.

"You look…"

Charlotte was anxious to hear Jay finish his sentence, but he trailed off, raising his gaze to something behind her.

She turned. Hugh was fiddling with a rolling cart or trailer. When she turned again, Jay's eyes met hers as if they'd been waiting for her.

"You look—"

"Ridiculous, I-I know," she cut in. "Birdie was adamant about this costume, and Mei and the girls swarmed around me with their brushes and powders and paints…They couldn't believe I didn't know how to apply mascara or rouge, but—"

"You don't look ridiculous. You—" He took his hand out of his pocket and reached toward her face.

Her heart was racing before his fingers landed in her hair. A tingling sensation ran up the back of her neck as his fingers combed through the strands at the bottom of the ponytail, and her shoulder shuddered beneath it involuntarily. She looked up at his face, her eyes following the strong lines of his jaw and smooth curves of his lips.

"You...you had some hay in your hair," he said, holding up a broken golden straw before tossing it on the ground.

Emotions ranging from excitement to embarrassment rushed through Charlotte as Jay put his hand back in his pocket and continued looking at something behind her.

"Speaking of guys you can't trust," he said, looking at Hugh. "I never know what he's up to anymore."

Charlotte hesitated. "Jay, I think I should tell you something."

Jay returned his attention to her.

"I...I found something. Maybe it's nothing. But Alex told me..."

"What did Alex tell you?" Jay asked sharply.

"He told me that he thinks you suspect the cannon accident...wasn't an accident."

Jay's posture straightened, and his voice took on a different tone. "Lottie, it's my responsibility to ensure safety and efficiency of—"

"No, no," she said, "I don't mean to...well, I-I..."

Charlotte reached into the bosom of her costume to retrieve the folded sheet of paper she'd stashed there. Jay's cheeks reddened when his eyes followed her fingers.

"I'm not sure what it means," she said, handing him the note, "but I found this in Birdie's trailer. Wh-when I was changing. I don't know what you think happened, but if it helps you...I...I want to help you."

She looked up at him, waiting for an answer.

Jay unfolded and examined the note. He slowly folded it back up, took out his black book, and tucked it between the pages. He stared at his book for a long moment before turning his attention to Charlotte.

"Well," he said, "for the second time today, I'm going to share thoughts with you that I haven't uttered out loud to anyone else."

Chapter 26

Left Pistol, Left Eye

Pete sighed with disappointment as he rolled the car to a stop in front of his little house in Ayer and surveyed the overrun garden. The neighboring gardens to either side were carefully weeded and organized. Beautiful displays of perfect order. His looked like it hadn't even been tended to.

Charlotte's too busy with that damn job. I'll talk to her about it tonight.

Pete had thought a lot about Charlotte while he'd been away in Fort Worth. What to do with her. He didn't like the way she'd been acting up lately. Talking back. Didn't like the way she thought she could make decisions about what was best for his son without him.

As he walked up the drive and opened the door, Pete decided there were a lot of things he'd be talking about to Charlotte that night.

"Time to get things back in order around here," he growled under his breath as he kicked a small tumbleweed from his path and marched up to the porch.

The inside was even more disheveled than the outside. He wrinkled his nose at the smell of staleness as he set his cowboy hat on the chair by the door and squinted through the dusty rays of light that broke in through the windows.

God, she really just cannot manage without me. Pete turned on the light and walked over to the sink.

Something wasn't right. The breakfast plates. He'd set them there for Charlotte to wash before he left for Fort Worth. Weeks ago.

The familiar thought returned to him then, that look in Charlotte's eyes at the circus after the murder, fear at the sight of the dead cannon girl.

Of course, she'd be afraid. She'd never seen anything like that before. She'd often tear up when he'd talk about shooting a horse, for crying out loud. When she took Alex and ran, he'd decided she was trying to protect their son. Bring him home.

But as he looked around at the dusty house, he wondered now. Was that look of shock from the sight of the dead girl, or was it something else? Pete's left eye started twitching.

He put his cowboy hat back on and walked out the door to the car.

****

The Winslow Inn & Cookhouse was full of people as usual, and there was no place for Pete to sit where he wouldn't have to make conversation with some godforsaken farmer or a ranch hand from Rex's place. He didn't have the time or the patience for that today.

He plowed directly through the tables and pushed through the swinging doors of the kitchen. He spotted Saul and Martha immediately.

"Where's my wife?"

Martha turned around, looking surprised, and mumbled something about Charlotte bein' gone. Pete looked away from her to Saul. He didn't give a damn what that woman had to say.

"I said, where's my wife, dammit!"

"Calm down, Pete," Saul said with an air of authority that set his teeth on edge. "It's just as Martha said. She ain't here. Let's sit down, and we'll get you a cup of coffee and some pancakes."

Pete looked around the kitchen and back at Martha. Covered in flour and a stack of dirty dishes a mile high by the sink. *It's no wonder Charlotte doesn't keep a clean house. Look at where she's at all day.*

"I don't want pancakes. I don't want coffee. I want to talk to my wife. I know she ain't at home, so where is she? She up in one of your rooms?"

"Pete, we haven't seen Lottie for weeks," the woman said. She sneaked a glance at her husband.

"But you know where she is."

"Listen, if Lottie—"

"Charlotte. Her name is Charlotte. Did she take my son with her?"

"No, you listen!" the woman said again. "If Lottie—"

Pete's jaw clenched, a slow pain spreading from the bottom of his ears to the top of his spine.

"We have not seen Charlotte or Alex," Saul cut in.

Pete's left eye fluttered open and closed again without his permission. How dare these people speak to him this way. How dare that woman—

"You need to get a handle on your wife." Pete turned toward the woman and pointed at her with a strong intimidating finger. "And you need to mind how you talk to me, you negro heifer."

But behind her on the counter, sitting between two cups of coffee, was a railroad map and a letter. Maybe a postcard. His left eye twitched again, and he turned back to Martha, who'd taken a step toward him.

"I think it's time for you to go, Pete," Saul said, folding up the map and tucking it in his pocket along with the letter.

"If I find out y'all are hiding my wife and my son, I'll sue," Pete said. "That's my property. Y'all don't have the right."

Pete walked through the kitchen toward the back door, looking for anything else that might give him a clue as to where Charlotte was.

"I'm friends with the sheriff," he said without looking at them. "I'll have him search this whole place top to bottom. Trust me, whether or not he finds my wife, he can find somethin' to hang you on. I'll have them return this building to the city or sell it to a white man for half the price you bought it for. Hell, maybe I'll buy it."

"Pete," the woman said.

He turned around to enjoy the fear in her eyes but instead saw a defiant glint that made him want to wring her neck.

"I hope you never see Charlotte or Alex again," she said. "You don't deserve 'em."

Pete's eye was twitching, but his hands were steady as he reached for his pistol. He'd learned that in the war, steady hands. Pete stopped before his hand hit his hip, remembering. He wasn't that good a friend with the sheriff. He reached instead for the counter, swept the dirty dishes onto the floor, and enjoyed almost instant relief as the ceramic shattered and scattered all over the dirty black and white tile floor. The twitching in his eye melted away, and his face spread into a smile as Saul and Martha took in the mess with a mixture of shock and anger.

Good, they'll have to pay for that at least. Pete took a satisfied breath in and let out a long whistle before turning back to the door. He made sure to shut it with a slam that would rattle the crummy little kitchen walls and hopefully the worthless Winslows within them.

Pete stomped down Main Street toward the sheriff's office, using every ounce of strength he had to maintain the façade of calm control.

He spotted the general store on the way and decided to make a stop there first.

The ding of the bell with the opening of the door rattled Pete's nerves. Every store seemed to have some annoying gimmick for announcing his arrival these days.

"Well, good mornin', Mr. Baxter," Bill said, pushing up his spectacles as he sorted through the mail behind the counter. "Haven't seen you in a while."

"Just got back from Fort Worth."

"Ah, off on business for ol' Rex again, huh. Well, I've got your mail here if you want it."

A thought occurred to Pete. "So Charlotte hasn't been in to get it, then?"

Bill stood up a little taller.

"Well, no, she has not," Bill said, setting down the stack of letters he'd been holding. "But again, I haven't seen her since she double-crossed me at the cookhouse, have I? Not since I turned her out of here."

"Tell me more."

"What's there to tell? She used her little charms on those fancy circus boys and seduced them into buying everything from Saul Winslow when they'd already made a contract with me. It's downright disgraceful."

"Fancy circus boys?"

"That's right, and I told her not to show her face in my store, and of course, she hasn't." Bill's smug smile crawled into a concerned purse of the lips. "Of course, that don't affect you, now. It ain't your fault your wife was outta line."

"Outta line," Pete snarled. His hand hovered just above the pistol on his hip that was calling to him.

"Not your fault at all. You can have anything you want," Bill squeaked. "On the house. What can I get for you?"

"Well, I need a drink," Pete said, "but I could settle for some tobacco."

Bill scuttled across the counter and began scooping tobacco into wax paper out of a glass jar.

"An' I'll take my mail," he added.

"Yes, yes." Bill's hands were shaking when he handed Pete the tobacco. "Here you are."

Bill gathered a stack of books, a few letters, and a parcel. Pete squinted at them as he shoved a wad of tobacco in his lip.

"What the hell is that?"

"It's those books she ordered for Alex. Looks like—"

But he shoved the parcels and books back across the counter at the silly little man before he could finish and stormed out of the store.

As Pete made his way to the sheriff's office to inquire about his wife, he mulled over what that little squirrel of a man had uttered to him at the general store. She'd been the one feeding Alex those garbage books. No wonder. Pete stopped.

There was no way she'd be clever enough to find the box, would she? No way she'd be that defiant.

Outta line.

Seducing circus men?

His eye started twitching again.

Pete turned back the way he came and quickened his pace to the car, squealing off toward home with one purpose. The image of the box beneath the boards burning in his mind.

Chapter 27

Leche y Manteca

"Well, what do you think, Sadie?" Jay squeezed his daughter's hand. "Was this a good parade?"

"It was pretty good. There are a lot of people here."

"You're right. It is a pretty good turnout." Jay kept his eye on the procession until the last Sahara Sister was out of sight and then looked down at Sadie, smiling.

"The parade is my new favorite part of the circus. I like watching it with you."

"I enjoy it too, Sadie-bug. You know what?"

"What, Daddy?"

"This might be the most enjoyable travel season I've ever experienced." *Despite the murders, accidents, and small fiascos.* "And you have a lot to do with that. I'm glad you came along with me this time."

"Me too. I wanna come with you all the time." Sadie looked up at her father. "Which city is this?"

"Pecos."

"It's too hot in Pecos. I like San Angelo better."

"That didn't have anything to do with that fancy toy store on Concho Avenue, did it?"

"Maybe..." She hugged the stuffed rabbit that had been among the many things she'd convinced her father to buy there. "You liked the candy sticks too, Daddy," she reminded him.

"That I did," he admitted as he checked his pocket watch. "Ready to head back?"

"Why do we never watch the end of the parade?" Sadie asked.

"Well, the best part is over, isn't it?" He looked over the top of the crowd. Benny was already waiting for them at the car. He'd asked him to follow Hugh again today, and he was anxious to hear what he might have discovered.

"Maybe we should invite Alex to come with us next time," Sadie said, looking up at her father, "so he can watch Lottie too."

Jay stopped and looked down at his daughter. "I don't know what you're talking about."

"Hey, you two!" Benny shouted as they reached the car. "Think we can convince your dad to buy us a sandwich, Sadie? I know just the place." He looked up at Jay meaningfully.

"I like sandwiches! Can we go, Daddy?"

"Sure thing, Sadie-bug." Jay pulled his black book and newspaper from his pocket, grimacing at the sweat beneath them. "Lead the way, Benny."

Sadie skipped along rattling wood boards with her stuffed bunny as Jay and Benny discussed the day's deliveries and the price of supplies in each city so far. Jay pointed out a few local events in the paper to Benny, and the two discussed the profits from 1926 and what they hoped to see this year.

"Pecos is a longer distance than the other cities"— Jay pointed to the notes in his book—"so we've got to make up the cost of fuel, but it's worth it to stay out of the Ringling Brothers' way. We don't want to get too close to their route or we'll have to deal with Verne."

Benny shuddered. "Is that guy still on their payroll? He was the only soldier in the AEF. that scared me more than the Germans."

"He is, but our deal still stands."

"Stay out of their way and they'll leave us alone?"

"Yep." Jay fanned himself with the newspaper. "And so we need to squeeze a profit out of Pecos."

"Plenty of people come out for that rodeo they have here, don't they?" Benny asked. "I bet we get the same crowd for the circus."

"Maybe, but our horse show really disappoints."

"We'll have to rely on Birdie to draw the crowds, then," Benny said.

Jay nodded. "Did the advance guys get everything wrapped up before they headed out for Clovis this morning?"

"They did," Benny said. "That reminds me, one of the books you ordered is in the car. Something about electricity. One of the boys brought it by before they left."

"Oh, thank you," Jay said.

"So you're reading about electricity now? In all your free time?"

"It's for Alex."

Benny raised an eyebrow.

"I like the kid. He's smart."

"Just the kid, huh?" Benny and Sadie exchanged sly smiles. "So that's why you have breakfast with his mom every day?"

Jay ignored his question. "You know Alex said he was halfway through that book and his father just threw it in the fire."

"I thought his dad was dead?"

"Well, I guess this happened before he died, obviously."

They walked under the balconies of a few two-story buildings that resembled lawless Wild West saloons, accentuated by the air vibrating in the blazing heat. Benny leaned in and pointed to a building at the end of the block.

"This is the place I saw Hugh sneak off to today," he whispered. "Our friend doubled around the back with one of our supply wagons and a few guys. I didn't see what he did after that, but I bet if we do some pokin' around…"

"Right." Jay nodded. "I'd like to have some evidence before I talk to Sonny."

The two walked up to a small sandwich shop with "Mobley Cafe" written in black and gold letters arching over the door. Benny pulled open the door, and the trio walked inside to the sound of a gently ringing bell and chose a round table near the window. Jay pulled out a chair for Sadie and sat opposite, with his back to the brick wall and eye on the door.

A waiter approached the table and filled the empty glasses with welcome ice water that Jay downed in one gulp before asking to use the phone.

"Of course, sir," the waiter answered. "It's in the back. I can show you to it."

"You think you two could hold down the fort while I step out for a moment?" Jay asked them.

"Daddy calls some man every day," Sadie whispered to Benny as she propped up her bunny at the table and set one of the empty cups in front of it.

"Me, Sadie, and bunny here will get you something

to eat." Benny winked at Sadie. "You go make your phone call."

Jay left his jacket on the chair and followed the waiter to the back of the shop where the telephone was mounted on the wall near the bathrooms. He thanked him and picked up the receiver, his other hand poised near the rotating wheel as if ready to dial. He waited until the man disappeared through the swinging doors of the kitchen. He replaced the receiver quietly and headed in the other direction, past peeling maroon and gold-striped wallpaper and dimly lit brass sconces, to a door at the end of the hallway. He moved a dusty valance to the side of the door window to reveal an empty brick alley.

There was no supply wagon, so if Hugh and his guys had been there, they were long gone now. Jay turned his attention to the wall on his right where the wallpaper wasn't peeling and the sconce wasn't lit. He twisted at the bulb in an attempt to test the light and looked down the hallway at the distribution of the doors.

"Three on that side…There should be a door or another hallway here," he mumbled to himself. Running his hand along the wall, he felt a seam where the wallpaper split and pulled at the dud sconce to find that an entire section of the wall swung out as a door. The kitchen doors at the end of the hall sat still. No one was watching. Jay stepped into the space beyond the newfound door and pulled it in behind him.

Jay went to take a step forward in the darkness, and his insides lurched when his foot had nothing beneath it to fall on. Regaining his balance, he placed his hand along the wall and tested the space below to find a stairway beneath his feet. He expected the hard concrete of cellar stairs, but instead soft carpet absorbed his steps.

Carefully, as his eyes adjusted to the dark, he descended. Jay's nostrils tickled with the dank moisture of an old cellar. Jay took another unfortunate breath in when he reached the bottom. *What is that awful stench?* He fumbled along the wall for a light switch and found one.

As an image of the room flickered beneath the dim light that shuddered to life, Jay reconciled the smell with the image before him. Sweat, salt, and sour booze.

Jay was standing in a makeshift speakeasy.

It had the stark eeriness of a room that looked out of place when fully lit and not swarming with people. To his left, a poorly made platform, scuffed and splintering, encircled in black tasseled cloth, served as a stage. The walls were covered in fabric that had weathered splatters of all kinds. In the light, rats and cockroaches scattered to their hiding places, awaiting the spills and crumbs that would inevitably form with the next round of visitors. Couches and chairs of every color clustered around chipped marble tables stained with berry-colored rings beneath crystal ashtrays, half-burned candles, and collected drips of wax.

Jay scanned the perimeter of the room and saw what he was looking for behind the bar. A stack of crates.

He crossed an ornate throw rug past sagging velvet couches and stepped behind the bar to examine the wooden crates. He opened one stenciled with LECHE on the side, but of course, he didn't find milk inside. Instead, there were rows of glass bottles full of amber liquid packed in straw. Jay stepped over a scampering cockroach to pry open another crate with the label MANTECA and found a similar setup. Beneath the muffled scraping of chairs and the distant sound of the dinging bell on the door above him, he continued sorting through the crates until he came to one that confirmed his suspicions. Stenciled on the top of the last crate was *Property of Sterling & Son's* in black with a stamp on the side that said FRAGILE. Inside was a similar row of glass bottles full of amber liquid. Jay pulled a stale cork from the bottle, and his suspicions were instantly confirmed. Whiskey.

Jay restacked the crates and crossed the room back to the stairs. He focused on the door and made a mental image of the steps in front of him, counting them before turning off the light. Jay placed his hand on the grimy railing and paused at the sound of footsteps and muffled voices above him outside the cellar door. He lifted his foot to take a quiet first step and cringed at the loud *scrick* of his shoe peeling from the sticky floor. He froze with his foot in midair, peering at the cracks of light around the door frame and bracing himself for a confrontation.

As he crept closer, he could hear the voices more clearly.

"Tell Jack when he takes deliveries down there, he's gotta close the door all the way." With a thud, the door closed completely, eliminating the last trickle of light from the stairway. "What happens when some copper comes poking around, eh?"

Jay crept closer to the door, hand balled into a ready fist. The grind of singing steel signaled the back door opening.

Jay waited for the clunk of the heavy metal door resting back in its frame before pressing the opening of the wall. He poked his head out to make sure the hallway was empty again before slipping out and pushing the door behind him back into place securely. He dusted at his white shirt, sticky with sweat and filth from the cellar, and walked briskly back to the phone.

****

"Sheriff figured out the answers to all your questions," Saul's voice informed him through the receiver. "First off, yes. The bullet matched the gun you brought us."

"I expected that it might," Jay said, keeping his eye on the kitchen doors. "And the girl, did the sheriff find out more about who she was?"

"Matter of fact he did," Saul said. "There was a lot more on the name Hazel Beauford. He called a buddy of his from the police department up near Fort Worth and found out she was one of a group of coochie dancers who'd get paid to bring chumps to a joint out there that ended up getting shut down on a Volstead violation."

"So she led guys to a speakeasy," Jay concluded. "What was she arrested for?"

"He said she did time for prostitution, and she was involved with a nasty group of rumrunners from Mexico."

"Does he think she was still involved with them when she died?"

"He acted like he thought she was. He said they never caught the guys she was runnin' with." Saul paused. "I gotta tell ya, Martha ain't real happy that we've got a dead prostitute in our ice house. I bet you could hear her hollerin' clear to Mexico when she went in there to get some bacon and—"

"Keep her on ice for a few more days, Saul," Jay said, rubbing at the grime on his fingers from his underground discovery. "I think I've got your murderer."

Chapter 28

Lipstick

"Ladies and gentlemen, the Sisters of the Sahara!"

"That's our cue," Mei said, leading the line of girls out into the center ring. Charlotte took in a deep breath and clicked at her zebra to follow, slipping him a sugar cube from a cloth pouch she'd fastened to her hip beneath the feathers. She'd learned over the past few days that her zebra would do just about anything if she gave him a sugar cube. So each morning at breakfast, before she sat down to have coffee with Jay, she'd ask Chuck to supply her with a few handfuls to get through the shows.

"Five princesses from the faraway desert, riding zebras from their palace. Here, tonight, for your entertainment!" Frank shouted, his extravagant showman's voice booming.

Charlotte waved gracefully at the cheering crowd as they cantered past, her zebra behaving well beneath her. Under the bright cannon lights that followed her, she couldn't make out any faces specifically, but she hoped Chuck had brought Alex to watch, and that he was smiling and clapping too.

As the riders before her dismounted and began to wrap themselves in the draping cloths that hung from the scaffolding for their aerialist acrobatics, Charlotte hopped down too and walked along the zebras to keep them in line while the other Sahara Sisters performed. The women ran in swift circles before being raised in the air by the fabric, sweeping above the audience with outstretched arms.

Wobbling a little in her heels, Charlotte missed the steady comfort of her boots more than ever. But she made sure to do her best to walk gracefully, extending her arms and making a show of the zebras as she'd been instructed by Mei and reminded by Frank.

Charlotte raised her arm in an exaggerated gesture to pet one of the zebra's noses with the back of her hand. Each pair of Sahara Sisters clasped hands in the air and twirled down in a circle toward the ground, hands held in the center and toes extended out horizontally while wrapped in the cloth.

She snuck a cube of sugar from her pouch to each of the zebras to keep them happy while the girls were twirling and cascading through the air in dizzying circles. She remembered her conversation with Jay at breakfast that morning. "Whoever it was, they shot Hazel right in the top of her head while she was loaded inside that cannon," he had said. "They did it with the whole crowd of people watching, innocent people behind the cannon who could have been hit. And they knew exactly when to pop that shot off so that no one would blink an eye when they heard the gun go off." Jay seemed to suspect Hugh after he'd found evidence that he'd been smuggling bathtub gin, wine, and moonshine at almost every stop along the circus route, but Charlotte wasn't so sure.

As she looked up through the swirling Sahara Sisters into scaffolding above, the only person she could see was Birdie, peering out before her with falcon-like focus, dusting her hands and adjusting her stockings in preparation for her act. Charlotte had done her utmost to avoid Birdie ever since she'd narrowly missed taking a glass of gin to the head in her trailer a few days ago. She still wasn't sure what she'd done to deserve that, but Jay didn't seem surprised when she'd told him about it.

"The other performers are scared to death of her. Truth be told, I think Frank is equal parts afraid and infatuated. He doesn't even know that she might have killed a man before."

"Killed a man?" Charlotte had let her coffee grow cold as she listened with interest.

"That's what Frank's fiancée claims. I called a detective she hired, and he confirmed that a person fitting Birdie's description may have committed a murder they looked into about ten years ago, although the police there didn't seem too keen on pursuing it further."

"Frank's fiancée? What a mess. I've got to be honest, I wouldn't put it past Birdie to shoot somebody. It doesn't seem to take much to make her furious to the point of fits."

"You might be right," Jay conceded. "It's worth looking into. I've got a few other things to check on in town first, though."

Charlotte never got a chance to ask Jay what it was he thought he would find in town, but knowing she could ask him about it at breakfast the next day gave her something to look forward to. She was beginning to feel safer and more at home on the train that carried them farther from Ayer. Her new greatest fear was running out of things to talk about with Jay, as if a lack of conversation would stifle this new spark that kept her up at night, yet still woke her up energized each morning.

Charlotte peeled her focus from Birdie and back to the act in front of her. The glittering purple tornado touched down, and the Sisters rose up with their arms extended to the cheers of the crowd while the crew silently and swiftly moved to pull the cloth away. Charlotte went back to her zebra and hopped on in unison with the Sisters, and the performers trotted the trail out of the center ring, still waving and smiling as the lights swung away from them.

"And now, in the center ring, witness the magnificent mistress of the trapeze with her extraordinary death-defying leaps and contortions! Birdie Bells! Watch her fly!"

The light swung onto Birdie, and she bounded out into the open air before her, no net below, catching the trapeze bar.

"The murderer had to know the show intricately," Jay had said, "and they'd have to be heartless, and determined, and bold."

Birdie whipped around in circle after circle before dangling from the trapeze bar precariously by the ankle. Heartless, determined, and bold. Charlotte felt certain she was looking at a murderer.

****

"Pack up, pack up!" a stage man shouted as the girls exited the big tent. Performers hastily moved toward the dressing trailers to pack away their costumes and get the carts ready for load-out.

Charlotte's zebra nuzzled her shoulder. "All right,

Whiskey, one more." She snuck him another cube of sugar and scratched the back of his ear. "You earned it."

"Whiskey?" the menagerie man asked as he took the reins. "Who the heck is that?" It was the same man who had introduced her to the beautiful white horse, Pegasus.

"Well, this guy right here!" Charlotte patted the zebra's head. "I thought we'd get along better if he had a name, and that was the name of my father's old horse."

"Well, sure, name a horse," the man said, "but these dumb animals already have names. I call this one Dumbass and that one Move-it, and that one over there is—"

"Name the others what you want. This one is named Whiskey now," Charlotte said, slipping her zebra one last sugar cube.

"All right, Whiskey," he muttered, walking away. "Sure. Why not? What do I know? I tell you what, I could use some whiskey. These broads are bonkers. I never know what they're talkin' about…"

Charlotte hustled over to the dressing area where the other women were taking off their costumes and placing them on a rolling rack for the crew to pack away.

The women were laughing as they undressed, lighting one another's cigarettes and congratulating each other on another great show. Charlotte wasn't alone in feeling like she might not make it through each day. Part of the magic of the circus for every Sterling & Son's performer was that each show survived was a death-defying miracle worth celebrating.

If only they knew there was a murderer among them. She found a chair to collapse into, kicked off her pinching shoes, and began undoing her buttons.

"Good show, greenie," the girl next to her said as she unhooked her own costume and flung it on the cart. The girl didn't have any undergarments beneath her costume, and Charlotte blushed at the sight of her bare breasts.

"Thank you," she said meekly, intently studying her own toes.

Mei and Sasha approached, each with a glass bottle in hand, and Mei with an armful of fabric.

"Oh my God, yes! I need a drink!" the girl said, arching her naked back against the chair with a loud sigh and reaching her arms out toward Mei and Sasha.

Sasha laughed and handed her one of the bottles. "Put those away, Ada. You're scaring the new girl."

Mei flung some clothing at Charlotte. "Here ya go, toots. I rustled up some clothes for you. Birdie says you're not allowed to wear that brown dress anymore. She told me to burn it."

"Thank you." Charlotte slid the purple robe Birdie had given her over her costume. The women exchanged glances as she squirmed out of the leotard while holding the robe closed.

"You could afford to loosen up a little, Miss Priss!" Ada leaned forward and flung Charlotte's robe open.

Charlotte gasped and pulled the robe closed. The girl laughed.

"Cut her some slack, Ada. She ain't a trouper," Mei said.

"It ain't no sin she don't want everyone on the lot seein' her breasts," Sasha joined in.

Ada shook her chest at Sasha, who batted her away and took the gin bottle from her hand. Ada laughed and picked up a silk bra from her dressing trunk and fastened it around her. "There's plenty of people in and outta this tent who have seen yours, Sasha."

"Oh, shut up," Sasha said playfully.

"Why? I heard Frank thinks they're pretty nice."

Sasha's face went white. She waited a long moment before exhaling the smoke. "Knock it off with that noise before Birdie hears you," she warned. "She's been in some kinda mood lately, and I don't want her comin' after me."

Ada took out another cigarette. "So you think she knows, huh?"

"Birdie thinks it was just Hazel seein' Frank when it wasn't her, and I ain't fixin' to set her straight. We're all sticking with that, right?" Sasha glared at Charlotte and extended a cigarette and lighter.

Charlotte waved away the cigarette and pulled the robe off her shoulders. "I-I don't talk to Birdie unless I have to, so you don't have to worry about her hearing anything from me." She slipped the new dress over her head. "And anyway, I'm absolutely exhausted. I'm going to go meet up with Alex at the cookhouse and turn in."

"You're not sleeping in the cookhouse car again?" Mei asked in surprise.

Charlotte shrugged.

"The cookhouse car?" Ada exclaimed. "With the roustabouts and stowaways? Never! Sleep with us! We got an open bed!"

"My bed." Sasha rolled her eyes.

"Oh, stop, you got a better one. Lottie used to sleep

in a train car full of hay," Mei said to Sasha, "until Chuck found out and insisted they sleep in his car."

"Oh my God, sister." Ada laughed. "We're a whole lot more fun than a stack of hay! You're with us tonight."

"Oh, no, I couldn't…It wouldn't be right for Alex to—"

"We could get Alex settled with Jay's daughter," Mei remarked with a coy glimpse up at Charlotte as she dropped her cigarette in the dirt and snuffed it out. "He'd do anything for you."

"You don't mean Jay Edwards?" Sasha exchanged glances with Mei, who nodded. "I thought he was off limits!"

Ada gasped and pushed at Charlotte's shoulder. "Oh, kitten, good for you! I wouldn't mind takin' a bite out of him. What's he like?"

"It isn't like that," Lottie protested, sitting back primly in her chair and smoothing at the lap of her new lavender tea dress. It had a dropped waist with tiered ruffles down the sides, so much softer and silkier than the old colorless wool thing she'd been wearing that collected hay, dust, and cat hairs like a magnet.

"Oh, it's like that," Mei said. "You should see her lookin' for him in the crowd at that parade every day."

"So that's it," Sasha said. "I wondered how you got your spot in the act."

"No!" Charlotte objected. "Jay did introduce me to Frank, but—"

Sasha and Ada nodded at each other.

"There's no shame in it." Ada handed Charlotte a bottle of gin that now had three different colors of lipstick on the neck. "We all gotta get our start somehow. Hard work and talent only get you so far out here."

"She's right," Mei agreed, taking a new cigarette from Sasha and lighting it.

"Well, I got my spot with hard work and talent," Sasha said. "I was born into the circus life. Traveled as a ballet girl, trained on trapeze and every animal. I worked my ass off for years to get into an act like the Sahara Sisters.

"But then I make one mistake, and I'm on the damn cannon. After the two dead girls." Sasha took Mei's lighter and threw it on her dressing table, knocking over a perfume bottle and scattering brushes and face paints. She fell into the chair in front of her dressing table and flicked the ashes off her cigarette into the sawdust.

Ada leaned over to place a hand on Sasha's leg. "You're a star, Sasha. A real professional! You ain't gonna end up like them."

"What do you mean, one mistake?" Charlotte asked, searching in the pile of clothes for a pair of gloves and a hat.

"She spilled a drink on Hugh Sterling at a party," Mei said. "It wasn't even her fault really, but he had one of his hissy fits and—"

"But I thought it was Birdie who put you in that act and—"

"Birdie put her in what act?" a shrill voice cut in.

The girls stopped giggling and chatting, and all heads turned to the open tent flap to see a glistening muscle man in a striped tank top holding a large trunk that reminded Charlotte of a treasure chest from one of the pirate stories she'd read to Alex.

A wisp of fiery red hair flashed behind him, and the voice continued, "What the hell are you chickens clucking about now?"

The man set the trunk down between the dressing tables. Birdie followed, wild red hair falling in curls over the straps of her glittering costume. She took the bottle of gin from Sasha's hand, holding it longer than she needed to and serving her with a long hard look before tossing the bottle back for a drink herself. She brought the bottle down and wiped at her mouth with the back of her arm, glaring at the man who stood staring at her after he'd put the trunk down.

"Shoo!" She lifted the bottle toward the man and pointed it toward the tent opening.

The man rolled his eyes as he walked past Birdie. Ada stood up and leaned against a chair in his path, biting her bottom lip and batting her eyelashes at him. The man sidestepped her and paused for a moment when she pinched his butt, slowly turning to look at her before stepping purposefully onward.

"Lottie was just about to tell us how she wound up on the circus train," Ada said, licking her lips and looking longingly after the man who'd just left the tent.

"Lottie?" Birdie laughed cruelly. "What kinda story can a Goody Two-shoes like you have to tell?"

"At least she's gonna tell us hers," Ada said, leaning over to Charlotte. "Birdie likes to keep it a mystery, what her life was like before she joined the circus."

Birdie rolled her eyes. "Who's got a cigarette? I need a smoke."

"Since when do you smoke?" Ada snapped but shrank back when she caught a reprimanding glare from

Birdie.

Sasha quickly pulled a cigarette from her garter and handed it to Birdie. Mei scrambled amongst her scattered things on the dressing table for her lighter. "Everybody's got a story," she said, holding a light to Birdie's lips.

"You know who had a story to tell?" Birdie patted the side of the trunk she was sitting on. "Hazel Beauford Stallman, that's who."

Charlotte looked up at the name Stallman.

"Is that her stuff?" Ada asked.

"Well, it ain't hers no more, is it, stupid? She's dead!" Birdie stood up and opened the trunk. "So I figured you gals might want some of it."

The women swarmed around the trunk, pulling out clothing and shoes and makeup. The tent was filled with the choking aroma of cheap perfume and sarsaparilla-scented tobacco as the women dragged out garment after garment.

"Hazel had some kind of a life herself," Ada said, picking up some lipstick and a handheld mirror. "Started dancin' in coochie clubs around the same age as me."

"I never liked her," Mei admitted, handing some shoes to one of her sisters. "She always thought she was better than everybody. Birdie can tell you. She was gone for that summer, that travel season. Got married and came back actin' like the Queen of Sheba."

"Except that she hated everyone," another girl said.

"She didn't just get married. She had a baby," Birdie said, breathing out a long puff of smoke that fell on the surprised faces of the women gathered around the chest.

Charlotte felt the bitter taste in her mouth that she'd felt when she opened the box back in Ayer. Was it the tang of vomit? Or the taste of something bitter that she didn't want to swallow.

"I never saw her with no baby!" one of the girls exclaimed.

"Well, of course you didn't, dummy. She got rid of it!"

"I can't understand why she'd give up her baby," Charlotte said in a low voice.

"What's she gonna do with a baby around here, little Lottie? Get a nursery train car? Wheel it out in a pram while she shakes her tits for money?"

Charlotte sat back down on the chair, feeling dizzy.

"That's the way it is. You can't have it all," Sasha lamented.

"No, you can't." Birdie glared at Sasha as she spoke. "That's why I decided a long time ago that family life ain't for me. That's where Hazel messed up. She wanted too much."

"You didn't tell her the best part," Ada said, breaking the tension. "Hazel's 'husband' was already married to someone else!"

The women laughed, but Charlotte's face went pale.

"She was so mad when she found out. Goin' around talkin' about how she was gonna go after him. Tell his wife an' all that." Ada laughed.

"Oh yeah, tell the wife," Mei joked. "That's always a good idea. Here ya go, Lottie. Try this on." Mei tossed a bunched-up handful of rayon, fringe, and fur onto Charlotte's lap.

"I don't want any of her clothes." Charlotte pushed

the pile into the dirt at her feet. "Did she? Go after him?"

"Who knows." Sasha shrugged, taking the clothes from Charlotte's feet. "Bet he was in for a big surprise if she did, thinkin' he got away with it." She shook out a fur shawl and flung it across her shoulders.

Charlotte coughed at the dust and clenched her jaw. "I bet it was a bigger surprise for the wife."

"Husbands are always full of surprises," Ada retorted, handing the gin bottle back to Charlotte.

"Well, we'll never know, will we," Birdie said, staring curiously at Charlotte. "Because little old Hazel is dead as a doornail."

Charlotte went to take a drink of the gin, but a new shade of lipstick was printed on the bottle. Magenta. The color she'd seen on the threatening note from Birdie's trailer. She looked at Ada wearing the lipstick she'd gotten from Hazel's box and back at Birdie whose face was settled in a smug malicious glare.

"So let's hear it, kitten," Ada said, turning to Charlotte. "What's your story?"

"Seriously," Sasha joined in, slipping a ring from the box on her finger, "we're all dying to know how you got here."

"And how you moved up in the world so fast." Birdie stared at her with narrowed eyes as she took another drag of her cigarette.

"My story?" Charlotte was reeling. Her head was spinning. "W-when I was a girl, I was in the rodeos. I wanted to be a star like my father, but I met this young bull rider…"

The girls all hmmed or clicked their tongues at that.

"Yeah, we know how that goes." Sasha sighed.

"He was so charming and romantic before the war, and then over the years…he just got colder. Distant. I used to think the war changed him, but I don't know. After that, the only thing that mattered was trying to make him happy, and he was just never happy. I became so pointless. I just…faded away…then when I learned there was another woman…"

The girls leaned in, eyes locked on her as she took another sip from the bottle and dabbed at her lips.

"You know what?" Charlotte stood up, swaying. "My life before? That was the real circus. Every day was just a show. An act."

"Oh, I see, so playing house was more bizarre than riding a zebra?" Ada elbowed Sasha. "Now she gets it!"

Birdie didn't laugh with the other girls in the spinning room. Just took a long pensive drag from her cigarette.

"Maybe I was unhappy." Charlotte went on. "Maybe it wasn't that I wasn't enough for him. Maybe that wasn't enough for me. Just being that man's wife. One person's happiness just isn't enough for two people. You said Hazel wanted too much, but what did she want? Love? Respect? Pride? Are you telling me you don't want that too?"

The women weren't laughing anymore. Ada sat frozen with her chin up, and Sasha examined the fringe on a new dress she was clutching. Mei and her sisters exchanged glances.

"Well, of course we do, hun, but you can't have all those things. Not like that. You have to choose," Mei said. "You can't have a husband and be on the road like this. You can't have men looking at you every night like they look at us when you're married."

"That's why none of us are married! They want you in the house, out of the spotlight," Sasha said, knuckles white from gripping the dress.

"I could never," Ada said, adjusting her bra. "This is the only place I can be who I want to be."

"I agree." Birdie tossed her cigarette on the ground and snuffed it out with her pointed toe. "I don't know about love, but pride and respect? Birdie Bells gets that in spades. Every night in the center ring. It's the only way."

"But why?" Charlotte exclaimed. "Does a man have the headliner on pride and respect while we're just the sideshows to support it? Why can't I be bright and free and be loved for it? I shouldn't have to disappear or flicker out to make space for love. There's room for all of it! And I want all of it too."

Birdie watched Charlotte like a hawk. She crossed one leg over the other, propped her elbow on her knee and her chin on her palm.

"Why can't I have it all if I want to?"

Charlotte searched the confused faces of the women looking up at her for some answer. Some confirmation. But each one reflected a different facet of her own doubts. The room pressed in on her, choking her. She collapsed back onto the rickety chair.

"You can try, kitten," Ada said gently, sitting beside her and placing a hand on her leg, "but that's a one-way ticket to heartbreak. It might not be right, but that just ain't the way the world works."

"Why? Why can't a man want me to be the same person *I* want me to be?"

"A man who wants you when you're one of us

don't want you because he respects you." Sasha shook her head.

"And a man who respects you won't want you to be one of us," Ada added. "You need to find your spot—whatever it is—and find a way to be happy in it."

"She's right," Birdie uttered tersely, chin on her palm. "People don't like it when we get outta place. Talking like that, acting like that. You might end up like Hazel."

Like Hazel.

Charlotte brought the bottle to her lips but couldn't will herself to take a drink. She lowered the bottle and sat silently for a moment. Birdie was right. Her husband never did like it when women got out of place.

"This gin is making me sick." Charlotte handed the bottle to the next girl. "I need to go get my son."

Chapter 29

Running

A low hum of curious whispers buzzed about the Sahara Sisters' tent as Charlotte stepped outside into the crisp night air. The breeze was cool against her chest. She'd been sweating. Suffocating under the stares of the performers in the dressing tent. Why did she say all those things?

The space before her was a dizzying swirl of colors and activity, from sideshows getting in a few more nickels to the crew hustling to pack up around them. She squeezed her eyes tightly to block out the overwhelming sights and sounds, and she jumped when she felt a hand on her shoulder. She turned to see Mei standing beside her.

"Are you okay?"

The familiar discomfort that always accompanied a concerned or caring friend crept up Charlotte's spine. But this time she didn't lie. "I don't know," she said, dropping her shoulders with a sigh.

"Why don't I walk with you to the cookhouse? We can get Alex where he needs to be together, and then you can come back with me to our railcar to sleep off all that gin you just drank in there."

Charlotte laughed. "All right."

As Charlotte and Mei meandered through the

sideshows packing up for load-out, they laughed about the girls from the dressing tent.

"I told Sasha to stay away from Frank, but she didn't listen." Mei gave Charlotte a side eye. "Some girls never listen…"

"What is that supposed to mean?" Charlotte asked, giving her a playful elbow.

"You know what it means. I've seen your big eyes fluttering at 'Jay—Mr. Edwards' every day. I've watched you giggle with him like a little school girl, and you mention him a lot…"

Charlotte blushed. "I know it's stupid. I'm sure a lot of girls—"

"No. For what it's worth, I've never seen him flirt with any of the girls. Sasha was right. He always kinda seemed off limits, you know."

"Really?"

Mei nodded.

"But you said that Hazel—"

"She tried." Mei laughed. "But, honey, she tried with everybody."

Wasn't that the truth.

"If I'm bein' honest," Mei whispered, "I was worried about Hazel as soon as I heard she was on the cannon. I heard it was Birdie's idea, putting her in that act. The girl who was on it before died, you know. They said it was an accident, but I was there. One minute Birdie had her by the neck, mad about who knows what, and then she was dead not an hour later. Her net just snapped loose, and she hit the dirt like a sack of potatoes."

"Really?"

"Yes, really! And nobody asked any questions

about that. Just like we don't ask no questions about why Hazel died."

"You don't think it was an accident?"

Mei shrugged. "Accident or no accident, crossin' Birdie is a death sentence. And Hazel crossed Birdie, that's for sure. She was always going on about being the next big star. And of course, everyone knows she was sleepin' with Frank. Think she mighta been sleepin' with Hugh too—"

"That's why you're so worried about Sasha." Charlotte stopped and looked at Mei, but her blood ran cold when a familiar shadow passed behind her friend. She gasped and ducked down behind a cart. Mei instinctively squatted down beside her.

Coming out of the shadows into the flickering light cast by the remaining sideshow acts was the silhouette of a lanky man in a cowboy hat. He had one hand on his pistol and a pipe in the other. Horses drawing a decorated clown cart passed between them, and the shape of the man was gone, leaving only the smell of his pipe tobacco behind. Sarsaparilla.

"What's the matter, Lottie?" Mei whispered.

Charlotte's eyes burned as she squinted into the intermittent light. "I...I thought I saw..."

Mei nodded in understanding.

"I'm s-sorry, it's just that..."

Mei placed her hand on Charlotte's arm. "We all have somebody we're running from," she said.

Charlotte gulped and peeked over the top of the trailer. She spotted the cowboy hat again. It was too dark to see the man's face, but he walked as if he were searching for someone.

"I-I can't be sure—"

"Let's cut around the other side, huh?"

The two women ducked down and crossed the path to the next cart before making their way to the other side of the big top. Charlotte looked over her shoulder to see if the man was still there, or if they were being followed, but in the sea of cowboy hats it was impossible to be sure.

"Look, up ahead, there's Chuck," Mei said. "That's where Alex is, right?"

Searching for her son, Charlotte forgot about the people in the crowd behind her and around her, and her swift walk broke into a trot.

"Hey, there, Miss Lottie," Chuck shouted joyfully upon noticing her. "I swear you look like a real star out there, girlie! I guess I'll never get my waitress back, will I?"

"Thank you," Charlotte said, looking around anxiously.

Mei caught up to them and frowned at Charlotte's trembling lips.

"Won't be long before you're twirling around up there too, I bet!" Chuck stacked a few crates of clean dishes onto a horse cart.

"Wh-where is—? Where is—?"

"Where's what, Lottie?" Chuck paused in his work and wiped at his concerned brow.

"Where is Alex?" she cried. "Where is my son?"

She didn't wait to listen to Chuck's answer when she heard Alex wasn't there. She stumbled backward in shock, fueled by fear, and fled from the cookhouse in the direction of the pipe-smoking cowboy she'd seen in the yard.

"He's taken him, Mei." Charlotte gasped as the

pair ran toward the load-out area.

"What?" Mei asked, panting. "You mean your son? Who's taken him? Chuck said—"

Charlotte was stumbling through the mess of the tear-down area now. Blinking rapidly, she could hardly see through the blur of her tears and the movements of so many people around them. Her lightheadedness seemed to separate her mind from her body. In her haste, Charlotte tripped over a stack of poles and toppled into the belly of a big bearded man in overalls.

"Well, hello there, pretty lady. Aren't you a doll?" he said, his glassy eyes flickering with a joke that Charlotte knew she wouldn't find funny.

Charlotte mumbled that she was sorry and attempted to push past him, but he grabbed her arm and yanked her back. "Hey now, where you goin' so fast?"

Charlotte squirmed to pull away.

"I asked you a question, you little slut," the man growled. He was breathing heavily now, his body wet with sweat and breath reeking of corn dogs and whiskey. He gripped her tightly in one meaty hand while sliding his other arm around her waist.

"Let me go!" Charlotte cried.

The man pulled Charlotte closer, licking his cracked lips to reveal putrid tobacco-stained teeth. He laughed. Breath rattled lustily with every deep chuckle.

"Get off-a her, you big brute." Mei slapped at the man.

The man laughed louder and knocked Mei's small body to the ground with the back of his hand as if he'd just swatted a fly. His focus didn't flicker but burned more intently from her protest. Charlotte turned her face away from him and squeezed her eyes shut as his sour breath fell over her.

Just as she thought she would feel the man's lips press into her face or her neck, his grip loosened. The rhythmic clicking of a thumb pulling back the hammer of a pistol punctuated the air behind her.

A voice followed. "I don't like the way you're treating this lady here."

"Get lost!" the man snarled. "This ain't none-a yer business."

Charlotte opened her eyes slowly. Behind her, a beautiful lady calmly held a gun aimed directly at the man's forehead.

"How 'bout you get lost before I make it my business," the woman said.

The man glared at the woman for a long moment before reluctantly letting go.

"I was just havin' a little fun," he said and shoved Charlotte toward the woman. "Dumb bitch."

The woman kept aiming her gun at the man and let him know which direction he could run in with two flicks of her wrist. The man ran his tongue over his rotten teeth as he stared her down before finally giving in and disappearing into the crowd.

Charlotte let out a rattled breath. She stared in awe at the woman, who lowered her weapon and lifted up her skirt to tuck it away on her thigh.

"You've gotta learn some self-defense, honey."

"Thank you so much," Charlotte said, her voice trembling. "I-I'm so sorry. I want to thank you, but I can't stay and talk. I-I have to find my son!"

"Chuck was trying to tell you, Lottie. Alex left with Mr. Edwards." Mei dusted herself off and rubbed her sore elbow.

"Jay Edwards?" the woman asked. "Well, I know exactly where he is. Come with me."

Charlotte's quick panting left her lightheaded as she and Mei walked briskly behind the woman toward the railcars. She walked up the steps to the door, knocked, and waited. Every second wound a tighter hold on Charlotte's heart.

"I was sure this was his car," the woman said, puzzled. She stepped gracefully down the mesh wire steps into the gravel. This woman looked more like a ballroom débutante than a pistol-wielding Annie Oakley.

Charlotte didn't have time to wonder at that now.

"He's taken Alex," she cried, holding onto her stomach and stumbling through the gravel. "We have to find him."

Mei placed a hand on Charlotte's shoulder. "Don't worry. We'll find him."

The woman walked up the next set of steps to a new railcar door as Charlotte looked frantically up and down the tracks. This time the door opened at her knock, and Jay appeared with a casual hand in his pocket. "Luella, what are you doing here?"

"I told you I come to every show, didn't I?" the woman said. "Do you know where a boy named Alex is? This woman is looking for him." She turned to gesture to Charlotte.

"Who's looking for Alex?" Pearl asked from inside the car.

"Alex!" Charlotte pushed past Luella and Jay into the railcar.

"Hi, Mom." Her son looked up from the table where he was sitting with Sadie and two other children, a book, various handheld tools, and a pile of wicks and wires before them. Pearl stood behind the children with an armful of glass jars.

"Alex!" Charlotte fell to her knees, hugging him and sobbing. "I thought I'd lost you," she cried. "I couldn't find—"

"I was right here, Mom," Alex answered, fiddling with a wire. Charlotte felt the eyes of everyone in the railcar on her as she wiped at her tears.

"What's going on?" Jay asked.

"We didn't know where he was, sir," Mei answered. "She was worried he'd been taken by someone when he wasn't with the steward."

Pearl laid the jars out on the table and turned to listen to Mei.

"Oh, I'm surprised Mr. Brown didn't tell you. I borrowed Alex after the show so I could set them up with—"

"I think he tried," Mei said, "but there was so much going on. She was attacked by an awful man."

"Attacked?" Jay balled up his fists. "By who? Where is he?"

"He's gone, sir," Mei said. "This lady here whipped out that gun, and he ran off like a thief in the night."

"Gun?" Jay asked.

Luella beamed. "Might be wise for you to carry a gun too, Jay. Rough crowd you're traveling with." Her eyes carried the weight of her meaning.

Charlotte sat on the floor in front of her son, unable to move. Unable to breathe.

"It seems like everything is all right now." Mei reached for Charlotte to help her up.

But she stood up on her own. She turned to Jay with an unbridled rage that swelled out of her fear. "You can't just take my son!"

Jay stood silently for a moment, clearly confused. "I'm sorry if I overstepped," he said slowly.

Blinking back hot tears, she took her son's hand. "Let's go, Alex."

"Mom." Alex tugged at her arm and reached for the book in front of him. *Electricity, the Science of the Nineteenth Century, a Sketch for General Readers* by Emma Marie Caillard.

She took in the book for a moment and the supplies on the table.

"You're making Leyden jars."

"Jay got us the supplies, Mom," Alex said. "That's why we're in here. Mrs. Pearl said we could make them in her railcar after the show."

Charlotte turned to Jay. "And the book. Did you get him that too?"

Jay nodded slowly, still confused.

"I…I…" Charlotte's throat felt too tight to speak.

"Why don't you two step out for a private chat," Pearl suggested gently.

"Yes, let the kids get back to their…whatchamacallits," Luella agreed. "I've gotta go find Frank, and I'm sure this lady has someplace to be."

Mei nodded. "Lottie, I'll wait for you over at the Sahara Sisters railcar. You know where it is?"

"I can help her get there," Jay said.

"No. No, I'm not leaving Alex," Charlotte said. "We should go together. To the—to the cookhouse car. To sleep. We—"

"Mom, please!" Alex begged.

"Please, Miss Cameron?" the other kids joined in.

Pearl placed a comforting hand on Charlotte's arm. "Let Alex stay with us tonight. He gets along so well with my children and Sadie. You can trust me, Lottie. I'll guard him like one of my own."

Charlotte looked at the eager eyes of the kids and back to Jay.

"Sadie is staying too. I'd trust Pearl with my life. Alex is safe here, Lottie."

"Please." Alex looked up at her with wide, hopeful eyes, completely ignorant of all of the fearful scenarios Charlotte had imagined he'd fallen victim to. All of the fears that were outside of the comfort of the railcar. He had one hand on his mother's hand and the other on his book.

She gave in. "All right."

The children cheered in unison. Alex gave his mother a quick hug and returned to the jars at the table. Charlotte tried to take comfort from the sound of Alex excitedly telling everyone who'd listen about electricity as she stepped out of the railcar and into the night air with Jay.

Chapter 30

Knock at the Door

Charlotte added a sigh of relief to the night breeze that fell fresh on her cheeks and brushed its cool fingers through her hair. She couldn't decide what Jay's expression held, so she glanced back down at the steps in front of her instead. She steadied herself on the railing with one hand, and the warm comforting grasp of his palm and fingers wrapped around the other as she made her way down.

After a long moment, he finally spoke. "Lottie, I'm sorry. I never would have let Alex come with me if I knew it would make you feel this way. But I don't understand why you were so worried. Don't you trust me?"

Facing Jay again, she was simultaneously chilled and flushed. Charlotte focused on the feeling of her toes in the cool grass instead, making every attempt not to vomit or sway. Why had she had so much gin? And no dinner. Charlotte closed her eyes.

"I was worried about my son," Charlotte said meekly. Her eyes blurred with tears as the waxy little body of a beetle rocked back and forth on spindly legs, moving toward the pointed toe of Jay's glossy black shoe. He could crush it, she knew. One step and he could crush that little bug with his shiny shoe. Two steady fingers gently lifted her chin up, and she had no choice but to meet Jay's concerned gaze. Something in his eyes made her bottom lip tremble.

"I hardly know you," she said. A wave of hurt washed through Jay's eyes, but she was unable to comfort him. Instead, she returned her attention to the slowly moving beetle. "And you hardly know me," she said. The little bug struggled in the dirt. *Why can't I just tell him about Pete?*

A heavy tear dropped in the dust in front of the beetle, sending it on a different course. The air was thick with the chirping of crickets and the rustling of load-out winding down. Dim darkness was settling over the tracks, lit only by the inside lights of the railway cars and the swinging lanterns of the load-out crew. Charlotte was reminded of the night she and Alex ran away and wondered where she could run to now.

"You don't mean that." Jay rubbed at the back of his neck. "It doesn't matter that we just met a few weeks ago. I do know you. And you know me too. Maybe better than anyone ever has."

She was mesmerized by the clouds that danced in his eyes. He let out an unexpected frustrated sigh that rustled the loose hair around her face and sent a tickle down the back of her neck. "Everyone is looking at us. I've got to finish load-out, and we've got to get you cleaned up."

Charlotte looked around at the crew who were sneaking furtive glances at their conversation and then back at Jay. She had forgotten there were other people around.

"You can use my railcar," he said, extending his arm. Charlotte slipped her hand through his elbow. She tried not to lean too much on his arm, but she was more and more unsteady by the moment.

In Jay's railcar, his scent enveloped her, the same rich woodsy smell she'd caught briefly before when they stood close enough. Jay took a handkerchief from his lapel pocket and tossed his jacket onto his bed. He dipped the handkerchief into a bowl of water at his dressing table.

"Oh, goodness," Charlotte said, catching a glimpse of herself in the mirror, "I look like one of the clowns!" She covered her face with her hands to hide the running mascara and smudged rouge.

Jay laughed and pulled her hands away gently. "You've had a rough night," he said, dabbing at her face with his handkerchief. "It isn't easy doing this on your own. Finding your way and raising your son. I know."

Charlotte fought against new tears as she swallowed the lump in her throat.

The flicker of a muscle in Jay's jaw defined as he took a deep breath in through his nose. "And what happened tonight with that reprobate who attacked you is unacceptable. I'll find someone I trust and reassign their duties so they can escort you to and from the tent. Nothing like that will ever happen to you again."

Charlotte's stomach turned. It wasn't the disgusting man from the circus grounds that worried her. She was afraid of the man she thought she saw. Of the feelings she had for Jay. Of getting too close when…

"I promise, Lottie, you and Alex are a priority for me now. I'll do everything in my power to keep you safe."

Charlotte's pulse quickened. Her lips parted

involuntarily as he dabbed at the corner of her lips with his handkerchief. Some feeble part of her held back, but it was overtaken when the warmth of his breath rustled her thick lashes. What would his lips taste like? She had to know.

Without knowing where she got the courage, Charlotte reached up to Jay's face and placed her hand on his cheek. The tension in his jaw relaxed beneath her fingers. Her heartbeat pulsed in the tip of her forefinger as she ran it gently along his jawline, tracing the lines of his smile. Tracing the shape of his chin.

Jay hesitated, biting his own lip as he pulled his handkerchief from her face. He started to speak and closed his mouth again without saying a word. He laughed and looked down at the ground.

Charlotte lifted her other hand to hold his face and stood up on tiptoes to kiss him. Slowly, gently, she met his lips with hers and took a deep breath in as the rich scent of his skin grew stronger. The smell of his face and the taste of his lips was different. New. She was dizzy. Wobbly. Scared. Like a little bug about to be crushed. But as she started to pull away, a strong hand at the small of her back steadied her and another between her shoulders pushed her forward, farther into the new kiss. She let herself melt into Jay, running her fingers through his hair and around his neck. He was gentle, and his lips tasted sweet on her tongue, like one of the candy sticks at Bill's General Store. She sucked his lip between her teeth, and he gripped her tighter, his gentleness growing into a hunger that excited her.

Goose bumps rose in waves over her body where Jay's hands ran over it, inciting a tingling through her spine that she'd forgotten she could feel. She stopped worrying about wobbling on her tiptoes. She closed her eyes and relaxed her body fully in Jay's sturdy hands, gasping for air as his lips moved to her neck.

Charlotte fumbled at his shirt buttons with her trembling fingers, slipping her hand under his shirt to feel his warm skin. So different from hers, tough and firm. As she moved her hands across his chest to push the shirt off his shoulders, she felt a ridge, like a scar. He slipped his arms out of the sleeves of his shirt and let the garment fall to the floor with a metallic thud. His watch had slipped out of his pocket.

Jay didn't glance down. His gaze was on Charlotte. He took her face in both hands and pulled her into another kiss, stronger now. Eager and purposeful. One hand on the back of her head, he ran the other down her thigh and lifted up the hem of her dress, hands climbing—

Knock-knock-knock. "Mr. Edwards, sir?"

Charlotte and Jay froze as they looked at the closed door, which rattled under another series of knocks.

The deep voice and thick accent of Joe, the strongman who'd helped her and Alex escape, penetrated the rattling door. "Mr. Edwards, load-out is complete. We need you for final check."

Jay sighed, and his eyes danced with laughter and longing as he looked back down at Charlotte. He kissed her on the forehead gently before reaching down to pick up his shirt.

"Thank you, Joe. I'll be right out."

Charlotte was swaying again as Jay buttoned up his shirt and tucked it in, slipped his suspenders back onto his shoulders and found his jacket. She looked longingly at his bed as he rustled through his jacket to pull out his little black book.

"Come on," he said, tucking his book under his arm. "We've still gotta get you to the Sahara Sisters car. We don't want the girls giving you a hard time."

Charlotte nodded and followed after him awkwardly, glancing at the watch that still lay on the floor of the railcar as they walked to the door.

Jay opened the door, and Joe was standing patiently on the other side of it with a lantern and a blank expression.

"Load-out is complete," he repeated. "Have you spoken with rail master, sir?"

"Not tonight. I had other things to see to." Jay looked back at Charlotte, and she knew she was blushing. "But he knows the plan. I spoke with him last night about the schedule for this week."

"Yes, sir. I'll tell him we're all boarded?"

"Yes, but walk with us to the Sahara Sisters' car first, please. I have something to discuss with you."

The Sahara Sisters' car. *You can't have it all.* What was she doing? *Talking like that. Acting like that. You might end up like Hazel.*

Jay turned back to Charlotte and took her hand. A thrill rushed through her at his touch. Walking along the tracks hand in hand with him, the warmth in his hand fought the frigid fear that gripped her spine. She felt out of place and right at home, unable to let in the comfort or the joy that she longed for. For some reason she couldn't understand, Charlotte again fought the urge to cry.

Jay let go of her hand and pulled his book from under his arm as he spoke with the strongman. "Joe, I'd like you to start escorting Lottie to the Sahara Sisters' railcar after the shows. We've had—"

"Because of that man?"

"Yes, so you've heard," Jay continued. "I'd like to—"

"Not heard, but I saw, sir."

"You saw him?"

"Yes. Could not go after him. Had to carry dead girl's palanquin."

Jay stopped walking, and the other two stopped with him. "The palanquin?"

"Yes, sir, as you ask, I carry the dead girl to medical tent. Just before that, I see a man, he was jumping from trapeze ladder, and he runs out of tent. Out into crowd and gone."

Charlotte and Jay exchanged glances. "You're not talking about tonight. You're talking about the night that Hazel died?"

Joe nodded. "Yes, sir."

"And you saw an extra man up with Birdie in the scaffolding?"

Joe nodded again.

The three walked in silence for a moment as Jay contemplated what Joe had told him, but all Charlotte could think about was the taste of Jay's lips. His hands, so strong and so comforting. She could trust him. Guilt returned, stinging at her temporary happiness. *He trusts me. He thinks he knows me.*

It was the night for courage.

"I need to tell you something," Charlotte whispered up at him after a moment.

Jay bent his ear and squeezed her hand, and the three of them stopped just short of the Sahara Sisters' railcar. Jay gave a nod to Joe that let him know they'd need a moment alone. Joe took a few steps slowly backward in the direction they'd come from.

Jay turned back to Charlotte and took her hand again. He waited patiently, with a gentle smile she'd never seen before. "What did you need to tell me?"

She took a step closer to him, her chest rising and falling with the quickening of her breath.

Charlotte opened her mouth to speak and closed it again. "The note," she said quickly. "There was lipstick…a strange color. I can explain later, but Hazel wrote it. To Birdie. I'm sure of it. She was threatening her, and I think that…"

Jay looked at her expectantly.

"I think that Hazel threatened other people too."

Jay nodded, contemplating what she'd said. Down the rail line, steel doors screeched shut and the muffled calls of animals rang out into the night air in chorus with the rising chirping of emerging crickets. A happy half-dressed clown with a brown glass bottle hung waist-up out of a railcar window singing a drunken ballad about a long-lost love while other performers either joined in or yelled at him to shut up.

"Let's sleep on it and discuss it at breakfast tomorrow," Jay said finally. "Don't worry, I'll check on Alex before I turn in."

Charlotte smiled. More than anything, she wanted to kiss him again. "Okay. I'll see you in the morning."

A wide boyish grin spread across Jay's face, and he squeezed her hand before letting go. "See you in the morning." His voice was something just above a whisper.

Jay walked back to Joe, looking back over his shoulder to smile at Charlotte one last time.

"All right, Joe, how did load-out go?"

"Smooth, sir. Everything is loaded, and three new stowaways join our train tonight."

"Good." Jay took out his book. "I'll check in with our crew master before the train departs, and I'll check in with our steward about the new stowaways in the morning."

"And the rail master, sir?"

"I'll leave that with you." Jay patted at his pockets for his watch. "Joe, can you describe the man you saw in the scaffolding on the night that Hazel died?"

The pair continued down the line of lighted railway cars, and the swinging light of the lantern grew dimmer and more distant. Charlotte turned back to the Sahara Sisters' sleeper car, where Birdie perched silently on the top step. She was smoking with narrow eyes, two long lines furrowed across her forehead, and two short ones squeezed between her eyebrows.

"It's time to load up, little Lottie," she said, tossing her cigarette into the grass. She descended the steps with a graceful agility that wasn't purposeful but seemed to exude from Birdie after all of her time on trapeze.

Charlotte nodded silently, feeling palpable tension in the night air. How much had she heard? The fear in her stomach tasted sour on her tongue as she moved past Birdie to climb the steps.

"Where are you going?" Birdie asked, putting out the butt of her cigarette with the toe of her glittery high-heeled shoe.

"Well, I—"

"No, no. You're coming with me."

Birdie didn't wait for Charlotte's answer but

marched instead toward her bright yellow railway car, kicking off the gray cat that circled her foot.

Charlotte jiggled the handle to the door of the Sahara Sisters' car, but it was locked and the lights were out. She wanted to call out after Jay, but they were too far down the line. Reluctantly, Charlotte stepped back down. Without knowing what else she could do, Charlotte bent over and let the vomit she'd been swallowing for the last half hour escape into the grass. It burned at her throat and her nose and her eyes. It tasted like fear and lies and doubt. But mostly, it tasted like cheap gin.

She stood up and wiped her watery eyes with her forearm.

Birdie was staring at her with an impatient hand on her hip.

"We ain't got all night." She flung open the door to her railcar and gestured for Charlotte to join her.

Charlotte wiped at her chin with the back of her hand, running through her options and realizing that she didn't have any. She stepped around the mess she'd made, picked up Printesa, and followed Birdie into her railway car, hoping to God that she'd step back out of it alive in the morning.

Chapter 31

Left the Station

Just as Charlotte shut Birdie's door behind her, a squeaking of iron signaled the train was departing. The room had undergone a change since she'd last seen it. There were gashes in the wall where the glass that was meant for Charlotte's face had landed a few days before, but the poster that had been there had been pulled from the wall in shreds. Broken glass littered the trailer along with torn fabric and feathers. The other posters had been ripped from the wall too, corners of them still dangling, leaving squares of slightly fresher paint on the walls where the images used to be. The mirror was broken. Still functional but with three large cracks radiating from a point somewhere near the middle where reddish smears signaled the point of impact.

"It looks like someone was murdered in here," Charlotte murmured to the cat.

Birdie spun around and glared upon hearing her. The gravity of Charlotte's situation settled on her as her body rocked and nearly tipped over with the jolt of the train starting. She would be stuck in this little lion's den with Birdie for the night. Birdie, who was so angry at Hazel that she probably killed her. So angry at Sasha that she wanted to. A murderess on the run from the law, who'd probably overheard that Charlotte suspected her. A new wave of nausea passed over her as the wheels started turning. This train was leaving the station.

"So you don't like my redecorating," Birdie cracked, pouring gin into two glasses and handing one to Charlotte.

"I, uh…No, thank you," Charlotte said. "I think I've had enough of that stuff. I'm not thinking clearly."

"No. You're not," Birdie said, dumping the gin from Charlotte's glass into her own and sitting down. "That's what I want to talk to you about. I saw you with Jay Edwards out there. You think you're any more special to him than any other skirt? He's five seconds a free man, if he even is divorced. You can't be so naive, not if you wanna survive around here. Those Sterling boys are all trouble. Trust me."

"Jay's not a Sterling boy." Charlotte crossed her arms. "You don't kn—"

"Edwards, Sterling, the name don't matter, Lottie. His mother was a Sterling, or don't you know? He, Hugh, and Frank…they're all the same. Fighting to be the next big shot and trampling any tramp in their way to get there."

"Like Frank? Did he trample you?" Charlotte asked, noting half a shredded dress shirt dangling off the dressing chair.

Birdie scoffed. "I'm done with Frank."

Charlotte considered Birdie's bloodshot eyes with compassion. She felt, for a moment, that she was looking at her own reflection. The reflection she'd seen the day she opened the box back in Ayer. The day she'd learned that she'd wasted years of loyalty on a man who didn't deserve it. "You're in love with him," she said.

Birdie slowly swirled the gin in her glass. When she tipped it up for another drink, Charlotte noticed the torn skin on her knuckles. Dried blood rested on her dainty fingers like circus makeup. "I won't deny it," she said. "But I hate myself for it."

"So Sasha…"

"Sasha be damned. And Luella too." The melancholy in Birdie's eyes was replaced by a look of fiery determination. "I made myself a promise a long time ago, toots. Never get too close to nobody."

She wished she didn't understand what Birdie meant, but the pit of her stomach was hollow where there should be butterflies. Moments ago, she'd had one of the most romantic moments of her life. Kissing the man she'd been dreaming about. She should be hopeful. Excited. But she just felt scared. And a little sick. She almost wished she could go back. Go home after the parade that day. Never meet the frustrating woman at the cookhouse. Never open the box. Never meet Rusalka. Go home that night. Never get to know Jay. Never experience these feelings. Never lean in for that kiss.

But that kiss…

Well, there was no taking it back now. That train had left the station too.

"I know why you look so sick," Birdie said.

"Do you?"

"You're worried. You've heard what they say about me. Those girls with their little whispers." Birdie stared at her intently. "They say that I'm a murderer."

A rush of fear rose up and settled in her chest. She continued petting the cat and tried to remain calm.

"They say that?" she asked casually, trying not to look like she was ready to throw up again.

"You know they do." Birdie looked at her frankly.

Charlotte held her gaze, heart racing. "Well, is it true?"

Birdie downed her drink and let the glass fall from her hand to the floor. "Yeah, it's true," she said. "I'm a murderer."

"You mean, you killed…you killed…" Saying a silent prayer of thanks that she'd declined the drink, Charlotte's thoughts were filled with a new prayer, pleading for her life as panic gripped her by the spine. Would Birdie poison her? Shoot her? Throw her off the train? Frantically, she looked around the train car for something she could use to defend herself if she had to.

"Don't you wanna know what happened? The real story?"

Charlotte nodded. Shards of broken glass were everywhere. She could wield one like a knife. Or perhaps she could pick up the chair and swing it at her.

"My momma had seven of us kids, and I was the oldest. Our daddy died young, and she couldn't manage the farm so she always had some new boyfriend around offerin' to help us out."

Charlotte leaned back, feigning mild interest while still surveying the room. Maybe her best option would be just to open the door of the railcar and push Birdie out if it came to that. *I won't end up like Hazel. I won't.*

"Momma was real pretty, always had herself done up real nice. Tight corset. Rouge and lipstick. That kept food on our table. Until it didn't. Some of them boyfriends started coming around for fun, but they didn't help us out no more, not like they used to. So

Momma told me to try her lipstick. Taught me to put on her rouge. I didn't know what she was doin', but she did. Soon Momma's boyfriends started helping themselves to me too."

Charlotte relaxed a little. "Oh Birdie, that's—"

"Save it," she said, slumping back onto the couch. "I told her the first couple of times it happened. But she didn't believe me. Or couldn't believe me. We'd started having food on our table again, and that was all that mattered to her for a while. Until she got a mean one. Real mean. He scared her off, and she left us all. No tellin' where she ran off to, but she left us with him."

Charlotte reached out to put her hand on Birdie's arm, but she pulled away.

"Soon as she was gone, the asshole stole our farm and our house with us in it. He forced us to work the fields, even little Maisy who was only eight. And every night, he…"

Birdie quickly wiped away an involuntary tear with a quivering pinkie finger. Printesa jumped onto Birdie's lap, curled up, and tucked her soft little gray head into Birdie's arm. Birdie looked startled, but slowly she began to pet her.

"But I could take it, you know? And that was our deal. He'd feed all of us if I let him have me. I hated him. But I could take it. For my family. So I'd do myself up like my momma taught me and that kept my brothers and sisters fed and livin'. My one rule for all my sisters was don't touch the damn makeup.

"But Maisy didn't listen, did she? No. She came runnin' in my room one night when I was sat up waiting for him. First, I saw the lipstick. That fool girl had put on my lipstick and my rouge, and she had a shiner to match it. Tears runnin' down her face. I knew he'd already helped himself to her too, even before she told me between all her sobbing and wailing about what he'd done. I could see it in the way that damn lipstick was smudged halfway down to her little chin."

Charlotte gasped. "What did you—"

"I shot him."

Charlotte took a sharp breath in and realized she'd forgotten to breathe during Birdie's story.

"Shot him dead with the gun we kept by the door for the wild hogs."

"Did he—"

"Never got to any of us again after that."

For a long while, the only sound in Birdie's car was the whirring of the steady wheels on the tracks and the purring of the soft gray cat in Birdie's lap.

"I trusted my mother, and she let me down. I trusted that man, and he let me down. I trusted Frank, and he…"

Charlotte put her hand on Birdie's arm, and this time she didn't pull away. Printesa hopped down and began tiptoeing around the broken glass and shredded posters, exploring the plush pillows on the floor by the dressing screen.

"It wasn't your fault, Birdie. You did what you had to," Charlotte said, looking at Birdie intently.

"I'll always do what I have to." Birdie clasped her own hands together tightly, running her thumb along the bottom of her palm and cracking her bloody knuckles. "That's why this is my last season with Sterling & Son's. I can't do this anymore."

"Oh, you don't mean that. Everyone knows Frank cares about you, he just—"

"Don't you get it? He'll never choose me. If I stay, I'll die. Like a light going out, I can feel it. I ain't never been nobody's first choice, and I—" She sat up and wiped away her tears. "I got too close to Frank, and I'm dead on the inside. The last two cannon girls got too close to Hugh, and they're the kinda dead you don't come back from."

An empty glass rolled slowly back and forth across the rug as the train chugged on.

"I've seen you with Jay," Birdie persisted. "What you're doing will kill you too."

"I know," Charlotte said. "Mei warned me too, not to get too close."

"That isn't just what I mean." Birdie shook her head. "What you were talkin' about with the girls back there. How you want everything. You want to be a mother and have your man and be a center-ring star."

"So what?" Charlotte felt her face grow hot. "You don't want me to do that either?"

"No, when you said choosing to be someone for yourself or someone for everyone else." Birdie searched around for a cigarette. "I tried to be something of a mother for my brothers and sisters but couldn't. Tried to be something of a wife to Frank, and I can't. It's fatal. Always kill or be killed. The only time I'm ever really living is when I live for me. When you're not the star of your own life, you die."

"And you can't have both," Charlotte said, thinking of how she'd choose to be a mother over a center-ring star any day.

"No, you can't. But sometimes the only way to learn who you are is to learn who you aren't." Birdie took a long drag from her cigarette and fell back into the sofa again.

"I guess I've been learning a lot about who I'm not," Charlotte said. "I ran away from home. Almost lost my son. Now I'm daydreaming about kissing my boss, drinking gin out of the bottle. Dressing up like a vaudeville harlot and riding around on zebras."

Birdie looked at Charlotte out of the corner of her eye and kept puffing on her cigarette.

"I'm supposed to be a mother. A wife. A small-town woman who works in the cookhouse."

"Sounds to me like you're still figuring out who you are." Birdie offered her cigarette, but Charlotte shook her head.

"You ever gonna tell me why you jumped the circus train in Ayer?"

Charlotte closed her eyes and leaned back on the sofa. "No," she said. "No, I am not."

Birdie shrugged. "Suit yourself."

Charlotte didn't try to fight the tears that ran down her face. She yearned for the simplicity of life before the circus with an intensity that gnawed at her stomach and bit at her throat.

She wanted her life back. The life she'd had before she'd opened that box. For Ayer with its wind and its dirt, Saul and Martha at the cookhouse, and the little street she'd lived on. For the comfort of her own bed. The kitchen table with Alex. A husband who loved her. The world she knew before.

Charlotte ached for home.

Chapter 32

Going South

Jay woke after a restless night of mind-racing wakefulness, and the lucid alertness that nagged him out of his drowsiness told him that nothing was as he expected it to be. He'd spent most of his sleeping hours savoring the lingering taste of Lottie's lips or thinking about her delicate face resting in his hands. Jay smiled. Lottie had turned his world upside down so quickly. Even the ground beneath him seemed to have shifted.

An electric pang of adrenaline shot through him. It wasn't just dreamy infatuation. That was the steady rocking of the train rolling along the tracks beneath him. Rolling along when it should have been resting at the station an hour ago.

Jerking upright, Jay reached over on his bedside table for his pocket watch, grasping across the table. It wasn't there. He lit the lamp and grabbed his alarm clock instead. Four thirty-seven? He slammed the clock back on the bedside table, shot out of bed, and sloppily shoved his anxious body into his clothes. *Where are we?*

Jay had been on this route enough times that he should recognize where they were, even in the dark. He pushed the window open. A thousand thoughts ran through Jay's mind as the unfamiliar landscape rushed past, and he searched for the crack of the sunrise or anything at all he might recognize. Nothing.

He closed the window slowly and gathered his map and his book from the table, turning over every other object in search of his watch. He stood up and patted at all of his pockets, panic crawling up his spine. When had he last seen it? He thought through the previous night. Load-out had been on schedule. He'd gotten the kids over to Benny and Pearl's car, and then Lottie...He closed his eyes and swayed slightly where he stood as he imagined Lottie's fingers tracing the lines of his face. Her lips on his. She'd pulled off his shirt. The train bumped along the tracks, and his eyes shot open as the weight of his situation fell on him like the thud of his watch on the ground. He picked up his lamp and knelt down to look under his bed.

There it is. The reflection from his lamp glinted off the gold case which sat open. Jay picked it up and turned it over. The glass was cracked, and the time was stuck at 11:03. His watch had broken while he was busy kissing Lottie. He hadn't had time to check with the rail master and now they were headed off route.

He carefully closed the watch and slipped it into his pocket along with his map and his book. He stood up and replaced the lamp to his bedside table. Letting out a sigh, Jay opened the door of his railway car and made his way across the platform of the moving car to Benny's door. He focused on the railroad ties beneath the car. The boards dashed through the opening between the platform and the step like morse code, and Jay marked their rate of speed. They weren't slowing down.

Benny answered before his third knock. "What's

going on?"

"I don't know."

Jay held up a rail map. Benny quickly kissed his confused wife and followed Jay back to his car.

Huddled over the railway map, Benny and Jay could only come up with two possibilities. The rail master had skipped Clovis and gone on straight for Albuquerque, or he'd gone south at the split on another line and he was taking them down to El Paso. Jay couldn't imagine why either would happen, but he felt sick with dread at the possibility of both.

If they skipped Clovis and went on to Albuquerque, they'd have supplies there ready for their stop the next day, and he could figure out what to do with the Clovis supplies. It would be inconvenient, but it wouldn't be the end of the world. However, Sonny would be arriving in Albuquerque in two days to check in on their progress and collect the earnings for the past few shows. Potentially, he'd even hint at who he'd be choosing to run the circus next year. Jay didn't like the idea of explaining to Sonny why they'd skipped a stop on the carefully planned route.

But he didn't think they'd skipped a stop. His gut told him they were traveling southwest to El Paso, near the border of Mexico, and there were about a dozen reasons he didn't want to go to El Paso. For one thing, it was four hours in the opposite direction of their planned route, and there was no turning around to head back up to Clovis. They'd be a day behind, and Sonny would be waiting in Albuquerque with a group of anxious investors and a lot of questions.

Then there were the supplies. There would be no food for them in El Paso, which would devastate the eating patterns of the hundreds of animals rolling along the tracks with them and greatly upset the hungry crew.

But the main reason that Jay didn't want to find himself in El Paso that morning was the fact that Ringling, Barnum & Bailey had a planned and well-advertised show there later that week. It was bad business to show up with their circus days before "The Most Wonderful Show on Earth," but more than that, Sonny Sterling and John Ringling had an understanding. Ringling wouldn't crush them—and they could—as long as the Sterling & Son's Circus stayed out of their way, kept to the less traveled cities, and didn't disrupt their travel routes or timelines. Having an unannounced show in El Paso days before the big Ringling, Barnum & Bailey show came to town was about as far from that understanding as it could be, and Jay was keen not to upset John Ringling or any of his cronies. Particularly his old comrade in arms, Verne Henry, who took pride in enforcing the treaty and working off borrowed power to intimidate smaller operations.

"Did the rail master understand the plan when you talked to him last night?" Benny whispered so he wouldn't wake Sadie.

"I didn't get to talk to him last night." Jay's knuckles were white around his pocket watch. "I was...with Lottie."

Benny paused for a moment. "He shoulda known anyway, Jay. You go over the schedule with him at the beginning of every week. Maybe he had a good reason for skipping Clovis."

"I don't think he skipped Clovis," Jay said through gritted teeth. "I think he's got us headed for El Paso.

Right into Ringling's territory. We'll nearly clap hands on the way through if that's true."

"But why—"

"I don't know," Jay said. "But if I hadn't been focused on Lottie, I never would have missed this. I shouldn't have let myself get so distracted."

Benny looked back at the map thoughtfully. "El Paso's awful close to Mexico."

Jay shrugged as he tucked his book and pocket watch back into his jacket.

"Didn't you say those crates at the speakeasy in Pecos had Spanish labels on them?"

Jay looked up at Benny, and they both arrived at the same thought, at the same time, as the train shuddered to a stop.

"Hugh."

****

The setup crew was already waiting for Jay when he opened the door.

"Hey, uh, there's no flares, boss. Where do we set up?"

Jay looked at Benny.

"Hang with me, boys," Benny said, trotting down the steps. "Jay's gonna confirm a few things with the rail master for us."

The men looked at one another in confusion but didn't seem to mind being told that they could wait to work. Every step he took in the desolate landscape around him added to the growing certainty and dread that they had landed somewhere between Texas and Mexico. When he arrived at the front of the train, the rail master was seated on the footplate in the cab, casually whistling a tune and filling out his paperwork.

"Mr. Edwards." He stood up straight, dropping his clipboard. "Everything all right, sir?"

"You tell me, Boyd," Jay said. "Where are we?"

"We're in El Paso, sir. Right on time."

Jay closed his eyes and took in a deep breath. "Can you give me an account of your decision to bring us here?"

"My, uh…my account? I wouldn't make a decision on the route, sir. I was…following your orders."

"And who gave those orders to you?"

"Well, that'd be Mr. Sterling, sir."

"Which one?"

"Mr. Hugh Sterling, sir."

Jay opened his pocket watch and stared at the long crack across the glass face as his lips pressed into a similar line.

"Thank you, Boyd," he said through clenched teeth.

The rail master scrambled to pick up his clipboard and pencil as Jay turned around abruptly and stepped out onto the platform.

"Oh drat, I've missed it."

Hugh's smarmy voice floated up to Jay's burning ears before his eyes had a chance to settle on his smug cousin.

"I was hoping to see your face when you realized there had been a little change in schedule." Hugh grinned wolfishly, all of his teeth reflecting the lights of the train back at Jay.

"Do I even bother asking why?" Jay stepped down past him and continued walking.

"I told you. There's nothing at all in or anywhere near Clovis. We'll get a bigger crowd here. And maybe it's a little fun to see you flustered."

Jay's simmering blood began to boil. He stopped and turned to face his cousin. "Hugh, this tiresome game of yours has very real consequences. Let's set aside the notion that, for one thing, the scheduling of our stops was carefully planned and determined months ago by Sonny and by me. That was never and will never be your decision. I can give you a list of about a dozen reasons why you've put us in a catastrophic mess with your newest antic."

"I don't have time for your lists," Hugh said. "I've got to meet the supplier to get our goods for the day."

Jay didn't manage to conceal his surprise.

"You think you're the only one who can coordinate our supplies?"

"Yes," Jay said. "Honestly, I do."

"And how very wrong you are. If you'd ever stop to notice, you'd realize I'm actually very savvy. Unlike you, I can pick up a phone, Jay. I didn't have to come out here and stir up curiosity and excitement or whatever it is you love to go on about. I called a store owner here, and he had all the supplies we needed. So I bought all of it."

"All the supplies he had?" Jay's boiling blood froze instantly. "Good God, Hugh. Did you ask why he had enough food and supplies for a traveling circus?"

"Why should I? That's no concern of mine."

"It's about to be a concern for all of us." He brought his fingers to his temples to soothe the pounding headache that was beginning to blind him. "I'm willing to bet the supplies you bought were intended for the Ringling, Barnum & Bailey Circus, which is set to come through here this week."

"So what if they are? That's their problem."

"Hugh, if you bought up their supplies and they find out about it, God help us. We'd be better off starving our crew and all of our animals than ticking off John Ringling. Take me to your supplier."

Hugh hesitated. "All right then, but you're overreacting."

"I wish I was. We'll see what Sonny says about it."

"If this is where the big boys come, then it's obviously a better venue. They bring in the big crowds and the big bucks. Sonny will see that. He'll have to respect me then." Hugh was beginning to sound less confident.

"But you're forgetting that Sonny's always told us to steer clear of any city Ringling plays at. He won't like you for putting us in this mess."

"Don't you think it's time for you to wake up? We don't have to live under Sonny's thumb anymore. Aren't you tired of being so small-time, Jay? So boring. So predictable. God, it's no wonder your wife left you. If something doesn't fit your plan exactly—"

"It sounds like you're the one with a plan, Hugh. So what is it? What is it really?"

"Do I have to spell it out for you? Frank will never take over for Sonny. He's an idiot who can't keep his pants on and doesn't know where we are or what to do until someone tells him. You're content to run the circus under that imbecile and let him take the credit and the money. Well, not me. I deserve that job, and I'm going to make Uncle Sonny see sense."

"He'll never choose you."

"Why not? I'm taking risks. Making changes. Making money. Sonny will see that, and he'll know he has to choose me. He wants someone bold. Someone to take charge."

As the pair approached the load-in crew, Jay turned to Hugh before they were within earshot of the men. "You wanna take charge? First problem. Where do we set up?"

"Set up where we always do." Hugh waved a disinterested hand at the desert before them.

"You wouldn't know this because you're never awake this early, but the crew needs a clearly laid out path. I always have the advance guys set that up before we get here. And we can't set up where we always do because we've never been here."

Hugh rolled his eyes. "It doesn't matter where we set up. Wherever we are, that's where the people will come. Honestly, Jay, stop making everything so hard. Do what you do, and make it work."

Hugh continued on past the load-in crew, who looked to Jay for instructions. Jay flipped open his pocket watch only to grunt and snap it closed again.

"What time is it, Benny?"

"Five to six."

"Looks like we're going to spend our day cleaning up after Hugh." Jay took out his book and began scratching out the old schedule in place of a new one.

"Wouldn't be the first time," Benny said. "Might be the last if you let Sonny know about his little side business though."

Jay considered for a moment. "You know, Benny, I think you're right. Not until we're back on track here though. What do you think about that lovely spot of dirt next to the cactus over there? Does that look like a planned circus setup spot to you?" He couldn't keep the bitterness out of his voice.

Benny nodded. "You gonna break it in for Ringling?"

"God help us, I guess I am."

Jay pushed away the voice that told him to load everyone back onto the train and speed out of town as quick as they could. Instead, he turned to the load-in crew to give them instructions on where and how to begin, pretending all along that everything was going according to plan, and saying a silent prayer that he wouldn't have to answer to John Ringling.

Chapter 33

Trouble at Breakfast

The whistle of the wind rushed through Charlotte's house, pushing her farther back into her pillow, forcing her eyes shut. The gust sat on her chest like a boulder, as if the air around her had been stolen from her own lungs. As she struggled to breathe, the swell of the wind rattled every wood plank in her tiny house. Shaking the floorboards violently. Bursts of dust breaking through to fill her nostrils. The whistle grew louder until it reached an ear-splitting pitch that forced Charlotte upright against the will of the wind.

The train whistle rang out again. Charlotte rubbed at her eyes and let the colorful patterns and textures of Birdie's railcar replace the image of her Ayer home rattling on a rail. It was getting old, waking up in a different place every day, never knowing what would be on the other side of her eyelids when she opened them.

Birdie was snoring loudly from under the pink silk sheets of her bed where Charlotte had wrapped her injured hand the night before and tucked her in like a child worn out from her tantrums. Watching the world-famous acrobat struggle to put one foot in front of the other after drinking buckets of gin had been quite a sight, but Birdie was no less threatening in her slumber.

More like a sleeping lioness.

Charlotte's own head was pounding, and her stomach was gnawing at her. She decided in that moment that she would never let gin touch her lips again.

I guess I'm learning who I'm not. She rose from the couch, bones aching. She carefully moved Printesa from her chest to a velvet pillow by her feet.

She went to wash out the grains of dust on her dry and sticky tongue but gave up when she realized the only water on the table was in the washing bowl. She settled for splashing a little on her face and patting it with the shredded sleeve of Frank's discarded dress shirt.

Charlotte turned her attention to the makeup, remembering the days she would peek over at the section of creams and tonics when she was shopping for potatoes and mouse traps at Bill's General Store. She'd never had enough money to buy any of them, and so she'd never wandered close enough to see the price. Now she sat at a table full of more glistening bottles, pretty powders, and creams than Bill had ever had on a shelf. All things she never could have afforded before that she could use for free now. She had a purse full of more money than she'd ever carried before, but she didn't need to buy anything. Free meals and someone else to cook them, but she still missed lighting the little stove in the quiet dark of morning and cooking eggs for her family. Her family.

She thought about Alex eating his meals timidly in the oppressive silence of Pete's stifling shadow and then remembered the way her son had laughed and lit up like one of his Leyden jars in the safety and comfort of Jay's railcar. What was family if it wasn't a safe place to laugh? A safe place to love?

She picked up the mascara that Mei had taught her how to apply but stopped. The eyelashes always made her feel ridiculous. She set the mascara back down and reached instead for a tube of magenta lipstick.

What if the train wasn't taking Charlotte and Alex to some destination like so many stops and stations? What if the circus train was the destination? What if these people were her family?

She carefully ran the lipstick over her lips in their natural shape instead of the cupid's bow that the girls had taught her to do. She pressed her lips together a few times on a napkin, set the lipstick back down on the table carefully, and considered her reflection for a moment. When she was in Ayer, she'd always gotten up so early that she'd rarely taken time to look at herself in a mirror. Maybe it was days or maybe it was years, but Charlotte had slowly forgotten what she looked like. And then recently she'd been wearing so much makeup, and that glittery costume, she didn't recognize herself.

She ran her fingers through a tangle of the sun-kissed hair that fell on her cheek and tucked it behind her ear, letting her fingers rest for a moment on her neck as she remembered the feel of Jay's lips pressed there. She moved her fingers to her lips and dropped them.

In the mirror now, she saw the woman that Jay had kissed. The woman who'd rubbed off the dust of her little Ayer life and shined up under the center-ring lights.

Charlotte decided she was pretty. Even without the

rest of the makeup. She liked the roundness of her cheeks, the fullness of her lips, and the creases by her eyes from where she'd been laughing so much lately. She liked the length of her neck and realized she seemed to carry herself a little higher these days. She thought of the way Jay's eyes had glistened and his face had warmed up into a gentle smile when he'd held out his hands for hers at the steps of the railcar. He had looked at her like their kiss had lifted the lid on a hidden treasure that he'd been searching for and no map could lead him to. His faith in her value had drawn her up, like wilted crops rising after a good rain. She sat up a little taller and pulled her shoulders back, but the posture felt like a lie.

A lie. She slumped down again. Guilt swelled up in her throat like the wind blowing up dust.

You've got to tell Jay about Pete, the girl in the mirror said to her. She squeezed her eyes shut and turned away.

Her stomach growled.

She had to eat something.

Maybe some bread.

Charlotte stood up, slipped into her shoes, and headed to the cookhouse tent toward Alex, Jay, and breakfast.

****

Charlotte had never been to Clovis before, but she hadn't imagined it would be so dry. Or so hot. It couldn't be far past nine in the morning, but she was already beginning to sweat under the dry heat. The air in front of her radiated, making the circus tent ahead look like a mirage from an Arabian Nights story. The familiar clinking of plates and rustling of working waiters compelled Charlotte toward Chuck in the kitchen.

"Mornin', Lottie!" he bellowed. "Here for your coffee or here for your son?"

"Both." She steadied her shaking hands to pour herself a cup of coffee. "Where is he?"

Chuck nodded to the egg crates as he flipped a pancake on the griddle. "Been busy since the poles went up. You've got yourself a hard little worker there."

They both looked over at Alex, who stacked crate after crate in the supply area.

"He's a good boy, Lottie. An' you're doing good too by how you're raisin' him."

Lottie looked up at Chuck gratefully, eyes stinging and stomach growling. "Can I have a plate of pancakes today, Chuck? A big ol' stack of pancakes?"

Chuck beamed. "Well of course! Why didn't you say so? You're always just drinkin' that coffee and nothin' else. I was startin' to think you didn't like my cookin', girl!" Chuck slid a stack of flapjacks onto a plate and handed it to her. The sweet smell of the warm plate signaled another growl from her stomach.

"Thank you." Charlotte took the plate and leaned over to kiss the big cook on the cheek. She picked up her coffee with her other hand and started toward Alex.

"Hey, Lottie," Chuck called out.

"Yes?" She turned around.

"Don't forget the syrup." Chuck smirked, winked, and turned back to the grill.

Charlotte gathered her strength and approached Alex. He looked so grown-up as he worked alongside the kitchen boys and dishwashers.

"Could you get us some syrup for these pancakes?" she asked, holding up the stack of pancakes.

Alex nodded excitedly as he set down his crate, and the two made their way to the breakfast table.

Alex ate ravenously, shoveling bites between updates on his new experiments from the night before.

"Don't tell Saul," Charlotte said, savoring a bite of the fluffy golden pancake, "but these flapjacks may be even better than his!"

"Will we ever see Saul again?" Alex asked through a mouthful of syrup.

"I'm not sure honey, I—"

"Are we ever going to see Dad again?"

Charlotte sat her fork down slowly, her appetite gone. "Alex, I know it's hard to understand. But your father—"

"I understand he isn't nice," Alex said. "I saw how he talked to you. How he hurt you. I know he was gonna take me out of school." His eyes welled up with tears as he stared at the table between them. "He burned my book."

Charlotte reached across the table for his hand. "Those things weren't nice," she said. "Alex, I...I don't want to treat you like you're not smart. You're so smart. I don't want to make you mad at your dad, I—"

"You want to protect me."

"Honey, everything I do is to protect you."

Alex poked holes in his half-eaten pancake. "Who's going to protect you, Mom?"

Charlotte patted his arm. "You don't need to worry about that. That's my job, okay?"

Alex smiled and took a bite of his pancake. "Maybe it can be Jay's job." He smirked.

"I can take care of myself," she replied, picking up her fork again.

"I know you don't want me to be mad at Dad. But I am," Alex said. "I know he must have done something really mean for us to leave."

The two ate their breakfast in silence for a moment, Charlotte pushing bits of soggy pancake bites around her plate while she thought about what to say. *How can I help him understand without hurting him more?*

"He wasn't a nice dad, but he was my dad," Alex said quietly. "I still kinda miss him."

"I'm sorry, honey. I…" The gnawing at her stomach returned. "I'm all done with breakfast—how about you? Ready to go to school?"

Alex nodded and picked the plate up to carry back into the kitchen. Charlotte held the mug up longer than she needed to when she took her last sip of coffee and didn't allow herself to cry until Alex was out of sight.

****

Though the stone never left her stomach, Charlotte enjoyed listening to her son talk about his plans for the day on the way to the school tent.

"Miss Pearl said we can try the next experiment for lightning rods tonight, and then Sadie said we can try what I learned about poker on the clowns after lunch. We're playing for money today, so when we win, we can use our money to buy cotton candy and…" The dull sadness that had briefly weighed his eyes down at breakfast had been reanimated with a joyful excitement that almost erased the guilt Charlotte felt for bringing him with her on this wild escapade. Would the guilt go away if she took him back home?

As Alex ran to join his friends in the school tent, a

swirl of emotions jostled for space in Charlotte's consideration on the way back to the cookhouse tent.

Charlotte's whole body was absorbed by the uneasy vibrations of her own fears. She desperately needed an encouraging word from Jay to calm her. Something to confirm that the things she felt for him weren't as ludicrous as Birdie had told her. Even a kind look would do. Charlotte took a deep breath in, imagining again the sweet gaze he'd given her when she stepped out of his train car and took his hand. Her determination couldn't be fueled on fear anymore. She needed something from Jay besides a reimagined look and a daydream worn thin. She was running on fumes.

When Charlotte approached the usual table where she had breakfast with Jay, she saw that he already had company that morning. Across from him sat a dark-skinned man in a black bowler hat and a striped suit that stretched across wide hunched shoulders. His left elbow was propped on the table, gold wristwatch glistening in the sweltering sun, and he pinched a stubby brown cigar between his fingers that sent up a stream of silvery smoke. Jay looked uncomfortable, sitting straight up with a blank expression on his face. His jaw was set, and his hand was in a fist on the table.

Charlotte chose a seat nearby and sat with her back to the pair so she could listen.

"I respect you, Jay. You were the best man in the 36th I ever worked with at the docks," the voice of the stranger said. "And Mr. Ringling respects you too. You've always honored our agreement. But you showing up here. Taking our supplies right from under us…I'd expect better from you. Mr. Ringling would be very annoyed."

"I can understand that," Jay responded rigidly. "I can't get into details as to how or why it happened, but I can assure you it is being handled and it won't happen again."

"I hope that's true. But I've got to protect my hide too. I'd find myself without a job if I didn't eliminate this annoyance before news of it reaches my employer."

"I can't undo what's already been done, Verne. I've reordered your supplies so you'll have everything you need when your crew arrives, and we're footing the bill for that as a courtesy. What else would you have me do?"

Charlotte waited, listening without watching as long as she could, but she couldn't endure the long silence between the men. She snuck a furtive glance over her shoulder. Just enough to see the man take a long puff from his cigar and blow the smoke between the two as he fidgeted with the ornate ring on his pinkie finger. She caught Jay's attention through the smoke, and he sent her a solemn stare that sent a new shiver of insecurity down her already weak spine.

He fixed his gaze back on the man with the bowler hat when he finally began to speak.

"Just know that whatever happens next, it isn't personal. I've got a job to do."

"And that job is to ruin us? Let me talk to Mr. Ringling. I'm more than obliged to provide an explanation—"

"This will never get back to him. My job is to ensure annoyances like this one are squashed before they do."

"Are you going to make me say it? You wouldn't even have a job if it wasn't for me. You wouldn't—"

"I've never forgotten how you saved my life in France. Why do you think I came here out of my way to warn you?"

"You're so kind," Jay said flatly.

"You don't know how kind. If I didn't handle it in the way I know how to handle it, what do you think would happen when it went up the chain? Ringling is the master of the ring, the most powerful man in the industry. You saw how he bought out Barnum & Bailey, the biggest transaction in circus history. Do you think he would hesitate to buy you out and shut you down? You'd be in for severe losses. Maybe a Ringling Circus will show up in every city on your route a day before you do. He could blacklist you with your suppliers. Buy all your prize elephants…He could squash your little family show with his pinkie finger. No, the kindest thing I can do is handle your punishment personally."

The man rose from where he was sitting and tapped at his cigar, dashing the ashes all over the table between them. "I'm just warning you as a courtesy because of our mutual respect, Edwards. My advice is to get rid of whatever caused this unfortunate mishap and brace for the fallout. I hope you and this charming little operation survive it, I really do."

The man tossed the butt of his cigar on the ground as he rose, grinding it out in the dirt with the heel of his dusty patent leather Oxford. "If Sterling doesn't make it, you could always come work for a real circus. Ringling would hire you in a heartbeat. I'd make sure of it."

The man ran his thumb and forefinger suavely along the brim of his bowler hat, examining the tent and everyone in it shrewdly as he walked away.

Charlotte was filled with fear and confusion. She turned to Jay and found that he hadn't moved at all. He was still sitting upright, with his hand balled into a fist amidst the ashes. She went to occupy the seat across from him that the man had left open and rested her hand on his fist.

"He didn't seem very nice," Charlotte said gently.

"He doesn't have to be nice." Jay pulled his hand from Charlotte's and pulled thin metal tools from his jacket pocket. "He's right, and we're wrong."

"I don't understand."

Jay popped open the back of his pocket watch and began poking at the fastener of a cog with a tiny flathead screwdriver. "It's pretty simple. Sterling & Son's operates on a predetermined route that avoids the Ringling Circus at all costs."

His tongue pressed in on his upper lip as he performed a minor surgery on the inside of his pocket watch.

"Ringling Brothers, Barnum & Bailey? The Greatest Show on Earth?"

"That's the one." Jay cursed under his breath when his tool slipped and a metal lever snapped back in on a cog he had loosed, rocking a delicate brass wheel at the bottom. He gripped the tools with white knuckles before setting them down deliberately. He looked from the broken watch to Charlotte with a chilling glare that reinvigorated the fears pulsing through her. "And because I've lost focus and allowed things to cloud my judgment, we went off our route last night. We've stepped right onto the toes of—as you put it—the greatest show on earth. We broke our deal."

"But surely that isn't your fault! Why would they—"

"I'm the managing director for Sterling & Son's. Everything that happens on the road is either my design or my fault. Last night they deviated from my design, and now I have to kowtow to one of Ringling's lackeys, beg forgiveness from Sonny, and find a way to get everything back on track. If there's anything left to get on track." Jay picked up the tools and pressed the small lever back again with the tiny screwdriver and pulled a metal splinter from beneath it. He rotated the cog a few times and closed the back of the watch.

Charlotte sat at the edge of her seat, feet planted firmly on the ground, though even the ground beneath her feet felt unsteady. She yearned for his eyes to shrug off their stony glaze and glow with the warmth she'd been so eager to see again. "It can't be as bad as all that. How can I help?"

He turned the watch over and wound it. "You can't help. This is what I get for spending my time and attention on you. On this investigation. Instead of being distracted, I should have confirmed the train schedule. Instead, Hugh confirmed it for me and—"

"Distracted? That was just a distraction to you?" Her face was burning now, eyes tingling ready to cool it with tears.

"Damn." He grunted, tapping at the glass and holding the watch to his ear. "You misunderstand me. What I'm trying to say is—"

"No, I understand you just fine. This is exactly what all the girls warned me about."

"All the girls?"

"Well, don't worry about me distracting you or

setting the whole circus off course again in the future. I'm leaving."

"Please don't be dramatic." He snapped the watch closed and set it on the table.

"I'm not being dramatic. I've come to tell you that we're leaving, Alex and I."

"That's absurd, where will you go?"

"We're going back to Ayer. Jay, I—"

"Look, I'm sorry I'm not pleasant this morning, but I…it's been a morning. That's no reason to threaten to run off. There's nothing for you in Ayer—"

"My husband is in Ayer."

Jay's shoulders dropped, and he narrowed his eyes before he spoke. "How can that be when your husband is dead?"

"I lied."

The storm in his eyes struck lightning in Charlotte that shook her to her core.

"He isn't dead. Maybe I wished he was, but he isn't. It's wrong pretending he's dead when he's not. That's why we're going back. I can't do this anymore."

Jay took in a deep breath through his nose that seemed to make his eyes wider. "You left your living husband and took your son to come—what, have a little excitement? See if you could feel pretty in scanty clothes? Find someone better?"

Anger and frustration swelled up in her chest. "No! That isn't it at all!"

"You lied to your husband, and you've lied to me. How are you better than Vanessa?"

"Vanessa?"

"Never mind." He tucked his watch and tools back into his lapel pocket. "Go back to Ayer then, and I hope you find whatever it is that you didn't find here." Jay adjusted the sleeves of his shirt at his elbows and stood up from the table.

"You don't understand—"

"Thank God you told me before I started having feelings for you." Jay looked down at Charlotte as he placed his hat on his head. "But now I still have to live with myself, knowing I'm the kind of scum who kept company with another man's wife."

Charlotte vibrated with shock and fear. She'd always known things with Jay would end this way. As he walked away, she burned his every feature in her mind. She'd never see him again.

Chapter 34

Moving On

Charlotte hurried back to Birdie's trailer with her head down, brushing past friends and strangers alike. She ducked in and threw herself face-first on the velvet couch to cry.

"So I was right. He's broken your heart already."

Birdie's silk-gloved hands buttoned a jacket over a silk blouse. She was wearing a light brown pleated skirt that went past the knee and a matching hat with a turned-up brim on top of the red hair that, instead of hanging loose about her shoulders, was tied back neatly into a bun. Somewhat stiffly, she handed Charlotte a napkin from the table. It was the one she'd used for her lipstick earlier that morning. She sat staring at the pinkish blur for a moment, trying to focus the definition of a print through her tears and thinking about the note she'd found in Birdie's trailer.

"What are you doing?" Charlotte asked. "And why are you dressed that way?"

Birdie went about the room gathering different things and evaluating their importance. Some items she tossed back down, and some she dropped haphazardly into an open suitcase.

"I told you last night that it was time for me to go soon," Birdie said. "Well, I guess lady luck was listenin', because I had a man come by this morning. Said he was sent straight from John Ringling himself, king of the Ringling Brothers and Barnum & Bailey circus, special for me!"

"Ringling? When did he—"

"He just left." Birdie pushed down on the pile in the suitcase and went back to pulling possessions from random nooks and crannies to add to the growing collection of clothes and shoes.

Charlotte looked behind her instinctively. *Did I pass that man in the bowler hat on my way back?*

"They want me for their star act. Said that he was authorized to pay me anything. Even Lillian Leitzel asked about me and wants to teach me how to use the Roman rings—"

"You're leaving? You can't be—"

"No. Sterling & Son's is leaving. I'm staying right here in El Paso—"

"El Paso?" Charlotte looked around her again, as if there'd be a city sign in the trailer to confirm her question. *I thought we were in Clovis.*

"—and tonight they'll roll out of town short one trapeze artist. Ringling is putting me up at the best hotel in town, and I'll join up with them when they get here in a few days." Birdie collected makeup, pausing to pick up a tube of lipstick, then placing it back on the table. She gathered a few perfumes carefully off the vanity table and wrapped them in one of her silk kimonos before pushing aside some of her costumes to form a little nest for the parcel, which she set in gently. She quickly tucked the dangling white sleeve of a man's shirt down into the mass of silk and sequins.

"Well, you look smart," Charlotte said. "I barely

recognized you."

"I can clean up like a fancy lady when I want to. I'm just partial to my leotard," Birdie said, brushing her gloved hands across the front of her tailored jacket. "This is the real costume."

"Aren't you sad?" Charlotte looked around at the trailer, all of its half-discarded knickknacks scattered desolately about the furniture and the floor. "About what you're leaving behind?"

"Not one bit," Birdie said sharply and snapped her suitcase closed. "I have everything I've ever been able to count on. Me."

Birdie looked at Charlotte with something like pity, and Charlotte shrank beneath her gaze. She wished Birdie would sit with her. Hug her. Cry with her. Offer her some sort of comforting advice.

"You'll tell them for me," Birdie said, still looking down on Charlotte as she sat clinging to the napkin. "I'd half like to see the look on their faces, but if Frank asks me to stay, I…"

Birdie adjusted her grip on the suitcase handle.

"You'll tell them for me," she repeated with finality.

"I'll tell them."

"Listen, little Lottie, you remember what I told you," Birdie said. "You've got to be the star of your own life."

Charlotte nodded and wiped the tears from her eyes.

"I want to tell you…" Birdie's voice faltered as she reached for her own hand, the one that Charlotte had tended to the night before. Her fingers quickly fluttered away. She patted at her hair and pulled her shoulders back, adjusting her posture. "Well, this place is yours now. Take what you want and give the rest to the girls."

Charlotte was speechless. She looked around at the trailer and back at Birdie.

"Everyone except Sasha," she said sharply.

Charlotte laughed. "You got it. Everyone except Sasha."

"Lottie…" Birdie stood looking at her, still clenching her suitcase tightly. Charlotte sat up and looked up at her hopefully. "Thank God you quit with that stutterin'. It was unbearable."

Charlotte sat back into the sofa, pulling her lips between her teeth and staring at the napkin in her hand, using all of her self-control to keep her eyes from rolling.

Birdie lingered for a moment, looking at Charlotte as if she had something else to say. Finally, she tipped her chin down sharply without speaking and stepped out of the private car into the sunshine. For the first time since she'd met Birdie, Charlotte felt jealous of her in that moment. She looked like a woman who knew who she was. A woman who knew where she was going.

Charlotte sat looking around the trashed trailer, ears ringing with the stinging words from Jay. *Did you just come here to wear a scanty costume and feel pretty? See if you could find someone better?*

She fixated on the ivory dancers amongst the trees on the ebony dressing panel.

"I never wanted to wear a costume," she told them. "I never intended to have feelings for Jay. Or join an act. I didn't ask for any of this."

What is it that you want then? they seemed to ask

in return.

The ivory dancers from the dressing panel looked upon Charlotte as she wiped the tears from her eyes. She turned her gaze from her friends on the panel to the stranger in the mirror. Smeared lipstick and purple sequins in disjointed shapes between the cracks. Charlotte washed her face. The shirt sleeve she'd used to dry it before was gone, but there were plush cloths in the drawers of the dressing table.

She stood up and fluffed at the feathers on her hips.

I'm a decorated flightless bird. About as useful as a horse with stripes.

Charlotte turned around and stepped past the dancers on the dressing screen. She sorted through the clothes behind them to find some wide-leg trousers and a silky beige button-up shirt that looked similar to the one Birdie had been wearing when she stepped out into the sun. And the boots, sitting together by the tall mirror. The boots had always been hers. Charlotte quickly changed into the clothes she'd found. This time she recognized herself when she looked in the mirror. She reapplied her lipstick with the tube Birdie had chosen to leave on the dressing table and stepped out of the trailer, not sure of her direction but sure of where she was going.

****

Charlotte moved mechanically through the circus grounds toward the horse tent, surrounded by a swirl of pandemonium. Performers with suitcases ranging from the brown square bricks that looked like Birdie's to bulging pillowcases or makeshift knapsacks were scuttling across the yard. Some were tugging on each other, pleading it seemed, responses ranging from refusal to surprise.

She recognized the old clown who sometimes played cards with her son. His frail body looked small in the oversized pants that hung gaping about his waist, and he shook his finger furiously at a younger clown who seemed to be presenting him with some sort of letter.

"It says anybody who leaves Sterling & Son's for Ringling gets twice their pay, in advance for the first show!" the younger clown said, shaking the paper in the old clown's face. "How can you turn that down, Maurice?"

"I've been loyal to Sterling & Son's for thirty years, that's how. And what do you expect they'll do when half their workers are gone tonight? How will we go on?"

"Exactly! That's why we gotta jump ship now. Birdie Bells is going, the Sahara Sisters are going, Serpentina's going—"

"Well, I'm not. And if you had any loyalty or any sense, you wouldn't either."

The young clown folded the letter and tucked it into Maurice's shirt pocket.

"Think about it. Get out while you can."

Charlotte surveyed the unorganized exodus around her.

The Sahara Sisters are going?

She turned away from her path and headed toward the performers' tents, where the girls should be getting ready for the parade at eleven. When she entered the tent, she found a similar scene. Half-dressed girls shoving their suitcases full and chattering excitedly.

"Can you believe it? The biggest circus in the

world!"

"We'll be famous! Really famous!"

Charlotte filtered through the flurry to find Mei, who, to her disappointment, was packing her suitcase too. She stood in front of her, not sure what to say.

"There you are," Mei said excitedly. "We've been looking for you—what are you wearing?"

Charlotte ignored the question. "Why are you packing your suitcase?"

"The real question is why you aren't packing yours? Haven't you heard?"

Charlotte shook her head slowly, looking around her again before returning her attention to Mei.

"Birdie got us all jobs with Ringling Brothers and Barnum & Bailey! Who knows how she did it, but that's Birdie for you! They arrive in town in two days, and they're paying us double!"

"But you've been here for years with Sterling & Son's. You…you can't just leave them…"

"We aren't leaving them; we're following Birdie. I know she's tough, but Birdie always takes care of us." Mei snapped her suitcase closed.

"But Frank found you. He gave you your big break…"

"He didn't give us anything, and he doesn't care about anyone. None of them do." Mei looked intently at Charlotte. "You know that, right?"

Charlotte bit her lip.

Mei's forehead furrowed. "You're with us, aren't you?"

Charlotte took a step back.

Mei's small mouth spread into a thin line. She picked up her suitcase and let out a sigh.

"If you change your mind," she said, resting a hand on Charlotte's shoulder, "we'll be at the Gardner Hotel."

"Thank you," Charlotte said, "for everything."

Mei nodded. "Good luck, Lottie." Mei gave her shoulder a final gentle pat and walked past her to the opening of the tent.

"Good luck," Charlotte whispered. But Mei was already gone, and so were the other sisters behind her.

Chapter 35

Get There First

Jay opened his pocket watch and scowled at the shaking second hand ticking under the broken glass. The parade was supposed to start in two hours, but the only procession in progress was the one happening before him. By his estimation, a quarter of their performers and workers were on their way either to wait for the Ringling Circus to come through or to take the train out of town, jumping ship altogether before the Sterling Circus could fold. Maybe the same train that would take Lottie back to her dusty old town and out of his life forever.

She's married.

"Jay! What happened? Everyone is leaving!"

Jay shut his pocket watch. His cousin approached in a panic. Frank looked disheveled and exhausted. His eyes had lost their jubilant energy, tugged down by the dark circles beneath them. His usually well-oiled beard was untamed and frizzing in all directions. His neat white shirt was unbuttoned at the collar.

"I know." Jay put his hand on Frank's shoulder. "It's Verne."

Frank looked about him wildly. "What are you talking about?"

"We're in El Paso, Frank. Hugh redirected the

train, and we infringed on the Ringling Brothers and Barnum & Bailey's Circus route. One of their guys came through to rattle us."

Frank's eyes widened, and he looked around him again.

"What's more, Hugh called the supplier here in El Paso and bought out all the supplies intended for their circus, which arrives in two days."

"We have to fix this! We have to leave!"

"It's too late," Jay said. "Your dad meets us in Albuquerque tomorrow with half the investors to collect the money we've made so far and check on our progress. What will he say if we show up with empty pockets and tell him we got lost and skipped a performance…"

"What will we tell him when he learns we pissed off the Greatest Show on Earth?" Frank ran both hands over his disheveled hair. "Hugh is trying to ruin me! My father is going to kill me!"

Jay put both hands on his shoulders. "We're going to salvage this. I've spoken with Verne. What you see before you is a warning shot; it's all they're gonna do. Our job now is to get things back on track and give El Paso a show that'll fill the tents. I need your showmanship, Frank; I need your charisma."

Frank shook his head in dismay. "I can't—"

"Round up the workers. Charm the performers. For goodness' sake, get all your girlfriends over here. Convince them to stay, Frank."

Frank nodded slowly. He took a deep breath in and nodded again more quickly. "I'll go find Birdie. She'll know what to do."

"Birdie's gone."

Jay looked over Frank's shoulder to see Lottie, standing alone in trousers and a man's shirt. Her hair fell about her shoulders in a way that made Jay forget to breathe. She was the only person he wanted to see. And the last person he wanted to see.

"What are you talking about?" Frank cried out. "She can't be! She wouldn't!"

"She asked me to tell you," Charlotte said to Frank. "She's joining the Ringling Circus."

"No!" Frank wailed and pulled at his hair. "No. No. No!"

"Who else?" Jay asked her calmly.

"The Sahara Sisters." Lottie bit her lower lip. "Serpentina. Half the clowns."

"Why would she leave me? Why wouldn't she come tell me herself?" Frank sobbed.

Lottie and Jay stood silently, looking past Frank and at each other. Jay swallowed the lump in his throat. "And you?"

"I want to stay. I—"

"What does your husband want?" Jay hated the bitterness in his own voice.

Lottie looked wounded, but before she could answer, Benny came running in.

"Hugh's loaded up one of the trailers, and he's headed into town," Benny said, panting. "If we wanna catch him in the act, this is our chance."

Jay nodded. He turned to Frank. "Birdie's gone. We'll need to feature a different act, Frank. I need you to figure this out, while I take care of business downtown. I need you to get the parade together."

Frank squeezed his red-rimmed eyes shut and shook his head back and forth. "I can't…I can't!"

"You can," Jay said resolutely. "You're Frank Sterling. This is your circus."

Frank wiped his face on his sleeve. "All right. All right." He took in a deep breath and looked around him.

"Frank, quit looking for Birdie and find Luella."

Frank started. "Luella?"

"Luella is here. She comes to all your shows." Jay nodded at Benny beckoning him onward with a jerk of his head and took a step away. "She's savvy, Frank. And she'd do anything for you. She'll help you figure it out if you let her."

Frank bobbed his head and took a few steps back.

Jay looked to Lottie, who'd stood silently watching. "Stay or go," he said. "But don't do anything for me. There's nothing here."

Lottie's jaw clenched. She didn't move or speak. She simply blinked and continued to stare. Jay felt he was looking at a stranger. How could she have kissed him so passionately the night before when she was married to someone else?

Benny placed his hand on Jay's shoulder. "We've gotta go! If we don't catch him in the act, it's all a waste!"

Jay turned to follow his friend to the car.

As he left, Lottie was speaking to Frank. "I can help you too. I have an idea. Let's find Luella together."

****

When Jay and Benny pulled up to the two-story general store on Main Street, he could have kicked himself. "Of course, this is who Hugh has a shady deal with," he said to Benny. "I thought the guy was out of his mind for selling us all of Ringling's supplies, but

Hugh had a hold over him."

Benny shook his head. "I never can understand that guy."

A black Model T and a paddy wagon rolled to a stop behind Jay and Benny, and the sheriff stepped out along with a few armed officers. The sheriff approached the men, shaking their hands. "Mr. Edwards, Mr. Brooks. Thanks for the tip." He placed a hand above his eyes and looked up at the building. "All right, we'll do this just as we discussed, Mr. Edwards. You go on in and engage the suspect in conversation. The owner of this general store is a big deal in town, and I'm gonna have a helluva time arresting him without a confession. Even if we do catch 'em in the act. Do the best you can. We'll be behind you. Outta sight." The sheriff turned to his men and gestured that they enter the building quietly. "We'll come out when the time is right."

Jay let out a sigh and nodded. He turned toward the building and slipped around the back. The Sterling & Son's delivery wagon was parked at the far end of the building in the alley, and he looked carefully around for anyone who might be lying in wait. *Pretty bold, Hugh. No lookout?*

He took off his hat and fidgeted with the brim as he made his way to the door, feeling the intense focus fueled by adrenaline that he'd learned to manage during the war. His breaths were measured, and his hands were steady as he slowly opened the screen door by the wagon and stepped inside.

The lights were off. Jay stood silently, patiently waiting for a sound. He stepped toward the sounds of clinking glass and murmuring voices to his left, rolling his feet at the heel so that his steps were silent. He stopped at the slice of light creeping out beneath a pair of wooden doors. Behind him, two police officers crouched with their guns drawn. Jay placed his hand on the doorknob and pulled the door open.

Inside the storeroom, Hugh stood with his back to the door. His jacket lay casually over a chair with his snappy hat placed on top, and he stood chatting with a large man in a wide-brimmed tan Stetson. Beyond them, a handful of young Hispanic men stacked the crates behind a false wall. One of the workers turned around and spotted Jay, his eyes growing wide. The man in the Stetson turned to see what had caught the eye of his crate carrier.

"Who the hell are you?" The big cowboy drew the six-shooter from his side holster and aimed it right at Jay.

"My name is Jay Edwards," Jay said calmly, still holding his own hat by the brim, "I'm the managing director of the Sterling & Son's Circus. And I'm Mr. Sterling's cousin."

Hugh turned around slowly and revealed his face. Jay couldn't hide his disappointment. He knew he shouldn't have been surprised at the scene in the storeroom, but a part of him had still hoped his cousin was innocent.

"What are you doing here, Jay?" Hugh sounded more annoyed than afraid. "Don't you have enough to handle back at the lot?"

"You've given me plenty of problems to deal with today, that's for sure," Jay said.

The cowboy with the gun pulled back the hammer. "Cousin or no cousin, I don't need nobody meddlin' in my businesses, fancy-pants."

"I'm not here to meddle." Jay held up his hands, an open right palm with his hat in the other. "I'm just here to understand."

"Understand?" The cowboy looked from Jay to Hugh.

"You've got it made, Hugh. You're one of us. Why do you need to smuggle—what is it? Moonshine? Liquor?"

Hugh rolled his eyes. "You really don't get it, do you?" He pulled a wad of cash from his pocket. "Money! It's not complicated. I'm not going to be left with nothing when Sonny hands everything to Junior, and then Frank blows it all. I'm taking care of me."

"You really had me fooled," Jay said.

Hugh smirked. "Well, you've been a little distracted."

Jay suppressed a wince. It was a punch to the gut. "So it's been going on all along? You sell booze at every town we stop in?"

Hugh shrugged.

"How?"

"How? What, is Jay Edwards the only one who can coordinate logistics? I have a system too. A whole team."

The cowboy lowered his gun and stepped back, looking past Jay to the exit.

"Sonny doesn't pay any of us enough. Turns out it isn't too hard to find employees willing to do a few favors for some extra cash. I send out a few of the girls to scope out a town and find out where the speakeasies are. And I pay the advance men extra to strike a deal."

"That's brilliant, Hugh. I underestimated you." Jay

set his hat on the table. "And how about you, Mr..."

"I ain't fixin' to tell you my name, or nothin' else." The cowboy gestured to the workers to close up the wall. "I think it would be best for everybody if you forget what you saw and skedaddle on outta here."

Jay nodded slowly and returned his attention to Hugh. "So is that how you tricked this redneck into selling you the supplies for the other circus? You blackmailed him?"

The cowboy grew red in the face. "Now hold on just a minute." He raised his gun again at Jay. "I don't like the word blackmail. I can have Miguel and his boys open that wall back up and stick your dead body right next to the moonshine."

Jay put his hands in the air and looked back at Hugh. "Was Hazel one of those girls? The girls who found idiots like this guy for you to sell to?"

"I don't like your cousin, Hugh. I think it's time for him to go. Time for you to go too, come to think of it."

Hugh sighed. "See what you've done, Jay. All right, Mr. Perry, pay the rest of what you owe, and we'll both be on our way."

The cowboy laughed. "Our deal was for a discreet shipment of whiskey and gin. I ain't payin' for your family reunion here."

Hugh took a step toward the cowboy in protest, but he swung the gun to aim at him. "Leave now, and count your lucky stars that you're leavin' with the same number of holes in your body that you came in with."

Hugh turned his back to the cowboy, collected his coat and hat, and glared at Jay as he walked through the doors. Jay picked up his hat, tipped it toward the cowboy and his workers, and followed Hugh out of the storeroom. Once in the hallway, the police rose from the shadows and entered the room Jay and Hugh had just left.

Shouts of "Freeze!" and "Hands up!" and "Drop your weapon!" rang out into the hall.

"Hugh Sterling?" An officer approached him calmly amidst the chaos.

Hugh's eyebrows flew nearly to his hairline, and he slowly extended his hands for the officer who approached him.

"You're under arrest, sir. Come with me." The policeman snapped the handcuffs onto Hugh's wrist and led him through the hallway. Jay walked alongside him.

"Did you kill her, Hugh?"

Hugh's eyebrows hadn't returned to their normal resting place above the eyes that now burned with hatred and glared directly at Jay.

"Hazel, the cannon girl. She was blackmailing you, wasn't she?"

Hugh looked back to the ground, shaking his head.

"Did you kill her?"

A slow chuckle rose up through Hugh. He looked back up at Jay with a smirk. "What's your next question?"

"My next—"

"Don't you want to know where I got the money? Who financed all this?"

Jay stopped in his tracks. "It couldn't be Sonny…"

Hugh laughed. "No, no, don't worry. Uncle Sonny hasn't fallen from grace…"

Benny came over to stand by Jay as the policeman pushed Hugh into the back of the paddy wagon.

"Then who?" Jay asked.

"Vanessa," Hugh shouted through the window. "Vanessa and her new husband, Butch McNeil."

"No more questions, please," the policeman said to Jay. "We'll give him the third degree at the station. Sheriff will want you to come in too. To give a statement."

The police cars rolled out of sight with Hugh, the cowboy, and the three accomplices from the storeroom in tow. Benny stood beside Jay, watching with his jaw hanging open.

The two looked at one another for a moment, exchanging expressions of shock, surprise, and relief. Finally, Jay broke the silence. "I suppose I should call Saul and let him know he doesn't have to keep that body on ice anymore. He'll need to meet us out here with the gun and a statement from their coroner now that Hugh's in custody."

Benny nodded and followed Jay inside the empty general store to look for a telephone.

The eerie silence of the store was a jarring contrast to the cursing, protesting, and the ringing commands of police, which had filled it mere moments ago. Jay turned to Benny, who was still walking beside him. "I'm glad to have you with me, Benny. You're a good friend."

Benny clapped his hand on Jay's shoulder with a lopsided smile. "Hey! There's a phone!"

Jay picked up the receiver and asked the operator for the Winslow Inn & Cookhouse in Ayer. He was ready to resolve all of this with Saul.

"Hello." A woman's voice answered the phone.

Jay was caught off guard. "Ah, hello, ma'am. Is

Mr. Winslow available? I—"

"He's not, I'm sorry. May I ask who's looking for him?"

"Yes, pardon. My name is Jay Edwards. I'm the managing director for the Sterling & Son's—"

"You're that circus man!" She took on an angrier tone.

Jay laughed. "I am."

"Y'all have brought us all sorts of trouble, and no mistake!" the woman exclaimed. "I always told Saul ain't nothin' good come from the circus. And here we are, aren't we? Here we are! You know we've got a dead girl in our ice house?"

"Yes, I…I'm sorry…"

"A dead girl! Not three feet from the bacon!"

"I've called to talk to Mr. Winslow about that. I believe we've caught the killer, so if I could talk to him—"

"Nossir, you can't. My husband ain't here, Mr. Edwards. Took a train two nights ago to get up to Albuquerque in time for your next stop."

"Oh. I…As a matter of fact, we're not in Albuquerque yet. We're in El Paso. But that is fortuitous because I do need to see him. Did he bring the gun with him? A statement from the sheriff, or—"

"I don't know. I don't know. But he's not on his way there to meet you. He's looking for a girl who used to work for us. She left town on the circus train when y'all rolled through, escapin' her no-good husband. Thank the Lord. He's a terrible man. Beat her, treated her like dirt."

Jay gripped the receiver tighter.

"He came lookin' for her the other day, that damn

fool of a husband, and he saw the letters she's been writing to us."

"Mrs. Winslow…" Jay took a deep breath. "What's the girl's name?"

"Lottie," she said, "Lottie Baxter. We think her husband has gone after her, and we think he's gon' kill her, maybe her poor boy too. Saul is trying to get to them before he does."

Chapter 36

On With The Show

Charlotte hadn't seen the whole parade, but from where she sat leading the zebras, it had gone well. They still had the jazz band to start them off and a series of talented acrobats. Of course, their little modified parade would be nothing compared to the Ringling Brothers and Barnum & Bailey's parade that El Paso folks would see in a few days—the million-dollar free show—but the crowd was happy today. So tomorrow didn't matter.

"Mom!" Alex ran over to greet Charlotte as she hopped off her zebra and handed the reins to the waiting menagerie man. "The parade was great! They showed every animal from the menagerie this time!"

It had been Luella's idea to fill up the parade by featuring more of the animals because it didn't take many workers or performers to roll them through the parade.

Charlotte hugged her son. "Want to help me with the horses? I think we have just enough time to run through the routine and still give them a little rest before the two o'clock."

On their way, Alex told Charlotte all about his morning in the school tent. All sorts of people had come in and nabbed their kids, telling Pearl that they'd only get the double pay if they were gone before the parade. "I turned around every time a new person came in. I was wondering if you were going to come get me too."

"I thought about leaving," Charlotte said, "but—"

"I'm glad you didn't."

Charlotte stopped to face her son. He seemed a little taller, a little more grown-up.

Alex beamed up at her. "I like it here. I want to stay."

It was a flash of lightning in a dark storm. *He wants to stay.* That hope energized Charlotte and gave her an idea. "Alex. I bet they're a little shorthanded behind the scenes. Would you like to work the lights during the show? I bet if you ask Jay—"

"Yes!" Alex clapped his hands together. "Oh yes, I would love that!"

"We'll find him when he gets back." A sad realization tugged at her. Conversations with Jay would be different now. There was nothing for her here with Jay.

When they entered the practice tent, the equestrian director was just leading in the line of white horses. Their elegant hooves trotted gracefully across the sawdust, hardly kicking up a speck from the ground beneath them. At the end of the line, she spotted Pegasus.

Charlotte strode over to the elegant horse. Just as her father had taught her to do, she took a calm breath. A deep breath. She looked deep into the eyes of the horse and waited to feel the trust between them.

Charlotte waved Alex over and gave him a handful of sugar cubes. She helped him hold his hand up to Pegasus so that the majestic animal could nibble at the sugar from his palm. "The thing about horses, Alex, is that there's no pretending with them. They see right through you to your soul."

Alex looked at his mother and back at the horse.

"And if your soul is true, they'll love you forever."

"They'll love you forever," Alex whispered. Her son ran his hand over the horse's neck like a natural, and Pegasus lowered his nose under the careful hand, trusting him.

He'll grow up to be a good man, a patient and gentle man.

"We'd better do that run-through, Miss Cameron," the equestrian director shouted.

"What is the signal for 'kneel'?" she asked without looking away from Pegasus.

The man flourished his arm, and the row of horses bent their left legs and extended their graceful noses to the ground. Charlotte kicked off her boots and gently climbed onto Pegasus's waiting back.

"Let's go," she whispered in his ear. Pegasus rose up and began to trot slowly around the ring. The line of white horses followed.

She kicked at the horse's ribs and picked up speed, the new wind rippling through her hair. Feeling bold, she gripped the horse's back with two hands and slowly rose up to place each foot on his back like she'd done when she was a child. Pegasus trotted calmly and confidently beneath her as she released her hands and stood up, arms extended.

Two horses flanked Pegasus as the team continued trotting, and another row of three kept perfect step behind them. Charlotte wasn't directing them. They were allowing her to join them. She raised one of her legs out behind her, toe pointed, and extended her arms gracefully to either side as Pegasus continued leading the horses around the ring.

After a moment, she sat back down on the horse and the team slowed to a stop. She leaned down to rest on his neck, tears in her eyes.

"Sir," she said without looking up, "could you teach me the rest of the cues?"

****

Charlotte stood next to Pegasus behind the tent flap, waiting for Frank to announce "Lady Lottie and the Liberty Horses" as Sasha and a team of aerialists performed in the center ring. In the ring to her left, clowns in cars put on a show, and in the ring to her right, elephants with dancers seated on their heads took graceful stomps around the circle. So far, the two o'clock show seemed to be a success. It wasn't a packed house, but there were plenty of people in the audience. Lottie hoped that Jay would be pleased. That he'd be able to face Sonny and the investors tomorrow with Frank at his side knowing they'd pulled it off.

"And now, ladies and gentlemen, allow me to direct your attention to the center ring for Lady Lottie and her Liberty Horses!"

Charlotte smiled and waved, leading the six white horses into the center ring to the triumphant tune of the band in the decks before her. She spotted her son as he wheeled the light cylinder toward her and gave him a wink before turning back to wave a graceful arm across the horses who stood in a perfect line facing the audience.

"Popcorn! Popcorn!" a pitchman hollered. Center ring sounds overcame the persistent whispers of doubt.

Charlotte's fears faded under the mixture of oohs and aahs from the audience as she stood in the center ring and gave the horses different cues, to trot or canter, to tap at the ground or step up on their hind legs. But the smell of popcorn along with cotton candy was poisoned by a familiar wave of smoky sarsaparilla. She froze. Squinting against the lights on her, she fought spots in her vision as she searched the crowd. What was she doing?

"Show 'em what you've got, girl," Frank hollered from the side.

Shaken from her trance, she signaled for the horses to kneel and walked up beside Pegasus. "Are you ready, pal?" Pegasus's patient waiting eyes calmed her nerves. She swung her legs over on his back, signaling for all of the horses to rise into a new formation as the band began to play a new song. Charlotte's heart swelled with pride, happiness, and freedom as she rode amongst the majestic horses through the center ring to the applause of the crowd. She placed her hands on Pegasus's shoulders and slowly rose up to place her feet on his back. She stood up to her full height and extended her arms, closing her eyes and hugging in the ecstasy of the air. The pure joy of doing what she was always meant to do in exactly the way she wanted to do it.

BANG!

The murmured awe of the audience erupted into screams. The horse next to her reared up and squealed.

BANG!

Pegasus trotted backward as the other five horses bolted around the ring in panic. Charlotte wobbled on his back, trying not to lose her balance.

BANG!

Pegasus wailed in agony and toppled forward, sending Charlotte flying to the ground amidst a stampede of horses and a loud and confusing blare of horns and screaming. The last thing she saw was the body of the goliath white horse tumbling down on her.

Everything went black.

****

Charlotte's ears were ringing as a memory tugged at her. Like a bell above a door allowing something to enter. Dazed, her eyes fluttered open, and the familiar walls of Saul's cookhouse materialized around her. Her hands were holding a cloth. Wiping a table. The door opened, bell clanging. The dull click, click, click of heels punched up dust on the wood floor as they made their way toward her.

"So you're Charlotte Baxter, then." The woman dragged the chair back and sat down at the table. "I've been looking for you."

"How can I help you?" Charlotte asked, setting down her dishrag and wiping at her forehead with the back of her hand.

"You'll wanna sit down too," the woman said, gesturing at the seat across from her. "Do you know who I am?"

Charlotte shook her head and sat down opposite the woman.

"My name is Hazel. I was born Hazel Beauford. Then I was married. I've been goin' around thinking my name was Hazel Stallman." The woman pulled her gloves off finger by finger with her teeth and reached into her purse to pull out a photograph. She slid it across the table to Charlotte. "But maybe you can tell me who the man in that photograph really is, because I met Rex Stallman this mornin', and that ain't him."

Charlotte stared at the photograph. In the picture, the woman before her stood in a delicate white dress with a bouquet of flowers in a church. Behind her was a balding man holding a Bible, and across from her—Across from her was…

"That looks like my husband, Pete," Charlotte said.

"Don't it just." Hazel leaned back in her chair. "Problem is, he's my husband."

Charlotte's trembling fingers picked up the photograph to examine it more closely. She flipped it over to look at the back. "When was this taken?"

"Last year."

Charlotte dropped the photograph. "Last year? That ca-can't be true!"

Hazel took the photograph from the table and put it back in her purse. "I met him in a speakeasy when I was runnin' rum for a fella named Hugh Sterling up by Forth Worth. Your Pete there fell in love with me the first night he saw me. Offered me the world just to get these knickers off."

Charlotte gasped for air. "This has to be a misunderstanding. We've been married for ten years."

Hazel tossed her head back and laughed. It was a wicked rueful laugh that chilled Charlotte to the bone.

"We have a son!" Charlotte said, slamming her hands on the table.

Hazel lowered her head slowly and glared across the table at Charlotte. "So did we. But I had to give him up. My husband left me pregnant and alone to run back to you."

Charlotte stood up. "N-n-no. You're lying. This

can't be true."

"You know I ain't lyin'! You're the one who's lyin'." The woman laughed. "Lyin' to yourself! You want proof? The picture isn't good enough? How about I describe the way his tongue tastes after he's been at that tobacco he used to smoke in the war…"

Charlotte's stomach turned as the woman's descriptions became more vulgar. "Why are you here? What do you want?"

Hazel leaned in. "I had to see with my own two eyes the woman Rex—or Pete, I guess—ran back to. I'd built it up in my head she must be some kinda Mata Hari. Some Queen of Sheba. But look at you! You're nothin' at all. Look at you, and look at me! Why the hell would he come back to you when he had me?"

The sting of tears was nothing to the way her body felt ready to eat her alive from the inside out.

"The way I see it, it ain't fair that you get to sit here with a husband and a son, and I don't have either. It ain't right for you to have everything when I got nothin'. And that's just what I'll tell Pete when I see him today. I ain't leavin' here empty-handed. An' I bet he don't leave here without his son."

Charlotte was unable to speak. She stood up, stumbled backward, and ran from the cookhouse.

Chapter 37

The Final Act

Adrenaline was pumping through Jay's body in a way he hadn't experienced since his time in the trenches. Performers and workers flooded to the center ring to pull the horse off Lottie. Others made a barrier around the ring to hold off the audience, pushing forward to get a better look at the bloody scene. *I'm too late.*

His next thoughts turned to Sadie and Alex, and then to the shooter. Jay narrowed his eyes, frantically searching for the children among the throng. He couldn't see them. "Benny—" He spun around.

"Go," Benny said. "You get the shooter. I'll take care of the kids."

Jay desperately wanted to run to Lottie. To see if she was breathing. To hold her hand. To—

There wasn't time for that now. She had help. Jay needed to find the shooter and take him down. He cut through the tent toward the exit closest to where the shots had come from. Jay thought he'd caught a glimpse of the shooter, but he couldn't be sure. What was he looking for?

His feet pounded the dry dirt outside of the tent, sun relentlessly baking the air in front of him so that any space between him and a hundred paces was rippling in the heat like a mirage. He shook his head and blinked hard, defying the haze. He stared through it until he spotted someone familiar.

Alex. He was being tugged along by a skinny red-faced man in a cowboy hat. Jay ran toward the pair. As he got closer, he identified the pistol in the man's right hand. A Colt .45 with a decorative cylinder. The same kind of gun that had been used to shoot Hazel. Jay didn't understand everything in that moment, but he knew this must be the man that shot Lottie. And if he shot Lottie, he must have killed Hazel too.

"Stop!" Jay yelled, closing in on them. "Stop! Let the boy go!"

The man wheeled around like a viper and aimed his pistol right at Jay's chest.

"This is my boy!" the man snarled. "Who the hell are you?"

So this is Pete. He looked to Alex. "Are you okay?"

Alex's eyes were filled with tears. "My mom—"

"Let's go back and make sure she's okay." Jay held out his hand toward Alex while sizing Pete up. Jay knew he could take him, even with the gun. But he wouldn't risk it with Alex in the middle.

Alex tried a step toward Jay, but Pete yanked him back and raised his gun up into the air, firing a shot.

"That was a warning shot, hombre. Scram, or the next one goes between your eyes."

"Why don't you let go of Alex, and we can talk," Jay suggested.

Pete pulled harder on Alex's collar, and his left eye began to twitch. "Listen, I don't know how you know my son. But I don't know you from Adam, and I don't owe you shit."

"I just want to know why you've shot two of my circus performers," Jay responded calmly as he edged forward slowly.

The man laughed. "I did what I had to, to get my son back. Plain and simple. Them girls are all disposable to y'all, so it don't hurt you nohow. I saw that girl in Fort Worth fly out of the cannon and break her neck when I was at one of your shows, but sure 'nuff, you've got another girl on it even now. When that dumb slut Hazel got ideas and came lookin' for me—well, I got an idea of my own, didn't I."

"So you shot her and made it look like an accident."

"Don't judge me! Sittin' there with your fancy suit. You don't know nothin'. That bitch was going to ruin me. And then Charlotte ran off with my son. My son! She deserved what she got too. She was outta line, so I put her down. I got my boy back, so I ain't gonna cause you no more trouble as long as you keep your nose out of it and let us on our way."

"I'll let you go. Fine. But I'm not letting you take Alex. If you want to go anywhere, you'll need to leave him with me."

The man snarled, "Who the hell do you think you are?"

Jay let out a long breath and rolled each of his shirt sleeves up to his elbows. "My name is Jay Edwards. I'm the managing direct…I work for the circus. I love Alex like he's my own son. And I'm probably in love with your wife."

Pete growled, throwing Alex across the dirt and putting two hands on his pistol. Jay stood firm as Pete took two long strides toward him. "Well, you can join her in Hell then." Pete spat in the dirt as he lifted up the gun to Jay's chest. He pulled back the hammer.

Jay went into action. He clapped Pete's wrists with one hand and pulled them down to his side as Pete pulled the trigger. The shot ripped through Jay's calf like a tiger's claw. Gritting his teeth through the pain, Jay finished the move and broke the wrist of Pete's gun-wielding hand, snapping the bones under his fingers like brittle branches as the gun fell from Pete's grasp. Pete wailed and cursed.

Jay searched around him while he still had Pete pinned by his broken arm and spotted Alex scooting backward away from the scuffle. Wide eyes watching in terror. "Run, Alex," Jay shouted. "Go find Benny. Get help!"

Alex nodded. He stood up feebly, stumbled backward, and ran back to the circus grounds.

Pete wriggled beneath Jay. "Alex, don't listen to him! Goddam it, get back here!" Pete stumbled back, watching his son run away from him. "Get back here, and help out your old man!"

But Alex didn't turn back.

A renewed rage flared in Pete's eyes as he narrowed them at Jay. He let out a yell as he took a swing at him. Blow by blow, the two did battle under the blazing sun, wrestling in the dirt between cacti and the red-flowering ocotillo bushes.

Jay pinned Pete to the ground with both knees and slammed his fist into his scowling face. Right fist, splattering blood. Left fist, crushing bone. He thought of the fear in Alex's eyes as he had turned to run away. He thought about the way this man had treated Lottie, how worthless he'd made her feel. How she'd been brave enough to get away only to be hunted down and shot like an animal by this selfish snarling redneck.

His muscle memory took over, and he was back in the war. Scrambling in the trenches with the enemy. Mad as hell. Jay punched him again. And again.

Jay knew what it felt like for a man's life force to fade from his body, and he could sense it in Pete.

Pete was minutes—maybe seconds—from death.

He had him. He could kill him. Just a few more punches.

Jay hesitated, fist in the air. Looking down into Pete's bloodied and swelling eyes, Jay got a sense that Pete had been wrought by the war too. The war, where they'd both been trained to solve their problems with a wary eye on the horizon and a quick sure bullet. Jay was sure. Pete had tasted death before the murder of Hazel. Before shooting his wife moments ago. Pete's eyes said he knew he wasn't long for this world. Something in him seemed to be begging for death when he should be fighting back.

Jay let his arm drop to his side.

"Enough." He fell back and stumbled over Pete's battered body, wincing at the pain in his leg as he stood up. Jay glanced down to see the blood rolling over his shoe as he rubbed at his jaw. "We've gotta take you in. Make sense of all this. You need to confess your murders to the sheriff and get this business wrapped up."

"No!" Pete reanimated and kicked at Jay's hurt leg, toppling him against his will back into the dirt, sending up a cloud of dust. "We ain't skippin' back arm and arm to chat with the law. You die, I die, or both of us do."

The two scuffled in the dirt, throwing wild punches. Both of them scrambling for the gun. Reaching.

BANG!

Pete groaned and gripped his belly. He collapsed and crumpled forward onto the ground, sending up a final cloud of dust.

Jay reeled and pushed back from Pete with open hands. He looked around him for the shooter.

Strutting through the dust, skittering lizards, and soaring grasshoppers was Luella. She tucked her gun back into the leg holster under her dress and reached her hand out to Jay to help him up.

"Alex was right, you did need help," she said to Jay, shaking her head. "Haven't I told you that you need to start carryin' a gun?"

****

Limping back to the circus grounds, Jay thought about what an extraordinary day it had been. He'd had a gun pointed at him twice. And now he'd have to call the sheriff and talk to him for the third time in one day. What Jay wanted to do was stop and examine his throbbing ankle, or maybe go back and kick the body in the dust with his good foot. But the pain of losing Lottie with so many things unsaid reduced Jay's ankle and his anger to a numb distant pain that he could deal with later.

To Jay's surprise, there were still people in the sideshow tents. Still people in the menagerie. They walked past a pitchman yelling. "Step right up, step right up! See the heroic horse who braved a bullet!"

A line of people waiting to pay the pitchman and

enter the tent wound through the circus grounds. Jay turned to Luella.

"People were lining up to see Pegasus after they took Lottie to the medic tent," she said. "And rumors started to spread, that the horse had deliberately gone up on two legs to take a bullet to the chest and save his rider. So I thought we might as well charge admission to see him."

"Save his rider?" Jay asked, looking over at Luella.

Luella smiled. "Lottie was unconscious when Joe carried her to the medic's tent, but she was breathing. The bullet didn't get her. Pegasus took the shot for her."

Jay brought his fist to his mouth and drew in a deep breath as his eyes filled with tears.

"Luella," Jay said when he could speak again. "You're an angel. A genius, and an angel."

Luella laughed.

"I mean it. You were made for this business. The way you saved Lottie. Saved me. You're helping Frank grow into the man he was always meant to be…thank God for you. When we roll into Albuquerque, I'll tell Sonny about everything you've done for us today. Who knows, maybe he'll choose you as his successor."

Luella nudged Jay with a sly grin. "Come on, Jay," she said. "Let's go see your girl."

****

Jay had to sift through a crowd of employees to get through to the medic tent. Everyone was pushing for a closer spot, asking one another what had happened. When he entered the tent with Luella, he found a crew of employees inside standing around a cot, hats on hearts. Obscuring his view were the large shoulders of the steward, a handful of cookhouse employees, Frank, and Saul Winslow.

Lottie's gentle voice floated through the crowd. Jay weaved through the cluster until he could see Lottie's face. She lay on a cot in the center of the tent, with her arm around her son. Her head was wrapped in white gauze above her ears. Lottie's eyes were weak, but her mouth parted in a slight smile at the sight of Jay.

A flood of relief washed over him, escaping the corner of his eye in a small teardrop that he allowed to run down his face and drip off his chin. Lottie was alive.

"How is she?" Jay asked the medic.

"Hit her head pretty bad. Might have a concussion," the medic advised him. "But other than that, she's really okay. She's got some bruises from her fall, but somehow no broken bones or damage to her back. That horse nearly fell right on top of her, but it looks like he rolled off her legs and missed her body. She's lucky to be alive."

"He saved me," Lottie said from the cot. "Pegasus saved me."

"What the hell happened?" Frank asked in a fury. "Who was that guy?"

"Pete Baxter," Jay said, brushing briars from his pants.

Charlotte's eyes grew wide with shock.

"The same guy who killed Hazel," Jay continued. "He admitted it."

Charlotte squeezed her eyes shut and put her hand to her head. "Pete is my husband," she said. "I didn't know he…I found out…right before…May I have my purse, please?"

Chuck nodded to one of his cookhouse employees,

who ran out of the tent. "You don't have to talk about it right now, Lottie. You need your rest." He took out his bandana and wiped at his red-rimmed eyes. "You gave all of us a scare there, girl."

"Mr. Winslow." Jay stepped over to Saul to shake his hand. "It's so good to see you."

"I just wish I'd gotten here sooner. I called Martha when I got to Albuquerque. When she said y'all were here, well, I jumped the first train. But I—" Saul paused. "I shoulda taken out that worthless husband of hers when I had the chance. He never did appreciate Lottie. Everyone who ever met her loved her, but he never did. He just…"

Frank took Luella's hand as he listened to Saul. "Forgive me, Luella," he said to her quietly. "I've been a fool. Can you forgive me?"

Luella bit her bottom lip. After a moment, she rewarded Frank with a subtle nod. He kissed her hand.

"Well, you don't have to worry about Pete now," Jay said, looking at Lottie as he spoke softly to Saul. "He's gone."

"Is he, now?" Saul stepped back and put his hands in his pockets.

"I'm sorry, I still don't understand," Frank said. "What does Lottie's husband have to do with Hazel?"

The kitchen boy returned with Lottie's purse. She thanked him and began digging through it to pull out a stack of letters and photographs. "Hazel came to see me in Ayer, the day the circus arrived. She believed she had married a man named Rex Stallman, who'd abandoned her. When she came into town looking for Rex, she found him. But he wasn't the man she thought he was."

"That makes sense," Saul said, "the sheriff said that she'd been out to the Stallman ranch and caused a ruckus."

"The man she'd really married gave her a false name, the name of his boss, because he was already married." Charlotte handed the photograph to Saul, who passed it to Jay. "To me."

"That's Pete, all right," Saul said. "But the sheriff said he probably never intended to marry her. Hazel had a track record for prostitution and blackmail. The sheriff imagines he got in too deep with her, that she learned some secret of his and threatened to expose him if he didn't marry her."

"I don't know, Saul. These letters…" Charlotte sighed. "It looks like they were pretty passionate."

"Pete said he had to kill her because she was going to ruin everything. So do you think she found him and threatened him?" Jay asked.

"I don't see how. He was out of town," Charlotte said.

Saul nodded. "He told you that, Lottie, but the sheriff and I talked to Rex and he said he hadn't sent him anywhere. Apparently, Pete had 'lost' a lot of money on the road the last time Rex let him travel, so he wasn't allowed to go out to Fort Worth no more. Sheriff reckons Pete was in Ayer that whole time, so he could have watched the first show and made a plan to kill Hazel in the second show."

"I knew I saw him," Lottie said. "I knew I saw him outside the tent. That's why we ran away, Alex and I. That's when we met you, Joe." Lottie smiled up at Joe the strongman, who blushed.

Jay desperately longed to receive a smile from

Lottie like that one.

"I saw him again in Pecos. Mei and I ran from him and...I wasn't sure then, but I'm sure now. He must have jumped the train and..."

"Waited for his chance to take a shot at you," Frank answered.

"He'll always be following me. He'll never leave us alone." Lottie's eyes overflowed.

Luella stepped in. "Oh, honey, didn't you know?"

Lottie looked up.

"Pete won't be troubling you anymore, darling. Jay chased him down and kicked the tar out of him, and I shot him dead."

A squeak escaped from Alex at the word *dead*, and he buried his face in his mother's chest. Lottie held him tighter and looked up at Jay. Her expression was something of gratitude and despair, and Jay wanted to run to her and wrap both of them in a protective hug. He remembered the room full of people and composed himself.

"You killed a man?" Frank asked incredulously, looking at Luella in awe.

"She saved me in Pecos, and she saved me here." Lottie wiped a tear from her cheek as everyone in the tent turned to look at the woman who'd surprised them all with her bravery and boldness. "Thank you, Luella."

Frank's eyes were still on his fiancée. "You are incredible, woman."

Luella smiled up at Frank. "Let's give them some room, huh? We've got to discuss the eight o'clock show."

"After you." Frank followed Luella almost in a trance as the two ducked out of the medic's tent, clapping Jay's shoulder as he passed. Jay winced with pain.

"Well, what's wrong with you?" asked the medic, eyeing Jay.

"I'm fine. I'm fine. Take care of Lottie—"

"He was shot. In the leg. My dad…Pete…" Alex swallowed hard, unable to speak further.

Lottie squeezed his hand, watching her son as he sat up a little straighter and settled his mouth into a thin line.

"Shot? Edwards, get over here," the medic barked as he pulled a cot alongside Lottie's.

Jay limped to the cot and lifted his pant leg.

The medic rolled his eyes and put out his cigarette. "All right, everyone, clear out. Let me do my job."

"Why don't you come with me, Alex." Chuck placed a gentle hand on Alex's shoulder. "You need a good hot meal."

"I'm not hungry," Alex said, wiping the tears from his eyes.

"Maybe a balloon?" Chuck suggested. "Come on, we'll get you some cotton candy or somethin'."

"I do like balloons," Alex said, still looking at his mother.

"I'm all right." Lottie smiled weakly, patting her son's hand and letting go. "I'm not going anywhere."

Alex nodded and rose to follow Chuck out of the tent. "Hey, Chuck, do you know how to play poker?"

Jay smiled as he watched them, thinking of Sadie and the clowns. It was cut short by the stinging burn of alcohol on his bleeding leg. He sucked air through his teeth as the medic tugged and dug at his wound.

"You need anything, Lottie?" Saul asked, kneeling

down to take her hand. Her eyes filled with tears again.

"I'm sorry I left," she said. "Saul, I'm sorry I—"

"Sorry? Shoot, Martha and I've been hoping you'd move on for years."

Lottie looked confused.

"When I heard you joined the circus, saw you up in your own act with those horses..." Saul drew in a whistle. "I thought, 'There she is. That's our Lottie.' "

"It was a silly dream, Saul. Now look at me. Honestly, it serves me right, lying here. Look what happened to Hazel. I'm lucky I'm not dead. You can't have it all, you know."

"Says who?"

"Says everyone! Pete, Birdie, Mei, Ada, the world...I need to go home, Saul. I need to be a good mom."

"And what makes you think being home in Ayer makes you a good momma when traveling on a circus train doesn't?"

Lottie paused thoughtfully. "Well, you know, nothing good comes from the circus." She laughed.

Saul placed his other hand on top of hers. "Listen, I don't know who Birdie or Mei or...well, any of those folks are. But I know Pete, and I think I know a little bit about this Hazel. Folks like those are chasin' at dust. Don't know what they want or how to get it. Like one of our Texas dust storms, they just make a mess for everyone else with their selfishness."

Jay considered that for a moment, the way Hugh seemed to spin a dirt devil of chaos in every dusty town he swept through. The way Vanessa had left a barren trail of frustration and brokenness for him and Sadie to sweep up in her pursuit of wealth and society. Jay had tried to clean up after them, but the only way for him to escape their scatter of debris was to leave them behind.

"Sounds like the people you been talking to think you can only be one thing or another thing," Saul continued. "Well, life don't work like that. You deserve everything you want, and you can have it too, as long as you believe you deserve it and you're willing to work for it. You just keep your focus and know your worth. Don't you always say a horse knows a person's soul? And didn't that beautiful animal give his life for you? Must be worth somethin', no matter what that good-for-nothin' Pete told ya."

Lottie squeezed his hand and whispered an almost imperceptible, "Thank you."

Saul winked at her, rose up, and looked meaningfully at Jay as the medic finished stitching up his leg. When Lottie turned to look at him too, Jay felt overwhelmed with emotion. The way he'd felt the first time she'd looked up at him at breakfast. The way he'd felt the night they kissed in his railcar.

"Lottie, I…" He paused for a long moment, searching for the right thing to say. "I should have…I'm sorry…"

She reached out to take his hand, six inches from hers on the neighboring cot in the medic's tent. "Me too," she whispered. "I didn't mean to—"

"Well, Mr. Edwards." Saul interrupted the moment. "Your jazz band didn't run off on you, did they? I believe I'm due for some good music." Saul replaced his hat and whistled as he ducked out of the tent. As he pushed the corner of the tent aside, a gray cat pranced through and hopped up onto Lottie's cot.

"How's your watch?" she asked. "Were you able to

fix it?"

"I was." Jay pulled his watch from his pants pocket, rubbed the dirt off the case with his thumb, and popped it open. "You know what? She's been through a hell of a lot, but she's still ticking."

Lottie laughed and leaned back, grimacing as her gauze-wrapped head hit her pillow. "I can relate."

"I bet." Jay tucked his watch back into his pocket. "I know you're thinking about going home. I don't wanna keep you from doing what you feel like you need to do. But you should know. Whatever you decide…"

Lottie sat back up.

"I'm so amazed by you. The things you've been through. This path you braved with your son. You haven't just survived, you…you're a triumph. And today with the Liberty horses. I know it was horrible, everything that happened. But I hope I get to see you on a horse again someday. You were just—you are—just…magnificent."

Lottie beamed and scratched the ears of the purring cat in her lap. "You know, maybe Madame Rusalka was right. Maybe I wasn't running from something." She lifted her gaze to Jay, and the brightness in her eyes made him forget his throbbing leg and aching body. "Maybe I was running to something. I guess since I don't have anything to run from now, I need to decide what I'm running toward. Whatever it is, I don't think I'll find it in Ayer. I think I can find it here."

Jay squeezed her hand. "Maybe we can figure it out together." He was filled with joy and warmth as she smiled gracefully back at him and returned to petting the cat, stirring up a question he'd had since the first time he'd seen Lottie with the cat. "Who is Madame Rusalka?"

Charlotte laughed. "The Romani woman from your fortune teller tent, of course!"

Concern pulled his eyebrows together. *Must be the head injury.* "We've…never had a fortune teller tent. Not since I've been running things anyway."

"That's impossible. They've been with us all along…"

Jay shook his head. "Not with Sterling & Son's. Trust me, I'd have to feed them if we did."

"But I…I spoke with her. Madame Rusalka. She told me…"

"I'm sorry, Lottie. Sterling and Son's doesn't have anyone by that name."

Lottie stared at Jay blinking, and then back down at Printesa, who hopped off her lap and trotted out of the tent into the clear bright sunshine toward the row of waiting railcars.

And so Jay and Lottie looked out toward the train tracks, hand in hand, wounds bandaged, deciding their direction as a gentle breeze ushered in the distant whistle of the circus train.

Epilogue

Birdie Bells slammed her trunk closed and flung herself onto the bottom bunk in the cramped performer's car, angry at the day's conversation.

"You said I'd be famous," she'd said to Verne as she put her clothes back on. "I've got nothin' to show for everything you got outta me."

"Bide your time, toots," Verne responded condescendingly.

"It's been almost three years! I should be front and center by now. You said I'd be a star!"

"This is Ringling Brothers, Barnum & Bailey, sweetheart. You gotta bring something fantastic with you to be a star here. You're in the big times now, toots."

"I am fantastic!"

"Not as fantastic as Lillian Leitzel, honey."

Birdie stared at the wood planks above her in a fury, every knothole vibrating in a mockery. As if the boards themselves, the very air in front of her, were all laughing at her. She had promised herself she wouldn't lose her temper. Not again. She remembered opening night with Sterling & Son's four years ago. How she had to turn away when the cannon girl soared toward the net. How she knew when she heard the unmistakable pop of a broken neck that the loosened ropes hadn't held.

The sickening sound of Zarina's bones breaking plagued Birdie relentlessly. When she was trying to sleep. When she soared from bar to bar. When she was getting dressed. When she put on her lipstick.

One moment she let her temper get a hold of her, and that was it. A lifetime of guilt. Like her stepfather when he'd gotten bored with her. Hadn't she wanted to kill Hazel too? Would it ever stop?

Of course, she'd gotten away with shooting her stepfather. She'd gotten away with Zarina's accident. If Lillian had an accident too, they'd need someone to take her place on trapeze.

Birdie squeezed her eyes shut and tried to blink the ghosts away. Tried to silence the voice. But the voice grew louder. And louder. Blinding her like the centering spotlight until she could only hear the whirring hum of the train on the tracks screeching in her ears.

We've all done things for the spotlight. Things we'd never dreamed we'd do to get to where we are. I could tell you stories you wouldn't believe.

Birdie's eyes shot open. She knew what she had to do.

****

The paper boy shouted his headline from the corner that cold February morning, selling papers quicker than he could cut the twine off. "Get your *New York Times* right here! Read all about it! 'Circus Fall Fatal to Lillian Leitzel.' That's right, folks. 'Famous Circus Star Dead from Fall!'"

Acknowledgments

Like any real-life circus, *Circus Train at Sunrise* was always a team effort. I'm grateful to so many who have contributed to bringing this story to life.

First I'd like to thank my husband, Jeremiah. For all of the encouragement, reading through draft after draft, brainstorming plots and ideas with me, your unwavering support, and for being the inspiration for a loveable logical guy who somehow manages a life circus while raising a family and helping his wife write a book. Thank you for being a life partner who always lifts me up and makes me better.

To my children, thank you for understanding when I had to stop what we were doing to make a note about a character or change something in the story. I'm so grateful for your patience, love, and support. Your bravery and curiosity inspire me every day to keep learning.

To my dad, Ray Box, thank you for introducing me to Sherlock Holmes and Hercule Poirot, and for sitting in long lines at bookstores with me for midnight release parties. My mom, Cathy Box, who is herself a published author and has always believed I would publish a book someday too. Thank you for being such a great role model, for taking me to writers' groups and journalism meetings before I could drive (and after). Thank you both for believing in me, pushing me to do my best, and reading anything I've ever written as if it belonged on a shelf. My sisters, Kristin Goen and Nikki Tekell, thank you for being the fiercest most loving supporters I could ever have in my corner, whether professionally or with anything life throws my way.

Thank you for cheering for Charlotte the way you've always cheered for me.

Thank you to the Shelf Indulgence Book Club: Jana Anderson, Julie Marshall, Yvonne Harwood, Ashley Cherry, Ronna Privett, Amy Smith, Jennie Dabbs, Meredith Hardy, Cathy Box, Cydney Martin, Carma McKenzie, and Susan Blassingame, for being discerning beta readers that I could trust with my manuscript when it was still a work in progress. Your invaluable suggestions helped shape this story into what it has become. To my other beta readers, Carol Denning and Cassandra Schmitt, thank you for the perspective and feedback you provided in the book's early stages.

To The Wild Rose Press and my fantastic editor, Eilidh MacKenzie. Eilidh, you're an absolute rockstar. Thank you for the hours you've poured into refining *Circus Train at Sunrise* as well as helping me to develop as a writer. Thank you for believing in this story and working with me to make it something I'm very proud of. I am honored to be a part of the rose garden!

Until next time.

Sarah Denning

A word about the author…

Sarah Denning is from Tahoka, TX, with a Bachelor's Degree in Art and Design from Abilene Christian University and a Master's in Literature from Wayland Baptist University. She is a middle school Language Arts and Reading teacher in Texas and a member of the Circus Historical Society. Sarah lives in Lubbock with her husband Jeremiah and their beautiful blended family that includes four children, Alleigh, Mason, Aubrey, and Brady.

Thank you for purchasing
this publication of The Wild Rose Press, Inc.

For questions or more information
contact us at
info@thewildrosepress.com.

The Wild Rose Press, Inc.
www.thewildrosepress.com

Milton Keynes UK
Ingram Content Group UK Ltd.
UKHW021614050624
443649UK00016BA/866